RESCUE
ME

MONTANA RESCUE Novels by Susan May Warren

MONTANA
RESCUE
+ 2 +

RESCUE ME

A NOVEL

SUSAN MAY
WARREN

Revell

a division of Baker Publishing Group
Grand Rapids, Michigan

Published by Revell
a division of Baker Publishing Group
P.O. Box 6287, Grand Rapids, MI 49516-6287
www.revellbooks.com

Printed in the United States of America

Library of Congress Cataloging-in-Publication Data
Names: Warren, Susan May, 1966– author.
Title: Rescue me / Susan May Warren.
Description: Grand Rapids, MI : Revell, a division of Baker Publishing Group,
    [2017] | Series: Montana Rescue ; book 2
Identifiers: LCCN 2016036310| ISBN 9780800727444 (softcover) | ISBN
    9780800728625 (print on demand)
Subjects: | GSAFD: Romantic suspense fiction. | Christian fiction. | Love stories.
Classification: LCC PS3623.A865 R47 2017 | DDC 813/.6—dc23
LC record available at https://lccn.loc.gov/2016036310

This book is a work of fiction. Names, characters, places, and incidents are the product of the author's imagination or are used fictitiously.

17 18 19 20 21 22 23   7 6 5 4 3 2 1

SAM WOULDN'T LOSE another kid on his watch.

If the homecoming queen was out here, he intended to find her. Even if he had to trek through the entire western edge of Glacier National Park, beat every bush, climb every peak.

Unless, of course, Romeo had been lying.

"How far up the trail did the kid say they were?" Behind him, Gage Watson shined his flashlight against the twisted depths of forest. A champion snowboarder, Gage looked the part with his long dark brown hair held back in a man bun. But he also had keen outdoor instincts and now worked as an EMT on the PEAK Rescue team during the summer.

An owl hooted. A screech ricocheted through the air, folding through the shaggy dark spruce, the skeletal white birch. Only a thin strip of moonlight managed to pierce the looming cottonwoods, the towering black pine.

This time of night, with the moon climbing and the stars waking overhead, the forest sounds could raise the hairs on a man's neck.

Especially while hunting for a so-called rogue grizzly.

See, this was what happened when kids like Romeo—stupid, arrogant, too-fun-for-their-own-good charmers—led with their impulses rather than their brains. They got themselves in over their heads, or worse, dreamed up things that went bump in the night.

Sam might be a bit jaded. It didn't help that the minute he'd pulled off the dirt highway onto the trickle of forest service road on the edge of Glacier National Park, memory flashed. He'd half-expected to see his kid brother Pete taking a giant leap over the lethal, flickering flames of the bonfire in the middle of the gravel pit. Or worse, to peel him off the dirt, burned, drunk, and surly, throw him in the truck, and drag him home.

But Pete wasn't sixteen anymore. And no longer his responsibility.

Still, more than ten years later, this after-homecoming pit party bore the telltale marks of trouble. Teenagers sitting around in their cars, the doors open, the twangy voice of some country crooner spilling out into the backwoods starry night.

As he pulled up, a few kids hid bottles of Jack Daniel's, Bacardi, and Jose Cuervo. Doused whatever other substances they'd brought to heighten their so-called fun. He'd wanted to call for police backup and start breathalyzing, see if he might scare a few of these teens straight. Maybe, once he found the supposedly lost girl.

Sam had a dark feeling he knew *exactly* what happened to send Romeo out of the forest, his shirt ripped, his face scratched. And it had nothing to do with a wild animal.

After Sam found her, Romeo would have some explaining to do.

Now, a crack from a broken branch sharpened the air behind him, and he stiffened, turned, and flashed his light across his brother, Pete, armed with an ax he'd pulled off the PEAK truck.

"You think an ax is going to take down a seven-hundred-pound grizzly sow on the rampage, there, Paul Bunyan?"

Pete's mouth tightened into a tight bud of defense. "Want to have a conversation about your dancing shoes?"

"I wasn't exactly planning this outing." Sam's first choice for callout attire wasn't his only pair of dress pants, jacket, and fancy church shoes, recently shined. In fact, had he not had his scanner on while picking up Sierra—and had Sierra, PEAK Rescue administrator, not heard the 911 call from a frantic teenager—he would be enjoying dinner at the Whitefish Golf Club, digging into a New York strip and a mound of garlic mashed potatoes.

Trying to figure out how to keep Sierra from breaking up with him.

"At least I have a gun," Sam said. His Remington rifle, which he kept in his trunk next to his police bag.

Just in case. Because bear or not, living in the shadow of Glacier National Park, Sam knew to expect trouble.

"Did you find her?" The voice ricocheted up the path and Sam turned. Grimaced.

The frantic and desperate Quinn Starr, aka Romeo.

About seventeen, with dark brown hair chopped short, wide shoulders, and a confident swagger, he played running back for the Mercy Falls Mavericks. Charming and cocky, the kid had Pete Brooks 2.0 written all over him.

Quinn wore desperation in his expression. It probably only halfway had to do with the fact that the kid had talked sweet Bella Hayes into hiking into the woods. The other part might have to do with the fear that once his former SEAL, senator father found out, he'd probably be shipping out to military school to finish his senior year.

Quinn's dress shirt hung open, the buttons ripped off and his shirt-sleeve ripped.

"Tell me again what happened," Sam said, his voice even, controlled. Later, all bets were off.

Quinn ran both hands through his hair. "We were sitting here, and all of a sudden, we heard this huffing noise, like heavy breathing—"

He made a funny sound, as if blowing out his horror. "Then it was just there! Just—there. Raging. It smelled like wet dog and just roared at us—"

He leaned over, gripped his knees, breathing hard, as if he might vomit.

Huh.

Pete looked at Sam, one eyebrow raised.

Okay, granted, the kid sounded truly terrified. Maybe his desperate tone *could* be attributed to the high adrenaline of life suddenly turning raw, out-of-control, devastating.

Sam well remembered that feeling.

"Breathe, kid," Sam said. "Are you sure it was a grizzly?"

Quinn looked up then, his expression grim. "Yeah. It had that ruff of fur between its shoulders." He stood up. "I yelled at Bella to run, and then I picked up a rock and threw it."

Sam might give the kid some props for trying to save his girlfriend.

"It grunted, and I just ran. Bella was climbing a tree, and I thought maybe I could give her time. So I ran toward the pit, hoping the bear would follow me."

Sam eyed him, his mouth tight. Probably panic had taken ahold of those running-back legs and set him sprinting.

What was the old adage? You didn't have to be faster than the bear, just the guy—or in this case, the girl—behind you?

Especially if said girl was wearing a homecoming dress.

Which only made climbing a tree that much more difficult.

"This tree?" Sam shone his light upward.

That's when he spotted a broken branch the size of his arm. As he dragged the light down, he made out claw marks peeling back the bark.

A cold hand wrapped around his heart.

Quinn pushed toward him, stared up at the tree. "Bella!"

"Here's Quinn's pack." Gage's light fell on the torn, mangled debris of a lightweight day pack. Nearby, a sleeping bag lay torn to shreds, the down lifting into the air like snowflakes against the harsh panes of night.

Which, if they didn't find the girl soon, just might turn real. Despite the late September air tinged with the scents of campfire, the breath of winter hovered.

"I found something!" Pete, banging around in the bushes, lifted a strip of fabric. A swatch of silky yellow.

"It's her . . ." Quinn's voice hitched. "Her dress."

"This way," Pete said and headed out, the ax easy in his hands.

Sometimes Sam forgot that Pete had spent the past seven summers as a smoke jumper for the Jude County wildland firefighters.

They followed the broken branches and bits of silky fabric into the tangles of the forest. The pine trees closed in, shaggy arms clawing at them, the spindly, crooked fingers of poplar saplings slapping his face, his arms.

Please, God, let her be alive.

The prayer felt too familiar—too futile.

"Bella!" Quinn tried to push ahead, but Sam caught him, shoved him back. "We got this, kid."

He heard sniffing and ignored it.

There would be plenty of time for blame and grief later.

"Bella!" Pete's voice boomed out.

"Here! Help me!"

The high voice shrilled into the darkness, and Sam turned, cast his flashlight over the limestone rocks, mossy-edged boulders, the ravine—*there*. She was huddled into a ball, wedged so far back under a ledge of rock that they might have never found her except for her call. Her bright yellow dress, neon under his light, dripped out from under the ledge.

Quinn raced over to her, hit his knees. "Bella, are you okay?" He reached in to tug her free, but she cried out.

Sam crouched next to Quinn. "Bella?"

Filthy, her hair matted with leaves, her dress torn, Bella appeared as if she had fled into the forest, come what may. Her mouth bled from the corner and her eye was blackened.

And then he saw the blood. It pooled into the loamy soil under the enclave.

"You're hurt."

She had her arm curled into herself. Sam shone his light on it. A long, nearly bone-deep laceration.

He winced and, not knowing what else to do, reached for his jacket.

But Quinn had his shirt off, had wriggled in next to her and was now wrapping the shirt around her shredded arm. "C'mon, baby. I got you." He took her into his arms and eased her out of the hole.

She whimpered, her breathing falling over itself, her pretty brown eyes wide with terror. "I tried to climb like you said, but my dress—it caught, and I fell. And then there was the bear, and I didn't know what to do—so I ran. I just . . . ran and ran . . . and . . ."

Quinn sat behind her, his arms around her, holding her as she shook.

"How did you find the hole?" Sam crouched down and examined the wound. So much blood had started to congeal around the edges. The rip in her skin—Sam guessed a claw rather than teeth—started at the shoulder, curled down in front of her bicep, and ended in the forearm. As if she'd been holding it up to protect herself.

"I fell. I just *fell* right off the edge and hit the rock. And I think I might have knocked myself out, but then suddenly, there was the bear . . . just on me. I thought—yeah, I should play dead. And . . ." Her eyes widened, and she closed her mouth, swallowed, as if she were sucked back to that moment.

"Bella," Sam said quietly. "You're safe now." He pulled off his jacket, wrapped it around her.

She looked at him. "He sniffed me. A lot. And . . . I don't know. Maybe I didn't smell good, because then suddenly he just walked away. And I thought maybe he was gone, so I scooted back, and

I found myself in this cave. And that's when . . ." She closed her eyes. "That's when he came back."

Behind him, he heard Pete on the walkie, calling in their position to PEAK Rescue HQ and asking Kacey for an extraction.

Yes, send in the chopper, soon. Because a press to her neck, at the carotid artery, told Sam that Bella's blood pressure was dropping.

She could go into shock.

"He slashed at me. I put my arm up over my head and tried not to scream. I don't know if he couldn't get to me, but he gave me another swipe and then just . . . left. And I couldn't move, couldn't scream because—because . . ."

Quinn pressed his forehead into her neck. He was sobbing.

And probably, Sam should forgive him.

Except, as he stared at this kid, a quiet rage boiled up inside him.

If Quinn hadn't been so—

"Bro," Pete said, "the chopper is on the way. We need to get these two down to the gravel pit—"

A roar echoed out of the woods, shivering the trees.

In the silence that followed, Sam's heart stopped in his chest.

"That's an angry bear," Pete said quietly.

Sam scrambled to his feet. "Get her up." Gage came over, lifted Bella into his arms, then he handed Quinn the flashlight. "Go."

Quinn took off through the woods, Pete behind him, clearing a path for Gage.

Sam's feet slipped on the loamy soil, his shirt catching on brambles. Another roar bellowed out, this time closer, and Sam could nearly smell the hoary breath on the breeze, skimming down his shirt, his sweaty back.

Then they hit the trail, turned, and headed toward the pit.

Sam nearly slammed into the back of Gage, who'd stopped.

"What—"

"Shh!" Gage was backing up the trail, Bella curled into his chest. Pete, too, began to back up.

Pete held the ax up in front of them like a shield.

Because there, in the middle of the trail, smelling rank, like pungent, rotted garbage, stood a mama sow.

And just up the path behind Sam, ten feet away, her two precious babes began to bawl.

The perfect night could be summed up with a bowl of popcorn, a Lord of the Rings marathon, a fuzzy blanket, and a golden retriever puppy named Gopher on her lap.

Never mind the bits of toilet paper the pup had strewn around the house; Willow would pick that up as soon as the movie ended. She didn't want to disturb the ten-year-old snuggled up next to her. Her brown hair tousled, her mouth open in sleep, Thea had surrendered to slumber long before the Orcs attacked Frodo's measly band.

Royal, age twelve, and too old for a babysitter, thank you, watched the Orcs with wide eyes as he fished out the last of the old maids from the bowl.

Willow still remembered the first time she'd watched *The Fellowship of the Ring* during one of those precious times when her father had been home on leave.

Willow glanced at the clock. Right about now, her father would be bending his knee and popping the question to Terri, Thea and Royal's mom. Digging out the black ring box from his flannel shirt. Just like they'd rehearsed.

Willow couldn't be happier for him.

She watched as Samwise Gamgee waded into the river after Mr. Frodo, until the hobbit deigned to reach out and drag Sam aboard his boat.

That's what friends—no, family did. They showed up to help each other. At least, that was how she imagined it.

She pulled a pillow from the end of the sofa, then eased the dog off her lap and put the pillow under Thea's head.

SUSAN MAY WARREN

Thea barely moved, and Willow pressed her finger to her mouth as she looked at Royal. As the final credits rolled, she picked up the remote from the coffee table and clicked off the television.

Quiet descended upon the small ranch house, only the refrigerator humming in the kitchen.

Royal picked up his phone and started up a game. Willow gathered up the pizza box and dropped it into recycling. Gopher danced around her feet, his soft brown eyes bright with excitement. He pawed at the door, nearly let out a yip, and she opened it. He ran out into the night.

She followed, prepared to call the pup back to the yard.

She loved where Terri and the kids—and soon her father—lived. A small home, yes, but on a street with other tiny ranch houses, each housing a family. Minivans in the driveways, a couple bikes propped up against garages, neatly clipped lawns. Lights glowed from over the doors, leaves blanketed the yards, the scent of pine stirred the air. And along the far horizon ran the jagged edge of the Rocky Mountains.

This was the kind of house, the kind of neighborhood she'd dreamed of growing up in. With welcoming porch lights, warm cookies after school, scary carved pumpkins on the stoop, and Christmas lights ringing the rooftops. And in the summer, sprinklers spraying emerald lawns, and kids running from one yard to the next playing Kick the Can.

Safe.

Willow tucked her arms around herself against a slight nip in the air. "C'mon, Gopher, do your duty."

The pup sniffed at her feet, then around the yard, probably revisiting old accomplishments. He'd found the proper place for his job when headlights cut down the street, then into the driveway.

Her father's truck.

Gopher chased it in, yipping. Willow lifted her hand, wanting to give Terri and her dad a minute to themselves, and headed inside, calling Gopher, who barreled in, nearly taking her out at the knees.

Thea leaned up, creases from the couch drawn in her cheek. She turned and looked out the window. "Mom's home!"

Willow held Gopher's collar as Terri and her father came to the door.

Willow liked Terri. Dark sable brown hair, not unlike her father's, with deep amber eyes and a wide smile, Terri worked at the church office, where Jackson part-timed as a handyman.

Although, to Willow's eyes, her father looked more war hero than handyman, with wide shoulders, strong hands, his brown gaze resonant with dependability and strength. He'd taken his breakup with her mother hard.

No wonder he'd run away to the military.

"Well?"

Terri flashed a solitaire diamond in a platinum setting that Willow knew set her father back about a month in pay. "Your father did it!"

He grinned at Willow, gave her a wink.

Thea had come off the sofa, the blanket wrapped around her shoulders. "Mom, does that mean you and Jackson are getting married?"

"It does, baby," Terri said and caught her daughter as she flung her arms around her waist.

Even Royal stood up, pocketed his phone, and walked over. He looked at Jackson, and a hint of a smile edged his face. "Cool."

He lifted his hand in a high five, which Jackson smacked.

See, that's what happened when you waited for the right man. Even after the tragedy this family had endured with the loss of their father three years ago in a wildfire, God healed wounds, offered a fresh start.

Willow just had to wait. Her happy ending was out there. After all, her sister Sierra, too, was proof of that. Who could be a better catch than Sam Brooks? Solid, strong, devastatingly handsome with his brown hair laced with the finest gold threads when he came in from the sun, and blue eyes that crinkled around the edges. His laugh was hard-won but oh, so worth it, rippling down right to a girl's insides.

His smile too. Gentle. Sincere.

And, not to mention, hot. Willow had nearly melted into a puddle when he showed up on the porch in a black T-shirt that outlined all those hours he spent at Ian Shaw's personal gym, pounding away on his heavy bag.

However, she loved it best when he wore his PEAK Rescue team uniform—brown jacket, Gore-Tex pants, boots. Capable and exuding the sense that if you were lost, he was the one to find you.

Yes. *Rescue me.*

Shoot. Even she knew that thought was inappropriate. Because, hello, Sam belonged to Sierra.

Full stop. Amen. And frankly, hallelujah, because Sierra deserved a man like Sam after pining for her aloof and unavailable billionaire boss, Ian Shaw.

So now, Sierra just might be the luckiest woman on the planet.

Next to Terri.

And maybe herself, because finally, Willow too was getting a family.

Gopher yipped at her feet, clearly wanting to join in the fun. In his excitement, he piddled on the linoleum.

"Oh no! Goph!" Terri picked him up, holding him out like he had a disease. "Really, Jackson. I think this is an outside dog."

"No, Mom!" Thea shrieked.

But Terri put the dog outside and headed to the kitchen for paper towels.

"He's too young—" Willow started, but then noticed her father returning with the puppy in his arms.

"He can come home with me, honey," Jackson said. "Don't worry. We'll get him house-trained. He's just excited."

Terri dropped paper towels on the floor. Stepped on them and looked at Jackson, her mouth a grim line. "I don't know, Jack . . ." And then her face curved into a smile. "Should we ask them?"

Jackson looked at the kids and then Willow, warmth and a tiny grin in his expression.

She knew that look. His I-have-a-surprise-and-you-have-to-guess look.

He toed off his boots and walked into the family room. Sat on the sofa.

The kids bounced in beside him.

Terri lowered herself onto an overstuffed chair. Her father took Thea's hand, moved her to the ottoman. Patted it for Royal to join her.

The kids faced him, wearing an expression Willow understood—like the time he told her he wanted to take her to Disney World.

If not for her mother's hatred of all things commercial, she might have gone on that trip.

Especially if he'd asked again later, when Mom stopped competing with her ex. When she stopped caring what Willow did altogether.

"So, you know your mom and I are getting married," Jackson said. He glanced at Willow, smiled.

Willow sat on the floor.

Jackson ran a hand over the pup, calming it. "And we've decided that, since we're all starting out as a family, you should come on the honeymoon with us."

Willow frowned at him. Her father *did* have a generous dose of unconventional. After all, he stayed with her mother for nearly seven years. Then, after he became a Christian, he had even proposed.

"We're going to take homeschool on the road, rent a motor home, and visit the Grand Canyon."

The Grand Canyon. Willow had only seen pictures, but yeah, it was on her list.

In truth, *anything* outside the borders of Mercy Falls was on her list. "Are you sure, Dad? That's very . . . generous of you."

Her father looked at her. "If we're going to be a family, we should start it together."

Gopher squirmed out of his hands, ran over to Willow. She let the pup climb into her lap.

"When?" Willow asked, mentally checking her schedule.

"Oh, next week," Terri said. "We've waited long enough, and we don't want a wedding. Just a quick ceremony, and then we're off." She reached over and caught Jackson's hand. Squeezed.

The timing wasn't great—not with the meeting about the new youth pastor position scheduled for next Friday. The church search committee hadn't asked her to present a résumé, but maybe they didn't need anything formal. She was a shoo-in for the job. She'd been at the church for three years, tirelessly working with the teenagers.

The kids loved her. Needed her. And the parents—especially Pastor Hayes and his wife, Carrie—treated her like family. If anyone would recommend her, it would be Walt and Carrie Hayes.

Probably she didn't even have to be there at the meeting. So, except for the upcoming youth trip, which she could possibly postpone . . .

Willow nodded. "I think I can make it work."

Terri turned to her. "Oh, really? That would be so fantastic, Willow."

"I'd be glad to. I can't wait. I've never seen the Grand Canyon."

Terri's mouth remained opened for just a moment. Then she closed it. Swallowed and looked at Jackson, wearing something of a stricken expression. She turned back to Willow. "I'm so sorry—we didn't think you . . . well, we know how busy you are, and . . ."

Oh.

"We were actually hoping you might watch Gopher for us."

Willow swallowed.

Watch.

Gopher.

Her throat thickened. She shot a glance at her father, who looked pained. "Willow, I didn't think you'd want to come along—I mean, you're so busy with the youth group and work and . . . I'm so sorry."

Willow cleared her throat. "No problem. Really. I am busy, and of course I'll watch this little guy." She leaned down to the puppy, blinking fast. "We'll have a great time, won't we, Goph?"

A lick across her nose. At least someone liked her.

"Oh, thank you, Willow," Terri said, relief in her voice. "You can even stay here, if you'd like. I know your own living quarters are a little iffy right now."

By iffy, did she mean the sleeping bag on a blow-up mattress at Jess's house, where they were holing up after Sierra's house collapsed from the flood earlier that summer?

"I'm fine."

"Oh, you're the best, just like your dad." Terri was beaming. "C'mon, kids, it's time for bed. Say good night to Willow." Terri got up, ushered the kids away.

Willow was going to rise, take her leave when, "Willow."

She couldn't look at her dad. Not without tears edging her eyes. "What?"

"I'm sorry. That was . . . I didn't think. I mean, *of course* you're part of this family."

"I'm not, Dad. And it's okay. I have a family. You. Mom. Sierra."

"It's not the same thing. I know you always wanted your mom and I to be married . . ."

She looked at him then, her eyes betraying her as they glossed over. "No, Dad. Actually, what I always wanted was for you to show up and rescue me, just like you did them."

Jackson's brow furrowed into a pinch. "What do you mean?"

She forced a smile. "Nothing. I'm just happy for you."

Gopher had one of her shoes. She wrestled it from his mouth and slipped it on.

"Honey, please tell me what you're talking about."

It was the softness of his tone that nearly broke her.

But she couldn't mar his joy with the wounds of yesterday.

"I just wish I'd had more of you when I was younger, is all. Like they will."

He sighed. "Willow, I wanted to . . . your mom—"

"Dad. It's all good. Listen, I gotta run."

And, as if the cosmos might be on her side for once, her cell phone buzzed in her pocket. She fished it out. Read the text.

Everything inside her stilled.

"It's the prayer chain." She looked up at her dad. "There's been a mauling."

2

TWO HOURS LATER, Sam still had to remind himself to take a breath.

To close his eyes, listen to his heart beat.

Remind himself that they'd lived.

Sam sat on a chair in the ER waiting room, his head sunk into his hands as he listened to the PEAK team talk about their miraculous escape.

Maybe not so miraculous as just darn lucky.

Sam wanted to kill Pete—or maybe hug him, he didn't know. For sure his quick thinking had given them an extra second.

Even if it had enraged the bear.

After all, an ax in the shoulder would probably peeve anyone, especially a protective mother sow. However, for a second, the injury had blindsided her, slowed her down.

Given Sam a chance to get Gage and Bella behind him, for Quinn to leap for the nearest tree, Pete close behind him.

Which left Sam staring down the beady dark eyes of an animal with incisors the size of his fist and claws that Wolverine would be jealous of.

If Sam stepped back from the emotion, slowed down the events of the attack, he could see it better—the hulking, rank mass of beast in the middle of the trail. Bella's piercing wail as Gage fled with her into the woods.

The thunder of his heartbeat as Sam leveled his gun, even as the animal bore down on him with a roar that ripped through his body.

The kick of his rifle against his shoulder, the shot reverberating against the night.

The bear, undaunted, despite what Sam knew had to be a hit.

The gun self-cocked, another round chambered, as the animal charged.

He pulled the trigger—the gun jammed. Right there in his hands, a dead stick. Sam tripped and fell on his back as the bear stood over him, roaring.

He heard a scream from behind, something feral and fierce, but all he saw were jaws and teeth and—

He shoved the barrel of the gun right into the bear's mouth.

The bear gagged, reared back.

Sam scrambled out from beneath the claws and simply ran.

He hit the nearest tree and scrabbled up it.

The bear rebounded, charging.

As Sam clung to the tree, certain the animal would knock it down, lights bloomed above them, bulwarked by the roar and wash of the PEAK chopper

Kacey Fairing, former military pilot, using the only tool she had to save him—a dual-engine Bell 429 chopper.

If they'd been in a field, Sam had no doubt she would have set the bird right down on top of the grizzly if it meant saving his sorry hide.

EMT Jess Tagg, hanging out the door, shot a flare at the bear, turning the forest into fire in a flash of brilliant light. The bear reared, and right about then, Ty Remington and Ben King ran up the trail wielding flare guns, having been dropped off by said chopper in the nearby pit. They shot the flare guns off, scaring the bear all the way up the trail to her cubs.

The last Sam saw of the animal, her grimy backside was fading into the darkness of a dying flare.

Sam wasn't sure if he had screamed, but maybe, since his throat burned and his entire body shook.

At the least, he'd *wanted* to scream.

Still felt it building inside. Despite the relative calm of the ER and the sound of his team reliving the story as they gathered near the nurse's bay.

"I couldn't believe it when Sam just shoved the gun into the bear's mouth," Pete was saying, looking unruffled, his blond hair held back by a baseball cap, just a good ole boy hanging out in the woods.

"And then, like Superman, Kacey came out of the sky." This from Ben King, and of course he'd say that. The guy still stood around with a half-dazed look on his face that Kacey Fairing had decided to give him another chance at being a father to their child.

It helped that their daughter, Audrey, thought her country star father hung the moon. But Ben was just a hometown cowboy, son of their founding pilot Chet King and a member of the PEAK team when he wasn't out singing about broken hearts and pickups.

Sam glanced up at the group, hoping to see Sierra. She hadn't arrived yet; she was still driving in from the base with Chet. The rest of the team came in on the chopper or the PEAK truck. Thankfully, Sheriff Blackburn and a few deputies had already put down the party by the time Sam returned to the pit. No doubt, more than a few parents were waiting for their kids at the station in town.

Sam didn't see Quinn Starr's father in the waiting room. He should probably let him know his son was safe, if not a little rattled. That would be a fun conversation. *Hello, Senator Starr. Yeah, your son was nearly killed tonight—oh, why? Because he was making out with his girlfriend, the daughter of the local pastor . . .*

Poor kid. Sam hoped Quinn had figured out a reasonable defense. After all, he did appear to care for Bella.

Sam looked at his scraped and bleeding hands. A tear in his palm burned—probably needed a stitch or two—and his forearms betrayed his fight with the brambles.

The others had suffered about the same, except for Quinn, who'd taken the brunt of the tree on his chest in a wicked scrape. Probably from Pete shoving him into a canopy of pine branches.

Sam got up and the world tilted. He pressed a hand against the wall, woozy. He just needed a soda, some sugar in his bloodstream.

"Sam, you're bleeding." This from Jess, a PEAK EMT. He frowned at her, and she raised a blonde eyebrow and pointed at the wall.

He'd left a red palm smudge.

She walked over to him. Uncomplicated, pretty, with long blonde hair and piercing green eyes that could triage a scene in a second, Jess had an easy smile and curves that should probably make a man take notice.

Not that he hadn't, but he was taken.

Sort of.

He hoped.

Jess took his hand and examined the wound. "This is pretty deep," she said. "Let's get it cleaned up."

"I'm fine."

"I know. But since I brought my first aid kit, let me play doctor, huh?" She pressed him down into the chair, then went to retrieve the kit.

Pete was leaning against the counter of the nurses' station, and his gaze followed Jess as she picked up the bag.

Interesting.

A blink later, Pete had turned back to the huddle with Gage, Ben, Kacey, and Ty.

Pete must have cracked a joke, because the team started laughing. Sam shook his head.

"You know Pete handles stress by being a clown, right?" Jess said, crouching in front of him, clearly able to read his mind.

"We nearly died. And Bella—"

"Is going to be fine. She's a toughie." Jess dabbed antiseptic on his wound.

Sam closed one eye against the sting and held in a word.

"You know, this is one of those few times you can say something unchurchy if you want. I know it's got to hurt—you've got bark embedded here."

She'd taken out tweezers and was tugging at the wound. He let out a breath, slow, through his pursed lips. "I got this."

"Mmmhmm. Of course you do." She blew on the wound, drying the antiseptic. "I think you need a couple stitches."

"Just butterfly it, Jess. I need to get home and out of this monkey suit. And—"

"Find your girlfriend. I know. Sierra radioed that she's on her way." Jess gave him a wink.

Girlfriend. Sam only wished he could call Sierra that. Even after three months of hanging out with the PEAK team at the Gray Pony Bar and Grill, listening to Ben try out his newest singles, or with the team at their Sunday barbecue, or even going on the occasional walk alone through downtown Mercy Falls for a malt at the Summit Cafe, Sam couldn't exactly call her his girlfriend.

But he wanted to.

Tonight, he also had this need crawling up inside him to talk to her, to see her smile, maybe finally find that spark that he'd first felt for her.

Back when he'd asked Ian Shaw for the right to date her. Not that the billionaire had any claim on her—after all, Ian was her boss, not her boyfriend. Still, they had history. And a weird connection, even after she quit working for him.

Could be simply the wounds associated with losing Esme, Ian's niece. They all bore them—even Sierra for her part in letting Esme run away and Sam for his inability to find her.

For at least a couple weeks this summer, being with Sierra felt like forgiveness. As if he might be able to let go of his mistakes.

Lately, however, he seemed to be making enough mistakes to drive her away. No matter what he did, he couldn't quite get Sierra's smile to reach her eyes, her laughter to ring authentic.

His kisses to light her on fire. He'd settle for a spark. Just a hint of smoke.

And now that the entire team, or maybe just Jess, had dubbed them boyfriend-girlfriend, Sam longed to make it work.

Sierra was a great gal. Pretty, organized, domestic. Everything a guy could want.

Jess closed the wound in his palm with a couple butterfly bandages, added some antibacterial cream, and covered it with a gauze pad and some tape.

"Sheesh, are you going to cast it next?"

"Maybe. But only if you give me trouble about dressing that scrape on your chin." She nudged his jaw up with her finger.

"I'm fine, Jess."

"My brother can handle a few little scrapes, Speedy."

Sam looked up and spotted Pete sauntering over. He had sustained the least amount of injury. The tree had manhandled his shirt, left a few tears along the body, but a scrape along the bridge of his nose was the only evidence that he'd scrambled up an old black spruce trying to escape a grizzly.

Pete looked every inch the guy who'd thrown an ax at death and walked away smiling.

Sam, on the other hand, had shredded his nice no-iron shirt, scraped up his only pair of decent shoes, and put a hole in his dress pants. He was soggy and sore.

"Enough fussing." Sam got up.

Jess frowned at him. "Fine. But I don't know if you two know how lucky you are. That's the second bear attack—or near attack—in three days," she said. "I was talking with the nurses, and a man and his daughter came in a couple days ago. She had broken her ankle running from a bear up near Grace Lake."

"I saw a bear there a couple days ago," Pete said quietly.

Sam glanced at him. "What?"

"My buddy Tucker and I were out hiking back from Vulture Peak, not far from Grace Lake, and we came across a grizzly."

Sam didn't ask, but he knew in his gut *exactly* what Pete was doing at Vulture Peak. BASE jumping was still illegal in the park, and really, he simply didn't want to know if his brother was throwing himself off a mountain peak like Superman, wearing only a squirrel suit.

"We weren't far from Grace Lake campground—maybe closer to Logging Lake—and we came across this silver-tipped sow. She was just standing in the middle of the trail, shaking her head back and forth, as if in warning. We had bear bells and stood on the path and yelled. But the bear didn't run off like usual. It stood there staring at us, and then suddenly it just started walking toward us. Unfazed. I didn't see any cubs, so I don't think it was our grizzly from tonight. I *was* carrying food in my pack, but I'd wrapped it up. There was no normal reason to attack."

Jess was staring at him, eyes big.

Good grief, all Pete needed to do now was to put his arm around her, whisper in her ear that he might have died . . .

It was simply too easy for him.

"I backed up," Pete was saying, "but Tucker totally freaked out. He pulled out his gun and shot at it."

Sam stiffened. "Are you kidding me?" His voice rose, and the rest of the team looked his direction.

"A lot of people bring guns into the park—"

He cut his voice down. "No, I mean, did he hit it?"

"I don't think so. But it did shock it. The animal stopped then, like it was startled. Then it took off into the woods."

"Did you call it in? Report it to a ranger? Anything?"

"We didn't hit it!"

"You *think*. Seriously, bro. One bullet is not going to bring down a bear—you know that. More likely is that you nicked it, and now it's in pain, and angry. And if it's wounded, it needs food—which means terrorizing stupid kids for their Hershey bars. Maybe even killing them."

Killing *him*.

"Nice work, Pete, as usual."

Sam hadn't realized how close he'd come to shouting, and now silence fell throughout the lobby.

Perfect. Never mind the voice of reason, he knew how the team saw him. Always riding his brother.

"I need coffee. Tell Sierra when she gets here that I'm in the snack area."

Sam pushed past them and headed toward the vending machine area, a room at the end of the hallway with coffee, snacks, and drinks. The space included two small tables, chairs, and a coffee machine with fixings on a counter. He didn't bother to turn on the lights—the vending machines glowed with their selections. The late hour pressed through the window.

He fished a buck from his wallet, approached the machine, and put the dollar in the feeder.

It spit the money back at him.

He pressed down the edges, fed the money back in.

The dollar slid back out.

He smoothed it on his pants leg, turned it over and fed it back in. It rolled back out.

"C'mon!" He slammed his hand on the machine, and the entire box shook.

He blew out a breath. Put in the dollar.

It came back.

He inserted it again.

Again, it came back.

His jaw tightened, and a crazy dark fist wrapped around his chest.

He pressed the dollar in again.

It churned back out.

He closed his eyes, crumpled the dollar, and then with a growl, threw the flimsy paper across the room.

He walked over to the window and put his forehead against the cool surface.

Footsteps in the hallway stopped. The door opened. He didn't turn, even at the voice.

"Sam?"

Shoot, his eyes were blurry, his cheeks wet. He wasn't sure how he'd dismantled quite so quickly, so thoroughly, but he couldn't look at her.

"Are you okay?"

"No." He wasn't sure why he admitted that, why he let his voice ring out, broken, febrile. But he just leaned up, stared out onto the lot, the lonely lights puddling against the blackness. "I'm not."

Silence behind him, but she hadn't left, so he took it as a sign.

Maybe if he let her in, just a little, they might get to that deeper place, stir something back to life . . . "I thought I was going to die tonight."

There, he said it. And now that the truth was out, the words kept coming. "I lay there on the ground, the bear standing over me roaring, and I thought—this is it. I'm dying, right here. And not nicely, either. It's going to hurt."

She took a step toward him.

"And I wasn't ready. I mean, who is, really, but I thought, *not like this*. Not when—well, my mom is still getting over her cancer. And Pete—" He closed his eyes. "Sometimes I think I hate him. So much it makes me want to scream. I want to throw my fist in his face." He closed his eyes. "I'm so . . . tired. Just tired of hurting and being furious and trying to hold it all together." He opened his eyes, stared out at the dark parking lot. "The strange thing is, I was lying there, and suddenly I thought of my dad—at least I probably did. Because his words came to me—the fact that bears, all large animals, really, have a pretty bad gag reflex. So, I guess my dad saved me." He hadn't thought about that until now.

"And the entire ride in, all I could think of was how much I'd failed him. And not just the night he was lost, but . . ." He ran a thumb and forefinger against his eyes. "Esme, of course. I'll never forgive myself for not finding her."

It felt good to say it, even though she probably knew it.

Except, she said nothing.

"And then there's Pete. My screw-up brother who I can't seem to save." Down in the parking lot, a truck pulled under the awning.

"I always thought that, after Dad died, I could figure out how to put our lives back together, you know? Take care of Mom and keep Pete from destroying himself. But—"

"You're just rattled is all, Sam." The voice came gently through the darkness, the sound of it different, as if she might be overcome by emotion.

Or compassion. Because that was Sierra, almost too willing to help others.

"You were afraid—that's normal."

Her soft tone made him grit his jaw. "I wasn't just afraid, Sierra. I was . . . I was terrified. I was out of control. I unraveled. I couldn't even shoot straight, and then I was at the mercy of something that simply wanted to tear me apart."

He shook his head, his stupid eyes burning again. Wasn't that going overboard just a little? Still, his breath shuddered, and he felt like an idiot, standing there weeping in front of his girlfriend.

What was his problem? He'd survived, for Pete's sake.

Maybe, literally, for Pete's sake.

"Sam, I'm not—"

"Don't tell anyone. I just need a minute, okay?"

She drew in a breath. "Okay."

"But come here."

She didn't move. And he didn't want to say it, but maybe in the darkness of the room, in this moment only, "Please?"

Then her arms were around him, and she was pressing herself to his back, holding him. "It's okay, Sam. You're not alone. And you're not going to die out there in the woods, mauled by some rabid bear. You're safe."

He didn't know why, but her words reached in, wrapped around him.

So he turned in her arms, put his own around her, and pulled her tight against him. Feeling her body, soft, molded to his, fitting so perfectly.

This was the moment he'd wanted for them, because holding her like this, he definitely felt some sparks lighting inside.

He closed his eyes, pressed a kiss to her head. Then felt her hand touch his cheek.

He leaned down, letting her kiss him, his eyes closed.

Her touch was sweet, kind, without the passion he hoped might be building inside her. He curled his arms around her, pulling her closer . . .

And then . . .

Yes. He could feel it, a shift in her touch, a little ardor, unfamiliar but, finally, *yes.*

She was moving in, wrapping her arms around his neck, pulling him down to her, deepening her kiss.

He sank into her touch, needing her comfort more than he wanted to admit. She tasted salty, like popcorn, and in his arms, she seemed taller, as if she hadn't changed out of her heels tonight into her Converse tennis shoes.

And then he realized he'd been running his fingers through her hair.

Her long hair.

He jerked his head up, stared down into her eyes.

Not Sierra's hazel-green, but . . .

Oh. *No.*

"I'm sorry! You were just so sad, and then—I thought you needed something more than a hug and—"

Willow stopped talking and started backing away.

Sam couldn't breathe.

Willow. His girlfriend's flower-child-turned-youth-worker sister. Willow, with the easy laugh, pretty smile, long chestnut brown hair, hazel-blue eyes. Willow, who was about six years younger than him.

Willow, his girlfriend's kid sister.

"Oh . . ." Sam swallowed, unable to move.

She held up her hands, bumping into the table as she backed away. "Listen, I tried to say something—"

"You *tried* to say something? When? I mean, I realize there wasn't a lot of time in between me blubbering about my dad and the part where you kissed me—but certainly you might have said something. Anything. Willow! You *kissed* me."

And how. For a split second, the kiss rushed back to him, and so did the feel of her in his arms, the stir inside him at her touch.

No, *no* . . .

She was pressing her hands to her mouth, her eyes wide in a sort of horror, even in the soft padding of darkness. "I know. I *know!*" Her voice wavered. "Let's just—oh, please, can we forget this? Just—I'm leaving. I am . . . so . . . sorry."

She turned then, knocked a chair over.

"Willow, calm down. Let's talk about this."

"Please don't tell Sierra." She hit the door, turned, and sounded like she might be crying. "I promise I'll never talk to you again if you don't tell Sierra."

Him? "Oh, don't worry, my lips are sealed."

Except they still tingled with her kiss. His entire body was on fire.

She slipped out the door and shut it behind her.

And he let out a long, shaky breath.

Oh no.

———— ✝ ————

Willow had completely lost her mind.

Simply experienced an out-of-body event, controlled by some apparently deep, dark fantasy.

Okay, maybe not that deep and dark. But nothing Willow had *seriously* entertained.

She rounded the corner, spotted the PEAK gang at the desk, ignored them, and beelined straight for the ladies' room.

Where she locked herself in a stall.

That seemed the safest place to let out a silent scream, press her hands over her mouth.

She rewound, trying to pinpoint just when everything derailed. Freeze-framed on the moment she stepped up to Sam, put her arms around his lean, muscled body, and held him as he trembled with adrenaline and emotion.

A precious, sacred moment.

And it hadn't mattered that she wasn't Sierra. He needed *someone*.

No, he needed Sierra.

She *had* been about to correct him, really. Truly.

Oh.

Willow leaned her head against the cool frame of the stall and was about to let out a groan when the door to the bathroom opened.

"Willow?"

She winced. Found her voice. "Yeah?"

"I thought that was you."

Jess. Her current roomie and landlord. Friend of her sister.

Everyone, apparently, belonged to her sister.

"I saw you come in. Were you looking for Sierra?"

Um, no. "The prayer chain called. I thought I'd come to the hospital and see if anyone needed anything."

As in food, or prayer, or sympathy, even a little comfort. Only not in the way she'd delivered it. Oh, for crying out loud, she'd practically attacked him.

Willow felt a little ill. Maybe she should just stay here, hovering near the commode. "How is Bella?"

"She's okay. I'm more worried about Quinn," Jess said.

Willow pasted on a smile, then flushed the toilet, just because, and opened the stall. "Quinn Starr?"

She glanced at herself in the mirror as she came out.

She definitely looked freshly kissed. Her hair mussed, her eyes wide, lips still tingling with Sam's touch. She nearly reached up to press them.

Jess was leaning against the row of sinks, her arms folded, looking capable and pretty. Not the kind of woman to throw herself into some taken man's arms.

"Quinn was with her tonight when they were attacked."

Interesting. Willow washed her hands. "Is he okay?"

"Probably will be, but he rode with me in the chopper and is pretty shaken up."

Golden boy, charming, wealthy. Hero running back for the Mavericks and dating Bella Hayes.

Willow grabbed a paper towel, dried her hands.

Maybe, with luck, she could simply sneak into Bella's room for a visit and stay put until Sam left.

And then, somehow, dodge him for the rest of her sorry life.

"Oh, and your sister is here. She and Chet just pulled up."

Perfect. "Thanks."

Which meant Willow would probably need to scuttle through the hallways, duck behind the nurses' station, and, well, get back to Jess's place, pack her gear, and start sleeping in her car.

Maybe move to Canada.

What was her problem that she so completely led with her heart and ditched her common sense like an ugly sock?

Especially when Sam was involved.

And practically crying.

And in need of a hug.

She gritted her jaw as she opened the door and, of course, right there in the middle of the lobby stood Sierra. Cute Sierra, dressed in a pair of faded boyfriend jeans, Converse tennis shoes, and a hoodie. She stood in the middle of the group, arms folded over her chest, listening to the recap of whatever had transpired this night.

Willow didn't know the details.

But she knew the effect it had on Sam.

Jess came out behind her and headed to the group. Willow knew that in about ten seconds, Sierra would look this direction and probably spot betrayal all over Willow's guilty face. Her Achilles' heel—she wore her heart on the outside of her body like a neon sign.

Flee. Willow was turning to scuttle her way to the ER in search of Bella when she spotted him.

Sam. Striding down the hallway, his jaw set, his eyes dark and composed. Quintessential Sam, the guardian of the PEAK Rescue team.

Not the man who'd practically clung to her.

Willow's stomach burned as Sierra turned to him, gave him a hug.

Sam closed his eyes, touched his lips to Sierra's head.

The perfect, right couple.

Yes, time to flee.

Willow found Bella in the third ER bay, propped up on a pillow, her eyes closed. She wore a hospital gown, and an IV line was running into her good arm.

The other arm was bandaged from shoulder to fingertips, encased in a protective plastic sleeve.

A dark-gray, purpled hue rose along her jaw, behind an accompanying gruesome scrape. And her eye—Willow wanted to wince at the sight of the red pinpricking her cheek, evidence of broken blood vessels, the rise of swelling along her cheekbone, the way her lip, swollen and grotesque, bore the marks of trauma. A welt along her upper brow had split with more swelling.

"They're going to move her upstairs, to another room. But we're waiting for the on-call plastic surgeon." This from Pastor Walter Hayes, who stood at the edge of the cubicle, his jaw tight. He gave her a tight-lipped smile. "Nice of you to stop in."

Next to the bed, holding her daughter's hand, Carrie Hayes sat with her back to Willow, barely glancing over her shoulder at her husband's greeting. But what little Willow saw of her face appeared wrecked.

Only daughter. Near-death mauling. Yeah, she'd be wrecked too.

"I know I'm not on staff yet, but I thought, well, church family has to stick together. And Bella's one of my girls." She touched Bella's foot.

At her bedside, Carrie stiffened.

Bella opened one eye—the good one—at Willow's touch.

"How you doing, honey?" Willow said.

Bella's mouth tweaked up one side, and then her eye fluttered closed.

"She's on morphine," Walt said.

Behind her, she heard a rattle, and she turned to see two orderlies pushing a gurney toward them.

Carrie got up and stepped back into her husband's embrace, and Willow hazarded a glance at her.

She had swollen eyes and wore a cardigan and a pair of yoga pants, as if she'd been yanked out of bed into her shattered world.

Willow hadn't a clue what to say. She stepped back, watching as the orderlies moved Bella, with all her tubes and bandages, over to the gurney. Bella groaned, and her mother winced.

They filed out, and Willow didn't quite know what to do. So, she followed. Maybe they just needed someone to sit with them.

Besides, they were going the opposite direction of the foyer, so that felt like the right direction. Willow got into the elevator, saw Carrie glance at her, a tick of a frown on her brow. But she said nothing as they got out at the second floor.

Willow stood back, behind the Hayeses as the orderlies settled Bella into a bed. A nurse supervised, checked her hospital bracelet, attached a blood pressure cuff, and drew the curtain across the other bed.

Quiet descended, with just the hissing of the automatic blood pressure cuff inflating, then deflating.

Carrie made no move toward her daughter, just stood at the end of her bed, a fragile sentry to the horror.

"What was she doing out there with Quinn Starr?"

The question came quietly, almost a whisper, and Willow nearly didn't hear it. Except, then Carrie turned, her eyes on Willow, a sharpness in them.

Willow frowned. "Because he was her homecoming date?"

Carrie's mouth opened, and with it came a huff of something— incredulity, disbelief, horror—Willow couldn't exactly place. Nor the look she gave Walt.

However, whatever it was, it sent a shiver through Willow. "You did know—"

"No, actually, we didn't," Carrie snapped. "Bella isn't allowed to date yet."

"But she and Quinn have been going out for about four months. Since they met on the . . . well, this summer." She suddenly didn't want to tell them how they'd met.

On the overnight camping trip that turned into a three-night encampment at the Granite Mountain Chalet, thanks to Willow's bad decision.

The one that stranded them on top of a mountain during the flood of the century.

Carrie's mouth tightened. "Really. And you knew about this?"

"Yes. I . . . Listen, Quinn's a good Christian kid—"

"Who nearly got my daughter killed tonight." Carrie cut her voice low. "Listen, I know Quinn comes from a good family, but he's a teenage boy, and that says enough. Besides, I think he's trouble." She shook her head, her mouth tight. "Did you know that the doctor thinks Belle might have even been doing drugs? He did a blood test. On my *daughter*!" She shook her head, her jaw tight. "If she was, I'm sure Quinn gave it to her. And who knows what he planned to do to her in the woods!"

"I don't think—"

"I know *exactly* what he was up to," Walt said quietly. "He's a teenage boy, after all. And clearly one with a problem."

"That's not fair. He's a good kid. I've never known Quinn to drink, let alone do drugs—"

"Apparently he's a good liar, and probably taught my daughter to do the same thing," Carrie retorted. "What's worse is that she's been lying to me all summer long. And you helped her do it!"

What? "I didn't know that she wasn't supposed to date."

"Really. After everything I've preached from the pulpit about courtship?" Walt said, and now she saw a spark of blame in his eyes.

"Pastor, listen, these two kids are crazy about each other, in a good way—"

"There is no good way when you're seventeen," Carrie said. "And you, as the youth leader, should know that." She crossed her arms. "At the very least, you should have told us."

"Told you what?"

"Anything. All of it. I am her parent, and I should know what my daughter is doing. I know there are a lot of kids, Willow, but when we send our children to youth group, we're trusting you to guide them." She took a step toward Willow. "And if they're going astray, we deserve to know about it."

"But they weren't—listen, I didn't know she wasn't supposed to date yet. But . . ." And apparently Willow hadn't a smidgen of common sense remaining, because in that moment, she heard herself, wanted to reach out and yank back the words. "Even if I did, I wouldn't come running to tell on them. These kids need to trust me. And they won't if I tell their secrets."

Carrie recoiled as if she'd been slapped. "What are you trying to accomplish here? Being a youth leader is more than just hanging out and being their friend. You have to guide them, Willow. Not just be their buddy. I know that's more fun, but we're expecting you to train them up in the ways of the Lord." She turned to her daughter and pointed. "Does this look like the way of the Lord to you?"

Her voice reverberated in the room, and like a hand, reached in and gave Willow a shake.

She had no words.

"As for being on staff—"

"Honey." This from Walt, who had stepped up, put his hands on her shoulders. "Not now."

"Really? Because now feels like *exactly* the time to tell her that no, she'll never be on staff at the church, because frankly, she can't be trusted to make wise decisions. Sure, you love these kids, but there's more to being a youth leader than just being one of the girls or planning fun events and object lessons. You have to actually know and *teach* the word of God. Because children's lives are at stake!"

Willow couldn't move.

"Willow. We all know your heart is for these kids," Pastor Hayes said quietly. "But you and I both know you don't have a Bible degree. Frankly, you don't even have a high school diploma."

If he'd punched her in the gut, it wouldn't have hurt her more.

Carrie cut in. "We need someone who can get through to these kids. Who will teach them to listen—and mind—their parents. And who will alert us if they decide to do something stupid like . . . like . . ." Carrie's breath caught, and she pressed her hand over her mouth. "Like get high and nearly get themselves killed by running off with some sex-crazed boy!"

Willow wanted to hold up her hand, offer some editing. But, really, what could she say, except, "I'm sorry."

Carrie could have turned her to stone with her glare.

Willow glanced at Walt, then at Bella. "Tell her . . . if you want . . . that I stopped—no, that I'm praying for her."

She bit her lip, blinking hard, and backed out of the room.

In the hall, she leaned against the wall, just for a moment, her heart thundering, and tried to keep her legs from turning completely liquid.

You have to guide them, Willow.

She could hardly guide herself. She pushed herself away from the wall. Then she headed to the stairwell.

Because, with Sierra and Sam congregated right by the elevator, she just might burst into tears, a full-out unravel at the sight of them.

All of them—the entire PEAK team, rescuing people from death and making a difference in people's lives.

While she, apparently, was just here for the fun.

Because, really, what else was she fit to do?

She opened the stairwell doorway and stepped out onto the landing.

Stopped.

Voices lifted and bounced through the metal and corrugated stairwell.

"What were you thinking, Quinn? No, scratch that. I know *exactly* what you were thinking."

"Dad, it wasn't like that!"

She held her breath and looked over the edge. Senator Wolfgang Starr had his hand fisted in his son's suit jacket and was pushing him up against the cold cement wall, just a floor below her.

Quinn didn't seem fazed. A good-looking kid with his short, tousled black hair, cut jaw, brown eyes—now fierce as he glared at his dad—he bore the physique of a kid used to workouts and not settling for halfway.

Probably just like dear old dad. Because in a way, Quinn was the image of his father—tall, wide-shouldered, confident.

No wonder Senator Starr had swept the last election. He simply had to smile into the camera and list his three bronze stars and four meritorious service medals and add in the fact he'd saved more than a few army personnel during his tours in Iraq.

She felt a little sorry for Quinn, trying to live up to all that.

"We were just out there because there's this great view of Huckleberry Mountain at the overlook. Willow was telling me about it, and I thought Bella would want to see it."

And she wanted to die on the spot. She *had* been telling the kids about the best views of the park, how God spoke to her when she was hiking or in nature. When she could get a perspective of God's world.

But—oh no.

"Listen, Quinn," the senator said. "I don't care about this girl—I care about *you*. And your future. You were at a pit party, with kids who were drinking and doing drugs. Do you realize how that might look on your Naval Academy application if you got busted?" He leaned into Quinn, whose jaw tightened. For Quinn's part, he didn't blink. "It means no naval appointment, no officer status, no future. All so you could make out with some girl—"

"She's not just some girl. I love her, Dad. And frankly, I couldn't care less about the Naval Academy!"

His father slammed his bare palm into the wall over Quinn's

shoulder. Even Willow jumped, pressing a hand over her mouth to keep silent.

Quinn swallowed and, despite his expression, seemed to pale.

Someone needed to intervene. Willow put her hand on the railing and was about to come to Quinn's rescue when the stairwell door banged open.

There in the doorway, the door softly shutting behind him, stood Deputy Sam Brooks.

He wore his law enforcement face. Solemn, his blue eyes piercing, his mouth in a tight line of warning.

Sam would protect Quinn—he wasn't the kind to flinch at trouble.

"What's going on here, Senator?" Sam said in his everybody-stay-calm voice. "We can hear you out in the lobby."

Wolfgang took a step back, considered his son, then turned to Sam. "A private conversation between father and son."

"Not if you continue to have it in a cement stairwell," Sam said. "There are reporters out there."

He glanced at Quinn, who'd taken the opportunity to take a breath. Then he ducked under Sam's arm and pushed out into the lobby.

"Quinn!" Wolfgang said, but Sam stopped his pursuit with a hand to his chest.

"Give him a second to cool off," Sam said. "And yourself."

See, this was why she'd kissed him—and would forgive herself for it. Because Sam was the kind of man she could—probably already did—love. Compassionate, strong, and safe, he gave people the benefit of the doubt. He didn't jump to conclusions but listened. Cared. Understood. And while he might be the law, he knew it wasn't about the rules but the relationship. Frankly, he'd proved that to her earlier, with his compassion to her after she'd kissed him.

Probably, he'd already forgiven her. Understood. *Let's talk about this.*

"You don't understand, Sam. He's going to destroy his entire life with this girl."

C'mon, Sam, tell him to calm down. True love is worth—

"I know. I couldn't agree more. Kids are stupid, and they lead with their emotions. Right now his emotions are making him impulsive and unpredictable." Sam clamped Senator Starr on his shoulder. "My advice—get him home. Calm him down. And wait until tomorrow to tell him you're sending him to military school, right?"

The senator's chuckle rattled up the stairwell, right into Willow's bones. Her throat burned, her breath caught.

And then her eyes blurred when Sam, too, laughed.

"Never trust anyone when they're emotional, Senator. Not even yourself, right? It only leads to mistakes, regrets, and most of all, people getting hurt. The best you can do is try to steer them away from trouble and hope they'll come to their senses."

He opened the door for Wolfgang and gave him a diplomatic smile.

It burned all the way through Willow.

She'd definitely come to her senses.

———— + ————

If she smiled any longer, her face might break. Jess Tagg gritted her molars, holding on to her final string of patience as Tallie Kennedy, reporter for the *Mercy Falls Register*, smiled up at Pete.

Out of all the PEAK team members still congregated in the ER, the former Miss Montana had cornered Pete Brooks as her spokesman.

And why not? Out of all her choices, Jess would have chosen Pete too, probably. If she were choosing.

Which she wasn't.

"How did you spell your name again?"

Right. How hard was it to spell B-r-o-o-k-s? Jess would lay heavy bets on the fact that Tallie wanted to say something else. Like, "Where do you live?" or even "Wanna go over that article later, maybe at your place?"

Jess closed her eyes, turned away, ignored the tiny churn of her gut. But what did she expect? Pete had been amazingly heroic tonight, saving everyone with his quick thinking.

Throwing an ax at a charging grizzly, like he might be Thor? He even *looked* like Thor, with his long, shoulder-length blond hair, now held back with his requisite baseball cap, and the slightest grizzle of crimson-gold whiskers.

Never mind the very Thor-like muscles and the blue eyes that could make a girl say yes to just about anything he suggested.

Other girls. Not her.

Sorry, but Pete Brooks could wield all his mystical charm on her and she'd simply suggest a night out, maybe a game of touch football with the guys.

The last thing she needed was to fall for a good-timing man like Pete. Not when she'd finally put her life, not to mention her broken heart, back together again.

She glanced at the door to the ER, hoping to see Gage or Ty edging out. Kacey had disappeared, probably to fly the chopper back to the base, and with her Ben King, her fiancé.

Which left Jess stranded at the hospital.

"Naw, I'm not hungry," she heard Pete say, and realized that Tallie had popped the question.

A little late for pizza, a burger, or really any food, wasn't it?

Although, admittedly, his rejection of Tallie's offer had Jess curious.

Not like charmer Pete Brooks to pass on a date with a cute girl like Tallie.

No, Tallie was more than cute. With her faded jeans and a V-neck T-shirt that looked more sorority girl than ace reporter, she had "Hot Night" written all over her. Her long golden-brown hair tumbled down in soft waves, surrounding big amber eyes and an I-like-you smile, and yeah, Pete must have come down with a raging case of the chicken pox to be walking over to *Jess*, his hands in his pockets.

Huh.

Even Tallie looked confused.

But if Tallie thought she'd been blown off for Jess, she clearly didn't know there was nothing but friendship between them. And Jess certainly didn't have anything on Tallie Kennedy. Not in her less-than-shapely blue jumpsuit and her hair pulled back in a ponytail.

She probably still had a dab of lavender paint on her chin. But when the team was called out, one didn't have time to scrub the paint off one's face. Jess had simply changed clothes and high-tailed it over to the ranch, where Kacey Fairing was running her last flight check on the chopper.

Mauling. That was the briefing PEAK boss Chet gave them, along with the fact that their team—Pete, Gage, and Sam—were hunting for a lost kid.

Her heart had kicked into high gear when they'd closed in on their LZ and she'd heard Pete over the radio shouting for help. Ben and Ty nearly leaped from the chopper. Kacey, with the steely-edged nerves bred from her years flying rescue choppers in Afghanistan, lifted back into the air.

On her way to help, any way she could.

Jess's breath stopped when the spotlights from the chopper caught the bear on hind legs about to tear into Sam.

For a moment there, it looked as if the grizzly might leave Sam in pieces.

And that would shatter Pete. She had fired the flare on pure reflex.

She put her hand on the nurses' desk, blew out a breath. Yeah, she needed to go home.

Probably, she also needed a pizza.

"Hey, let's get out of here." Pete had stopped right in front of her, leaned down to meet her eyes. "Wanna get a pizza?"

What, did the man have the ability to climb inside her head and poke around? She hoped not, because then he'd see the way just his presence had all her synapses firing. Her heartbeat kicked up a notch, and her body hummed.

Oh, she was a magnet for men who would break her heart.

Still, she managed a smile, her years of society-page training saving her hide once again. "Really? I thought Tallie—"

"She's not my type."

Huh. She wanted to ask what his type was, but—

"Besides, we should probably finish that bathroom before the paint dries, right?"

Oh, she was in trouble when he talked like that. "It probably needs a second coat."

"Then we'll order an extra-large pizza." He winked and turned to the group. "Hey, Sam, gimme your keys."

Sam stood with Sierra, dressed in the unlikely Search-and-Rescue attire of dress pants, scuffed-up dress shoes, and a ripped shirt, over which he'd donned a dirty suit jacket.

He frowned at Pete.

"You're riding with Sierra, right? I need to ditch, man."

Sam's mouth tightened, but he reached into his pocket and tossed Pete his keys. Pete caught them with one hand and headed out.

"Poor guy. He was out on a date with Sierra when the call came in." Pete held the door open for Jess as they stepped out into the cool night air.

The stars were now fading as the night began to wane, the half-moon glimmering against the darkness, its glow puddling on the dark parking lot. A slight breeze carried the scent of pine and the hint of a wood fire in some hearth.

Pete tossed the keys in his hand.

"You okay?" she asked.

"I'm good." He looked over at her, winked.

There it went again, the very forbidden thrill. Because they were teammates. Buddies.

Just a couple of guys, hanging out late. With pizza and lavender paint.

She got into Sam's truck and unzipped her jumpsuit, pulling off the arms, rolling it down to her waist. She wore a blue PEAK T-shirt underneath.

Pete pulled out, and she took off her hat, tossed it on the dash, then tugged out the tie from her hair, running her fingers through the strands to work out the snarls.

Only then did she see Pete glancing at her, more than once.

"What?"

"Nothing, I'm just wondering what's on your agenda. 'Cause we have work to do."

She stared at him, and then he smiled. "I'm just kidding, Speedy. I wouldn't think of hittin' on you."

She laughed too, because this was their game.

He flirted, she pushed him away, and round and round they went.

"I wouldn't date you anyway, Pete Brooks."

"Aw, c'mon. I'm fun." He pulled into the Griz, an all-night convenience store.

"Believe me, I know. Word gets around. Pete Brooks, all fun, all the time."

She got out of the truck and headed to the door.

He didn't join her. He just sat looking at her, his smile gone.

"What?" She held up her hands. "I'm just kidding."

A strange half smile curved up his face, and he got out.

He put his hand on the small of her back as he reached out to open the door.

Inside, he headed over to the prebaked pizzas, wrapped and under the heat lamps of the twenty-four-hour kitchenette.

"Pepperoni?"

"If that's all they have." She grabbed a couple Cokes from the cooler and they met at the checkout.

Her stomach roared as she got back into the truck.

She stared out the window as they drove toward Mercy Falls, passing the local VFW and out in the distance the glimmering lights of the PEAK Rescue ranch. Beyond that, Ian Shaw's place remained dark—he'd been out of town searching for leads on his lost niece most of the summer. Last she'd heard, he'd been placing missing person ads in the paper and was trying to get his now-twenty-one-year-old niece listed on the national missing person's registry.

"I have to know, Pete. Why isn't Tallie your type?"

The padding of darkness had made her brave.

"Tallie? Oh, she's nice. I supposed she *might* be my type. I just wanted to get out of there."

Oh.

Well, what did she expect him to say? That he only liked—

"But if you must know, I'm partial to blondes. Grimy, sort of feisty ones with no real social life. The kind I can beat in a game of horse."

Her mouth opened. "I have a social life!"

"Right. You and your Skil saw."

"I happen to like home repair."

He was grinning, and as they passed under streetlights, his eyes were so blue they shimmered. Her heart skipped one beat, two.

"Good thing you're not talking about me," she said then, finding her voice. "Last time I remember, I kicked you up one side of the court and down the other in one-on-one."

"I let you win, Speedy. You whine when you lose."

"I don't lose."

"Because I let you win." He reached over to the pizza. "Gimme one of those pieces. I could eat a grizzly."

"That's not funny." She dug into the box, pulled out a piece. The pizza was soggy, a little overcooked, but she too could eat a large animal.

Maybe not a grizzly.

He folded the pizza in half, eating it like a sandwich, one hand on the wheel.

"Besides, you're not exactly *my* type," she said.

"Which is?"

"Oh, I don't know. The kind of guy who won't let me win, maybe? Who can simply acknowledge that I'm better than him?"

"Right, honey. Okay, we'll have another go. When and where, name it."

She liked how he said it, with a little growl to his voice.

"Anytime, Michael Jordan." She dug a piece of pizza out of the box, took a bite. "This isn't terrible."

"The Hotline Grill over in Ember makes awesome pizza."

"That's where you were based when you were smoke jumping, right?" She caught a piece of dripping mozzarella, tucked it in her mouth. "Do you miss it?"

"A little. But it's better that I'm home. For Mom, you know? She's still pretty weak from the chemo."

She had to admire a guy who came home because his mom needed him.

Her mother might speak to her again someday. But Jess wasn't exactly waiting by the phone.

They wove their way through town, along the side roads, until he pulled up in front of her house.

Her glorious, ramshackle, someday-gorgeous 1907, three-story house, with the front porch, gables, clapboard siding, formerly crumbling foundation, and a stripped and dilapidated interior.

48

A house that no one could ever kick her out of, and paid for in full, thank you, for the grand sum of $1.00 from the city of Mercy Falls.

Formerly condemned, and now with a little help from her team, sporting a new roof, new insulation, and new windows.

Although, granted, she was still sleeping on the floor and generally living like a squatter. At least she had a working kitchen and plumbing.

Most important, it was hers. Bought and remodeled with her own hard-earned money.

As far from her father's influence as she could get.

"It's late, so maybe painting can wait. But . . . I'm walking you in."

He grabbed the box of pizza and got out.

"What's with the chivalry? You're suddenly worried about my safety?"

Although, come to think of it, he'd been here most evenings, fixing the roof, porch, siding, adding insulation, repairing the plumbing, re-ducting the heating system, even rewiring a couple rooms for electricity. Frankly, he spent more time at 303 Sycamore than he did at his mom's place.

"I can take care of myself," she said as she climbed up the steps.

"I know." He held out his hand, waggled his fingers.

"Fine." She handed him the keys, and he opened the heavy vintage door. It creaked on its hinges, and she could admit that any time after 2:00 a.m. was a creepy time of night. He flicked on the overhead light, and the newly washed leaded glass fixture sprayed light down the hallway and into the family room.

Three sleeping bags atop air mattresses lay on the floor in front of the hearth. Beside them snaked cords that plugged into outlets for their chargers and lamps.

Pete headed straight back to the kitchen and turned on that light too.

He put the pizza down on the Formica table she'd picked up

at the Goodwill. Table and four chairs for twenty bucks. Paid for in full.

She put the Cokes down on the table. "You going to walk Gage to the door for safety, too?"

Strangely, he didn't smile. "No," he said quietly.

He stood so close she could just reach out and touch him, just lightly run her hand down his chest.

She felt it then, the tug of longing, the game suddenly crashing down between them. The darkness of the hour folding in, inviting her to take a chance.

Teammates. They'd been dancing around that word for months now and—

"Jess."

His soft, low voice just sort of slid into her, around her, and she caught her breath. Oh shoot—if she looked up at him, she knew he'd see it, no more acting. All her emotions right there on her face.

He took a breath too and took a step toward her.

His hands fell on her shoulders.

She closed her eyes, lifted her face.

He was going to kiss her. She could feel it in the simmer between them as he stood there. And she was going to let him.

No, she was going to kiss him back.

"I need to ask you something."

She opened her eyes. Swallowed. Met his beautiful eyes with an imperceptible nod. *Yes, Pete, you can kiss—*

"I think I'm going to apply for incident commander for the PEAK team."

She blinked at him.

"And I was wondering if"—he drew in a breath, his face solemn—"you might help me write a résumé. It's required, and I wasn't so great in school."

He walked over to the pizza, leaving her standing there, the heat of his hands still on her shoulders.

"Résumé?"

He dug out another piece of pizza and leaned against her table, looking so relaxed, his blue eyes innocent and easy, as if he hadn't just tilted her world off its axis. "I've never done one—just sort of worked odd jobs, and then I was a smoke jumper, so I didn't have to. The Forest Service kept us pretty busy, even in the off season. But I need a real job. Not just working for my uncle down at the lumberyard, but something I'm good at."

He was serious. And being strangely sheepish about it, with his furtive looks and wry smile.

"Yeah. Of course," she said, her voice rebounding. "I think it's a good idea."

"You do?"

His question rocked her, as if he actually needed her input. Or approval.

She wanted to retrieve her own piece of pizza, but probably it wouldn't make it through the knots in her stomach. She plastered on a smile, shrugged. "Yeah. Of course. You're a quick thinker, and you always know what to do. I think you'd make a great IC. I mean, your brother would probably have to hire you, but that's no problem, right?"

Pete looked away, his jaw tight. "Shoot. You're right." He tossed the pizza in the box. "I gotta go."

Oh. "Pete—"

"I'll come back in the morning, see if we can knock out that second layer of paint."

She frowned at him, but he flashed his killer smile, reached out, and touched her chin. "Only you, Speedy, would paint a bathroom purple." He kissed her forehead. "Thanks for saving my hide from the grizzly tonight."

And then he left her there, closing the door behind him.

Anytime, Pete. Anytime.

3

IT FELT DOWNRIGHT SINFUL that the search committee for the new youth pastor should meet in the back room of the Summit Café at lunchtime, on a Friday afternoon.

During Willow's shift.

In her area.

It was probably God's punishment for her betrayal of Sierra. Not that God was vindictive, Willow knew that. But she'd been walking around with the memory of kissing Sam in her heart for a week now—a sharp-edged burr that stung every time she looked at Sierra.

Willow deserved a little punishment, and would take it with a smile. Even if it nearly dismantled her watching her dream job being handed over right before her eyes to a twenty-year-old preppy Bible school youngster in blue jeans rolled up at the ankles, a printed black T-shirt, and suit jacket. He had such a baby face he could double for Justin Bieber. He drank a caramel latte as he talked about his plans for the youth program—to start a Bible certificate program and a youth choir.

She put his Reuben sandwich in front of him, then looked at the gathering around the table, doing a quick appraisal.

Grilled cheese and tomato soup for Pastor Hayes, a pastrami

on rye for Nora Webster, the associate pastor's wife, and a chicken salad sandwich for Chet King—he looked up and smiled at her. At least she had one friendly face in the crowd.

Her jury, the ones who had ruled her unworthy.

She pasted on a smile. "Can I get anyone anything else?"

"I'll take more water," Nora said, tapping her glass.

"Can I get some Coke?" This from the youngster. Oh, she should probably start calling him by his name. "No problem, Josh." She headed out of the room to the long soda fountain counter.

The Summit Café hummed with conversation on this Friday afternoon, a day off for Mercy Falls schools for some sort of teacher training day. The smell of burgers on the grill, crunchy onion rings, fresh-spun malts, and house-ground coffee made the café one of her favorite places, ever, to work.

She'd made the rounds, from the convenience store, working at their twenty-four-hour kitchen, deep-frying wings and assembling pizzas, to summers working in the park as a trail guide, to pulling espresso shots at the Last Chance Coffee Shop. Even that one stint as a waitress at the Gray Pony Bar and Grill. After all, a girl without a formal education couldn't turn down a job.

She should probably see if she could get back on staff at the Pony for the winter. After all, given the conversation in the next room, she'd no longer have to keep her weekends free for youth activities.

Apparently, they didn't need her anymore.

Willow filled a glass with Coke, grabbed the water pitcher, and headed back to the room. The group stopped talking when she entered—small mercies—and she set the glass down in front of Josh, then filled Nora's glass.

Pastor Hayes touched her arm as she passed by. "Bella comes home today," he said quietly. "She was hoping you'd call her."

Willow smiled, nodded, crazy tears burning her eyes as she fled the room.

Silly. It wasn't like she wouldn't see these kids again. But Carrie's words had rung in her head all week. *"She'll never be on staff at the church, because frankly, she can't be trusted to make wise decisions."*

She tried not to let the words dig a hole in her chest but . . .

It might be true. After all, she'd stranded them on a mountaintop only a few months ago during the flood of the century.

She wandered by the rest of her tables—a family on vacation, a group of teenage boys fresh in from some grass-stained practice. Maybe rugby players. She thought she might have recognized one from a youth event, but he said nothing. Another table of ladies—they held books and were in rapt discussion—ignored Willow as she filled their glasses.

She put the pitcher down on the table at the booth where Jess and Sierra sat. Sierra was finishing the last of her banana chocolate shake, and Jess was picking at her tater tots. As usual, Jess hadn't quite gotten all the paint off her hands—Willow spotted a smudge of pink.

"Paint break?" she asked.

Jess looked up at her, her mind clearly somewhere else because she blinked a moment, then smiled. "Yeah. I think Pete is coming over later to start tackling the upstairs. We need to gut the bathroom."

"I can't believe he's doing all this for free," Sierra said.

Willow glanced at her tables and slid in beside her sister, just for a moment. "Oh, I know why he's doing it—he's getting paid in hang-out time with Jess."

Jess's mouth opened, then closed, and she frowned. "No—I mean, sure, we're friends, and we have a good time together, but we're teammates. I promise you, he doesn't think about me in any other way."

"Right," Sierra said, and Willow glanced at her.

"Seriously," Sierra continued. "I see the way Pete looks at you at

54

the ranch. And yeah, you two have fun, but under all that teasing, I think he's looking for a way to ask you out."

"Oh trust me, that's not what's happening here." Jess added a shake of her head, a wry smile, and picked up a tot.

Silence filled the wake of her denial, and she looked up. "What?"

"No, you tell us, *what*," Sierra said, and Willow nodded.

Jess lifted a shoulder. "Nothing, just . . ." She sighed. "After the bear attack, he brought me home and . . ."

More silence.

"Jess, do I need to take those tots away?" Willow said.

Jess looked up, wrinkled her nose. "Fine. I thought he was going to kiss me, and . . ."

For a second, just a flash, Willow was back in Sam's arms, tasting his mouth on hers.

"He kissed you?" Sierra said.

"No. I *thought* he was going to kiss me. We were goofing around, as usual, and then things just got real serious, real fast, and he took a step toward me—close enough so that we probably *could* have kissed . . ."

"Would you have let him kiss you?" Willow said.

Jess looked past her, out the front window. "Maybe."

"Jess," Sierra said.

"Why not? I mean, I know you guys say he's such a womanizer, but really, I haven't seen it. Yes, he flirts—but that's just his personality. And . . . oh, I don't know. You're probably right. I don't want a guy who just wants to have fun. I'm not that kind of girl. Except, maybe I am, because the last thing I need is to get tangled up in a relationship."

Willow watched her as she wiped her mouth, crumpled her napkin. "Jess, why didn't he kiss you?"

Jess tossed the napkin on her plate. "He asked if I'd help him write a résumé. He wants to be an incident commander for the PEAK team."

"That's a great idea," Sierra said. "Sam's always saying that they need a backup, in case Miles is unavailable."

"Yeah, well, I mentioned that Sam would have to hire him, and Pete sort of shut down. There's bad blood between them, but Pete never talks about it."

Sierra was nodding. "Sam doesn't either. I don't know what their problem is."

Willow stared at her sister. "What are you talking about? Of *course* you know—it's about their dad. And the fact that he got lost on the mountain chasing Pete."

Sierra frowned at her. "I guess I thought he was over that."

"What are you talking about?" Jess asked.

"What do you mean *over that*?" Willow said to Sierra.

"I don't mean losing his dad, but the fight between him and Pete—"

"*What* fight?" Jess said.

"I guess I didn't realize he really blamed Pete. I thought it was an accident," Sierra said.

"They got in a huge fight. In front of everyone!" Willow said.

"Pete and Sam?" Jess interjected.

Poor Jess. Willow turned to her. "Yeah. It was about twelve years ago—I remember because I was at Dad's that weekend. He was called out to find a skier who'd gone missing in the backwoods off a nearby ski resort. A storm blew in that night, and they didn't find the skier for two days. He'd fallen in a tree well and frozen to death."

"Oh my gosh—and that was Pete and Sam's *dad*?" Jess said.

"Yeah. Apparently, when they found him, Sam blamed Pete, publicly. It was pretty ugly." She left off the rest, the more private information he'd shared with her in error. "*Sometimes I think I hate him. So much it makes me want to scream. I want to throw my fist in his face.*"

His wretched tone could still shake her. Oh, Sam.

She refused to think about the rest. Especially when she was sitting next to Sierra.

But her throat burned.

"Sam was out of school for about two weeks, right in the middle of our senior year," Sierra was saying to Jess, finishing the story. "His uncle took over the lumber company. Maybe that's why Sam didn't go to college. Stayed local."

"Probably to help his mom. Especially after Pete took off." Willow saw the teenagers in need of a checkup. She got up and delivered them more water, then fished around in her apron for the check. Ripped it off. "No hurry."

She swung by the counter, picked up the coffeepot, and refilled mugs for the book ladies. Then stopped by the family, whose children were still finishing their chicken nuggets.

"Don't forget to pick a candy from one of the bins. It comes with the kids' meals," she said and pointed to the baskets of old-time candies, one of the Summit's novelties.

She debated swinging into the back room and instead headed back to Jess and Sierra. She picked up Jess's plate.

"Hey, what's happening back there?" Sierra said. "You get a glimpse of the new youth pastor?"

"Yeah. He's about three years old. Perfect Bible name—Josh Blessing. He's a newlywed and apparently he and his wife, Ava, just found out that she's expecting."

She stacked Sierra's malt glass on the plate. "I shouldn't judge— they're probably super nice. The kids are going to learn lots. I'm just going to miss everyone."

She turned, but Sierra reached out, touched her arm. "Willow, what are you talking about? You're not stepping down as a youth leader just because they have an official youth pastor, are you? Those kids know you—they *need* you. Probably Josh could use your help settling in. Don't let the committee's rejection keep you from doing what's right for these kids."

And see, *this* was why Sierra deserved a happy ending—although maybe if she'd heard Sam's words in the stairwell, she might not be so thrilled with him. But still, Sierra had nothing but mercy, nothing but a generous spirit.

Case in point, her almost tireless search, on and off the clock for the last three years, looking for billionaire Ian Shaw's missing niece, Esme. If they hadn't called off the search, and if Ian hadn't fired her, Sierra would probably be at the Shaw ranch right now, making calls, following leads.

Unable to extricate herself from her crush on her billionaire former boss.

No, Sam and Sierra had to work out—for Sierra's sake. She needed a fresh start, something to show her she didn't need to be at Ian's beck and call.

Besides, Willow just knew Sam wasn't the guy she'd heard with Senator Starr. She'd worked it all out as she stared at her darkened ceiling so many nights this week. Sam had just been trying to appease Senator Starr. Trying to tell him what he wanted to hear.

Because Sam was a cop and knew how to talk people away from their dangerous emotions.

Unlike her, who apparently dove right in.

"Don't you have a hike scheduled for this weekend into the park?" Sierra asked.

Willow set the dishes down. "I did. I thought maybe I could use it as an object lesson—something about teaching the kids to look at life from God's perspective. To let him guide them, since he sees the entire picture."

"Right—see, that's good. And *exactly* what they need. You should go in there and tell Josh and the committee that you'll take them on the hike. Josh can go with you, a sort of introduction to the group. Then, on the hike, you can prove to Josh that he needs you. That you're still part of the team. You want that, right?"

She didn't want to admit it, but . . .

Okay, she might just be feeling a little sorry for herself. It just felt that, with her father finding a new family and Sierra finding true love with Sam, the youth group seemed the only family she had left.

"They'd never let me be the only adult who knows the park on the hike."

"What if I went with you?"

Ah, see, she didn't deserve her sister. "I don't—"

"And I'll get Sam to join us. They can't turn down Sam's involvement. Who better than a cop to keep them safe?"

Willow managed to find a smile. "Yeah, but he's so busy."

"No, he's not. He just doesn't slow down. It would be good for him, I promise. I'll ask him tonight, on our date."

There it went again, the burr crawling through the walls of her heart. Somehow she managed an "Oh . . . okay."

"Go in there—right now," Sierra said. She actually slid out of the booth, pressed her hand to the small of her sister's back. "I'll go with you if you want."

"No. I . . ." Willow blew out a breath. "Okay, fine."

But she picked up the water pitcher on her way, just for fortification.

Most had finished their food. Chet asked for a box for his chicken sandwich and chips. Josh had left half his Reuben on his plate.

She filled Pastor Hayes's water, then stepped back, waiting for a pause in the conversation—an innocuous discussion about the current winning streak of the Mercy Falls Mavericks.

Nora was the first to look up at her. She gave her a smile. Willow tested it for warmth, couldn't decide.

"The check is on me," Pastor Hayes said quietly, glancing up at her.

"I know," Willow said. "Actually, I wanted, while you were all here . . ." She swallowed. "I wanted to talk about the youth hike we have scheduled tomorrow."

"It's not another overnight, is it?" Nora said.

"No, just a day hike. Sort of an end-of-the-season wrap-up. I wanted to take them up to the lookout on Huckleberry Mountain and talk about God's perspective and . . ."

Now it sounded so lame. A feeble attempt to build some faith activity into a fun trip. *"There's more to being a youth leader than just being one of the girls or planning fun events and object lessons. You have to actually know and teach the word of God."*

"I don't know, Willow." Nora was shaking her head. "With the recent bear attack, and the last hike you were on . . ."

It didn't help that Nora's son, Nate, had gotten lost on said hike and ended up breaking his ankle in two places.

She should probably slink from the room.

"That sounds fun." The voice came from the other end of the table. Josh, slick, skinny, and about as city-bred as a guy could get. "I've never been in the park, and it would be a great way to bond with these kids. Nothing builds friendship like a challenging activity together."

"Not too challenging, I hope," Nora said.

"I don't know," Pastor Hayes said. "Josh doesn't really know the park—"

And that's when Willow got desperate, when Sierra's idea suddenly turned from wretchedly awkward to brilliant. "Deputy Sam Brooks would be going with us, along with my sister, Sierra."

It had the effect she was hoping for.

Nora settled back in her chair, nodding. Chet glanced past her, perhaps at Sierra, and offered a shrug.

"All right, Willow," Pastor Hayes said. "You coordinate with Josh. But yeah, if Sam's going, then you can take the kids up the mountain."

She was reaching to gather up their plates when she heard Nora add, "And back down again, safely."

Willow had a feeling she wasn't kidding.

———— + ————

He wasn't going to sing hallelujah or anything, but Pete could admit to a rush of relief when Jess didn't answer her door.

At least then he didn't have to spend the day pretending that something hadn't changed between them the night he'd driven her home.

He pulled out his cell phone, checked for a text from her, but his messages were empty.

Huh. She was probably out getting supplies. Which meant he could sit on the porch and wait for her, or . . .

Or maybe she, too, felt the awkward shift in their friendship.

Which meant he should leave it alone. Give them time to find their footing again. He didn't know how the teasing turned from fun to fire. Probably when she'd asked him what kind of girl he wanted and he'd answered with the truth.

He blamed it all on fatigue and nearly being eaten by a bear—but he'd let it spill out. *"I'm partial to blondes. Grimy, sort of feisty ones with no real social life. The kind I can beat in a game of horse."*

Really? Oh, he wanted to bang his head on something solid, maybe the oak doors to her house, and knock his brains back into place.

She'd laughed it away, but it was too late because she'd already stirred up longing like a live coal inside him when she'd shaken out her long blonde hair.

His heart had thundered, his entire body began to hum, and it turned deafening when he'd walked her to her door, despite his instincts screaming at him to run. Or actually that was his brain—his instincts whispered a completely different song.

Then, in the kitchen of her wreck of a home, she stared up at him, her beautiful aqua blue eyes in his, her golden hair in waves, and he heard the whispers begging him to weave his fingers into her soft mane, to pull her to himself.

The desire crashed around inside him, tried to take control, and he'd nearly surrendered. Nearly put his hand to her neck, touched his lips to that beautiful mouth.

Shown her *exactly* the kind of girl he wanted.

In desperation he'd come up with the lame question about the résumé. Not that he hadn't been thinking of asking her for help—but suddenly, it became his lifeline.

He needed something, *anything* to save their playful, perfect friendship, to keep himself from doing something stupid that would someday make her regret knowing him. Because eventually he'd end up hurting her—he knew that too well about himself.

What was it that his smoke jumper friend Kate had once said to him? *"Pete gives them just enough to stay interested, but not enough for them to show up on his doorstep the next day."*

He'd laughed it off then, but really, his image as a good-timing guy protected everyone, including himself. He could admit that having women jockey for a turn with him on the dance floor put a Band-Aid on the wounds. It kept him smiling. Moving forward.

Until Jess. She'd somehow made him believe that he could actually *be* a good guy. It started with him fixing up her house, but since then had morphed into a late-night, pizza-eating, basket-ball-shooting, let's-watch-football, buddy friendship, the kind he hadn't had since leaving the Jude County Smoke Jumpers last fall.

He wasn't going to jeopardize that. Besides, how could they work together if they were, well, *together*?

It had been heaps easier when his teammates consisted of just the guys—Reuben and Conner, even Jed, fellow members of the Jude County Smoke Jumpers. Maybe he should have stayed, but coming home to help his mom recover from her fight against cancer seemed the right move.

The fact that Sam hadn't sent him packing only lit the crazy hope inside Pete that he could actually repair his mistakes, restart his life, become that guy he thought his father would want him to be. Dependable. Serious. Responsible. A guy who valued relation-ships and stuck around for the hard stuff.

Instead of running.

Although, as he pulled away from Jess's house and headed for the PEAK ranch, he could admit that, given the amount of relief that gusted through him when Jess didn't answer, running felt like the right move.

He still felt like a jerk. He should probably stick around and wait. Or . . . maybe he'd double back later.

He turned out onto Main Street, away from town.

Truth was, not only did he want to take a sledge to that rank bathroom, but he really did need Jess's help with the résumé, despite the fact that her comment about his brother choosing the new incident commander pulsed in the back of his mind.

Sam probably wouldn't hire him to park cars, let alone lead the team during a callout.

Unless Pete could prove to his brother that he had changed.

He turned onto the highway and flicked on the radio. Chuckled when a Ben King song came on. One of his new singles, cut right here in his new studio in Mercy Falls.

> We said good-bye on a night like this
> Stars shining down, I was waitin' for a kiss
> But you walked away, left me standing there alone
> Baby, I'm a-waitin', won't you come back home.

Pete found himself tapping his hand on his steering wheel. See, if Ben King could turn his life around after getting his high school girlfriend pregnant, after leaving her for a decade, only to come home and woo her back into his arms, then certainly Pete could figure out how to earn Sam's forgiveness.

Maybe.

He pulled off the highway toward the PEAK ranch and slowed as his tires rumbled over the cattle grate, then crunched on the dry dirt road. The ranch house and barn had once belonged to the family of Chet's now-deceased wife, and when billionaire

Ian Shaw bought the ranch, he gave the ranch house and barn to PEAK Rescue.

The white barn loomed pretty and clean against the backdrop of blue sky and the hazy purple rise of the Cabinet Mountains to the west.

Pete had spent most of the last five summers fighting fires in those mountains.

The words "PEAK Rescue" written in red against the white of the barn shone against the morning sunshine, a beacon of hope.

In a way, the team had pulled Pete back from the crazy, dangerous edge he had treaded, jumping from planes and fighting fires.

That part of him that loved the taste of danger, the rush of holding his life in his hands.

Okay, he *still* loved it—hence the BASE jumping trip a couple weeks ago with Tucker Newman off Vulture Peak. But he'd mostly agreed to the trip because Tucker was passing through and needed a jump buddy.

Pete had told Jess where he was going, just in case their jump went south. But he'd been extra careful, even attached a secondary chute.

See—responsible.

Although today, he could taste the need for *something* to take the edge off this crazy, frustrating week.

Maybe purge the roar of the grizzly from his brain too.

He pulled up to the white, two-story ranch house next to Kacey's Ford Escape and Gage's Mustang.

Pete checked his phone one more time before heading inside.

Still no text from Jess.

Really, it was for the best.

The renovation of the ranch house included a new kitchen area, open to the main room. A huge map of the entire Glacier Park area spanned the far wall, with radios and Doppler radar and two computer stations that fed information about current weather conditions.

A scanner hummed in the corner, quiet for the moment.

Chet King, their boss, stood at the counter in the kitchen, putting a Styrofoam takeout box in the refrigerator. "Pete," he said as he closed it, then moved over to reach for a freshly poured cup of coffee.

"I got that," Pete said, and reached for the coffee to carry it into Chet's office.

"Thanks," Chet said. "My physical therapist says I can upgrade to a cane soon."

The fact that Chet had not only survived a chopper crash last spring but managed to be moving around after breaking both hips spoke to the toughness of the old Vietnam vet. Chet swung himself into his office, set the crutches against his desk, and eased himself into his seat.

Pete set the coffee down. "What are you working on?"

"Next year's budget," he said. "Now that we're under the control of the city government, we have to submit an open budget to the city council for their approval. It was a lot easier when Shaw footed the bill."

Back when his niece went missing, Ian Shaw founded PEAK to search for her. He kept the doors open when the search came up empty.

After three years, they'd located a body earlier this summer in the park. While Sheriff Blackburn wanted to close the case, the body still hadn't been identified. And Shaw refused to give up hope that he'd find Esme alive.

"Kacey and Audrey are in the hangar. I think Ben's out there too—they're doing some inventory for us."

"I saw Gage's Mustang."

"Yeah. He's resupplying some of the packs."

Pete looked out the window toward the barn, which housed their chopper, the pretty blue Bell 429. "Chet, can I ask you something?"

"Mmmhmm." Chet put down his coffee.

"I'd like to be an incident commander." Pete turned and sat on the sill, his arms akimbo. "Do you think Sam would hire me?"

Chet considered him a moment, then reached over and picked up the newspaper folded on his desk. "You're certainly on your way to proving yourself."

Pete took the paper, unfolded it.

And there he was, just below the fold, a picture of him in all his bear-tousled glory, ripped shirt, the scrub on his chin, his long hair down and scraggly. He was looking away from the camera as if contemplating his next big save.

If he remembered the moment correctly, he'd glanced at Jess right about then, seen her edging toward the door and wanted to catch her for that late-night pizza run.

"Nice write-up. Makes us look good—and good timing too," Chet said.

Pete handed the paper back to Chet without reading it. "Hopefully Tallie didn't embellish too much."

"Well, I think she's taken a shine to you—there is a smidgen of a heroic slant to the piece. But pretty much all true."

"Yeah, well, what can I say?" He wasn't sure why those words emerged—habit, maybe.

Chet rolled his eyes.

Pete turned away, and through the window he spied Ben coming out of the barn, a football in his grip. A moment later, Audrey came running out, Jubal barking at her heels.

Even from here, he could make out the words from Ben. *Go long*, with the wave of his hands. *I'll catch it*, from the way Audrey raised her arm.

A beautiful spiral, and Pete laughed when Jubal left the ground, arching for it.

Great defensive play by the chocolate lab.

"Everybody deserves a shot at a second chance," Chet said

quietly, and when Pete glanced at him, Chet too was watching the scene.

Then his gaze fell on Pete. "I know it feels good to be liked. But the question is, are you interested in the IC position for the limelight? To be the hero?"

Pete frowned. "Of course not." He didn't know why Chet's words irked him.

"Good. Could you bring this out to Kacey?" Chet handed him a clipboard. "I need a list of all the improvements and supplies she needs to procure this year."

Pete leaned up, took the clipboard. Headed outside.

He *didn't* have to be the hero.

In the yard, he nearly intercepted another pass from Ben to Audrey, who bumped him out of the way for the catch. "Good nab."

She giggled, and he winked at her.

He found Kacey in the barn and handed off the clipboard.

Gage had supplies from their packs spread out on the counter in the back room and was methodically repacking the overnight packs.

Binoculars, a folding saw, fire starter, webbing, cookstove, one-man tent, chemical light sticks, trail tape, along with maps, first aid kit, signal mirror, space blanket, MREs.

"Need help?"

Gage pointed to a pack. Pete began to fill it.

"By the way, nice write-up, Pete," Gage said, looking over at him. "You get all the love. It's just not fair."

"The reporter has a mad crush on me, so what can you do?"

He wondered why those words chose to come out of his mouth.

"I think you need to call her, tell her 'thank you' for making you look like a SAR god. You'll have women lining up outside the barn. Maybe we should set up a kissing booth, make some money."

Pete laughed, but Gage's words burned a little in his chest.

A little shorter than Pete, Gage had honed his body and reputation on the slopes as an all-terrain snowboarder and champion freerider. Pete couldn't imagine the steel nerves and concentration it took to ride down a powdery, jagged-edged mountain face, do a flip or two off a fifty-foot cliff, land in a pillow of white fluff, and make it look good. Not only that, but Gage could also work the half-pipe—had landed a McTwist on national television. Gage Watson had lived in the world of sponsors, posters and interviews, winning two world freeriding championships before heading home for a different life.

Pete knew a few of the details; an accident that cost Gage his life savings and his reputation. But he hadn't put all the pieces together and more, appreciated Gage's need for privacy. They all deserved to keep a few secrets, nurse their wounds in private.

Pete looked at the checklist, the order of packing, and put the heavier items in first. "So, what if—hypothetically—you had a friend who you liked, but you weren't sure she liked you back. What would you do? Go for it?"

Gage tightened the top cord on the pack. "Well, how good of a friend? And has she already put you in the friend zone? Because if you're there, pal, you're stuck. If you try to move out of that zone and she gives you the stiff arm, there's no going back."

Right. *"You're not exactly my type."* Jess had been uber quick to point that out, hadn't she? Gage was probably right—they were stuck.

If Pete hadn't already destroyed it.

"Besides," Gage was saying, "why would you ever venture into that no-man's land when you have someone like Tallie hunting you down?" Gage was looking past Pete and gave a little nod. "Howdy."

Pete turned, and there she stood, Tallie Kennedy, dressed in a pair of jeans, cowboy boots, and a T-shirt that hugged her in all the right places. The kiss of the sun streaked her doe brown hair, and she leaned against the doorjamb, holding out a manila envelope, her blunt fingernails a shade of red.

"Hey, Pete. I'm not sure if you subscribe to the paper, so I brought you a copy of the article."

Oh. He reached out for the envelope. "Thanks."

"You're welcome." She glanced at Gage and stepped into the room, closer to Pete. So close, actually, that he could smell her perfume, sweet, with enough spice that it twined around him.

A whir of curiosity stirred inside him. Her eyes were shining, and a tantalizing smile tugged up her face.

"I saw Ben in the yard, and he said he was releasing a new single tonight at the Gray Pony. I was thinking that maybe I could buy you that pizza . . ."

It feels good to be liked.

Yeah, it did, actually. Felt *real* good to have a pretty girl like Tallie look at him with a smile that suggested anything but the friend zone.

He swallowed, felt himself relaxing into old habits. "I might like that."

A lot. In truth, he hadn't had a date in months.

All his time was spent at Jess's.

No wonder he'd let himself read too much into that friendship. He just needed time with a girl who didn't see him as a teammate. A buddy.

Pete wanted, suddenly, to be the guy he saw in Tallie's pretty amber eyes.

She had inched closer now, raised her face to just inches from his. "And maybe, before that, we could take a drive into the park? You could tell me all about what it feels like to wrestle a grizzly?"

"I have to help a friend with her . . . bathroom."

Wow, that sounded flimsy, even to him.

"Really? C'mon, Pete. It's a gorgeous afternoon, and I have it off. Spend it with me."

She put her hand on his chest, right over his heart.

He exhaled, glanced behind him at Gage, who had his attention buried in the packing list.

But Gage gave a furtive glance at Pete, a tiny nod of *go for it.*

With Tallie, there were no games, no threats.

Pete could spend the day, even the evening with her, laugh, dance, have fun, and walk away.

He fished his phone out of his pocket and turned it to "do not disturb."

"Okay, Tallie. I'm all yours."

---+---

A Friday night, burgers on the grill, tickets to Ben King's debut single party at the Gray Pony Saloon and Grill, the sun dropping lazily behind the hazy purple outline of the Rocky Mountains, and Sierra in the kitchen with his mom, tossing a salad. Yes, tonight Sam would finally shake off the stress of the crazy week.

Break free of the lingering effects of the bear attack, his horror at kissing Willow, even his residual frustration at Pete for not reporting the wounded bear.

Sam didn't want to blame his brother—probably just a coincidence, the two bear attacks. But the fact that his irresponsible brother got his mug on the front page of the weekly *Mercy Falls Register* irked him more than he wanted to admit.

The angle of the article made it sound like Pete alone had saved them all from a mauling. Pete could have probably left out the part where Sam came to a callout dressed for a dinner party.

Tonight Sam planned to resurrect the abysmal crash-and-burn date from last week with romance, country music, and hopefully Sierra in his arms on the dance floor.

He'd finally burn from his mind any lingering memories of kissing Willow, and along with it, the ember of shame in his chest.

"How are the burgers coming along?" Sierra stepped out onto

the deck carrying the Caesar salad. She wore a lime-green Ben King T-shirt, fan gear she'd probably procured from Kacey, faded jeans, and a pair of cowboy boots. He liked her dark hair shorter, hanging in soft waves around her face, reaching to her chin. It made her appear sweet, just a little fragile. Like she might need protection.

Like she might need him.

Except Sierra didn't possess a fragile bone in her body. Small but tough, she'd spent the past five years organizing Ian Shaw's life as his personal assistant, and the last summer turning PEAK Rescue into a shipshape operation.

Probably that's what drew him to her—she reminded him a little of himself.

From organizing their weekly barbecues to putting together the early-alert system, from PR to baking cookies, Sierra stepped into the role of den mother for his sometimes unruly crew.

Not that he didn't appreciate their skills, but every one of them, starting with Pete, had the mind-set of a star football player: *Give me the ball, Coach! Put me in, Coach!*

They needed teamwork. As the liaison between the team and the sheriff's department, Sam kept pounding the word into their heads. He understood, really. The team had fractured after the chopper crash last spring. The frantic search for Chet and Ty, the differing opinions of how to find them. Sam hadn't made any friends when he brought in Miles Dafoe as incident commander this summer.

Pete had wanted to take point—Sam knew that. But his brother was the most alpha of them all, always fighting to be lead dog. If he wanted to lead, he had to prove he was trustworthy.

As if.

Sam flipped the burgers, the smell of hickory rising in a rush of smoke. Flames curled around the meat, sizzling. Sierra brought a tray of buns over and set it on the side table. "Looks good."

"Thanks for letting my mom join us. Pete was supposed to

pick her up from her chemo today, but as usual . . ." He lifted a shoulder.

"I think it's sweet how you help your mom," Sierra said, smiling up at him.

And in that moment, Sam let Pete live. This time.

"But should we be worried about him? Because he was supposed to show up at Jess's today and help her tear out her upstairs bathroom. Last I saw her, she was wrestling with the old commode by herself."

"That's typical Pete—his promises are sort of like wishes on stars. Don't count on him for anything."

Sierra frowned, then gave a nod and headed back inside.

Maybe his words *had* emerged too sharp, but really, Jess should figure out she couldn't count on Pete to help her fix that money pit.

He was probably out doing something crazy—BASE jumping, fatbiking down some trail, maybe even speed-climbing Grinnell Glacier.

Or, more likely, he'd picked up some girl along the way, ditched the hike for a more scenic view.

Poor Jess. Sam dearly hoped she didn't expect more from Pete than he could give.

Sam pulled the burgers off the grill, slipped them into the buns, and set them on the glass deck table. Sierra had set a pretty table—red place mats, white dishes, a spray of white hydrangeas in the middle, probably cut from his mother's bush out in front of the townhouse.

He rapped on the sliding glass door, spied his mother laughing with Sierra.

It warmed his entire body to see his mother smile. She looked good today. Despite the chemo, she hadn't lost her dark hair, although the treatment had definitely stripped pounds from her already thin frame. She always took time to look her best too—putting on her makeup before she went into the clinic. She simply refused pity for the cards life dealt her.

Thankfully, the worst of it was over—now, she just took chemo once a month to keep the cancer from resurging and stopped in weekly to check her blood levels.

Sierra opened the door, carrying a pitcher of iced tea. "Oh, that smells so good, Sam."

He took the tea from her, set it on the table, then came back to steady his mom, putting a hand on her elbow.

"I'm fine, Sam," she said. But Rachel Brooks had been saying that since the day his father died. *"I'm fine, don't worry about me, Sam."* She'd smiled through her grief, helping his uncle take over the Sweetwater Lumber and Construction Company. She hadn't deserved what Pete put her through, or his absence during her year-long battle with cancer.

Sam didn't know how she'd opened her arms, welcomed his kid brother home without a word. But Sam had done the same, just for Mom.

She deserved at least a snapshot of a happy family.

He slid a chair out, held it for her.

"Sam, I feel terrible to cut in on your date with Sierra," she said as he scooted her up. "You don't have to cook for me."

"Aw, Mrs. Brooks, I love seeing you," Sierra said, so much warmth in her voice, Sam believed her. "And we love to eat together."

She left unspoken the fact that Rachel still struggled with a meager appetite, probably wouldn't eat at all if Sam, or Pete, didn't cook.

When Sam took his place at the table, his mother took his hand and said grace.

He tried to concentrate on the prayer and not on the fact that if Pete had shown up when he was supposed to, he and Sierra might be having dinner at *his* place.

Although, Mom's view was definitely better than his untamed backyard forest.

Mom squeezed his hand, then reached for the iced tea. "I hear you're going to listen to Ben King tonight."

Sierra helped herself to salad. "He has a new single. He's releasing them one at a time, sort of like teasers to his new album. He's only doing three releases. The rest will be on his album. It comes out next spring, I think."

"How are Ben and Kacey's wedding plans?" Rachel asked.

"Kacey's fully recovered from her injuries, so I think they're planning a wedding sometime this spring."

Sam well remembered Ben's panic when Sierra's rickety old house collapsed after a flood, trapping Kacey and their daughter, Audrey, in the basement.

"I love happy endings," his mother said. She looked at Sam. "Speaking of, did the forest service track down that bear?" She kept her smile, not mentioning how close she'd come to losing both her sons.

"No. I went out with some forest service trackers. Usually bears stay in one area, but they must have wandered back into the park." Sam loaded his burger up with onions, lettuce, mayo. "Those kids were lucky. They shouldn't have been out there in the woods alone."

"Oh, that reminds me, Sam," Sierra said, reaching for her burger. "Willow is taking her youth group on a hike tomorrow and she needs adults to go with her. I told her I'd go, and . . ." She made a face, looking up at him as she cut her burger in two. "I volunteered you."

He kept his smile.

Perfect. He would have been content never seeing Willow again.

Yes, *never*. Because he still couldn't purge from his mind the way that, for the briefest of seconds, Willow had awakened in him exactly the sparks he'd hoped to share with her sister. Worse, she'd left a residual strum inside him that was only just starting to subside.

Oh boy.

"It's just a day hike up to Huckleberry Mountain Lookout," Sierra said.

"I heard we have a new youth pastor at the church. What happened to Jared?" his mom asked.

"He left for a year of missions in Scotland. Apparently this new guy—Josh Blessing and his wife, Ava—are fresh out of Bible school and full of ideas. Willow was hoping they'd hire her, but she isn't exactly qualified, so . . ."

"Why not?" Sam didn't know what made him ask.

"Well, for one, she never graduated from high school."

Really? "She didn't?"

Sierra took a bite of her burger, washed it down with iced tea. "It's my mom's fault. She didn't believe in formal education—preferred the unschooling approach. Took Willow out of school right after I graduated, kept her at the commune, insisting she'd learn more there."

"Your mother is so interesting." Mom, the polite one.

"She sings her own tune, that's for sure. She and Willow are actually a lot alike. They both sort of live by their passions. Except Willow's is Jesus and the youth group. She loves these kids—understands what it feels like to be forgotten, I think. She has a real heart of compassion."

That made Sam temper his judgment, just a little.

Whatever offense he'd taken to her impulsive kiss, probably it had something to do with the way he'd unloaded his fear, his frustration, even his hurt, on her.

So maybe he'd forgive her. And himself. Because it meant nothing—he loved Sierra.

Okay, *love* might be too strong, but he *wanted* to love Sierra.

"I know it's an imposition, Sam, but would you come with me on the hike?"

Sierra looked at him, her hazel-green eyes in his, her dark hair in soft, touchable waves around her face, her smile whispering up on one side . . .

"Yeah. Sure. I could use a hike in the park."

Her smile widened, and with it came the slightest simmer he'd been hoping for. Yeah, this night had the makings of romance.

———— .+ ————

Pickups, 4Runners, and SUV hybrids jammed the parking lot of the Gray Pony Saloon and Grill, just outside Mercy Falls. The sultry country tones of some warm-up artist spilled out of the doors into the star-sprinkled night as Sam went around to help Sierra out of his truck. They headed inside, his hand tucked into hers.

Ben had rented out the saloon for his release party, and Sam handed over his tickets to the bouncer at the door. The Pony hummed with conversation, the air smelled of beer, onion rings, burgers, and Roy's famous tangy-sweet barbecue sauce. Sam searched for—and found—the PEAK team, or at least a few of them, in their familiar alcove near the front. Kacey sat next to her daughter, fourteen-year-old Audrey, who was wearing a cowboy hat and a plaid snap-button shirt, her dark blonde hair in braids. Like father, like daughter. Audrey had made her debut only last month, recording a duet with her country star dad.

Ty, the team's bona fide cowboy, was shooting darts with Gage. Ty's family owned a cattle ranch south of Mercy Falls. Clean-cut in a dress shirt and jeans, Ty still hadn't shaken off the accident that had nearly cost Chet his life.

Even if he'd hiked out in a blizzard, on a broken knee, to save him.

"Bull's-eye," Gage said as his dart landed in the circle. "That's twenty bucks, Rem."

"Game's not over yet," Ty groused.

Gage grinned, glanced at Sam, and raised his hand in greeting. Sam nodded at him.

Willow sat on the windowsill nursing what looked like a Coke, every inch her hippie self in a pair of cutoff overalls over a sleeveless white shirt, her long tanned legs bare all the way to her red Converse tennis shoes. She sported a thematic black cowboy hat, and her brown hair was down and tumbling over her shoulders.

He had the sudden, very vivid memory of the silky feel of her hair between his fingers.

Willow had followed Gage's wave, and for a second, her gaze fixed on Sam.

Deer in the headlights.

He tried not to have the same panicked expression. Found a smile.

Willow looked away, back at the game, but he saw her entire body stiffen. *"I promise I'll never talk to you again if you don't tell Sierra."*

No problem.

"Let's go sit by the team," Sierra said, and tugged him toward trouble.

"I'll get us drinks," Sam said and escaped.

On the front stage, on the far end of the room, the warm-up singer—a clean-cut cowboy with styled short brown hair wearing a white shirt, jean jacket, and tie for his set—settled into a cover.

"Who's that?" Sam said to Gina after he ordered a couple sodas. Her dad, Roy McGill, owned the place.

Sam remembered a few times, back in high school, when Gina would open up the place after hours, let them dig in to the leftovers. She'd lost about fifty pounds since then, dyed her hair black, added a couple tattoos.

"Easton somebody, up from Nashville. Mountain Song Records has tryouts here sometimes."

"Be my love song, my all night long . . ."

Gina handed over the drinks, and he gave her his card, started a tab. Then he headed over to the table, eyes on Sierra, who was laughing with Kacey and Audrey.

Willow sat at the edge of the group with a tight-lipped smile.

Sam set down the drinks, slid in next to Sierra. Put his arm around her.

"I told Willow that you said yes, by the way," Sierra said, smiling up at him. Sierra had such a pretty smile, the kind that told a guy he could hang the moon.

Almost on reflex, Sam glanced over at Willow. She was staring into her cup, looking miserable.

He felt like a jerk. Because clearly she felt as wretched about her actions as he did for reacting to them.

The kissing part ended up being just as much his fault as hers.

"We're going to have a great time, Willow," Sam said, raising his voice over the music.

She looked up then, startled, with the slightest hue of fear in her hazel-blue eyes.

He gave her a smile, offered a message in it. *See, we can forget the past, just move on.*

He received a hint of a grin in return, sweet relief in it.

Easton wrapped up the song, started another, something slow and romantic.

"Your sunset kiss, on a night like this, come on over, we'll stay up late . . ."

Sam leaned over to Sierra, whispered in her ear. "Let's dance."

She looked up, her eyes shining.

He took her hand, and they slid out of the booth.

Apparently, they weren't the only ones with the idea, because as they scooted around tables and chairs to the front, the dance floor began to fill up with couples swaying to the music.

"It's a perfect night, out in the moonlight . . ."

Sam found them a pocket near the back corner, and Sierra wrapped her arms around his neck, tucked her head into his shoulder.

Yeah, a perfect night.

Sam closed his eyes, sinking into the music. And wouldn't you know it, there was Willow smiling up at him.

He opened his eyes. Swallowed against the tightening in his chest.

In his arms, Sierra stiffened, and for a second he thought maybe—crazily—that she could see inside his mind.

But as he lifted his head, he saw her look away. He followed the trail of her gaze, and a fist landed in his gut.

Ian Shaw, back from his hunt for Esme, taking a turn on the dance floor with a blonde caught in his arms. Her high heel boots, shimmering black tank top, and tight sequined jeans over her too-thin model form evidenced that the woman wasn't from around here.

Sierra turned her face the other way, settled her head back onto Sam's chest, and Sam suppressed the urge to go over and tell Ian and his floozy to get lost.

That would only bring to a fine point the fact that it still bothered Sierra. Which meant that she probably wasn't over the man.

Someday, Sam hoped to make her forget Ian Shaw.

Sam turned his back to Ian, protecting Sierra from the view, and Sierra looked up at him, smiled.

He should kiss her. Erase, finally, the feeling of Willow in his arms.

He leaned down, brushed his lips against Sierra's. Softly, sweetly.

She kept her mouth closed, but she received his kiss, a gentle, polite response.

Okay. They were in public, so . . .

Still, when he lifted his head, she gave him a smile so darned perfunctory that he suddenly felt patronized. Like, *Phew, we got that over with.*

Huh.

It didn't help when someone bumped into him. He nearly stepped on Sierra's foot, and caught her as she fell back.

"What the—" He rounded on the club-footed dancer.

Stopped.

Pete held up his hand in surrender. "Sorry, bro. Tallie and I are just getting our dancing legs."

Sam stared at his brother. Pete wore his baseball cap backward, and he had that reporter from the other night in his arms. She giggled as she stared up at Pete, so much infatuation on her face it was embarrassing.

"Just stay in your space," Sam said, turning back to Sierra.

But Sierra was standing there, her mouth open. "Are you kidding me?" She glared at Pete. "You told Jess you'd help her today. The only time we were gone was for lunch. And now she's at home, tearing out tile, and you're here . . . dancing?"

He didn't want to, but Sam gave Pete credit for the flash of guilt that crossed his face. It vanished in a second, replaced with a shrug. "That house is her mess. I didn't sign on to spend every waking hour repairing it."

Sierra's mouth opened, and even Sam stared at him.

Huh?

Pete turned back to Tallie, who wrapped her arms up around his neck. He leaned into her for a very slow dance.

And that was just it.

"Seriously, Pete? It's not just Jess—you were supposed to pick up Mom today too." Sam didn't know why he suddenly had his hand on Pete's shoulder, turning him. "I swear, you're the most irresponsible person I've ever met!"

Pete came around fast, his eyes dark, sparking.

Sam couldn't stop himself or the derision in his voice. "You're just out for yourself—always good-timin' Pete, right?"

A moment too late he recognized Pete's expression, the same defensive posture he'd seen so many nights when he dragged the idiot home from one too many parties, even a few ER visits.

Guilt.

Masked oh-so-perfectly by anger. "Step back, Sam. I know you think you're the boss of me, but guess what, my private time is *mine*. I'm sorry I forgot to give Mom a ride, okay?"

Sam should have just left it there, ignored the shove Pete gave him, maybe pulled Sierra off the dance floor.

Anything, really, to grab the fraying ends of his perfect night before it all unraveled. After all, he was a deputy and knew how to rein in trouble.

But not tonight. Because it all piled up—fear, guilt, frustration, and not a little disappointment—and came out in a fist, balled and headed for Pete's chin.

Pete ducked and hooked him around the waist, tackling him back into the wall, slamming him so hard, his breath whooshed out.

Then Pete planted his fist into his gut, and Sam doubled over.

But he hadn't been Pete's brother without learning his tricks. Sam rebounded fast with an uppercut that had Pete spinning.

"Stop it!" Sierra leaped in front of him, cutting through the haze of fury.

Heaven help him, Sam nearly pushed her aside and went after his brother on the floor.

But Tallie was screaming, and the party had come to a screeching halt. The dancers parted, and Ian grabbed Sam by the collar and pressed him up to the wall. "Let it go, Sam!"

Pete pinched his nose, blood flowing into his hand. He climbed to his feet, and Tallie tried to help.

Pete brushed her off. Came at Sam.

Ian stopped him with a hand to his chest.

Pete shoved it away. "I don't know why I bother to try and impress you," he spat. "I'll always be a screw-up to you."

"Yeah, actually, you will. And seriously—impress me? We're *way* past that, Pete. Now I just desperately hope that you don't kill anybody."

Gage and Ty broke through the crowd; Gage headed for Pete, Ty for Sam.

Gage worked Pete into his corner, shoving napkins at him for his nose.

"What's the deal?" Ty said, his hand on Sam's collar.

Sam shook free of them all. "It's nothing." He pushed through the crowd, headed for the door, and didn't stop until he was on the porch, bent over, still trying to catch his breath.

His insides ached.

And not only from Pete's punch.

Sierra came out. She said nothing as she stood there.

Finally, "You want to talk about it?"

He looked up at her, the grim set of her mouth, tight expression of disappointment, her arms folded over her chest.

"No."

She sighed and looked away, her eyes bright with tears. "Then I think this night's over, Sam. Take me home."

4

It didn't seem quite fair that while the rest of Mercy Falls swayed to the music of Ben King's newest single, Willow ended the evening snuggled up with a hot date who had floppy golden ears and an insatiable urge to eat the gelato turning to mush on her car seat.

"Stop it, Gopher." She pulled the puppy onto her lap and earned a swipe of love across her chin. At least he had pretty eyes and adored her with abandon. "We'll be home in just a minute." And yes, she could have house-sit, but when Jess heard about her agreement to watch Gopher, she practically begged Willow to bring him home.

Apparently, Jess had a soft spot for troublemakers with big sad eyes.

Willow braked at the light, glancing at the crumpled bag from the Griz containing their specialty, Simeonson's caramel gelato, with chocolate chips. And, for Gopher, puppy treats and food.

Peace offering or therapy, Willow wasn't sure just how to present the treat to Sierra. Please let Sam have kept his promise to not tell Sierra about her impulsive kiss.

Not that she wanted to keep secrets from Sierra, but . . .

Gopher jumped up on her shoulders, and she had to press the

brakes, move the dog back onto the floorboard. "I appreciate the enthusiasm, but you were not the plan tonight, Goph."

However, her father's text, shortly after Sam and Pete's epic fight, had given Willow exactly the excuse she needed to cut and run.

Are you coming to pick up Gopher?

Um. Apparently when her father's new family said they were leaving tomorrow, they meant 4:00 a.m. tomorrow. Not conveniently tomorrow night after her hike into the park. They'd tied the knot quietly, two nights ago on the lookout over Blacktail Mountain, only the kids and Willow in tow.

Distraction accepted and appreciated, because the last thing she needed was to stick around and join in on the musing of why Sam had decided, finally, to lay out his kid brother.

Do the math, she wanted to say to Ty and Gage.

Because Sam dated Sierra. Who lived with Jess. Who had been noticeably absent tonight.

Instead of here, with them. With *Pete*.

Even Willow wanted to land a kick in Pete's shins. Had he no clue how Jess felt about him?

Willow pushed the golden retriever's snout away from the bag as she turned off the highway, toward town and Jess's place. Lights blazed out the front windows of the kitchen and the bedroom-slash-family-room. It cascaded onto the dilapidated porch, out into the barren yard.

Admittedly, Jess's house looked like a place where squatters might reside, but then again, since Sierra's house had sunk into the earth after the flood four months ago, Willow and Sierra had become exactly that—squatters. They'd even purchased their sleeping bags from the local Goodwill.

Thankfully, the place was insulated, had a decent roof and the camaraderie of Jess and Sierra. Willow could think of—had experienced—worse, *much* worse, accommodations.

Gopher had the determination of many of the SAR guys she

knew. He was licking the bag where the moisture from the cold gelator turned it soggy, but she'd reached the house and stopped at the curb. "Sorry, sweetie." She grabbed the bag in one hand, the puppy in the other, and headed into the house.

A song drifted down from the stairs, a country-western tune. She recognized it as a Ben King original.

"Hey there, pretty girl, let me sing you a song . . . In this mountain boy's arms is where you belong."

At least some people ended up with the one they loved.

The thought came fast, sharp, and she shook it away before she entered the kitchen.

Before Sierra could see her face. While Willow felt fairly sure that her guilt wasn't tattooed on her forehead, if Sierra told her that she and Sam had broken up, Willow just might burst into tears.

Good thing she had purchased an entire half gallon of gelato.

Gopher wiggled out of her arms, hit the floor, and scampered toward the kitchen. Sierra looked up from where she was emptying the trash.

"You're home early," Sierra said. Her gaze landed on the gelato. "Oh."

"Are you okay?" Willow asked, testing her sister's expression for anything amiss. Sierra nodded, and her smile seemed warm, authentic. The fist in Willow's chest loosened just a little.

"Gelato?"

"Caramel and chocolate chip."

"You are my hero."

While Sierra took the garbage outside, Willow found a bowl, filled it with water for Gopher, added food in another, and set them by the back door.

Gopher scampered away into the next room, and she chased him down, fished a sock from his mouth.

Sierra had produced two spoons when Willow returned, Gopher squirming under her arm.

Sierra came over, flopped the puppy's ears, pressed a kiss to his snout. "Hey there, big guy."

Willow put Gopher down, and the dog sat and started to whine.

"Shh," she said, taking the carton to the table. She set it in the middle and opened it while Sierra sat down opposite her.

Sierra dipped her spoon right into the carton. "Yum."

Willow did the same, then scooped gelato from her spoon onto her finger, reached down, and let Gopher lick it off.

"Willow—that's not good for him."

"Aw, it's just a little treat. Look at those eyes. How can I say no?" Gopher licked his lips.

"You are too much of a softie," Sierra said.

Silence, except for the music drifting down from the bathroom remodel upstairs.

"Are we going to tell Jess about seeing Pete with Tallie?" Willow said, her voice low as she reached for another spoonful.

"I could murder Pete Brooks. Especially after he nearly kissed Jess."

"*Nearly* being the important word," Willow said. "Besides, sometimes a kiss doesn't mean anything. It can be an accident."

"Are you kidding me? A kiss *always* means something." Sierra shook her head. "That's the problem."

Willow froze. *The problem?*

Sierra was staring at her empty spoon.

"I think Sam is going to break up with me," Sierra said. "And I'm going to let him."

"What? No. Sam is a great guy, so worth fighting for."

The words seared a little coming out, but when Sierra sighed as if in disbelief, Willow pressed on. "Why would you break up with him?"

A knock sounded at the front door, and Sierra put her spoon down as Gopher raced toward the sound, yipping.

Willow heard Jess coming down the stairs.

Shoot—what if it was Pete? This wouldn't be pretty. Willow got up to follow, intercept, maybe call 911.

Where was Sam when she needed him?

Sierra reached the door first and opened it.

Froze.

Ian Shaw, billionaire and Sierra's former boss, stood at the door. Six foot two of dangerous playboy charm, honed muscles that photographed well in the tabloids, and tonight, looking way too devastating in a starched white dress shirt and a leather jacket, the light on the porch picking up the gold threads of his tousled short brown hair.

As if that tootsie he'd been dancing with might have run her fingers through it.

Willow wanted to slam the door.

"Hello, Ian," Sierra said, way too much warmth in her voice for Willow's taste.

"Hey," he said, and Willow had the crazy urge to search for his Vanquish, see if Tootsie might be hanging out in the front seat.

"What are you doing here?" Willow said instead, and Sierra glanced at her, frowned.

Oops. But Willow gave her an "are you serious?" expression.

Which Sierra ignored. "Come in, Ian."

Ian the Destroyer stepped foot over the threshold.

Sic 'em, Gopher.

But Ian only crouched and ran his manicured hands over the pup, picking the animal up, laughing as Gopher gave him a slurp.

Apparently, Willow would have to teach Gopher some discernment.

"I didn't know you got a dog," Ian said, looking at Sierra with those dangerous, hypnotizing eyes.

"It's my dad's dog," Willow said and swooped the animal out of his embrace.

Sierra shot her another frown, but Willow lifted a shoulder.

Ian got up. "I was hoping Sam might be here."

If he'd driven a knife into Sierra's heart, it would have probably hurt her sister less. Maybe only Willow knew it, but Sierra was only dating Sam in a desperate attempt to rid herself of her feelings for Ian—feelings that clearly Ian didn't share, for him to so casually accept her dating his close friend, Sam.

As if he didn't care that Sierra had loved him during every minute of his journey through suffering and back, had sacrificed her social life during the last three tense years helping him search for his missing niece, holding his life together as his executive assistant for Shaw Holdings.

And after he'd fired her, she'd managed to land on her feet and put her life back together, thank you.

Sierra, the consummate peacemaker, however, kept her smile. "Sam's not here. Why?"

"Oh, I saw you two leave together from the Gray Pony tonight, and, well, I wanted to talk to him about—"

And Willow could have stepped in, filled in the words for him.

"The hunt for Esme."

Yep. Willow glanced at Sierra, testing her expression.

It stayed sweet, soft, even willing to help. Because that's who Sierra was, even when someone betrayed her.

Right then, Willow determined to throw her heart in front of a bus if that was what it took to keep Sam and Sierra together, if only to show Ian that he didn't own her sister's heart. Not anymore.

Willow sensed Jess behind her, mostly because Gopher was rooting to get to his next love interest.

"How's it going?" Jess said. "Have you tracked down any leads?" Covered in dust and plaster, Jess's hair hung down around her drawn and tired face.

After Willow dismantled Ian, she'd track down Pete and run him down with her car.

Men.

Except for Sam, of course. She was a little worried about him too after the fight tonight, but she could hardly go running after him.

"Nothing," Ian said in reply to Jess's question. For the briefest of seconds, the flash of despair on his face turned a knife in Willow's heart.

Maybe he deserved a little grace—after all, she couldn't imagine someone she loved going missing. She, too, might spend every waking hour trying to find them, for as long as it took.

"I submitted Esme's name to the registry for missing persons and got an artist to run an age-progression sketch. Right now I have ads running in all the major papers and on the internet. Now I just have to sit back and hope I get a call."

"I'm sorry, Ian," Sierra said quietly.

"Yeah, well, they ruled out her DNA as a match to the body Ben and Kacey found this summer, so, I'm not giving up hope. Especially not after the eyewitness at Saint Mary Lodge."

An eyewitness who supposedly spotted Esme and put her on a train heading to Chicago. With that news, Ian simply couldn't let go of the search. Even if it seemed Esme had *wanted* to vanish.

"She's out there, and I plan to find her," Ian said. He offered a quick smile. "If Sam stops by, can you ask him to swing by the ranch? I tried his cell, but he's not answering. Then again, after tonight, maybe he's just at home, cooling off."

Sierra nodded. "Thanks for being there. I don't know why he freaked out on Pete tonight."

"Sam freaked out on Pete?" Jess said, and Willow wanted to wince. "Why?"

And how could Ian know about the near romance that went on only a few nights ago in Jess's kitchen? So, of course, he spilled the beans.

"I'm not sure. Pete was dancing with this girl, and I think he bumped into Sam. Sam freaked out—"

"He did not freak out!" Willow couldn't just let Ian throw Sam under the bus.

Willow glanced at Sierra for a little support. But Sierra shrugged. "He did freak out. I mean, yeah, I was a little mad at Pete too, but—"

"Why were you mad?" Jess said. "What was Pete doing?"

Willow set Gopher down, and he scampered away, probably to the kitchen to finish off their gelato.

Willow suppressed the urge to follow him.

"Nothing. Dancing," Ian said.

"With Tallie Kennedy," Sierra added quietly.

Jess stared at her, only her lips betraying her reaction to Sierra's words. A quivering smile, a glance at Ian. "Oh."

"Jess—" Willow said, but Jess held up her hands.

"That's great for him. Pete's been single way too long." She blew out a breath, and on the tail of it created an Academy Award–winning grin. "Seems like a strange reason for Sam to hit him."

"Indeed," Ian said.

Sierra offered a tight smile. "I'll let Sam know you dropped by."

Ian gave a quick frown, then nodded. "Okay. Good to see you . . ." He cast his gaze around, as if he didn't know how to end that sentence.

"You too," Willow said bluntly.

She gave in to the urge to check out his car as he left.

No bimbo in the front seat. So maybe he'd dispatched her before coming to harass the woman he should let go of.

Sierra shut the door, and Jess headed to the kitchen.

"Jess . . ." Willow said.

"It's fine." She stopped at the utensil drawer, however, and pulled out a spoon. "Pete is just a friend."

Ho-*kay*, so that's where they were going to land tonight.

Willow returned to the table. Sierra sat down opposite her.

Jess dug into the gelato.

"Tallie is—" Sierra started.

"Cute," Jess finished. "And it doesn't matter. Like I said, Pete's been single way too long. How was your evening? Ben's new song?"

Sierra let the question sit for a minute, and Willow didn't know what to say.

Finally, Sierra picked up her spoon. "Sam brought me home before Ben took the stage."

"Really?"

"The fight managed to kill the mood," Willow said. "Especially with Pete bleeding."

And Tallie fawning over him, although she kept that aside to herself.

"I was pretty disappointed in Sam," Sierra said. "Sure, I wanted to choke Pete, but Sam nearly took his head off. I have a feeling there was a lot more to that fight than just Pete showing up with Tallie Kennedy. Something else is bothering him."

Willow lowered her spoon down, found Gopher, let the dog lick the spoon. Closed her eyes.

"Did he say anything?" Jess asked.

Willow braced herself.

"He was fine earlier—we were at his mother's house. He agreed to go hiking tomorrow with Willow's youth group. Then we got to the Gray Pony and suddenly he turned dark and possessive. Even kissed me on the dance floor."

Willow let the dog finish cleaning the spoon, then got up to put it in the sink.

At the mention of the kiss, a tiny fist had latched onto her heart, started to squeeze.

Probably the claws had been there all night, digging in the minute Sam walked in and sat down in the booth, his arm around Sierra.

Sure, he'd tried to make it all okay—he gallantly looked at Willow, flashed her a smile.

For a minute, made her believe that yes, she could forget the way he'd kissed her, hungry, as if she'd awoken something inside him.

As if he wanted her.

Thankfully Willow hadn't seen the part where Sam kissed her sister in just that way.

She braced her hands on the sink.

"Are you okay, Willow?" Jess, the EMT, too observant.

"Fine." Willow turned to face them. "Don't be too hard on Sam. He *did* nearly get eaten by a bear last week. That has to be hard to shake off. And he's usually such a gentleman. He's trying to woo you, Sierra. You need to let him."

Crazily, her eyes pricked, burned. "Sam Brooks is the most honorable man I've ever met. Self-sacrificing, kind, patient, and responsible. Not to mention cute, right? With those pale blue eyes and that hard-won smile?" She met Sierra's gaze. "Give him a break. I'll bet that tomorrow he shows up with apologies and spends the day trying to charm you." Willow finished with a smile.

Sierra was staring at her, wearing an enigmatic look. Slowly, she nodded. "He is all those things, isn't he?"

Willow slid into the chair. "If anyone can make you forget stupid, arrogant Ian Shaw, it's Sam Brooks. So let him, okay?"

Jess wore a strange frown.

"Okay, Willow," Sierra said. "You're right. Sam *is* worth fighting for. I'll give him exactly the chance he should have."

Oh. Willow should be cheering. Instead, her throat turned thick—she'd call it relief.

"I'll make sure that tomorrow everything gets sorted out during the hike, okay?" Sierra said.

"You're going on a hike in the park tomorrow?" Jess asked.

"Willow planned a youth group trip, a hike to Huckleberry Mountain."

"You know you shouldn't take this little guy in the park, right? He'll be a bear snack." Jess leaned down, picked up Gopher, put him on her lap. Casanova batted his big brown eyes at Jess. "Maybe you should stay here with me, huh?"

Willow grinned. Disaster averted. Tomorrow, as they hiked, and under the lure of the park's inspiration, Sierra and Sam could find the footing they needed for a fresh start.

And once and for all, Sam could forget about the sister who shouldn't have kissed him.

———— ✦ ————

With the sun high, the temps in the valley rising to the mid-sixties, and the air smelling sweetly of pine, Sam just might have a chance at redemption.

He pulled his day pack from the bed of his truck, hiked it over his shoulder, and walked up onto the porch of PEAK Rescue HQ.

He'd agreed to meet Sierra and Willow here, on their way into the park after picking up the youth hikers from the church.

Meanwhile, he'd pack a few other essentials, just in case something went south today. Not that he expected trouble, but . . . lately he seemed to find it without looking.

Like last night. Trouble simply slid into his periphery.

He may have slightly overreacted.

He spent the entire night wrestling through any of the other reactions he might have attempted, ones that didn't include laying out his kid brother.

Or resulting in Sierra looking at him as if he'd turned into a grizzly.

Yeah, he'd made a fantastic impression on Sierra. But today bore all the earmarks of a fresh start.

He'd simply show her that he could be the kind of relaxed, easygoing guy who didn't let circumstances have their way with him.

The bright, sunny day confirmed it. Hiking into the beauty of the mountains, the clean forest air, a day of simply exercising, working out the kinks of the last week . . . He planned on wooing his way into Sierra's heart by the end of the hike.

Sam opened the door to the house, and the smell of fresh-brewed coffee reached out, tugged him in.

Chet sat at the table, nursing a cup of java and reading the weather and incident reports in the park. He looked up, gave a one-sided smile. He wore a PEAK Rescue hat over that salty gray hair and a jacket with the logo on the breast. He always reminded Sam of the older version of Harrison Ford, a wry, hard-won wisdom in his eyes. His crutches leaned against the table.

"Hey, Sam," he said and nodded toward the kitchen area.

Sam took the hint and poured himself coffee. "Heading into the park with Willow's youth group today. I was hoping we might take an emergency pack with us, just in case."

"Help yourself," Chet said. He scooted his chair out and massaged his legs for a second. "But before you go, I wanted to talk to you about something."

Sam leaned against the counter, glancing out the window as he saw the church van pull into the yard. "Sure."

"Your brother wants to be an incident commander."

Sam jerked his gaze back to Chet. "What?"

"Yeah," Chet said, reaching for his crutches. "He was hoping I might put in a good word for him. I told him it was up to you, of course, but if you're wondering, I think Pete is ready—"

"You've got to be kidding me." Sam leaned up. "Pete is not ready to command the local Boy Scout troop, let alone lead a callout. And he never will be."

Chet frowned. "With his smoke jumper training and the courses he's taken this past year—"

"What courses?"

"FEMA has an emergency management course online. He's nearly finished with it."

Sam just stared at him.

94

"He's current on all his EMT certifications, as well as his Wilderness Rescue Technician training, and a few specialized certifications, like swift water rescue and mountain search and rescue."

Sam took a sip of coffee, just to clear his head, make sure he heard Chet right. "When did he have time to do this?"

"The last couple years, during his off seasons from the Jude County Smoke Jumpers. It's one reason why I hired him on last spring."

A decision Sam hadn't been involved in, as back then, Ian Shaw controlled the PEAK team resources and the SAR team was not yet under the funding and jurisdiction of the Mercy Falls Sheriff's Department.

Too bad Pete hadn't given Sam an on-the-job reason to fire him.

He took another sip of the bracing, dark coffee, then set the mug on the counter. "I can't have Pete in charge of anything, Chet. He might pull his weight here, but away from here, he's reckless and irresponsible." Sam walked over, poured out the coffee into the sink. "I'd put my life in the hands of one of those high school kids before I'd ever trust my brother to find me."

Harsh words, he knew, but someone had to speak the truth. He turned, met Chet's eyebrows-up gaze. "I'm sorry, but the answer is no."

Chet's mouth tightened in a grim line. "I don't think you really know your brother, Sam. Pete is—"

"Trouble. Full stop. Trust me, I *do* know him."

For a second, he was standing over his brother, breathing hard, watching Pete stare up at him, holding his bloodied nose. He couldn't believe Tallie and the entire community of Mercy Falls fawned over the jerk, as if he were the one who needed understanding. As if he wasn't the one who'd started the entire thing.

Sam must have settled in memory too long because when he looked up, Chet had a concerned gaze on him.

"You keep feeding that anger, Sam, and someday it's going to consume you."

Sam looked out the window and spotted Sierra and Willow in the yard with a handful of kids. "I'm not angry. I'm just stating the facts."

"Oh, you're angry, Sam. You just can't face—"

"Okay, fine. I'm angry." Sam turned back to Chet. "But there's nothing I can do about it. I don't know how to forgive him. Every time I try, he does something stupid, and there it is again. Like yesterday. Pete was supposed to pick up my mom from the hospital—"

His phone vibrated in his pocket. He tugged it out and read the text message.

Of course. "And he did it again." He shook his head. "Pete's not home, and Mom needs a ride to Bible study—she's still too weak to drive." He pocketed the phone. "There goes my hike."

"Sam—"

"No, there's not a snowball's chance that I would hire Pete. For anything."

"I was going to say that I could drive your mom to church. Ty is on call today."

That was Chet. Always trying to help people. As Sam glanced again outside, trying to locate Sierra, he wanted to take him up on it.

Just once, let someone else share the mantle.

The door opened and he looked over just in time to see Sierra come in. She held a puppy in her arms, a cute little golden retriever who squirmed free. She put it down, and it scampered over to Chet.

"Whoa, who's this?" Chet leaned down to scoop the dog up.

"It's Gopher, Jackson McTavish's puppy. We're dog-sitting." Sierra looked at Sam. "Which is what I have to talk to you about, Sam."

As a SAR professional, used to hunting for clues, he should have seen it coming, especially with Sierra dressed in a pair of yoga pants, flip-flops, and an oversized T-shirt.

Not exactly hiking attire.

"I'm not going with you today."

Despite the warning, her declaration felt like a punch in his gut. He even emitted an incoherent, "Huh?"

"Jess doesn't think we should take Gopher on the hike and she was going to watch him, but the bathroom sprung a major leak this morning, and she needs help—"

"Call Pete!"

But he realized his folly as soon as the words emerged.

"We're not going there, Sam. It's the least I can do after her letting us live there. And Willow can't stay back because, well, she's in charge. So . . ." She lifted a shoulder, an easy shrug as if she hadn't decimated his entire day. His hope of redeeming their wretched date.

"I'm not going if you're not." The words came out more rebellion than clear thought.

Sierra frowned. "Sam, you have to go. Willow needs you."

Willow *needs*—and that put a very fine point on exactly why he *shouldn't* go. "Your sister has been a trail guide—she knows how to handle herself in the park. Besides, it's just a day hike. It's not like anyone is going to get hurt. And isn't the new youth pastor going with them?"

Sierra put her hands on her hips, gave him a look she'd probably used on Ian for years to get him to snap out of his despair about Esme and rile him back into the land of the living. "You can't abandon her."

Abandon. Interesting word.

"Besides, have you taken a look at the new youth pastor? He'll probably get blown off the top of the mountain by a stiff wind."

He looked out at the group, couldn't spot any adult but Willow.

"He's the ten-year-old wearing jeans, his Cons, and a You-Don't-Scare-Me-I'm-a-Youth-Pastor T-shirt. Very hip and most likely to be the one to perish."

"No one is going to perish today."

"Because *you'll* be with them." Sierra stepped closer then, her voice softening, her gaze in his. "Please? Willow and I sort of promised the pastor that you'd go. Besides, I won't feel okay about Willow going out there if you're not with her, either."

Oh man.

Then she touched his arm. "And when you get back, come over for pizza. I'll make it from scratch."

She offered a smile, so much warmth in her eyes, what could he say?

"No black olives."

"Deal." She looped her arms around his waist, leaning in for an embrace. "You are my hero."

Oh. Well.

He gave her a quick hug back, his day suddenly brightening.

"So that's a yes on picking up your mom?" Chet said.

Sam felt fairly sure Chet didn't mean it like it sounded. "Yeah, that would be great if you drove her to Bible study."

Chet winked then, and Sam hadn't a clue what to make of that. Then, "Where are you headed today, just so we know?"

"The Huckleberry Mountain Lookout trail," Sierra said. "It's one of Willow's favorites. It's an easy six-mile hike, nice views."

"There might be snowfall higher up," Chet said. "We're starting to get some dusting in the mountains, so keep an eye out for weather."

"Willow and I looked at the weather this morning," Sierra said. "Looks like a chance of rain tonight, but you should have a nice day."

Nicer with her along, but . . .

Sam picked up his pack. "I'll grab an emergency pack from the barn."

Sierra opened the door for Gopher, who bounded toward the barn, his big paws and floppy ears a magnet for the high school girls.

They, at least, resembled hikers. In fact, as he joined Willow, it seemed she'd given them instructions to dress like she did because all of them, except for Youth Pastor Blessing, wore layers—thermal shirts, fleece jackets, windbreakers for a couple, and sturdy boots.

He'd have to keep an eye on the pastor, make sure he didn't turn his ankle or slide down a scree of rocks in his hipster shoes. Sam would grab a fleece for him instead of the canvas jacket.

"Hey, Sam," Willow said. But she looked at him as if he might bite.

Oh, this would be fun. "I'll grab a pack, meet you back here."

She nodded, her smile wavering, but as he stepped away, she got up, jogged after him.

"Hey," she said, catching up and walking with him to the barn. "I just wanted to say thank you for coming with me. I . . . I tried to talk Sierra into going, but she has a high responsibility gene and feels like Jess needs her more." She made a wry face. "I told her I'd stay but—"

"You can't stay. This is your trip." He stopped, put a hand on her arm. Met her eyes. "It's okay, Willow. It's all okay."

She stilled then, her breath catching. Swallowed. For a second, he thought he saw tears glisten in her eyes.

His frustration softened. "We're going to have a great day. Fun, sunshine. A beautiful view. What could go wrong, right?"

She grinned, the sun in her eyes turning them a deep blue, rich with hope. It took another layer off his darkness. "Right."

———✚———

Jess didn't want to believe that her house had betrayed her, but frankly, after an hour of trying to figure out where the leak was coming from, she felt pretty sure 303 Sycamore had it out for her.

This was what happened when she tried to prove that she didn't need help.

Especially from a six foot one, too-charming former smoke jumper.

Jess stood on a folding chair in her grimy basement, fighting with the wrench that would cut off the water, once again. Soggy to her bones, she'd worn her tennis shoes into the murky, primordial sludge in her search for the broken pipe. A dim shop light illuminated the debris, and she could see the lath ripped out as she followed the pipe through the ceiling.

So much for her spectacular installation of her new toilet and sink in the upstairs bathroom. She wanted to kick herself for not checking the pipes to the upstairs before turning on this section of plumbing.

The wrench slipped off the bolt and she lost her balance, fell back, hit an old sheet metal sink. In a flash of heat, the rim sliced across her back.

She let out a cry that echoed through the house. She followed it by flinging the wrench at the pipe. It clanged and the copper shuddered. The wrench skittered off into the recesses of her dungeon.

"Stupid house, stupid pipe, stupid . . ." She didn't know how to finish, except maybe with *life*. Because despite her stiff upper lip, she just wanted to sink down into the dirt and fold. More, she longed to call home and hear her father's voice on the other side.

But that wasn't going to happen, was it? Not ever.

And she only had herself to blame.

Jess blew out a breath, put a hand on her back. She hoped she hadn't cut herself—the last thing she could afford was a trip to the ER.

Although tetanus might be more expensive.

She heard footsteps upstairs and she closed her eyes, willing herself to pull it together. Sierra didn't need her unraveling today—not when she'd given up her perfect day in the park with Sam.

At least she had one loyal friend.

"I'm down here!" she shouted but headed for the stairs.

Please let Sierra have brought donuts.

The door to the basement hung ajar, and light was streaming down the steps when a shadow crossed it.

She looked up.

Pete stood in the doorframe.

Her night of tossing and turning, telling herself that she didn't care that he'd been out with Tallie, because she most definitely did *not* have feelings for him, died at the look of worry on his face.

He wore a pair of faded jeans, a gray Mavericks T-shirt under his jean jacket, and worry in his pretty blue eyes. "Are you okay? I thought I heard a cry?"

"I'm fine." She didn't mean to snap at him, but yes, she'd most definitely hurt herself. Her back felt like it was turning to fire as she hit the top of the stairs.

Pete stepped back from her, and he looked even better in the light, wearing a layer of golden-red whiskers, his blond hair wavy and loose behind his ears. Worse, he held a bag of donuts from the Avalanche Bakery.

Jerk.

She grabbed the bag and walked past him to the kitchen. Set the bag on the counter. Lifted the back of her shirt. "Am I bleeding?"

Pete didn't move, so she turned, glanced at him.

He had his hands in his pockets, his expression just a little undone.

"Pete. How bad is it?"

He glanced up at her. "You've got a pretty good bruise there." He moved into action then, opening her freezer and pulling out a bag of peas. She reached out for it, but he shook his head, put his hand on her shoulder, and pressed the vegetables to her back.

She jerked, but he held her steady.

"Don't be a baby."

And just like that, she thought it might be okay. She might be able to live with the image of Tallie in his arms, come to terms with the fact he'd chosen a night out with a reporter over fixing her plumbing with her.

Because he was still here. Her friend. She at least had *that*.

Now she just felt pitiful. Jess put her hand on the peas and inched away. "Thanks for the donuts."

"Aw, Jess, I'm sorry."

Huh?

She just stared at him, his words so unexpected she felt as if he'd reached into her heart, put a hand around it. Squeezed.

"Um, for . . . what?" She tried a casual, easy smile, but heat had rushed to her face and she knew he could see right through her.

Crazily, she thought she just might start to cry. Talk about an overreaction.

She grabbed the donut bag, brought it to the table, and opened it. She stared into the bounty without seeing it.

"For not showing up to help you with your plumbing yesterday."

Right. *That.*

Not for the Tallie thing, because, really, why might he apologize for taking out a cute girl on a date?

"It's fine, Pete," she managed, and thank you, even kept her voice even.

She pulled out a raised glazed. Handed him the bag. "You are most definitely forgiven."

He had a sort of sweet confusion in his eyes, and it flushed all the annoyance out of her.

Then, "Really?"

"Pete, you don't have to apologize. You have your own life and are under no obligation to help me put my house together."

She looked down at her exceedingly grubby clothing. Paint had covered her T-shirt, turning it hard and crispy. And her jeans were so soiled with dirt, grease, plaster, and dust she could probably prop them up, assign them their own project.

Pete selected a cake donut with chocolate frosting. She could have predicted that.

"I did stop by yesterday around lunchtime, but you weren't here. I probably should have simply made myself at home."

Oh, he hadn't a clue how his words stirred hope in her.

A home. Preferably with Pete in it.

Yep, she was going to cry. She walked past him to the fridge, hunting for a container of orange juice, blinking fast.

"Like I said, Pete, this is my mess. You don't have to help." She put the orange juice on the counter, found a napkin, and set the donut on it, then wiped her fingers and found two glasses.

Pete leaned against the counter. "I know. But that's what friends do, right?"

Hmmm. "Right." She poured the orange juice.

"Besides," he said, "when I didn't see you last night at the Gray Pony, I thought maybe, well, I should probably stop by today and see how it's going." He made a face as he took in her appearance. She had so much grit in her hair, she should call it a spa treatment. "Losing the war, are we?"

"Just the battle." She lifted her glass to him. "But I am undeterred. There is a plumbing leak in them thar walls and it can't hide from me."

His mouth tweaked up and again, strangely, all was right with the world.

He drank to her toast, then shucked off his jean jacket. "How about if we hunt it down together?"

Oh, her traitorous heart. "Pete, you don't have to do that."

"I *want* to do that. Besides, if I go home, Sam is going to kill me for not picking up my mom yesterday from the hospital." He shook his head. "I can't believe I forgot. I . . ." And then it appeared like maybe he'd gone too far into that conversation because he blew out a breath, gave a half-chuckle. "Okay, I drove into the park with Tallie Kennedy for the day, and sort of . . . well, lost track of time."

And if she needed proof that they were Just Friends, that was it. Pete, telling her about his romances. Super.

But she could take it, because Pete was here with her, *not* with Tallie, at least right now.

She didn't want to think beyond that fact.

"Did you have fun?" Her words came out on their own, clearly unattached to her heart, from the part of her that was just Jess, his buddy. Then, "Tallie's really cute."

Pete glanced at her, then gave a quick shrug. "She's okay."

Okay. And the green-eyed monster inside Jess wanted to give a fist pump.

"She wrote an article about me."

"I know, I read it." She held the glass to hide her smile. "You're such a hero, Pete." She batted her eyes at him, affected a damsel-in-distress voice. "Will you save me?"

"Oh, you're hilarious." But he grinned, and finally, *finally*, it all reset. Their friendship, the easy flirting and banter between them.

They would be okay. And when he picked up the peas and tossed them to her with a "Don't make me dig out the carrots," she stopped feeling pitiful.

"Let's see if I can find that leak and put a plug in it," Pete said. He touched her shoulder as he walked past her. "And yes, I will save you."

5

WILLOW REFUSED to let today's hike end in epic failure. Even if Sam's words contained an eerie, haunting prophetic doom.

What could go wrong?

She could start with the arrival of Quinn Starr, who was dropped off by his senator father at the PEAK ranch just as they were leaving.

The fact that Quinn had other plans became evident the minute he got in, pulled out his cell phone, and began to text. Even Josh Blessing's attempt at a name game got little response.

At least the rest of her youth seemed on board with today's agenda—get to know Josh, enjoy nature, maybe even be inspired.

Seven kids in total. Dawson Moore, sixteen, son of a local doctor, and Vi, his twin sister. Gus Blumer, senior nose guard starter for the Mavericks, a youth group faithful. Zena Lynch, tall and dark, from her dyed hair to black fingernails. She probably came simply to escape a Saturday at home. Whereas Riley Rigs, video gamer, was most likely forced into the light. Maggy Nichols sat eating a bag of Cheetos in the back. The daughter of the choir director, she never missed an event.

They played the game with Josh as Willow drove them into the park, Sam riding shotgun. He'd offered to drive, but she knew exactly where she wanted to take them today.

Except, that turned out to be the next fateful mishap.

105

"What does it mean, 'Closed Due to Grizzly Danger'?" Josh asked as they parked in the gravel lot at the Huckleberry Mountain trailhead.

Sam shot him a look.

Willow suppressed a smile. "Don't worry, I got this."

Which only meant she had a reason to take them to a better hike, one she'd always wanted to take them on—the Numa Ridge Fire Lookout.

"Are you sure?" Josh asked as she drove them north, past the town of Polebridge, her old haunts, and of course, the commune.

"Yes. It's a steeper hike, but so worth it." She glanced over her shoulder, met eyes with Quinn.

He still bore the scars of last week's terror—not only on his body but in his eyes. Shame, and she wanted to shake it out of him.

Show him that he didn't have to let his mistakes consume him. Sorry, but she still didn't believe he'd meant Bella harm. She had it on good authority that he'd camped outside Bella's room at the hospital for three days until she was discharged.

Willow could only imagine what Bella's mother thought of the senator's son hanging around. She couldn't put a finger on why the senator had dropped off Quinn for the day, but if she could nudge Quinn out of his funk, get him to talk about it—even with Sam—she'd count the day as successful.

"Eyes on the road, Willow!"

Sam's voice jerked her back to the moment, to the fact she may have edged over to the side a smidgen. About six miles into the park, they were gaining altitude, with Bowman Creek falling into the valley below them. Pine trees intersected the rocky debris, and the road wound through forest and along the cliffside.

Spectacular.

"Sorry," she said.

Sam folded his arms over his chest, stared out the window.

Which hinted at the third disaster of the day. Because she'd heard Sam's call to Sierra as they'd left Huckleberry Mountain, and the fact that it went to voice mail. He hadn't left a message.

Worse, when he'd called Jess, Pete had picked up her cell phone and told him Sierra wasn't there.

Sam turned dark and moody.

Willow wanted to offer the easy explanation—Pete had decided to show up at Jess's house, and seeing that he had it covered, maybe Sierra had gone to the ranch to catch up on administrative work.

Although, it had her feeling a little dark too.

So much for her grand plan to give Sierra and Sam a magical day.

Her spirits lifted when they reached the trailhead. The day was bright and the air was crisp. The kids seemed eager to get out, stretch, embrace the challenge of the hike.

A slight wind bullied them as they walked along Bowman Lake, with Rainbow Peak rising in majestic glory, her ridges covered in rich green pine and spruce.

They reached the ridge, and the panorama began to open up, tiny glimpses of the lake below, a deep turquoise blue surrounded by the rich glacier forest. The terrain turned rough, and they stopped for lunch in a field with a view of golden larch and aspen.

Sam sat away from them.

Quinn, too, didn't join the group, though his phone was now useless with the loss of signal.

"He's been really upset since Bella got hurt," Maggy said as she peeled back the wrapper on her cheese stick.

Zena took snaps with her phone. Vi read a book on a boulder nearby. Josh sat with Gus and Riley, and Dawson stood not far away, nursing his water bottle.

So much for bonding, but Willow planned an inspirational speech when they reached the tower.

Yet, when they reached the Lookout Tower, her exhausted crew barely noticed the glorious view—Rainbow Peak, already snowcapped, the falling scree-side of Kintla Ridge, and the blue radiance of Bowman Lake, now a puddle in the distance. Yes, she noticed the gray clouds to the west, tumultuous and dark, tasted the menacing bite of the wind, but she refused to let it deter her words.

Josh didn't seem eager to take ahold of this moment, so she dove in.

"I brought you here to make a point—that when we were down in the valley, we had no idea of the beauty of being on top of the mountain. Bowman Lake looks tiny, and even Rainbow Peak feels close enough to reach out and touch. Psalm 61 says, 'From the ends of the earth I call to you, I call as my heart grows faint; lead me to the rock that is higher than I.' The reason David asks God to lead him to a higher rock is so that in his weakest, most over-whelming moments, he can get a new perspective. A divine view of his problems. See, when we're stuck in our everyday troubles, we can get focused on them, and that's all we see. We don't see God at work in our lives, just the darkness around us. But if you turn it around, look up, start finding a way to thank God, even praise him, you'll discover a different view."

Quinn sat with his back to the lookout tower, not looking at her. Gus leaned against the rail, and Dawson and Riley threw rocks off the tower, watching them crumble below. Zena played with her phone, taking shots of the view. Only Maggy and Vi seemed to be listening.

Strangely, when Willow glanced at Sam, he looked like he was frowning at her, although he'd put on his sunglasses, so she couldn't be sure.

"A different view can also show you the truth of your situa-tion. And a path out. Just remember, God has this view all the time. No detail of your life is unseen by him. He is your guide and your protector through life's journey. The great part is that he says 'don't worry.' He'll take care of us. All we have to do is be still and know that he's God."

She thought it went well, given the fact that Josh looked up then, nodded, gave her a tight smile.

Epic day achieved.

Except for the sleet that hit on the way down. Willow had checked the forecast before the hike, saw the chance for rain that evening, long after they would have returned. Willow had never seen a storm cloud roll in so quickly, the wind change, the temperature drop.

Only a mile from the lookout, tiny shards of ice began to pepper them.

"Faster!"

This from Sam, who was practically running down the path, but with the boulders and rocky ledges—and Josh's pitiful Converse shoes—she refused to let them go too fast.

"We are not running. We're going to be fine."

Sam slowed, but with his long legs, she still felt like she was sprinting to keep up.

Quinn, however, decided to keep up with Sam. Probably as eager to escape this dismal day as Sam was.

By the time they reached the forest cover, they were shivering, soaked through. Worse, halfway down the trail, Dawson had tripped and fallen into Josh, who slid and skinned his knee.

She gave him points for being a trouper and not whining, especially when he started limping.

Willow caught up to Sam. "I didn't know it would sleet," she said. "I'm really sorry."

He looked at her, did a double take. "This isn't your fault," he said quietly, walking steadily on the path.

"It sort of is. I pushed us all to come here. If we'd turned around to go home, we'd all be at a movie right now."

This got the slightest tweak of his mouth. "Yeah, well, we wouldn't have heard your inspirational talk."

Funny how his words could light her from inside. "Did you like it?"

"It was fine."

Or not.

"I just wanted these kids to know that God is watching over their lives, even if they feel like they're lost, or alone, or overwhelmed."

That made his smile vanish, his mouth tighten into a grim line. He nodded.

Sped up.

There went her opportunity to tell him that maybe he needed to give his relationship with Sierra another chance. That just because they'd had a rough start didn't mean they didn't belong together. That if he could just hang in there, he'd discover that she was an amazing, kind, patient, awesome human being.

Although probably Willow was the last person he would listen to, because even in her own mind, her words sounded pitiful. The girl who kissed him telling him—practically *begging* him—to date her sister?

Clearly she had issues.

By the time they reached the van, the sun was nearly gone and the brisk wind was snaking through the trees and into their bones. Willow couldn't feel her hands and fumbled with the keys in the lock.

"I got this, Willow," Sam said and took the keys from her hand. She let him, because frankly, she couldn't take any more failures today. She just wanted to climb inside, blast the heat, and dry off. Maybe curl in her seat and hope that Josh wouldn't report her sad, barren youth event results to the church board.

Sam fired up the van, let the heat blast.

"Seat belts," he said, and glanced back, waiting.

Even Quinn obeyed. Sam put the van into gear and started back to the main road.

Miserable silence descended.

Willow simply couldn't take it. The darkness, the pinging of the sleet on the windshield, the shiver that shook her entire body—

"We have to sing something."

Sam glanced at her, shook his head.

Well, *he* didn't have to sing anything—and really, she didn't want him to. Not with the road slick and his headlights cutting through the sleet like he might be in the Millennium Falcon, about to zap into warp speed.

But he wasn't a sixteen-year-old youth in need of cheering up. She pulled out her iPhone and cued up her playlist. "Okay, how about 'Don't Stop Believin''?"

Fourteen eyes looked at her like she might be speaking another language.

"Seriously, you don't know this? It's an epic eighties song my mom loved. C'mon, I bet you do." She pressed play, began to sing.

"Just a small town girl . . ."

Nothing.

"Livin' in a lonely world . . ."

She kept going, turning up the volume. Noticed Maggy bobbing her head, Vi frowning.

Quinn looked away, and Josh was shaking his head.

Gus, however, began to hum. "I know this one."

"Right?" Willow said. She kept singing. Louder.

And then, miracle of miracles, next to her, "Just a city boy . . ."

No. Seriously?

Sam glanced at her, and the slightest of smiles creased his face as he sang along with her iPhone.

With her.

And she couldn't help it. She wanted to kiss him all over again. Especially when he raised his voice on the chorus.

And caused Dawson and Riley to sing along, Dawson reaching dangerous off-tune decibels.

"Some were born to sing the blues . . ."

And that's when it happened. Maybe Sam drove too close to

the edge and overcorrected. Maybe he hit an ice patch, tapped the brakes too hard.

Maybe he simply stopped thinking about the road, got distracted.

Suddenly they were sliding down the highway, toward the edge of the embankment.

Willow screamed, grabbed the armrest as the van hit the ditch, barely shuddered, then with a sickening crunch on gravel, spun out over the edge.

Then they were rolling. Hard edges, stunning blows, chaos, and broken glass as they careened down the mountainside.

———— ✛ ————

Needles in his skin, so cold they found his bones, turned him brittle. Sam fought the darkness, lashed out, heard a scream, maybe his own. He could feel the snow on his face, the heat of his own tears on his lips, the desperation clawing at his chest.

Dad!

"Sam!"

The voice reached in. "Sam!" A hand on his arm, squeezing.

He jerked, the voice familiar enough to arrest his panic, and he struggled to catalog it.

"Sam, wake up!"

He shook himself free of the darkness.

Just a dream.

Or . . . no, something else. A gasp and suddenly he jerked awake.

Darkness still folded in against him, ice pinging his skin, his face, but the cold air filled his lungs and he realized.

Not dead. And not lying in his room in the wee, brutal hours of the night reliving a familiar nightmare.

For a second, the final moments before the crash flashed— singing, a quiet stir of surrender as he'd turned to Willow, her smile reaching in to loosen the darkness—

"Willow?"

"I'm here," Willow said, her voice shaky. "Are you hurt?"

Someone in the van was whimpering; maybe others were moaning, even crying, but in the darkness it all felt jumbled, chaotic. He put his hand to his forehead, found a bump blooming. His hand felt cool against the heat of the hematoma. He tasted blood and ran his tongue tentatively over his lip, found it tender.

They'd ended up with the passenger side to the ground. His body dangled over the armrest of his captain's chair, his seat belt imprisoning him. He let out a moan against a bone-deep ache, the spur of pain in his side.

His hand went to hers, found her fingers. "I'm okay." Maybe. "How hurt are you?"

"My shoulder's a little banged up, but . . ." Her voice caught, and it seemed she might be about to cry.

That seemed the perfect way to end this miserable, disaster-wrought day. Sure, he could have tried harder to make it a win for Willow, but when Quinn Starr had shown up, it yanked Sam right back to his frustration with Pete, accentuated by the fact that it looked like Sierra had lied to him.

So much for her staying home to help Jess. Pete, the hero, had arrived and, judging by the laughter behind the phone call, Jess had clearly forgiven the jerk.

He didn't care what Jess did. He just wanted to get them home, track down Sierra, and get to the bottom of why she didn't want to spend time with him. Why they couldn't seem to get their relationship off the ground.

It didn't help that Willow's inspirational talk had driven a knife into his gut. And now Sam had nearly gotten them killed. So much for Sierra's assertion that the kids would be better off with him on this trip.

Sam's vision began to adjust to the darkness. From what he could tell, the front windshield was still attached, although spider-webbed. The acrid odor of gas hung in the air, but he didn't smell smoke, didn't hear sparks.

"I'm going to unbuckle," he said, letting go of Willow's hand and reaching for his seat belt. He winced, leveraging his feet against the floorboard, glass crunching as he wrestled with the latch.

He forgot, however, to brace himself and nearly fell into Willow's lap. He caught himself on the dashboard, his other hand clinging to the armrest.

Her hands came up to brace his chest. "I got ya," she said, her voice shaky.

"I'm okay," he said and carefully scooted down, stepping on her door, then moving so he crouched on her passenger side window. She lay crumpled against it, but he could barely make her out in the swath of dark shadow, night falling fast with the storm.

"I have a flashlight in my backpack," she said. "Under my seat."

He carefully moved his hand through the rubble and found the pack. He fumbled with it, then opened the zipper and reached inside. His hands closed on a small cylindrical object, and he pulled it out, found the rough edge of the Maglite and turned it on.

Light pieced the darkness, and Willow winced, averting her eyes.

"Sorry," he said and flicked the light over her body, making a quick assessment.

She lay on her side, of course, her shoulder wedged hard into the door. She offered him a tentative smile, courage in her eyes.

"You're cut," he said, holding the light near, but not in, her face. He reached out to move her hair away from the wound just below her hairline. Broken glass was embedded in it, but he didn't want to touch it, fearing digging the glass in deeper. The blood had matted her hair.

"The kids," she said then and he nodded.

"Call out when I say your name!" He flashed the light into the back and called out their names, one by one.

Thin voices, shaky, a few hiccupping back sobs as they called back, but everyone was awake, albeit scared. He flashed the light on each one of them as they answered.

As a whole, they lay crumpled together, still buckled in their seats. Vi sat closest to him, her hands over her face, whimpering but otherwise okay. Maggy, next to her, had her arms wrapped around herself, her expression stricken.

Behind them, Gus and Quinn and Riley were trying to untangle themselves.

"Don't unbuckle yet," Sam said, glancing behind them to Zena, Josh, and Dawson in the last row. Zena, nearest the window, seemed dazed, with Dawson trying to push himself off her.

Blood ran from Josh's nose. He pinched it, held his head back, moaning.

"Okay, everyone stay put." Sam looked again at Willow. "I need to see how bad it is."

Willow nodded but grabbed his sleeve. "Come back."

He frowned at her request. "Of course."

But she held on, so he gave her hand a little squeeze. "I'll be right back, I promise."

Then he stood up, put the flashlight in his teeth, and using her seat as leverage, pulled himself through the broken driver's window.

The sleet and wind whistled outside the van, blinding him, and he nearly slid off down the roof.

He grabbed the mirror, clamping down hard on the flashlight to stifle a grunt, and scrabbled back to the side of the van.

His heart jammed into his throat as he cast his light around.

They'd come within two feet of careening off a cliff. Save for the shaggy arms of a white pine which, to his quick survey, had saved their lives, they would have slid all the way down the side of the mountain and into a black abyss. Now, the van lay in the embrace of the tree, its nose jutted out into thin air.

How long the tree could hold them, he couldn't guess. He

couldn't see anything beyond the precipice, the cloud cover obscuring any moonlight.

Working his way over the slick body of the van, he slid toward safety into the bushy grasp of the tree.

The tree cracked, and he froze, his heart in his ribs. The van didn't budge.

He shined the light on the trunk of the tree.

The van had taken it out at the roots, which were thick and twisted and jutting from the ground. He took one step—the tree held—then another, and finally scrambled along the length, the needles pricking his face as he wrestled free of its grip. He tripped out onto the rocky ledge and stood up, breathing hard.

Taking the light from his mouth, he walked over to the edge of the cliff, not too close, and flashed the light into the gorge.

The tree obstructed his view, but from what he could tell, the drop could be fifty feet or more. Despite the ice in his hair and his eyes, a thin, hot trickle of sweat beaded along his back.

"Tell everyone to stay perfectly still!" he shouted to Willow. He didn't want to tell her why.

He shined the light toward the road. The light couldn't peel back the darkness enough to spot it, but he guessed they'd slid nearly fifty yards, maybe more, taking with them saplings, boulders, and not a few bushes.

It left a trail that any good SAR team could follow.

Which meant that if they just stayed put, the team could find them.

That was, if they knew where to look, or even that they were missing. Maybe he should hike up the hill and get help.

Come back.

Willow's voice, soft and plaintive, whispered in his ear.

What if he tried to get the kids out? The emergency pack contained climbing rope, webbing, carabiners—everything he'd need to rig up a belay system.

Or maybe he could simply try to secure the van, buy them time.

116

But if he didn't go for help, they might all freeze to death. With the cloud cover closing in and the wind gusting, the sleet could turn to snow. An early season blizzard.

He was standing there doing the math on his options—distance to help, time of exposure, probability of the van going over—when he heard the shout.

"Vi, come back here!"

He flashed the light to the driver's window, and his entire body jerked when he spotted Violet Moore edging her way out. Sobbing, nearly hysterical, she screamed, struggling hard as she fought to free herself. The van shook with her efforts.

"Violet!" Sam climbed onto the tree, trying to get back to the van. "Get back!"

Even as he broke through the branches, he spotted Quinn Starr behind her, pulling her in.

Sam's feet steadied on the back door handle, and he launched himself to the upward side of the van.

"Quinn—get her inside!"

His gaze connected with Quinn's one brutal second before he heard a great, ripping crack. The tree shuddered.

Sam scrambled over the top. *Come back.*

Quinn pulled Violet inside, and Sam lunged for the door.

The tree started to give, and he slid forward, toward the front of the van.

Toward the edge of the abyss.

The tree began to tilt.

Sam dropped the flashlight and grabbed for a hold. His hands closed over the side mirror.

With a deafening crack, the tree surrendered and heaved the van over the edge, into the black, steel-edged night.

6

SHE JUST HAD TO STAY CALM. That one thought centered Willow as she shook herself out of the panic, the shock of plummeting— well, she didn't know how far—into darkness.

They'd landed with a bone-jarring crash, Quinn pinning her.

She should have never let Sam leave the van. Okay, it wasn't like she could stop him. And her pitiful "come back" had her cringing.

Of course Sam would come back. He wasn't the kind of guy to leave her in the woods in the middle of a storm.

Willow fought to control her breathing. Her shoulder ached, her sternum burned, and her head thundered as the blood pumped against the heat of her hematoma.

"Vi! Are you here?" Vi had totally freaked out, started climbing out the window. While Willow struggled with her seat belt, Quinn had launched himself at Vi.

Which shook the entire van.

Then, Sam's voice, and thumping across the van just before whatever held them aloft broke with a night-shattering crack as the world dropped out beneath them.

They couldn't have fallen too far because the van still shuddered with the impact. Thankfully, they landed wheels down, but the jolt of the fall jerked her away from the door, and the pain in her shoulder had her gasping.

Especially with Quinn on her lap, his arms still around Vi.

He was already trying to untangle himself.

Except Vi was writhing, wailing in pain. "My foot—it's caught!" Her words ended on another scream as Quinn tried to move her.

"It's stuck," he said.

Someone from the back flicked on a light—a phone, maybe— and it illuminated not only the wreckage but Vi's injury.

Her foot was twisted in the steering wheel at an angle that made Willow a little queasy. Quinn struggled to stand up, his arms around Vi's waist, then leaned over to work her ankle free.

"Don't touch it!" Vi screamed, and Willow had to agree with her.

But Quinn ignored her and eased it out of the entrapment.

Only when she stopped screaming did Willow hear the yelling.

"Willow!"

"Sam?"

Quinn moved Vi back to the bench seat, and Willow gritted her teeth, fought with her buckle.

It came free, and she scrambled over to the driver's window.

Oh . . ."Sam!"

He looked up at her, his hands gripping the side mirror of the van as he dangled out over the edge of whatever ledge they'd landed on.

"Hold on!"

He started to pull himself up, and she leaned out the window to grab him, but whatever she'd done to her shoulder made her arm fall limply at her side.

Quinn put his hand on her waist. "I got him! Move, Willow."

She stumbled back to her seat, watched as Quinn leaned out.

In a moment, he'd dragged Sam through the broken window, then fell back again onto her lap as Sam climbed in.

Sam collapsed into the seat, breathing hard.

He'd nearly gone over the cliff trying to get back to her—no, to them.

"Are you okay?" Her voice trembled, and when Sam looked at her with a tight shake of his head, she put her hand over her mouth. *Stay calm.*

But Vi was crying, nearly screaming, and when Willow looked back at her crew, they all wore whitened, stricken expressions.

Quinn knelt beside Vi, grabbed her hand. "Calm down. You're going to be okay."

Sam found Willow's gaze in the erratic wash of light and, for a second, his fierce concern, so much sheer worry in his eyes, reached in, took ahold of her.

Stopped the shaking.

"Are *you* okay?" he said, his baritone tending her raw, fragile places.

She managed a nod.

He cut his voice low. "Listen. The van is mostly on a little ledge about ten or fifteen feet down from the top. I might be able to climb back—"

"Don't leave!" She cringed at her tone. "I mean—yet."

Bless him, he reached out and took her hand, squeezing it. Kept that solid gaze in hers. "I'm not leaving you, Willow. We're in this together. We'll get out together."

Right. She swallowed, nodded.

Except this was all her fault. If she hadn't demanded, well, togetherness, with her crazy song . . .

"There's an emergency first aid kit in the back," Sam said, turning his attention to Vi, his hand releasing hers. "Someone find it and pass it up here."

Selfish of her, yes, to want him to simply hold her.

Sam moved toward Vi, and Willow knelt next to him.

Quinn moved away, and Dawson crawled around in the back and found the backpack, passed it up. Next to him, Josh was still trying to stop the bleeding in his nose. From the angle, Willow had a feeling it might be broken.

Gus had his big arms around Maggy, who had moved to the middle seat. She had her face buried in his lineman chest, sobbing quietly.

Zena, the source of the iPhone light, passed her phone up as Sam eased off Vi's boot.

Vi whimpered.

"Yeah, her ankle, even her leg might be broken." Sam held her foot in his hand, gently probing. "We'll need to secure it—"

"No!" Vi reached out to grab his wrist in a lethal clamp. "Don't touch it."

"Violet," he said in his impossibly calming voice, "I'm going to get a cold pack on it first, see if we can ease some of the pain. Then we'll figure out what to do. But we have to protect it from getting jarred, right?"

Her face crumpled, but she nodded.

"Thatta girl," Sam said and dug out the emergency ice pack. He wrapped it around her ankle and secured it with an ACE bandage.

Willow gave Vi a smile meant to tell her she'd be okay, but frankly, right now, she needed someone to tell *her* that.

Sam motioned to Josh to come to the front.

He worked his way forward and collapsed in Willow's captain's seat.

Sam put his arm around Willow to gather her into their huddle. "We're on a cliff that's not much bigger than the van. I don't know how precarious the ledge is, and in this weather, the van could slide right off."

"How high are we?"

"I don't know. I couldn't see the bottom. If I lean out the window to check, it might jar the van loose."

Oh.

"The storm is picking up. The temperatures are dropping, and the sleet is turning to snow. If we leave the van, we'll be sitting out in the weather, exposed. And we have no idea how long it will be until they find us."

"*If* they find us," Josh said. He checked his bleeding—it seemed to have stopped. He looked at Willow. "I can't believe I let you talk me into this—"

"That's enough, Josh," Sam said.

Willow could collapse with gratitude. Probably she should stop thinking about throwing herself into his arms, for Pete's sake. "But is it safe to stay here?"

"I don't know. I do know that we can't climb up the embankment in this storm. I suppose I could try—"

"No!"

He frowned at her.

"I mean—like you said, exposure. Even if you miraculously made it to the road in this storm, we're miles from Polebridge. The road is practically deserted this time of year. You'll walk all night and not find help. Better to wait until morning, right? By then, Sierra will know we haven't made it home and alert the team . . ."

Which only made his face pinch into a tight knot. "I didn't get ahold of her, remember? They have no idea where we are." He shook his head. "I should have left a message."

Oh. Right.

Because Willow had decided to drag them to an uncharted hike. And now, when they didn't come home, sure, parents would get worried, start wondering, and maybe even head into the park looking for them.

But they were thirty miles from where they said they'd be.

Willow grimaced, shaking her head.

"How's your shoulder? Is it dislocated?"

"I don't know."

"Can you move it?"

She wanted to say yes, but when he reached out as if to touch it, she jerked away, held her arm to her body.

"Willow."

"It's no big deal." Really, it wasn't. Her shoulder was the least of their problems.

He ignored her and touched her shoulder, his thumbs pressing into the joint. She ground her jaw to keep from crying out as the pain speared down her arm, into her neck, through her body.

"I don't think it's dislocated. You might have torn a few ligaments, though."

See, she was such a baby. "I told you I'm fine."

"You will be." He met her gaze with such compassion in his eyes—yep, hers welled up.

In fact, she hiccupped, and her breath trembled out in a cowardly sob. "I'm so sorry, Sam."

It just wasn't fair that she'd dragged him into this mess with her. "For what?"

"For everything. For making you go on this trip, and for taking us to the Numa trail instead of turning around and going home, and for . . . singing. I can't believe I thought singing was a good idea! I am so . . ." She shook her head, her hand over her eyes.

She couldn't even mention the Other Thing, although that seemed so far down the list of her sins, it felt nearly incidental.

"Hey, Willow . . . *Willow.*" Sam touched her hand, pulling it down so her eyes met his. "You are not to blame for this accident."

"Uh—" Josh started, and Sam gave him a look that suggested he might be the first one off the side of the cliff.

Then back to Willow, with a solemn look. "It was an accident, right?"

"Yeah. I guess."

"And we're okay."

Mostly. For now. "I think so."

"What was it that you were saying before? We just need a different perspective, right?"

She let out a breath.

"So, here's what we're going to do. I'm going to climb out, see if I can somehow secure us into the rock with our climbing gear. We'll all pile in the back, keep the weight away from the front driver's side, and wait out the storm. Our body heat should keep us warm. Then, in the morning, we'll see where we're at, okay?"

"Yeah."

"So . . . huddle up?"

"Yeah."

And that's when he wove his fingers through hers, solid, tight. Calming.

She clasped her other hand over his, held on like a three-year-old. Oh, she was pitiful, but she didn't care. She managed a tight smile.

He held her gaze, a resoluteness in his eyes, unflinching against her fear. "I'm going to get you home, Willow. All of you. I promise."

Then he kissed her, sweetly, on her cheek, like he would a sister.

And for the first time since they'd left for their outing, she started to believe that maybe today wasn't a complete disaster.

One wrong jostle and, frankly, they might topple right over the edge.

That thought, even more than the icy rain soaking Sam through, turned him cold.

If Willow knew the precarious nature of their situation, she'd unravel even more than she already had.

Not that he blamed her for crying—he sort of felt like crying himself. Because Sam had gotten a good look at their situation as he'd dangled from the mirror, fighting his icy, numb hands for a grip, and knew that they had just about perished.

And still would if they weren't careful.

They'd fallen onto a lip in the rock barely bigger than the van. The lip jutted out just beyond an overhang, and miraculously the tree hadn't flipped them like a coin into the ravine below. Instead, as they slid forward, the tree had broken in the middle with the weight of the van and slid them backward, toward the enclave of the rock.

Which meant they had shelter, albeit meager, from the storm. Still, with the temperatures dropping, it could be a long night.

A long and slippery night.

Sam dropped the rope, slick with ice and water, and blew on his hands, wiggling his fingers, trying to steam life into them. But he might as well give up. Although he'd managed to tie webbing around the back axle, attach a carabiner, and then weave the rope through it, the attachment he made to the rock seemed akin to using dental floss to hold up a semi. He'd used one of the larger SLCDs, a good-sized cam anchor, leveraging it into a horizontal crack in the rock wall behind the van.

It might slow down a fall, but eventually, with enough pressure, the cam would rip out of the rock.

They might have a better chance praying for the PEAK chopper to appear in the sky and whisk them all home like Dorothy in her hot-air balloon.

The cold had apparently gotten to his brain. So much so that he'd considered, way too long, just evacuating them all onto the ledge. But the space behind the van couldn't accommodate all of them, and with the wind and snow driving down on them, they had their choice between hunkering down in the van and hoping the edge didn't give way and dying of hypothermia.

He should have talked to Pete, told him where he was. At least then the team would know where to start looking. But he'd heard Pete's voice on the other end of the phone, and Sam had simply stopped thinking. Shut down.

The fight rushed back with sudden, brutal clarity.

He'd asked for Sierra, and when Pete said she wasn't there, he'd simply hung up.

"You keep feeding that anger, Sam, and someday it's going to consume you."

Chet's voice, in his head. Sam shook it away as he climbed around to the passenger door.

He opened the passenger door and got in, maneuvering over Josh, who was curled up, fighting a shiver.

Willow sat on the floor next to Vi, her forehead against the seat.

The rest of the kids had piled into the back two seats. Sam glanced at Quinn and noticed the kid was awake, his phone glowing as he played a game with his last juice.

He wanted to tell him to turn it off, to save the batteries, but maybe Quinn was feeling just as buzzed, restless, and battered as Sam was.

He could go for a turn at Ian's workout bag.

Probably, tomorrow, Sam would find the words to thank Quinn for grabbing his hand just as it slipped from the mirror. In short, saving his life.

Josh grunted as Sam finished climbing over him. "How did you do out there?"

"We just need to lay low until morning," Sam said.

"And pray," Josh said.

"That too." Really, it couldn't hurt.

Although, frankly, Sam had his doubts. He'd tried that route—a few times, actually, starting with his dad and most recently his mother's cancer.

But if Josh wanted to pray as his way of coping, then, well, whatever it took.

Sam scooted by Willow and sat down behind the passenger seat, his back to the side door. She drew her legs up and wrapped her arms around them, giving him room. "You're shivering."

He hadn't noticed, but yeah; he couldn't seem to stop.

She reached out and cupped her hands around his, the warmth seeping through him. He debated a second, then didn't pull away.

He needed the warmth in her touch, and with it, calm resonated through him.

Whatever had happened to Willow earlier, she'd reverted back to her normal, positive, hopeful self. Despite sitting in the frigid darkness of a battered van, with hurting, terrified kids on the edge of a cliff.

Sam had always appreciated that about Willow—her cheerful adaptability. Sierra had the world neatly folded and in its place, but Willow exuded an amenability about her; she was almost always smiling, despite what life threw at her.

He finally let go of her hands. "Thanks."

"I should be thanking you," she said. "Sorry I freaked out earlier. My shoulder is feeling better."

"Willow, you took a hard fall. It's okay to be freaked out. And hurt."

"No, I'm fine. And tomorrow we'll climb out of here, get help, and be back to Mercy Falls by dinnertime."

He could nearly see her smile. "Right. Well." He didn't know how to tell her this. "We're under an overhang of sorts, and I'm not so sure we can climb up."

"I'm a pretty good climber," she said. "One of my brothers at Ainihkiwa taught me how."

"Your brothers?"

"The commune where I grew up. We were all considered children of the Source—or what they'd call the Great Power. We called ourselves Mukki. It's a Blackfoot name for children."

"Sierra mentioned a commune . . ."

"It wasn't a cult—just a community. We had communal ecological living—gardens, livestock, a common kitchen and eating area, and in the winter a lodge we all lived in. There were about forty of us. I was the oldest child for a while, so some of the younger men and women took me along on their activities. My brother Arank taught me to climb."

He didn't know why, but he had a sudden stirring of curiosity about this Arank. "You can't climb with that shoulder."

She emitted something that sounded like a grunt or a chuckle. In the dim light he saw her shake her head. "Have you learned nothing from dating my sister? You don't tell the Rose girls what to do."

"Fine. We'll see how you feel in the morning." But really, over his dead body was she climbing up that overhang and hiking out to find help.

That was his job.

"Sierra, Pete, and Jess will figure out we're lost when we don't come home tonight."

"When *you* don't come home tonight, maybe. Pete and I don't keep tabs on each other. Well, rather, Pete doesn't keep tabs on me. I usually have to trail after him and pick up the debris."

He didn't mean it quite how it sounded.

Okay, maybe he did, but hated it a little when she went quiet.

Then, "I'm so sorry about your dad, Sam."

Huh?

"I saw the fight last night. I know that . . . well, there's history there."

"It was a long time ago," he said. "It's not about that anymore. It's about . . ." But really, he couldn't finish the sentence, not knowing exactly where to start.

It felt like everything arrowed back to that day on the mountain.

Willow shifted, straightened her legs out under the van seat. "I was angry at my sister for a long time too." She tucked her hands into the fold of her legs, probably for warmth. "After my mom and dad split, Mom took us to Ainihkiwa. I was seven. Everyone in the commune homeschooled, but Sierra got it in her head that she wasn't going to miss school in Mercy Falls, so Mom let her drive this old station wagon to town. I went with her, every day for four years. Then she graduated."

On the bench, Vi sighed and Willow leaned up to check on her. But the girl had dozed off, covered in the emergency blanket from his pack. He'd have to take another look at her foot in the morning and put together a splint.

"Sierra moved to Mercy Falls the day after she graduated and never looked back. Since I was only eleven, I couldn't drive. My life stopped that day. And I hated her for it."

He had heard the rest, only a different version. "Sierra thought your mom didn't want you to go to school—"

"She didn't, but she would have let me if it didn't inconvenience her. Mom is . . . a free spirit. She doesn't believe in attachments or responsibility."

"Sounds like Pete."

"Oh no, Pete is nothing like my mom. Pete shows up, even if it's late. He's been at the house helping Jess nearly every day this summer. I know he messed up last night, but that wasn't Pete. Or at least the one we know. The fact that he's back at Jess's says that he might have shown up with an apology."

"Pete doesn't apologize. Ever."

"Sam. Pete is a good guy—a little bit of a Casanova, yeah, but really, the guy is adorable. And is it his fault that he only has to smile at the right girl and she'll fall into his arms?"

What was it about her that always found the best in someone?

"But he'd leave his date in a blinding second if there was a callout." Willow touched him, and the heat of her touch traveled up his arm. "If anyone can find us, Pete can."

Sam couldn't place why her words sat like barbed wire under his skin. Nor why he felt the need to add, "He won't have to. I'll get us out of here."

Her silence needled him until, "I'm sure you will." Her voice was soft, so much confidence in it he probably didn't deserve it. "Because if I were lost, you're the one I'd want trying to find me."

He stilled, and her words landed in tender, surprisingly unprotected places. "I didn't mean it like it sounded," he said. "It's just—"

"I was serious."

Oh. When he searched her face, she met his gaze with a tiny, encouraging smile.

Problem was, he didn't quite recognize the hero reflected in her eyes.

She simply didn't know him, didn't see his failures.

Then her voice fell, and, as if she could read his mind, she said, "I see how hard you've searched for Esme and how much Sierra has appreciated it, and I know you don't give up easily."

Her words slid into him, heated him softly from the inside. And freed him, just a little, from the knot of worry that had crept in during his trek outside.

No, he didn't give up easily.

He stretched out his legs, curled his arms around himself. Found words rising to the surface without restraint. "Sometimes, on nights like this, I go right back to that moment when I realized they were going to call off the hunt for my dad, and I think, I should have fought harder. I should have told them he was still alive, that I knew it in my bones."

She nodded, her eyes looking into his.

He looked away then, not sure why he'd brought this up. Except she was so easy to talk to, just like she'd been a week ago, when she'd kissed him.

This almost felt like a continuation of their conversation. "I should have meant it when I said that if they weren't going to look for him, then I would," he said, his voice thick.

"You were a kid."

"I was eighteen years old. Not a kid."

130

"There was a blizzard that night," she said. "Even the rescuers were afraid to go out."

"I wasn't afraid." But his tone had him clenching his jaw, softening his voice. "They didn't believe me. And even Pete gave up. But I should have kept searching."

"And you would have ended up frozen to death too."

He winced.

"Oh, Sam, I'm sorry. I didn't mean it." Her hand touched his leg. "I say stupid things—it just comes out of me. I do know that finding your dad in the middle of a blizzard, in the dead of night, would have taken a miracle."

He looked at her hand on his leg. "And that's exactly what I asked God for." He gave her a tight, wry smile.

She swallowed, dropped her hand away.

"Aw, don't worry about it, Willow. I get it. God doesn't show up for bitter, angry guys like me." He leaned close to her. "So, I'm counting on you to pull in the miracle card for us."

She gave him a small smile, shook her head. "Well, then we're in big trouble, because have you met me? I never seem to make the right decision. I have too much of my mother in me—impulsive. Rash. I don't think things all the way through. Case in point, today's hike. Or, how about . . ." She drew in a breath, wrinkled her nose at him, cut her voice to a near whisper. "Well, last week in the hospital."

With her words, he was transported back to the hospital, and she was back in his embrace, his hands tangled in her soft, silky hair as she kissed him with an ardor that made him feel wanted.

Whole.

He drew in a long breath, looked away, a little unnerved at the memory and what it stirred in him.

"Let's chalk it up to a moment of weakness for both of us," he said quietly.

"You're a nice guy, Sam Brooks," Willow said softly. "My sister is a lucky woman."

Oh. Right. Her sister.

"Try and get some shut-eye," he said then.

"I don't think I can sleep." She rubbed her hands up and down her arms. "I'm too cold."

And then, his brain stopped working just a little because he reached out. "C'mere."

She frowned at him, almost recoiling. That might have slowed him down, but he saw her shiver, and sorry, but some things were more important.

"No, I mean, turn around. Scoot next to me."

She shook her head. He actually had to press on her legs, moving them. "You can't sleep on that side of the van. And we need to keep warm."

Someone had shoved a backpack into the step-down by the door, and he moved over, directing her next to him.

Then, before she could get too far away, he put his arm around her waist and pulled her against him.

"Oh," she said.

"To keep away the cold," he whispered, and indeed warmth sank into him as she leaned against him. He needed her more than he realized.

Just for tonight. Because they had to survive.

"Close your eyes. Get some sleep. I'm not going anywhere without you."

When she gave a tiny sigh of release, he thought maybe he had a hope of being the guy he saw in Willow's eyes.

7

WILLOW COULD WAKE UP EVERY DAY right here in Sam's embrace, his body warm against hers, the twitter of birds cheering them into the day.

A day they'd get all these kids home safely, if it was up to her.

Sam stirred next to her. The dawn had just begun to illuminate the sleeping visages of her youth group.

Maggy leaned against Gus; he had his arm around her, his head propped on hers. Zena had curled up next to them; Gus was big enough to support both of them. In the backseat, Dawson lay with his head back, his mouth slightly open, as if completely passed out. Next to him, Quinn curled into a ball, his hands tucked under his arms. Riley, however, sat up straight, his eyes bloodshot, his jaw tight.

Sort of how she'd felt last night. If not for Sam's calm presence, she might still be an unraveled mess.

She didn't know why she'd lost her grip on herself last night, practically begging Sam not to leave her. She'd been alone plenty of times before.

Although not on a cliff's edge, in a brutal storm, with darkness enclosing, entrapping her.

Oh God, listen to my cry! I cry to you for help when my heart is overwhelmed.

Her words at the lookout came back to her, and with them a rush of peace. It seeped through her, into her bones.

Yes. Today they would be rescued.

She gave Riley a smile of reassurance.

He looked away.

The storm had died sometime in the night, but it glazed all the surfaces with ice. Her breath formed in the air, her fingers stiff and cold. But her shoulder ached less now—maybe she *had* only torn a ligament.

Vi groaned, and Sam came awake. Willow leaned away from him, scooting to Vi. "Hey, Vi, how you feeling?"

Vi, with her short brown hair and delicate features, always seemed a little fragile to Willow. Smart—straight A's—but delicate. Apparently Dawson had gotten the brawn.

"My leg hurts," Vi said.

"Hang in there while Sam and I figure out what to do."

Sam and her.

And Josh. Oops.

She glanced at the youth pastor, who was curled into the front passenger seat, his hands tucked under his arms. Oh my . . . Willow grimaced at the purple bruises blooming under his eyes. Most definitely a broken nose. His eyes were open, and he looked at her, no smile. She wondered if he'd gotten any sleep.

Sam leaned up, and for the first time since the accident she got a good look at him.

A cut across his cheekbone, a bruise forming underneath, and an ugly bump just over his left eye.

The damage, plus his five-o'clock layer of dark whiskers, turned Sam Brooks positively, devastatingly fierce. The kind of man who wouldn't quit.

"You look like you've been in a street brawl," she said to him.

He raised his non-wounded eyebrow. "Yeah, well, you're not much better there, Fight Club." His gaze went to the wound on her head. "We need to get that cleaned out this morning, then wrapped up."

She could feel her hair matted on one side from blood, but the throbbing had mostly stopped, leaving behind a dull ache.

"The good news is—look." She moved her shoulder up and down, slowly, yes, but with enough movement to suggest healing.

Relief crested over his face. "Good. How's Vi—"

His question broke off with the shout from the back of the van.

Riley was on his feet, opening the back hatch of the van—and he wasn't alone. Dawson too had turned in his seat, fighting the door.

"Stop! You're going to jostle us loose!"

As if reading Sam's mind, Quinn grabbed Dawson by the belt. Willow winced as Dawson elbowed him in the face.

Quinn recoiled, but he had the grit of his father, apparently, and held on.

Riley kicked at the door, and it swung open. He slithered out onto the ledge.

"Riley!" Sam shouted just as Dawson rounded on Quinn with a fist.

Quinn dodged it but fell back, his grip on Dawson breaking free.

Dawson climbed over the seat, out into freedom.

Sam turned and opened the side door to the van.

Willow gasped. Whatever ledge they'd landed on couldn't be more than a foot wider than the van. She nearly made a leap for Sam to pull him back.

He stepped out, hanging on to the door. "Stay here!"

Then she heard shouting as he headed back to recover the fugitives.

Gus, Maggy, and Zena sat up in their seats.

"Stay put," Willow said, even as she got up to disobey Sam.

Josh's hand on her arm slowed her down. "He said to stay."

She shook out of his grip. Sorry, but not when World War III was igniting outside.

"Let go of me! I'm not getting back in there!" Riley said, his voice tight and edgy.

Willow clamored to the back, put a hand on Quinn's shoulder. "Stay here," she repeated and pushed open the back door.

Their position on the ledge could turn her legs to wax. They were perched precariously on a lip of rock, with no more than five feet of space behind the van. They'd dropped at least fifteen feet, the cliff arching over them.

A rope ran from under the van and disappeared into the rock face behind the van, affixed by a rather large cam anchor.

Ingenious but precarious. Especially since ice and frost layered everything—a thin skin of danger.

Riley had backed up to the cliff wall and was crouching down, his arms folded over him. "I'm staying right here. Try and move me."

Sam stood at the end of the van, on the passenger side. Gave her a frown and a shake of his head as she got out. But he didn't know these guys like she did.

"Riley. Listen. It's cold out here—"

"I don't care. I'm not staying one more second in that van."

By the look in his eyes, she believed him. She didn't blame him, really. She glanced at Sam; his jaw was tight, as if he just might throw Riley over his shoulder and manhandle him back into the van.

Dawson wasn't helping. He stood right next to the edge. She noticed how Sam kept eyeing him, his footing on the rocks.

"Daws, get in the van," she said softly. "Please."

Dawson glanced at Sam, back to her. Shook his head, a quickness in it that suggested he was simply trying out rebellion for size.

"Dawson—"

"Willow." Sam reached out and caught her arm. "C'mere."

And it wasn't the soft, gentle "c'mere" from last night, but one that issued from a clenched jaw of frustration.

She stepped up to him.

"I think they might be right. We don't know how long this van is going to stay put—maybe we get everyone out and then figure out how to get up the cliff."

She examined the cliff overhead. It was slick with ice and projecting out like an overhang, and she couldn't spot one decent handhold. "Can you climb that?"

He drew in a breath, and she knew that was the wrong question. Better was, *"Are you willing to die trying?"*

To which, in her gut, she knew the answer was yes.

And that's when the van jerked.

"Hey!" Sam said, looking inside. Willow spied Josh headed to the back. The displacement of his weight, however meager on the passenger side, had redistributed the weight.

The rope jerked.

"Josh, stay put!" Sam yelled, but the youth pastor kept coming.

In his widened, red eyes, Willow saw his youth. He was barely older than Quinn or Gus, and in this moment showed his fear as he went over the seat and out into the crisp air.

She had to give him props, however, for standing up to Sam, who looked like he wanted to turn him to ash with his glare.

"I can't stay in there—none of us can."

"That's not a choice now," Sam said, glancing at the anchor and then to Willow. "I'll get Vi."

"No, I'm lighter. You stay here, get the kids out the back. Gus and I will hand her to you."

Then, because she knew he'd put up a fight, she simply climbed back in, over the seat. Zena hopped out in Willow's wake.

The van shook as the weight again redistributed.

"Hurry up!" Sam yelled.

Vi had sat up and moved her foot off the bench. Willow knelt in front of her as Maggy climbed out.

"Gus, let's do this together."

Gus nodded and leaned down, grabbing Vi under her arms. "Sorry, Vi."

Big teddy bear of a guy, he winced as Vi cried out. But Willow had her leg, trying to immobilize her ankle as she worked her backward. Gus stepped over the backseat, Vi cradled in his big arms.

"Easy," Sam said.

Gus stepped down, and Vi moaned as Willow directed her foot over the backseat.

She didn't know how it happened—maybe Gus lost his footing on the icy ledge. Maybe she accidentally bumped Vi's leg, making her jerk and twist in Gus's arm. Suddenly Gus was tripping back and Vi was screaming, grabbing at the van.

She tore away from Willow's grip.

The force of it toppled Willow back. She slammed against the front passenger seat. Pain exploded in her shoulder, and she fell to the floor.

"Willow!"

She lay dazed for a long moment before she climbed to her feet.

When she looked up, she spotted Vi clinging to Sam, caught in his embrace. Of course.

The van started to roll, easing toward the edge.

"Willow—get out!"

Her gaze landed on the emergency pack.

Vi—maybe all of them—would need that. Willow scrabbled toward it, hooked her hand on the strap, and hauled it up, groaning.

"Hurry!" Sam stood at the door. Beside him, Quinn had ahold of the bumper as the van slid along the icy surface.

The anchor ground against the rock.

"C'mon!" Sam lunged toward her, and it only made the van jerk.

The anchor ripped from the icy stone.

"Willow!"

Gus scrambled to grab the bumper beside Quinn, but they only slid across the jagged surface.

She lunged toward the back, the backpack catching on the seat—Gus tripped, fell.

Sam jumped onto the bumper, reaching for her. "Leave it!"

But—

His expression told her that if she didn't drop it, he would come in after her.

The front wheel bumped over the edge, tilting the van, and the girls began to scream.

"Drop it, Willow!"

Willow let the backpack go, launched herself at Sam.

He grabbed her hand, yanked her hard as the rest of the van slipped away around her. She hit the door coming out—

Sam's arm circled around her.

Then they were falling to the ground, Willow's face buried in Sam's muscled, safe chest, his arms tight around her. Clutching her to himself as the van crashed into the ravine below.

She couldn't breathe. Her heart thundered out of her body, her hands slick.

Sam lay there, his arms around her, his breath razoring in and out. He pressed her to his body, as if afraid to let go.

"I'm not going anywhere without you."

Apparently, she wasn't either.

———— + ————

Sierra's sister had nearly died on his watch. Twice now.

Sam closed his eyes, not sure if it was Willow shaking, or him. Because with their feet dangling off the edge of the cliff, he couldn't slough off the residue of terror that lay just under his skin.

Willow Rose would *not* die out here.

Even if he never made it back to Sierra, which, at the rate his luck was holding, might be prophecy, Willow had to survive.

He owed Sierra that much.

Especially after the way he'd practically clung to her sister all night long, needing her warmth as much, more maybe, than she'd needed his. Willow had relaxed into him, sweetly surrendering. If Sierra was here, she'd be organizing them into groups, maybe assigning duties. Which, of course, he'd appreciate.

But Willow had simply let him hold her.

And then, *catch* her.

Thank you, God, he'd caught her.

"What were you thinking?" he said, more roughly than he felt. "Why didn't you get out?"

Willow finally raised her head, her hair falling around her face. "Sorry, but I thought we needed that backpack."

He exhaled long and hard, and finally sat up. She disentangled herself from his embrace, but he held on to her arms, made sure she sat far enough away from the edge.

Behind them, the kids were huddled together, a few crying. He felt like crying too.

Or maybe just hitting something, letting out a yell of frustration.

Their emergency pack, including their ropes, had taken a dive with the van.

Quinn and Gus sat on the ground, looking stripped, and Sam didn't want to think how close those two came to going over too.

Which brought him right back to Willow and her struggle with the backpack.

"We do need it. But not enough for you to nearly die." He softened his voice. "You okay?"

She nodded, more calm in her eyes than he felt. "Thanks."

Uh, anytime?

She crawled to the edge to peer over. "Oh my."

He couldn't help it—he took a look too.

The van lay upside down, nearly smashed flat, wheels up, forty feet down in a jagged ravine littered with boulders and knife-edged rocks.

Yeah, that would have been lethal, left them all in pieces.

"Now what?" Willow said. "Our gear is down there."

He just needed a minute to regroup. His hands shook, and he shoved them in his pockets. Stared out into the tangled forest across the ravine. His breath formed in the air, the chill of it calming after the heat of his pulse, the sweat beading his skin.

Now what?

In the light of day, their survival seemed, well, miraculous, but he wasn't going to go that far. Without the tree to stop them, they would have sailed right over the edge, a drop of sixty or so feet.

They would be dead, or mostly dead, at the bottom.

Instead, despite being chilled, they'd survived the night and even emerged from the van intact.

Now it was up to him to figure out how to get them all to safety.

He got up and took a good look at the overhang.

Next to him, Willow also got on her feet.

The overhang, maybe five feet long, hung out over the top of the rock, extending thirty feet or more wide from the ledge. From there, the land sloped uphill, dotted with rock, pine, and brush. No sight of the road.

They stood on the only ledge for miles; the cliff dropped away on either side. The fact they'd fallen in exactly this spot—

He glanced at Willow, who had folded her arms over her chest, her lower lip caught in her teeth.

"It looks much worse in the light of day," she said quietly. "Maybe we should be glad it was so dark last night."

He distinctly remembered stumbling around in the brutal cold, perfectly aware of the situation, but said nothing.

"We can't go up," she said then, speaking his thoughts.

She stared over the edge.

"And we can't go down," he finished.

"Maybe we wait for help," suggested Maggy behind them. "My parents will know we're missing."

"I'm sure the PEAK team has already been alerted," Sam said.

"But . . ." He didn't want to tell them about the fact that no one knew where they were.

Apparently, that wasn't a problem for Willow. "Because we changed hikes, unfortunately no one knows where we went. Which is on me. I should have called the pastor and told him about our change of plans. I'm so sorry. Because now they think we're at Huckleberry Mountain, which is about thirty miles from here. And that's a lot of area to search."

Except.

She looked at Sam as if hearing it too—the *whump-whump* of a chopper. High altitude, yes, but—

"Quinn, give me your jacket!" Willow said, and Quinn shucked off his red windbreaker.

The kid only wore a thermal shirt underneath. He wrapped his arms around himself as Willow took the jacket, began to wave it.

"Here," Sam said and grabbed a broken tree limb from their life-saving pine. He took the jacket, wrapped it around the tip of the limb, then raised it over his head, began to wave it.

And that's when he felt it—the pinch inside that went from a dull ache he'd barely noticed to a knife-edged pain.

"Oh!" He nearly dropped the tree limb to bend over and grab his side.

"What?" Willow grabbed the limb before it toppled over the edge. "Are you okay?"

"Yeah." No, he wasn't. And it only took a second for her to figure out he was lying, because she crouched in front of him, even as he slid to his knees. "I think I might have broken something."

"Or maybe it was already broken, and saving my life made it worse." She turned to Gus. "Wave this thing, see if you can get their attention."

The hum of the chopper grew louder, and Gus picked up the branch.

But even as he waved the limb, the red jacket affixed to the top, even as Sam cupped his hand over his eyes, wincing with the shards of pain in his side, the chopper swept away from them, farther south into the park.

Gus lowered the tree limb. "Sorry, Deputy Brooks."

"It's okay, kid," Sam said. "Give Quinn back his jacket."

"But how are we going to get out of here?" Riley scooted up from where he'd been regrouping. "They didn't see us!"

Sam pressed on his side, gritting his teeth.

"That really hurts, doesn't it?" Willow said.

He shook his head.

"Okay, if that's how we're going to play it, then I should probably tell you that I'm going down there."

It took Sam three—maybe five—complete seconds to wrap his brain around her words. He even uttered a confused, "What?"

"I'm going down the cliff. Listen, climbing down is the easy part—"

"No, it's not. Not with your shoulder."

"And you're going to climb down when you can't even stand up straight?" She put her hands on his shoulders, reasoning with him. "Listen, I don't have to put any weight on my shoulder. I'll go down—"

"And then climb back up?"

"I'll rope up, use the cams to anchor me." She met his eyes, a surety in them he hadn't seen last night. "This, Sam, I know how to do. Let me."

His jaw tightened, and he looked away. "If anything happens to you . . ."

"It won't."

He hadn't quite realized just how amazing her eyes were. Hazel-blue, with shades of amber and gold flecks, and in the morning sun, nearly hypnotizing.

Someday, some guy would fall into the spell of her smile, those pretty eyes.

He groaned against a spasm inside, adding a growl to his words. "I hate this idea."

"I know," she said. "But you can't be the only one doing the rescuing around here."

Uh, yes, he could.

"Come back to me," he said, his mouth a tight line.

"Promise."

———— + ————

The all-fun, all-the-time guy who helped Jess repair her plumbing, all the while fighting with her over appropriate pizza toppings, vanished when he put on his PEAK jacket.

No, it had vanished late last night when she'd called him with the news that Willow and Sam, along with the youth group, hadn't returned.

Pete had shown up at her house an hour later, freshly showered after a day working on her house, grim and wired.

By 4:00 a.m., he'd rustled Kacey Fairing out of bed and convinced her to take the chopper into the park. Now, six hours later, Pete paced the office, clearly edgy and frustrated as he debriefed Miles on their cursory airborne early morning search.

Jess finished pouring herself a cup of coffee, set the pot back, and picked up the other cup before heading back to the huddle of her teammates listening to Pete.

Country singer Ben King leaned against the wall, looking every inch a PEAK team member in his baseball cap and his blue jacket. Next to him, reading the weather report, stood Kacey. Gage and Ty had just walked in, both holding coffee from the Summit Cafe. And Miles stood at the center table, laying out a map.

Jess cast an eye toward Pete.

He'd changed into his fleece SAR jacket for their flight over Huckleberry Mountain, wore a wool hat, his blond hair sneaking

144

out the back. He hadn't shaved, and behind that tight jaw, she knew he was working out the scenarios.

If Sam was truly lost, Jess had no doubt Pete would find him.

More, he had incident commander written all over him. He simply needed the chance to prove himself. And with Sam in need of rescue, well, it just might be Pete's opportunity to heal old wounds and start over again.

Not that he'd said that, but after the fight Friday night, the bruise still healing on his cheek, she didn't have to be a doctor to diagnose the situation.

Even if she did, actually, have the degree to back it up.

"You're sure the van isn't in the lot?" Miles was saying.

"We flew over it a few times, but of course, we were in the air . . ." Pete stepped up to the map. "We really need to get better eyes on Huckleberry Mountain."

It seemed as if the youth group had simply vanished from the planet. When a cursory search of the trail—and the parking lot— came up empty, Kacey agreed to Pete's urging to head farther into the park, along the inside North Fork Road, nearly to Quartz Creek. But as the sun hit midmorning and their fuel reserves dropped below the halfway point, Kacey turned them around.

Besides, the snow cover and ice suggested a road untraveled.

They returned to the PEAK ranch only to be met by a congregation of worried parents jamming the front porch. Senator Wolfgang Starr appointed himself spokesman, holding coffee and wearing an expression not unlike Pete's.

None of them had heard from their kids since the moment they'd left the church parking lot, under the care of Willow and Josh.

"We have no PLS," Miles said. Point last seen. As in, no way to start their search grid. They needed clues—a discarded wrapper or a sighting from a fellow hiker. But with the lack of traffic in the park this late in the season and Willow's history as a park guide, finding a PLS might be akin to locating the Holy Grail. "We'll need to follow our gut here. Right now, we're searching for anything that might help us establish a search grid."

Outside, Sierra talked with the parents, getting descriptions of the kids, their clothing, as well as any other information that might be useful.

But they all knew the same thing.

They'd headed for Huckleberry Mountain, dressed for a day hike.

The temperatures in the park had dropped below freezing, and a layer of sleet and ice covered the roads, at least to the north. With no sign of the van in the parking lot, it could be that they'd slid off the road.

Which was why Miles was running his finger along Camas Road, to Huckleberry Mountain. "Kacey, get back up in the chopper, take Ben and follow along the road," Miles said. He looked over at Ty, who'd shown up shortly after Gage. "You take the truck, drive the road. It's possible they slid off and are hidden from overhead."

Miles looked over at Pete. "You're right. Somebody needs to rule out Huckleberry Mountain as a possibility. Even if the van is missing, we don't know what happened. Could be someone got hurt and others hiked back to get help. They could still be on the mountain."

"You want us to hike the trail," Pete said. "Look for clues." He glanced at Jess when he said it, clearly choosing her as his partner.

"Yeah. And get a move on." Miles picked up a piece of paper Chet had handed him. "According to the weather report, we have about a twenty-four-hour window before another storm hits us. And this time, it's an actual winter storm warning. We need to find these kids and get them off the mountain, because they won't survive another storm like last night."

Miles had always seemed to Jess like a man who should have

been in the military—maybe he had been, she didn't know. But with his short dark-brown hair, his piercing pale gray-green eyes, and unshaven face over a firm jaw, he reminded her of a cop or an FBI agent.

When in fact, he'd spent the past ten summers chasing down fires and riding bulls in his spare time. Because it was *fun*.

If he weren't married, with his second child on the way, Jess might accuse him of being an older version of Pete. Only Pete's idea of fun included leaping off tall places—cliffs, mountaintops, planes—like he might be a superhero.

"That coffee for me?" Pete asked.

"Yep," she said. "So, we're going up the mountain."

He nodded, took a sip. "Thanks." He didn't stick around for chitchat but headed out to the barn. She followed, dodging the grouping of worried parents still peppering Sierra with questions.

Inside the barn, Pete grabbed two packs—one filled with first aid supplies, the other with survival gear. Jess added a warm jacket and a hat. Despite the warm temperatures in the valley, the mountain could be topped with snow and ice.

"I'll get the radios," Jess said.

"I'll grab some water bottles." He left to dump the supplies in his truck while she checked out two radios, confirming their battery life.

Finally, she grabbed a radio harness and was walking out from the barn when she spotted Pete talking with . . . no, *seriously*?

"Hey, Tallie," Jess said.

Tallie wore a sweatshirt, jeans, and a frown on her face, and now looked at Jess with the tiniest of glares. "Hi."

Oops. Jess had clearly walked in on something. By the expression Pete wore, it was a conversation that he seemed itchy to leave.

Pete had one hand on his door handle; the other held his radio vest.

Jess raised an eyebrow and climbed into the truck.

She could barely hear the conversation. Pete's voice was low, Tallie's a little more animated.

Something about not returning her calls. And expecting more from him. And how she knew he didn't make promises, but . . .

Jess looked away.

Tallie might have gotten the all-fun version of Pete, but this was the version Jess preferred. The hero who kept his promise to save the day.

Pete slid in next to her, putting his harness on the seat, and closed his door. Tallie stepped back, her arms folded.

"Everything okay?"

Pete glanced at Jess, an emotion in his eyes she didn't recognize. "It's fine. I, uh . . ." He blew out a breath.

"She's nice," Jess said, then wanted to kick herself.

He glanced at her, frowned, then put on his aviator glasses and put the truck into gear.

Gage and Ty pulled out in front of them. Kacey was on the pad doing a walk-around flight check on the chopper.

Jess stared out the window, the silence humming between her and Pete as they pulled out toward the highway.

"If you want to talk about it, we can," she said.

"Talk about what?"

She glanced at him. He was staring straight ahead, those blue eyes shaded by mirrors, balancing his coffee cup on his knee.

"You? Tallie? This thing between you that has you upset?"

"I'm not upset."

"You seem upset—sort of grumpy."

He shook his head. "No. I'm just . . ." He sighed. "There's nothing between me and Tallie. She's just . . . Aw, fine. Apparently she's mad I didn't call her yesterday."

Jess took a sip of coffee. "Are you planning to go out with her again?"

"What is this, the Spanish Inquisition?" He stopped at a light.

Looked at her. "No, okay? Or, probably not—I don't know. Tallie is the last thing I'm thinking about right now." The light turned green. "Why?"

Oh. "No reason. Just trying to be a friend."

"Yeah, well, I don't need friends, Jess."

She turned away, her mouth tight.

"I didn't mean it like that. It's just—okay, I find myself sometimes wishing I could rewind time. And Tallie is one of those times. She's fun, yeah, but I think I hurt her a little, and I hate that part. I'm not the kind of guy who calls back the next day. I never have been. I like a girl, we go out, and that's it. I don't want more, okay? Like my brother always says, I'm just out for a good time."

Maybe, but that *wasn't* the Pete she knew. Jess held up her hand. "Okay. No judgment here—"

"Really? Because it sort of feels like judgment. Like you think I should have, what, kissed her good-bye? Told her I'd call when I got back?"

Actually, no, that was the last thing she wanted, but . . . "Maybe you could give a girl a longer tryout than twenty-four hours."

"Eight. We didn't spend the night together, Jess."

The way he said it made her feel a little ashamed.

"Sorry."

He drew in a breath, slowing at the turn into the west park headquarters. "I'm doing Tallie a favor, I promise. I'm just not the guy you want to build a life with. I don't see a home or a family in my future."

She looked away, blinked. Right. Silly her.

"As long as we're on the subject, why aren't you dating anyone? I noticed that Ty had his eye on you."

The fact that he'd even asked that made Jess take a quick breath.

All this time she'd thought Pete had been dodging asking her out because of their teammate status. Apparently not.

"I can't date a teammate." Although, out of all the choices of potential dates, Ty might be the best. At least she had nothing to lose with Ty—he already knew her secrets.

She took another sip of coffee. "Besides, I'm too busy fixing my house to date anyone. Maybe after I have furniture."

She'd tried to make it light, funny, to ease the sudden darkness between them, but Pete only pursed his lips.

She finished off her coffee as he turned onto Camas Road. In the truck in front of them, Ty and Gage had slowed, so he passed them, gunning it toward the Huckleberry Mountain trailhead.

"I know I already said it, but thank you for working on my house so much. I know you could be spending time doing—"

"It's no problem." Pete took a sip of coffee. "Actually, it reminds me of working with my dad. He was a general carpenter in the valley, and both Sam and I were going to go to work for him—or at least, that's what I had in my head. He used to take me on jobs with him, taught me how to run wiring, lay tile, frame a wall, put up Sheetrock."

The slightest hint of a smile edged up his face. "Our last project was a home theater in our house. We three were covered head to toe with Sheetrock dust. Mom took a picture, just our eyes showing—we looked like ghosts." His smile died. "Dad was killed about two weeks later."

"I'm sorry, Pete."

He lifted a shoulder. "It was my fault. A stupid decision . . ." He turned onto the dirt road that led to the lot.

But she couldn't move. Her breath scraped out at his casual words. "You don't really think that, do you?"

He seemed almost to not hear her as he slowed the truck.

"Pete, it's not your fault."

He turned into the parking lot. "Actually, yeah, it is. I decided to ski down into the trees on the back side of Blackbear Mountain. Dad came with me. I didn't realize he was lost until after I got down the mountain. He never showed up." He pulled into a parking space. Put the truck into park. "It was the last run of the day, and a storm was closing in." He turned the truck off. "They had to give up the search. He fell into a tree well, upside down, and froze to death." He said it almost clinically, no emotion. "Did you check the radio?"

Did she . . . ? "Uh. Yeah, but—"

"Let's go."

She couldn't move, his story pinning her heart to her chest.

He slid out, shucked off his jacket, leaving just his fleece on, and shut the door.

She blinked back the moisture in her eyes.

Thankfully, with the bright sunlight, she also needed her shades. She took off her outer jacket and wore only her black fleece.

She had a feeling this would be more of a sprint than a hike.

Pete was strapping on the survival pack—the heavier of the two.

She grabbed the emergency pack. Added a bottle of water to the side pocket.

The sun had burned off the frost and the layer of ice from the dirt lot. A crisp wind shivered the pine trees.

It rippled a notice tacked over the entrance to the trail.

"Did you see this, Pete? The trail's closed due to bear activity."

Pete had started walking through the empty dirt parking lot, head down, searching for signs of the van in the now-soggy ground.

He came over and stared at the sign. Blew out a breath as he looked up the trail.

"They're probably not there, but . . ." His mouth tightened into a grim line. "I'll regret it if we don't look."

She nodded, hearing more than just the regrets of this moment.

"Please let this not be a stupid idea," Pete said, then turned and started jogging up the trail.

8

COME BACK TO ME. Willow knew Sam didn't mean it the way it sounded, his voice soft, even intimate. As if he meant it.

Of course he meant it—in a practical, we're-on-the-same-team-so-stay-alive kind of way.

Not in the way her heart longed for him to mean it.

Silly, stupid—she'd clearly banged her head too hard against the glass, a wound, actually, that had started to burn with the sweat beading along her forehead.

Sam belonged to Sierra. More, Sam's hero gene was probably twice the size of the average male's. Of course he'd be giving off vibes of protection.

"Ten more feet. You're doing great, Willow!"

Sam, encouraging her as he leaned over the edge of the cliff.

The harrowing part—where she scaled her way down the cliff one scrubby hold at a time—was over. Now, she wore a harness attached into a self-belay system, using the cams in the equipment pack to secure herself as she climbed back up the face. The emergency pack hung from her shoulders and was clipped around her waist.

This could have been the easy part if her shoulder wasn't sending fire through her body, burning tears into her eyes, tempting her to let out a groan.

But she couldn't slow down, couldn't surrender. Not with Sam leaning over the cliff with such agony in his pale blue eyes, looking like he might do something crazy.

Like climb down after her, drag her up to the top.

She'd never had anyone look at her like that before—like he had to forcibly hold himself back from rescuing her—and frankly, it undid her a little.

Not unlike his Superman leap for her as he dragged her out of the van.

They needed to get back home, and fast, before her heart started to skew all this focused, devastating attention and convince her it was something more.

Sorry, Sierra. Willow shouldn't even allow herself to think of Sam as anything but taken—should not be having memories of his arms around her last night, the heat of his body keeping her own alive.

And especially not while she fought to find a grip for her left foot, her hands grimy and sweaty, slipping a little on the tiny lip of a handhold.

She curled her thumb over the top, trying to add reinforcement to the bare hold, looking down to find a groove or a slit—

"To your left there's an indentation."

"My legs aren't that long." Still, she reached out for it and nearly slipped off her current hold.

"Sorry!"

"I'm okay, Sam." Even if she did fall, her last cam was only a body-length away. She wouldn't go far.

It might, however, hurt.

She brought her knee up, found a groove, and used it to leverage herself up to a pocket in the rock for her left hand.

Eight more feet. Sweat dripped down her back, along her forehead. The wind had turned brittle despite the warmth of the sun. She guessed they might be in for another storm.

They couldn't spend another night on this ledge. Especially exposed.

The fact that she'd again risked the lives of her youth shook her to her core. Thankfully, they were in good hands—when she'd left, Josh had them circling to pray for her.

That was the kind of leader they needed, someone safe, who didn't risk their lives.

Willow found a nice thick jug hold for her right hand. She pulled up, put her foot in the previous lip.

Four more feet, and now Sam did lean down, put his hand on her pack.

"Sam, you're going to hurt yourself."

But her words didn't seem to matter as he practically hauled her up over the edge of the cliff.

Dragging her to safety beside him.

He was breathing hard, his face grim, sweat around the edges of his hairline.

"You okay?"

"That has to be the worst two hours of my entire life," he said bluntly. "Are you okay?"

With him looking at her like that—as if he'd tear his heart out of his chest and give it to her if she asked? Um, yes.

"That was scary brave, Willow, and I'm a little sick for letting you do it. I don't know what I was thinking."

"You were thinking that I knew what I was doing. Now, help me off with this pack." She reached for the belt, but her shaking hands gave her away.

Sam reached over, unbuckled the pack. Eased it off her shoulders. Quinn and Gus stood behind him, and now Quinn grabbed it from him.

She sat there, her legs drawn up, her arms circling them, her head bowed, just breathing.

Sam didn't move. When she looked up, his blue eyes were in hers. He gave a little smile. "You did good."

Her heart gave a traitorous leap of joy.

"Now we have to get these kids down." He stood up and headed over to the pack. "But first, we clean you up. And secure Vi's ankle."

Vi whimpered, but she played the trouper as Sam dug out a cravat from the pack and wrapped it around her ankle, securing her foot.

"That should keep it from moving. Try not to bang it."

He moved over to Willow. "Your turn." He touched her chin, angling her head to take a good look at her wound. "I'm afraid of grinding the glass into the wound, so I'm just going to irrigate it, then cover it with a bandage."

"Sam, we don't have to do this now."

"Shh. I know it hurts."

It did hurt, but in light of . . .

His thumb ran across her cheek, a quick tender swipe that probably didn't mean anything at all but had her breath squeezing out of her chest. "It'll just take a minute. I hate looking at it."

He didn't say why, he just grabbed a travel bottle of saline. "Close your eyes. This might hurt, sorry."

She closed her eyes. He grabbed her good shoulder and gave it a squeeze as he squirted saline over her wound. More surprising than painful. She inhaled as the saline dripped down her hair. He used a gauze pad to flick away the glass.

"It looks pretty clean, but you've got a vicious gash there. I wish I had ointment."

She grabbed his wrist, eased his hand away from her head. "It's fine, Sam. Really." She met his eyes, just so he'd believe her.

His mouth tightened into a grim line, as if he didn't want to accept it. Then he sighed, nodded. But for a second, she thought she saw his eyes glisten.

As if it pained *him.*

"Let's get these kids off the ledge," she said before her emotions could find her voice.

He began to root through the pack. "I'm sure Gage packed

a mechanical descender—it's standard in all our packs . . ." He unearthed a metal belayer/descending device. "We can lower each person down with this."

She unhooked the rope from the harness, and Gus and Quinn pulled up the slack.

Sam went to work rigging a belay system using the webbing and the rope and more cam anchors. When he finished, he climbed into a second harness and hooked himself into the anchor.

"Are you sure you want to do the belaying? Your ribs—"

"I'm sure." His tone cut her off, betraying again just how hard it had been for him to watch her sidle down the cliff and climb back up. With the harness sitting at Sam's hips, maybe he wouldn't injure himself further.

"Who goes first?" she asked.

"I think we need to have an adult at the bottom," he said and glanced at Josh.

Josh stiffened but nodded.

"Have you ever been climbing, Josh?" Willow asked as he tugged on the harness.

"A few times at a gym."

"I'm sure they lowered you down, right? Once you reached the top?"

He nodded. She wanted to wince at the brutal angle of his nose. Up close, he looked like he'd done time in a UFC ring and lost in a knockout.

"So, just lean back and Sam will lower you down. When you get to the bottom, unhook the harness, then climb out of it and send it back up."

He swallowed, nodded.

To her eye, he still looked like a sixteen-year-old kid.

He walked over to the edge of the cliff.

"There are a couple of footholds just over the edge. Step on those, then lean back. Sam will do the rest."

Josh gave her a tight nod, then stepped over the edge, visibly trembling.

Sam just sat there, his mouth a tight bud of impatience. "Ready?"

Willow put a hand on Josh's shoulder. "Look up, Josh. Not down. That's the key."

He found her eyes, his gaze latching on to hers. "Good advice," he said and flashed her a smile.

Then, slowly, he leaned back, his hands on the rope. "Ready."

Sam slowly let the rope out, sliding it through his gloves.

Willow got on her knees and leaned over the edge to watch. Josh worked his way down steadily, walking with the rope.

He settled at the bottom, not far from the destroyed van. A few minutes later, Sam started hauling up the harness.

"Maggy, you're next."

Maggy had slammed her mouth against something in the accident, so her lip was fat, and her eyes were reddened from crying. Willow pulled her into a quick embrace, smoothing her curly brown hair, then took her by the shoulders.

"Sometimes, when I'm afraid, I sing," she said, and began to hum the only thing that came to mind.

Amazing grace, how sweet the sound.

Maggy picked up the tune and began to hum as Willow outfitted her with the harness and gave her the same instructions as Josh.

The song rose to her as Maggy descended, humming, then mouthing the words.

Dawson went next, eager to get off the cliff, then Riley, who caught her arm. "Sorry," he said.

"Nothing to be sorry about. We're in God's hands."

He wore a tight-lipped disagreement as he headed over the edge.

But really, she meant it. The fact she wasn't shaking with fear filled her with a strange sense of power.

Especially when she glanced at Sam, and he winked.

Huh. Maybe they would live through this.

Yes, of course they would.

Zena, then Quinn and Gus. Willow winced at the gritting of Sam's teeth, the sweat that beaded on his forehead when he lowered the big guy.

Finally, Vi. Willow got her up, gently worked on her harness. "Vi. You are stronger than you think. You can do this. Sam will lower you slowly . . . just sort of hop down. Lean back, let him do all the work."

She helped Vi over the edge, held her arm as she leaned back. Kept her gaze in hers as Vi descended.

"Now what?" Willow said as Vi reached the bottom, collapsing into the arms of Gus. Josh was helping her off with her harness.

"Now you go, Willow," Sam said.

"But—"

"When you get to the bottom, I'll rappel down. It'll be easy with the descender, I promise."

He wore his Deputy Brooks face.

He pulled the harness up, and she took it and climbed in, cinching it tight. Clipped in the rope.

She was just walking to the edge when he added, "We're going to make it, Willow. We're going to get home, and everything's going to be fine." He offered a smile, so much warmth in it, it almost turned her weak.

But even as she nodded, even as she stepped over the edge, her life in Sam's strong hands, Willow knew that no, after today, with Sam back in Sierra's embrace, Willow would probably never be fine.

Sam sat in the rocky wash, his back to a boulder, staring at the crushed remains of the van, unable to find words.

Just in case he was caught in some crazy nightmare, he blinked.

The van remained, the front windshield blown out, the top pancaked in, glass scattered, oil and gas blackening the earth.

He couldn't move. Or take a full breath.

Never mind the ache in his side whenever he inhaled. Or exhaled. Or really, thought about the fact that they could have slipped right over the edge in their initial career down the hillside, ended up dead under a twisted coffin of metal.

Willow's words yesterday on the mountain had an ironic twist.

"See, when we're stuck in our everyday troubles, we can get focused on them, and that's all we see. We don't see God at work in our lives, just the darkness around us."

In this case, the light of day told him exactly how God, maybe, had saved them. That was the only answer to why they hadn't perished or at the very least ended up with more than a few scratches. Yes, Vi probably had a broken leg, and they all appeared banged up—split lips from hitting the seat in front of them or from flying debris, Josh's horribly broken nose, Willow's shoulder, clearly still aching judging by the way she favored it.

But all of them were breathing, and, save any more crazy accidents, would stay that way.

Against his gut advice, Quinn and Riley had shimmied through the dented window frames in search of their personal belongings—backpacks, iPhones, food. Probably a good idea, because now the youth group sat around finishing off the hiking lunch leftovers, drinking water, and adding layers that they hadn't been able to locate last night.

Someone had given Willow a brown wool stocking cap for her wound. Her golden brown hair cascaded down over her shoulders. She sat with Vi and Maggy, sharing a cheese stick and a package of Oreos, probably speaking words of encouragement.

The woman who'd nearly shaken apart after the crash, or even the one who'd leaned into his embrace last night, had vanished when she'd climbed down to retrieve the pack. Determined. Brave. Risking her life for her youth group.

His stomach still roiled at the memory of it. The second she started climbing down, his gut knotted, his hands turned slick, and he'd wanted to reach down, yank her back.

Some hero he was.

A little broken rib—and he felt pretty sure that he'd managed to break at least one, given the radiating pain under his arm—shouldn't have kept him from taking her place.

He glanced at Willow now, the way she leaned her head back against the boulder.

He hadn't realized, really, how amazingly pretty she was. With the slightest smattering of freckles across her nose, and lips that curled up into a smile almost on their own. Her hair took on a burnished gold sheen in the sun, and a warmth shone in her hazel-blue eyes that pressed him to keep looking, discover that light that glimmered inside.

He exhaled, pulling himself back. It was just the emotion of the crash, the relief at being at the bottom of the cliff. Safe.

Josh came over, sank down next to him. "Now what?" He offered Sam a beef jerky roll, and Sam took it. "Wait here to get rescued?"

The PEAK chopper did have a better chance of spotting them in the ravine—if it happened back on its search. Still . . . "I don't think so. They're not looking for us this far north. Once they figure out we're not at Huckleberry Mountain, they'll spread out, but my guess is that they'll go east, deeper into the park to the more travelled hikes. The Numa Trail Lookout isn't a hugely popular destination."

"We should have turned around at Huckleberry Mountain," Josh said darkly. "We never had permission to take the kids to Numa. I should have stepped in, but I wanted to trust Willow. Frankly, I don't see what Willow's point was in taking us to such a remote location."

Sam couldn't exactly place the rise inside him, why he felt the sudden need to come to her defense. He'd been thinking the exact same thing no less than twenty-four hours earlier.

"The remoteness is probably why she took us there—so we

didn't have any distractions." He looked at Josh. "Willow loves these kids. I think she was just trying to help them see beyond their lives—high school, if I remember correctly, is a bit of a war zone. You never know when you're going to get blown up."

"I was homeschooled," Josh said, "but I doubt a little hike in the mountains is going to keep these kids from sleeping around or doing drugs."

"Maybe not, but it might help them get ahold of their lives afterward, when everything is in shambles." Not that he knew, exactly. He'd packed his shattered life into a hard ball, shoved it deep inside to simmer like a peat fire. Maybe he should have taken his brother on such a hike, back in the day, helped them get a different perspective, find their footing.

Except Pete would have been like Quinn, sitting apart from everyone else, aloof, alone. Not in the least interested in what Sam had to say.

"We need to help them make right choices at the beginning. So they don't find themselves picking up the pieces."

Funny, it seemed that life was always about picking up the pieces. He frowned at Josh. "We're talking about teenagers here. They live from one impulse to the next."

"That's why you get into their lives and help them curb the impulses."

He glanced again at Willow. Maybe teenagers weren't the only ones in need of curbing their impulses. Because his current impulse had to do with Willow, and the fact that he couldn't get his mind—or gaze—off her.

He could probably blame it on his need to get them all to safety.

Or not. Because right then, she looked at him and met his eyes. Smiled at him.

Heat shot right through him.

Sam swallowed hard. This was simply a reaction to the stress of the last few hours.

The fear that she'd plummet right off the cliff and he'd have to watch Sierra's sister die.

Although, for a while there, he'd forgotten that part—Sierra's *sister*. She'd become just Willow. His partner in getting these kids home.

Something about being with her, despite the trauma of the past day, seemed . . . healing maybe, and didn't that sound crazy? Because he should be taken apart by their predicament.

Instead, for the first time in as long as he could remember, he felt less shattered, and the angry burr under his chest seemed to have shifted.

But then what? In a few hours, they'd be back in Mercy Falls and life would reset. He'd find Sierra, figure out how to make it work between them. According to his calculations, it *should* work. Sierra was exactly the girl he'd waited for. She fit perfectly into his life. Organized, capable, a little domestic, kind, patient.

Willow was—aside from being Sierra's kid sister—messy, impulsive, reactive, emotional. She wore her heart on the outside of her body, taking no care to protect it. Frankly he'd always be a little worried about Willow that way. Sierra could take care of herself. Hadn't she walked away from Ian when she realized he didn't have the same feelings for her?

Although, knowing Ian like Sam did, there was more underneath Ian's polished exterior than he let on. If he'd only reached out to Sierra, let her glimpse his heart . . . Which meant that maybe, to keep Sierra, Sam would just have to be more forthcoming about his feelings. Maybe if she knew . . .

What? Because at this moment, the only emotions he could pin down had everything to do with wanting to pull Willow back into his arms.

Oh no.

"We need to get going," Sam said now, to Josh.

"To where?" Josh said.

Willow had gotten up, dusted herself off. She had added a windbreaker over her fleece pullover. That, a pair of Gore-Tex hiking pants, sturdy boots, and she appeared ready to hike Everest.

Sam got up. Stared up the cliff, trying to spot the road. But with the cliff and overhang . . . Farther ahead in the distance, the mountains curved, and he spotted the hazy outline of a cutaway that could only mean the highway. If he could find a place where he could hike up, he could get help.

Don't leave. Willow's voice. He shook it away and gestured to the youth to gather in. All but Vi got up and walked over to him. Even Quinn joined them.

"We can't stay here. The chopper doesn't know where to look for us, and there's no shelter. But if we head down the ravine, maybe we can find a place to hike up to the highway, okay?"

Nods all around. "Gus, can you carry Vi for a while?"

"Sure, boss," Gus said.

"Okay, let's gather up the gear. Quinn, could you take the emergency pack?"

To his surprise, Quinn nodded. Not that Sam expected him to flip out or anything, but still, the way the teen walked over and put on the pack without a moment's extra thought, that, and the way Quinn had saved his life last night—maybe Sam had judged him wrongly.

Gus picked up Vi, who looked like a three-year-old on his back, and they all started hiking down the ravine.

Sam fell in step next to Quinn. "Hey."

Quinn glanced at Sam, one eyebrow up.

"You okay?"

"Yeah, sure. Why?"

Sam walked along, his hands in his pockets. "I dunno. A grizzly attack last week, a car accident this week, just sort of wondering what you had on the schedule for next week."

A twinge of a smile.

"Maybe don't get in any airplanes."

Quinn chuckled. "Right?"

Sam looked ahead, checking on their motley crew. Willow hiked behind him, still talking to Maggy, but Zena, Dawson, and Riley headed up their trek, with Gus and Vi behind them. Vi hung on like a trouper.

"How's Bella?" Sam asked.

"She's out of the hospital," Quinn said. "Still hasn't been back to school. Her parents won't let me see her." He lifted a shoulder in a shrug. "I guess they're right. If I hadn't dragged her out into the woods . . . But it wasn't what they think. I wasn't trying to . . ." His mouth tightened. "Anyway, I just want to apologize to her, but they won't let me near her."

Something about his tone gave a tug on Sam's heart.

"I didn't mean for anyone to get hurt."

How many times had he heard that in his career as a deputy? People just didn't think about their actions, ended up in the wrong place at the wrong time. And that's where he and his team came in.

Sam couldn't deny a small niggle of annoyance every time he got a call. If people just obeyed the rules, thought before they acted, no one would need to be rescued in the first place.

Like them. If he hadn't been hurt by Sierra's absence, the feeling that she'd lied to him, hadn't let his emotions take over, he would have left a message, at least alerted someone to their whereabouts.

He looked at Quinn, understanding his sigh completely.

"Hang in there, kid. Everyone lived, and in time, Bella's folks will come around."

"I doubt it. They have me pegged as trouble in their minds. My dad too." He glanced at Sam. "Thanks, by the way, for calming him down the other night. He gets pretty . . . Well, he's all Senator Starr in public, but sometimes he acts like he's still in the military at home."

Quinn walked out ahead of him.

His words, however, unsettled Sam.

He heard scuffling behind him and looked over to see Willow catching up to him.

"Hey," she said, a little out of breath. She jutted her chin toward Quinn. "I saw you talking to Quinn. Thanks."

"For what?"

"Well, things aren't always easy for him with his dad."

"I got that," Sam said. "You don't think that . . . Senator Starr isn't the kind of guy who would add a little physical incentive to get his way, is he?"

Willow glanced at him, her eyes wide. "I don't know. Why, do you think that . . ."

"No. I don't. But Quinn just mentioned how his dad is still pretty military."

"Oh yeah. He wants Quinn to attend the Naval Academy and follow in his footsteps. He rides Quinn pretty hard. But Quinn loves music—he's been hoping to get a job at Ben's studio, maybe as an intern, so . . ." She lifted her shoulder. "I'm sure the senator is thrilled. I can bet the disagreement has made for a few battles."

"When Pete said he wanted to be a firefighter, I wanted to throttle him."

"And yet, he became this amazing smoke jumper."

"I suppose. I always thought we'd both go into the family business, with my dad. After he died, I thought that Pete would want to take up the mantle. Especially the building side of the company. He and Dad shared that—a love for building."

"Why didn't you take over the company?"

"My uncle ran it with Dad, and he just took it over. I graduated just a few months after Dad died. My uncle didn't need me in the business, and frankly, working construction just opened the wounds. Pete and I used to go out on jobs with Dad—worked every summer alongside him. And doing that without him . . ." He shook his head.

"In fact, I couldn't do anything we used to do together—fish, ski, even hike the park. It was just a reminder of what I didn't have. I joined the Mercy Falls Sheriff's Department right out of high school, took classes, became a peace officer, and worked my way up. I like working with the PEAK team."

"It allows you to do what you couldn't do for your dad."

He looked at her.

"Save people."

Oh. Right.

She cringed. "I did it again. Spoke without thinking. Sorry, Sam—I didn't mean to open wounds."

"No, you're right, Willow. I couldn't save my dad—"

"That's not what I meant. You have hero written all over you."

He went warm at her words, all the way through to his core. Hero. Written all over him.

When she said it like that . . .

"I'll bet your dad would be really proud of you."

The words turned sour in his gut. "I don't think so. My dad and I were very different. He was more like Pete—loved to laugh, have a good time. They were risk takers—both of them. When Pete went down the mountain that day, I wanted to go down a different, safer way. We had an argument, and Pete won. Dad went his way."

"Why? Was he afraid Pete would get hurt?"

Around them, the ravine had started to narrow, and the breeze brushed the pine trees. Behind the rush of wind, Sam picked up the sound of water. Maybe they could find a creek, fill their water bottles.

"I used to think so, but Pete was sixteen and an accomplished skier. I think Dad just . . . wanted to. He chose Pete over me."

He'd never really heard himself put it that way, and the rawness of his words turned his throat thick. Oddly, he couldn't stop. "Dad's last words to me were, 'Live a little, Sam.' Then he took off.

And somewhere in that back country, he got lost, fell into a tree well, and froze to death."

Sam blinked away the sudden burn in his eyes, shook his head. "So no, I'm not sure he'd be thrilled with my life."

"Why? Being a cop is an honorable profession."

"It's not the cop part he would hate. It's the fact that . . ." He looked away, not sure how they'd gotten so far into his life, digging around in places he'd rather stay buried. But Willow made it okay with her soft gaze, the way she listened.

"I don't think I've let myself really live since he died. I had Mom to take care of, and Pete just went off the deep end. Someone had to pull our lives together. But I can't shake off Dad's words, that I'm missing something. Not living . . . if that makes any sense."

She nodded slowly. "And that's what makes you so angry at Pete. Because he is *always* living life."

He blinked at her. "Yeah. Exactly. He apparently had no problem getting over losing Dad. It's almost as if he's *more* alive. BASE jumping. Skydiving. And don't tell me that his long list of women isn't another way of living life in the moment." He shook his head. "I don't want to be like that."

"But you resent that he is."

"We can't end up with another death in our family. It would put Mom under. She's been through so much. Dad. Her cancer. She deserves a chance to be happy. She can't lose Pete . . ."

"Or you," she said softly.

He frowned. Lifted a shoulder. "She won't lose me."

"Because you don't take chances?"

"No, I don't. I think before I act. I don't put myself in danger." He gave a rueful smile. "Usually."

"I know."

Something in her eyes, the way they reached out with such a look of pure admiration, had that band around his chest tightening.

Willow was so easy to talk to, a guy could get himself in over his head. He'd just told her more in ten minutes than in all his dates with Sierra.

With that knowledge, Sam's mouth went a little dry. He looked ahead, terribly aware of the thunder of his pulse. Good grief, he needed to get ahold of himself.

"That's probably why Sierra and I are so right for each other. Because she too thinks through everything. Plans it out, organizes it. I really respect that about her."

Wow, his chest ached, especially when he chased his words with a polite, distant smile.

Willow nodded, her own smile fixed. "Yeah, I know. You and Sierra are perfect for each other." She looked out ahead, picking up the pace just a little. "And she'll be so glad to see you when we get back."

He didn't know why, but frankly, at this moment, he couldn't care less.

———— + ————

The SAR professional she was, Jess practically ran the six miles up Huckleberry Mountain.

Right on Pete's tail.

No complaining, just her breath huffing out as they pressed on, past McGee Creek, through the towering stands of lodgepole pines, then along the saddle beneath the towering Apgar Mountains. They'd stopped for a brief water break when they hit the ridgeline, then Pete couldn't help himself and practically ran the quarter mile to the summit.

Now, beside him, Jess gripped her knees, catching her breath as they stared out at the magnificent panorama.

At the top, a fire lookout offered a view of the Livingstone Mountains rising gray and rugged against the sky, now tufted with heavy cumulus lying low against the peaks.

A winter wind bullied his fleece, and despite his desire to shed his outer layer, Pete didn't want the sweat turning to chill.

Good way to catch a cold, and frankly, he needed all his energy.

Sam was out there, somewhere, maybe hurt. Maybe *dying*. It felt just like the past repeating itself.

"I know we were walking fast, but I had my eye out for anything—fibers, a wrapper, even footprints," Jess said, standing up and digging out her water bottle. "I don't think they've been up here."

Which meant, of course, he'd wasted the past two hours on a fruitless search.

Pete checked his watch, then pulled out his walkie and tried to connect with his team.

Nothing but static, and he moved around the mountaintop, trying for reception. No surprise; the mountains probably obscured the signal.

"We'll try a little farther down," she said. "I got a signal in the parking lot on my cell. I'm sure we'll be able to catch it there."

Pete slipped the radio back into his vest pouch. "Where could they have gone?"

Jess stood staring out at the view, as if lost in thought. The wind tangled her blonde hair, which was caught back in a wool hat. She held a water bottle, her thumb running up and down along the surface.

"I can't date a teammate."

He didn't know why those particular words thundered back to him in this instant. Maybe it was the fatigue.

Or maybe it was because the incredulity in her voice still rocked him.

Really?

Good. If he were honest, the idea of Ty dating her put a fist in his gut. Pete had seen the guy checking Jess out—and frankly, who wouldn't?

169

The woman was the complete package of fun and steel-edged determination. The kind of girl a guy wanted on his side, during—and after—a callout. Funny, compassionate, easy to talk to.

Breathtakingly gorgeous, even with paint on her chin. Especially when she looked at him, gave him an encouraging smile.

He wanted to take back his words in the truck, egged out of him by her probing. *Tallie is nice? Really, Jess?*

Which was why he gave her the knee-jerk response.

"I'm not the kind of guy who calls back the next day. I never have been. I don't want more, okay?"

With her, he'd nearly forgotten that.

"I'm just not the guy you want to build a life with. I don't see a home or a family in my future."

Call him crazy, but he'd sort of felt like that was *exactly* what they were doing, fixing up Jess's house. Picking out tile and paint colors and even talking through future improvements. Like they might be a couple investing in a house. A future.

The one Pete wanted to deserve.

"Let's get going," he said.

Jess took another drink, capped the bottle, and slipped it back into her pack.

He stood there, staring at the view of the park, the endless jagged crevices, the undulating foothills covered in lush, impenetrable pine. The foamy, nearly frigid rivers, and above it all, the tumble of gray storm clouds.

Jess touched his arm, squeezed, and he came back to himself.

"We'll find them, Pete."

The knot in his chest released, just a little. "The sooner we get down, the sooner we can figure out a new strategy."

"Maybe Ty and Gage found something."

She set off down the trail, picking her way over the bouldered path, her steps sure as she jogged down.

The trail ran along the ridge, then dropped down into the scattered forest. Spires of black pine and Fraser fir jutted up, edged by thick tangles of scrubby huckleberry bushes still laden with blue, plump fruit. The trail rambled down between the bushes, mountain ridges rising on either side, the glorious jagged Apgar Mountains in the distance.

Jess stopped once, held up her phone to the air.

"Any signal?"

"Nothing."

He wore a lightweight wool hat and kept it on, despite the sweat at his temples. He blew out a breath.

Jess's expression softened. "If anyone knows how to survive in the woods, it's Sam. He's not going to let anything happen to these kids."

"That's the thing—you're right. Sam's always been the one with the level head. He's not going to do something stupid, ever. So the fact that they aren't here feels so . . . irresponsible." Pete gave a wry smile. "Something I might do."

"You're hardly irresponsible." Jess started down the trail again.

He fell in behind her, kept her killer pace.

The woman just might be bionic.

"You clearly haven't been listening to my brother, then." He didn't know why the wounds of his father's search felt suddenly so raw. "When we lost Dad, Sam told me that all I wanted was to have fun, that I didn't care who I hurt. Maybe he was right."

She rounded on him so fast he nearly knocked her over. He grabbed her arms to right himself, to keep her from going flying. "What—"

"Are you kidding me? He's *not* right. Look at you—nearly frantic with worry, climbing a mountain in record time to try and find him."

"I'm not frantic," he said. Except, well . . . "It's just . . ." He shook his head.

"What?"

"It's just that Sam's pretty much hated me from that day on. And the thought of him still . . . I shouldn't care, I guess."

"You don't want your fight at the Gray Pony to be the last time you ever saw your brother."

Somehow Jess had that power to look right through him, part the clutter, and get to the bones of the situation. He gritted his jaw and looked away. "I had no idea how much he hated me until Friday night."

"Sam doesn't hate you."

"Really? You didn't see his expression. The guy would have mopped the floor with me—or tried—right there if Ian hadn't pulled him off."

The fact he'd admitted that took all the energy out of Pete. And now his eyes burned. "The worst part is, we used to be friends."

She took his hands, squeezing them. "No, the worst part is that Sam is your big brother. You admired him. You loved him, and . . ." Her words stopped then, her breath tremulous, and her teeth caught her lip, as if fighting a strange surge of emotion. "And he betrayed you when you needed him most. Your dad was . . . in trouble. Lost. Dead. And you needed Sam to *not* blame you—you were already blaming yourself enough. But he did. He turned on you, pointed a finger, and decided you were a blemish on the family. Pushed you away."

He had a feeling they weren't only talking about him and Sam.

Still, her words gathered inside him, forming into a hot ball in his throat. "Sam changed after that. He was already so serious, but after Dad died, he became almost driven. Wanted me to go to college—which I didn't. He started policing my life." Pete shook his head, the heat settling into his chest. "Probably that's why he became a cop—to keep me out of trouble." He gave a wry grin, trying to ease the moment. "Apparently, that didn't take."

"Pete."

"I can't . . ."

"Lose him?" Jess said, her voice trembling. "No. Because if you do, then you'll forever live with the what-ifs. Wonder what you could have done differently."

They were definitely not only talking about him. He fought the desire to put his hand to her cheek, thumb away the moisture he saw forming in her eyes. "Are you okay?"

"Sorry—it's just that I think you're wrong about one thing." She reached up, wiped her fingers under her eyes. "Sam loves you. Or at least, doesn't want to leave things like they were, either."

He frowned.

"He called you. Yesterday, right? We were in the bathroom."

"No. He called on *your* phone, looking for Sierra." Pete stilled then. "Jess. When exactly was that?"

She pulled out her cell phone, scrolled down. "Around 9:30 a.m."

"When did we lose reception here?"

"We had it in the parking lot. But pretty quickly after we started the hike, I think."

"Right. When did they leave for the park?"

"Sierra and Willow left at 6:00 a.m. They picked up the kids at 6:30 and were at PEAK around 7:00 a.m. They probably left soon after that."

"An hour more to the trailhead, at the most. Even if they were delayed, there's no way he could have called you at 9:30. He would have been out of cell phone range by then."

Her eyes widened. "Right. All we need to do is find the cell phone pockets in the park—the places he could have traveled to by 9:30 a.m. that still had reception. We need to get a map, start tracking down all the lookout towers."

"Why lookout towers?"

"Willow is obsessed with them. That's why she climbed to Granite Chalet earlier this summer."

Right. When the same youth group got trapped by an early

summer flood. Willow had some kind of crazy bad luck when it came to youth outings.

"And that's why she wanted to come here."

"So, you're thinking that—"

"They saw the grizzly warning sign and turned around, went to a different hike. And maybe that was Sam trying to call Sierra to tell her."

"And got me," Pete said. "Only to hang up when I told him she wasn't there."

Jess put her hand on his arm, squeezed, her beautiful eyes shiny, a deep aquamarine in the sunlight, the kind of eyes a man could lose himself in. Especially when her lips curled into a delicious smile.

For a second, all Pete could think of was lowering his mouth to hers, tasting that smile, letting it seep through him, fill him with her touch. He wanted a piece of all that sunshine, the way she could make him feel like he wasn't the guy who broke hearts, but the one who fixed them.

He couldn't stop himself. "Jess," he said softly, his hand reaching up to touch her face. His gaze roamed her face, stopped at her mouth.

She stiffened. "Pete."

Oh. His breath trickled out, and he caught himself. Right. What was he *doing*—

"Don't move."

It was the way she said it, softly, her eyes not on him at all, but past him, her gaze widening with a flush of panic.

"What?"

She reached out and gripped the front of his jacket. "Move very slowly and keep your voice down."

Now she was scaring him. Especially when she met his gaze. "I don't think she's seen us yet—we're downwind."

Downwind? He frowned at her, then very slowly turned to look over his shoulder.

Froze.

Forty feet away, ruffling around in the huckleberry bushes near the top of the ridge, a silver-tipped grizzly sow rooted for the plump berries, fortifying herself for hibernation.

And lost in the bushes beside her, two hungry cubs.

He put his arm around Jess. Pulled her to himself. "Stay with me," he whispered.

She nodded.

Very slowly, he crouched down onto the ground, urging her alongside him.

Then he began to crawl, low, toward the shelter of the brush, through the ferns, the huckleberry, the sparse low-hanging pine.

Jess scooted in beside him, wordless, wincing when branches cracked under her.

He reached a thick, towering pine tree, scuttled underneath, and without a second thought, pulled Jess in beside him, nestled her under his arm, protecting her with his body as they hid under the tree. Ferns and huckleberry rose around them, scant protection on the scrubby trail.

However, if the animal wanted to get to Jess, it would have to tear Pete off her first.

"Maybe the pine scent will cover ours," he said quietly into her ear, his gaze on the bears. They rooted around the faraway huckleberry, taking their time.

"Is that the same bear as—"

"I don't think so—maybe. We're about ten miles from the pit, and usually grizzlies stay in a smaller area. But with the berries . . ."

He couldn't see any wounds, but a bear didn't have to be wounded to protect her young. He tightened his grip around Jess.

She didn't fight him, fitting, of course, perfectly into the curve of his embrace.

"What are we going to do?" Jess said, turning her face to his, only inches away.

He tamped down the urge to simply get up, run down the trail. That would only alert the bear, and while he'd gone to state on his high school sprinting team, he couldn't outrun a grizzly.

And he wasn't leaving Jess.

The other urge he couldn't do anything about, either. The one that had him wanting to capitalize on this crazy, unforeseen moment where he had her in his arms.

Pete swallowed and closed his eyes before she saw exactly that thought in them.

"We stay here and wait her out," he said, the sweat on his forehead starting to cool, run a chilly finger down his spine.

Talk about needing rescue.

9

WILLOW'S BRILLIANT PLAN worked better than she could have imagined.

Sam, fighting to get back to his One True Love. Sam, realizing that Sierra was worth fighting for. Sam, dedicated to wooing her sister, making her happy.

Oh, Willow was such a fool.

She fought the crazy, impulsive urge to simply sprint down the ravine, put as much distance between herself and Sam as her energy would muster.

Instead, his words curled around her, squeezed out her breath.

"That's probably why Sierra and I are so right for each other. Because she too thinks through everything. Plans it out, organizes it. I really respect that about her."

Willow had to knock the words out of her head, but really . . . Sam nailed it. Beautiful Sierra, with her short dark hair, her exotic hazel-green eyes, her quick wit, the way she knew how to untangle a problem . . . She and Sam were a perfect match. Sierra never did anything rash, never lived by her impulses, never went anywhere without a backup plan.

Sierra would have never distracted Sam when he was driving with a stupid song, in a wild, impulsive hope to help the kids see beyond their current troubles.

What troubles did Willow think they truly needed help with that so necessitated this trip? Maggy showed up like a Girl Scout to every youth meeting. Sure, her father was the choir director, but Maggy had a natural goodness to her, two parents and a younger sister who loved her.

Dawson probably came because of Vi, who clearly adored her brother, hovering over him. Dawson suffered from a hint of a learning disability, and Vi was constantly helping him with his homework.

Quinn—well, he might have jumped at the chance to be away from his father for the day. So his father wanted to send him to college—what a tragedy. At least he had a father who showed up.

Of all of them, Zena came from a home she could complain about. She'd probably signed up for a chance just to get away from the crazy, the fighting. The neglect. Willow got that too, having leaped at the opportunity to live with Sierra when she turned seventeen.

Her mother, admittedly, hadn't put up much of a fight.

As for Gus—always a charmer, the guy was a big teddy bear, his blue eyes sparkling with a can-do attitude both on and off the field. He had parents who loved him, a couple older brothers, a sister. A family that took up the second pew in church for as long as she could remember.

To be honest, out of all of them, Gus bore the marks of a true man of God. Dependable. Self-sacrificing.

And, apparently, hungry.

"I would give my entire collection of NFL footballs for a double cheeseburger and a basket of curly fries from the Summit," Gus said as he readjusted Vi on his back, his shirt sodden with sweat, his forehead glistening. He'd taken off his jacket, tied it around his waist at the last break. The big guy could decimate the forest with his football-player redolence.

Poor Vi hung on like a trouper.

"Give me a plate of endless spaghetti," Dawson said, a few steps behind him. He stumbled on a rock, righted himself fast.

"I'll take a pizza from the Griz," Zena said.

"Ice cream sundae, lots of whipped cream," said Vi.

"Chocolate shake for me." Maggy's voice drifted up from beside Willow.

Josh shoved his hands in his pockets, said nothing.

"Pizza rolls," Riley said. "And Mountain Dew." He'd slowed, and now walked just ahead of Willow. She knew that most likely his parents had pried him away from his Xbox. More than once, Kendra Rigs had mentioned her worry about Riley making friends.

Up ahead, Gus, too, stumbled, and Vi let out a little shriek as he pitched forward, nearly going down.

The beast he was, he saved them both, but worked his way to a boulder, set Vi down, then leaned over, breathing hard.

Sam came up from behind, having been quiet for the past half mile. Probably dreaming of when he'd see perfect, amazing, organized, put-together, non-impulsive Sierra again.

"I'm sorry, boss," Gus said to Sam. "I just need a breather."

"You've carried her at least a couple miles, Gus," Sam said, clamping the linebacker on his shoulder. "I'll take a turn."

Of course he would. Because Sam naturally defaulted to "I Will Save You."

"No. Sam, *no way* are you carrying Vi," Willow said, unable to stop herself.

He looked over at her, frowned.

"You're hurt—maybe even have a broken rib. And carrying Vi isn't going to help."

A voice spoke up. "I'll do it."

She couldn't have been more surprised if a unicorn had suddenly appeared to grant all their wishes. "Riley?"

"I can carry her," he said.

Indeed. Riley wasn't a small guy, just . . .

She probably shouldn't judge a man's heart by the size of his shoulders. He unhitched his backpack and handed it to Gus.

"Trade ya."

Gus grinned. Riley looked at Vi and smiled, his expression warm, almost glowing.

With a whoosh of illumination, Willow got it.

The kid had a mad crush on Vi. How had she not seen it earlier? Clearly she was too wrapped up in her adoration of a man she couldn't have.

Riley had apologized to her earlier, and with another rush of understanding, she realized . . . he blamed himself for the van going off the cliff.

And wanted to fix that.

Riley leaned down, and Vi climbed on his back. He staggered under her weight a second, but got up. Seated her better with a little wiggle of his hips. "You okay?"

By the expression on Vi's face, Willow had to wonder if maybe Vi wasn't nursing a small crush in return.

Huh.

Sam had stepped back, his gaze on Riley. "You good?"

He nodded.

The ravine they'd started down only deepened into a gorge the farther they trekked; the mountains rose in cliffs that towered over them. Only the mountain in front of them gave her any hope that they weren't getting themselves horribly lost.

The last thing Sam needed was someone second-guessing him. That's not what *Sierra* would do—she'd stand by him, plan with him exactly what to do when they got to the road.

Most of all, she wouldn't be terrified, her heart nearly giving out at the prospect of Sam leaving her—them—to hike out for help.

Because Sierra wasn't the weak link. Ever.

But Willow wasn't anything like Sierra. She didn't think past her first thought, she let her emotions be her trusty guide, she considered organization to be any pile in which she could find her shoes, her watch, a hat. And as for smarts . . .

No wonder Sam looked so crazy afraid when she'd climbed down the cliff. Probably thought she'd lost her mind.

Maybe still did. After all, a smart person would have suggested turning around at the first hint of trouble back at Huckleberry Mountain.

Sam waited for her to catch up, fell in line with her. "I think I can hear a river up ahead. Maybe there will be a bridge or some way to hike up to the road from there. If not, we may have to cross it."

She gave a nod, no hint that her entire body coiled tight at his words.

A river.

Oh, please, no.

She let out an exhale, harder than she meant to because he looked over at her.

"You okay?"

She offered a smile, felt it quiver on the edges. "I was just thinking . . . are you sure we all need to cross? Because maybe some of us should stay on this side."

One eyebrow dipped down in a frown.

"We should stay together, Willow, if we can. We don't know how long it will be until we find help, and we're stronger, and safer, together."

Right. Okay. She *wouldn't* fall apart. Besides, she could dog paddle. Had a couple times in McFarland Lake, back when Arank had thrown her in.

Of course, he'd had to swim out and grab her when she went under.

No problem.

"I'd order the pulled pork sandwich," Sam said quietly.

She looked over at him; he was trying to make friends.

"Macaroni and cheese," she said. "And Oreos dipped in milk."

"Can I change my answer?" A broader smile, his eyes sparkling, and she wanted to cry.

Nodded. *You can change your answer anytime, Sam.*

She looked away, her jaw tight.

And that's when she heard it—the sound of a river rushing over rocks and boulders. She smelled the freshening in the air, heard the rush of the trees.

Sam picked up his pace, striding through the dry bed, nearly running ahead.

Wow, he really wanted to get back to—

No, that wasn't fair. He wanted to save them. She blinked back the stupid burning in her eyes and also picked up her pace.

The ravine ended at a drop-off with a tumble of boulders down to the river's edge.

Sam stood on one of these boulders, staring at the watery expanse.

She climbed up behind him, followed by Josh.

Thirty feet wide, the river didn't look that deep, but it washed over boulders and downed trees in a rush of foam, white water, and icy blue.

On the other side lay the forest, tangled and foreboding.

Beyond that, however, she could see the mountain, and the road chipped along the edge.

"According to my memory of the park," Sam said, "if we cross the river and head due west, we should eventually hit the road to Polebridge."

"Cross the river?" Josh said.

"It doesn't look deep," Sam said. "I think if we're careful, we can go slowly . . ."

Josh stiffened but nodded, apparently not wanting to be the weak link, either.

Except the youth pastor had managed to keep these kids calm on top of the cliff and down below. He was forging a bond with at least Dawson, if not Maggy and Zena.

And anyone could form a bond with Gus.

Riley had set Vi down, was catching his breath. Now, Gus and Dawson climbed up to take a look.

"Piece of cake," Gus said. He turned. "Dawson, you or I will take Vi—give Riley a break, okay?"

Riley looked up as if to argue, but Gus shook his head. "Just let us get her across."

Josh was rolling up his pants legs.

Sam stepped back, frowned. "You do know your shoes are going to get drenched—"

"I'll take them off."

"Josh," Sam said. "Besides being glacial cold, the river is filled with rocks that could slice through your feet. Should you lose your balance and get caught in the flow, you'll need to catch yourself, push off the rocks. You can't do that if your feet are frozen."

Josh stood up, looking a little white. Once again, Willow wanted to apologize for getting him in over his head.

He stepped down into the water, and it crested up over his shoe. He took a breath, recoiled.

"You got this, Josh," Sam said, and Willow noticed how he leaned toward Josh, as if ready to go in after him.

Not unlike he had for her on the cliff.

So, yes, indeed, she'd been reading into his concern way too much. Sam was just a good, amazingly brave, kind, self-sacrificing man.

Who loved her sister.

"I'll go next," Riley said, scrambling down the rocks.

Josh had worked his way to nearly the middle, gasping with the cold as the water came up to his waist. His arms wobbled as he tried to keep his balance. "It's slippery, and—"

That's when he went down. His feet slipped out beneath him, and he splashed hard into the river.

"Josh!" Sam leaped out for him, but Riley was two steps ahead of him.

"I got him!"

Josh popped up, scrabbling for a hold as the flow tried to whisk him downstream. Riley grabbed his arm, his other hand clutching a boulder.

Josh set his feet down and flung himself at a nearby boulder. "It's deep here!"

"You got him, Riley?" Sam said, still poised to leap in after them.

"Yep," Riley said. Josh was working his way back around the boulder, to shallower ground. He sat on the boulder now, propping himself there. Water ran down his face, his body, and he shook with the cold.

"I have a better idea," Josh said through his gritted teeth. "I'll stay here. Riley, you keep moving and find a spot a little farther on. Then we'll get the others across—they can hang on to us."

Sam nodded, a quick decision that probably had something to do with his shaken expression.

Maggy went first, crying out at the cold but holding on to Sam's hand until she could reach Gus, who planted himself in the middle, between Sam and Josh.

Then to Josh. The current nearly knocked her over. But Josh guided her to Riley, his hand gripped to a tree that jutted out over the water.

Riley helped her to the final boulder, and she climbed ashore, shaking.

Zena went next, making it look easy, and then Dawson, his sister on his back. She clung to him as she reached Gus, gasping as Dawson slipped.

Gus was right there, catching her. She fell between Dawson and Gus, one arm over each boy's shoulder. They struggled across. Josh walked behind them, clearly afraid the trio would go down.

Riley met them on the other side, picking Vi up in his arms, holding her as Gus and Dawson scrambled up.

He transferred her—probably reluctantly—to Gus, who carried her into the woods.

Which only left Willow and Sam and Quinn.

She turned to Quinn. "You go."

Not procrastinating. Not at all.

Quinn handed the emergency pack to Sam, then struggled out into the rapids, slowly, carefully. He'd made it to the middle when Sam turned to her.

"Can you make it, Willow? Or do you want Quinn to wait—"

"I'm fine."

Just fine. No problem. But a fist closed around her chest, squeezed as she looked at the river.

She could nearly taste the grimy water in her mouth, filling her nose, blinding her—

"Willow?"

Oh. She took a breath, stepped down into the water.

Ice. The cold turned her foot nearly numb. She held on to the moss-covered boulder as she edged her other foot out.

She put her hand down to steady herself as she searched for footing. The water crested up to her knees, over her arm.

The next step brought her to her waist. She gasped with the rush of cold.

"I'm right behind you," Sam said.

She didn't look back, just reached out for the next boulder, took another step and nearly lost her balance, her arms windmilling.

Quinn had reached the shore on the other side.

She was just reaching out for the boulder, her hands grazing the rough edge when she heard it—Sam's cry of surprise, the splash.

She turned. He'd fallen, feet upstream, the rapids yanking him into the froth.

"Sam!"

Then, as usual, because she was *not* Sierra, Willow simply reacted.

She reached out for him, one hand on her boulder, the other groping for him.

He was sputtering, fighting, and she leaned out farther. "Grab my hand!"

Except, then, she was no use at all. Her feet slipped on the slick rocks, and she plunged into the rapids.

A thousand needles of pain made her cry out just before the current sucked her under.

———— + ————

Sam popped his head up, shook the water from his face, and gasped as the cold raked over him.

He slammed into a boulder, pain ripping through his body, and he went under again. But he had the presence of mind to reach out and grab for the rock before the river took him.

His feet came around, and he forced his legs up, kicking against the current, his arms straining against the cold to hold on.

Only then did he hear her scream.

Willow?

Last he'd seen, she'd been clinging to the rock. Now, as he hugged his own boulder, he blinked, clearing his vision. He heard more shouts, yells from shore.

The kids, screaming, pointing downstream.

Oh no. "Willow!"

Willow's head bobbed just above the surface some twenty feet away as the river swept her downstream. She writhed in the water, hitting boulders, debris, going under, popping back up.

"Put your feet up! Float!" But the river chewed up his words.

He had no choice. He launched off the rock after her, ignoring the burn in his side. "Willow, hang on!"

Water filled his mouth, and he sputtered as he pushed off boulders, raised his feet.

186

Let the current carry him toward her.

"Willow! Lift your feet, find a boulder to brace yourself on!"

He was paddling hard toward her, pushing away from rocks and ledges, trying to stay in the flow.

Willow thrashed in the water, screaming, slamming into boulders, going under.

It was like she couldn't swim.

She disappeared in the foam for so long that the panic reached up, cut off his breathing.

Then she appeared, clawing at a downed tree, scrabbling for a grip on her only lifeline.

Thank you, God.

"Willow, I'm coming!"

He began to swim, using the current to maneuver around the danger. He sat back as he washed over a tiny falls, his feet up, directing himself into the V, the deepest part of the river.

He spotted her ten feet ahead in a whirlpool, fighting to stay afloat.

"Stay there, Willow!"

He launched himself toward her, nearly got a hand on her, but the current yanked her beyond reach.

"Sam!" Her voice was feeble. "I can't swim!"

If he weren't already frozen to the bone, he would have gone numb with her words.

He had no time to wonder at why she'd keep that essential piece of information from him and kicked hard toward her outstretched hand.

She went under in the vortex of the whirlpool.

Willow! He took a breath, dove.

Found her just below the surface, grabbed her jacket, and yanked her to air.

She came up sputtering and gasping, and he turned her in his arms, her back to him. "Just kick," he said. "Don't fight me."

She obeyed, holding on to his arm clasped around her shoulders as he paddled toward an eddy where the shore jutted out.

He fought over the eddy line and into the opposite swirl of water, catching his breath in the sudden release of the current.

He could touch ground here. He stood and turned her in his arms.

She was shaking, and her hair was plastered to her face. She wrapped her arms around his neck and held on, breathing hard.

Willow. He clutched her to himself, trembling so hard in the cold he thought his teeth would rattle out.

Somewhere in all that, he managed to keep the emergency pack strapped to him.

No wonder he'd nearly gone under. What kind of idiot crossed a river with a backpack strapped to him?

Apparently, him.

He pushed her toward shore and then out onto the mossy surface. She turned, grabbing his arms, as if to help him.

He needed it, because his adrenaline had dropped and his bones had given way, turning to rubber. He barely dragged himself up onto the spongy shoreline. He fell into a heap and pulled his arms from the straps of the pack.

"Sam—I'm sorry—I'm so sorry."

"For what?" He looked up at her, still unable to move. "I went down first." To his recollection, she'd reached out, put a hand on him to help him. "You fell in trying to help me," he said, the words emerging in near disbelief.

"I know! I don't know what I was thinking."

He sat up then and took her face in his hands. "You can't swim, Willow. What *were* you thinking?"

She looked wretched. Shivering, her face pale with the cold, her brown hair stringy, her hazel-blue eyes—oh her eyes, so wide, so amazingly beautiful, and so much emotion in them. Too much, maybe.

Because he saw it, right there. Not just concern, but fear, and admiration, and desperation, and . . . a nearly raw longing.

His mouth opened. Because he knew exactly how she felt—those same emotions piled up in his chest, tumbled over, taking him under.

He held her gaze only a second before she started to cry. She bit her lip, but her face crumbled, her breath catching.

"Willow, don't cry."

She had her eyes shut tight, gulping breaths as if trying to obey him, but it didn't work as the sobs started to tumble out.

"Willow, please." He ran his hands down her arms, not sure what to do.

He couldn't take it. Not one more second of seeing her unravel, knowing he wanted to comfort her. Tell her they'd be okay. And then, even that stripped away, leaving only the impulse, the swift, burning desire to—

He kissed her. Not the sweet, soft, tentative, completely mistaken kiss they shared at the hospital, but something intentional.

Something he'd probably wanted to do for—well, he didn't know exactly for how long, but definitely since she'd looked at him on the cliff and promised to come back to him, not a hint of hesitation in her gaze.

Frankly, he was tired of trying to woo a woman who thought of him as a second choice.

He barely had his hand behind her neck and was pulling her close when she sank against him, tightening her hold on his shirt.

He lost himself in the rush of emotion. Probably relief and not a little adrenaline, but she tasted of the wild abandon and crazy hope that was Willow. He tangled his fingers into her wet hair, aware this time of exactly who he was kissing, her mouth soft and willing under his.

Willow.

He ignored the pulse of guilt in the back of his head, the one that said *off-limits* and *you traitor* and instead gave in to the pull of something else.

Live a little.

She made a little sound of desire deep down inside. Then she moved her hands around his waist, molded her body to his, angled her head up for him to slow down, savor, enjoy.

It only ignited something deep inside him. Kissing Willow was a lot like taking a full, pine-scented breath while standing on top of a mountain. Invigorating. Tempting him to stretch out his arms, maybe take a leap off the edge.

Freeing.

This was how it was supposed to be when a person loved—

Wait.

Oh. Wait . . . what was he *doing*?

He must have stiffened, or maybe she just possessed the ability to read his thoughts, because she loosened her hold.

Leaned back.

She lifted her gaze to him, caught her lip in her teeth.

"Whoops."

Yeah. Just a little. He loosed his embrace, his heart thick in his chest.

"Sam, I'm so sorry. I did it again." She shook her head, moving away from him. "I don't know what my problem is—"

"Stop. Willow." He caught her hands. "Just stop, please."

She took a tremulous breath but closed her mouth. Such a fragile expression, and he hated everything about it.

He could way, *way* too easily fall in love with Willow. Probably was halfway there already. He let his heart bleed a little. If only he'd known, before . . .

He sighed, slid his hands up her arms. "It's okay, Willow. This time that was me kissing you."

He wanted to blame the adrenaline, the fear, even the hero worship in Willow's eyes. But none of that excused the way he'd completely trampled over his values and turned into, well, Pete. A guy who moved from one relationship to the next like changing songs on the radio.

He wasn't Pete. "We can't, Willow."

She clamped her mouth shut. Nodded.

"Right?" he added then, and hated himself. Because the hope lit back in her eyes.

And inside him too.

No, *no.* He would not live by his impulses, despite how right, how amazing she'd felt in his arms. And despite the dangerous fire she lit inside.

"Yeah, right. We can't. We shouldn't," she said. "You . . . I was just scared. And you saved me—"

"And I was scared too," he said, because, well, it was so terribly easy to be honest with her.

Except it took everything inside him not to wrap his arms back around her and kiss her again.

Forget, once and for all, that he ever dated her sister.

She looked down at their clasped hands, gave a squeeze, then let go. "Thank you for rescuing me," she said softly. Looked up. "That's a first."

He blinked at that. "What do you mean?"

She shook her head. "Nothing."

It wasn't nothing. And frankly, he didn't want to move from this spot, even though he knew they should probably get up, find their way back to the kids.

Funny, he didn't seem as cold as before. He tucked her wet hair behind her ear. She'd lost her hat in the river, but at least the water had washed out her wound. "Willow . . ."

She sighed, looked at the river, wiped her hand over her cheek. "I always had this, I don't know, dream. Fantasy. Wild hope that my dad would show up at the commune and tell my mom that she couldn't keep me there, that . . . that he wanted me, I guess."

This might be worse than seeing her swept downriver—the image of a lonely, scared little girl waiting for her daddy to find her, tell her she mattered.

That he chose her, and not, say . . . well, adventure.

Maybe Sam was more like Willow than he realized.

"I saw him, of course—he'd come up to the commune when he wasn't deployed, we'd go out for lunch, or I'd stay with him on an occasional weekend. And he'd write me letters. But he didn't know how to fight Mom, and frankly, I'm not sure he wanted to." She shrugged. "I knew he loved me. It's just . . . well, I was probably being silly. I was safe and healthy—"

"And you wanted him to show you that he would change his world for you. That's not silly, Willow."

She looked up at him, a brokenness in her gaze that he longed to fix.

"Willow—"

Crashing in the woods near them, shouts.

"Sam!"

Quinn.

"Willow!"

Gus.

"Apparently we have rescuers," Willow said. "When it rains it pours."

He blinked at that, and for a second just wanted to grab her and tell her, in a crazy, impulsive declaration, that he *would* change his world for her.

That he wanted *her*, not Sierra.

Live a little.

"Over here!" Willow shouted.

Then, whatever moment remained died with the breathless arrival of Quinn and Gus. Their heroes.

———— + ————

Admittedly, Jess had dreamed about being in Pete Brooks's arms. More than once.

But not quite like this. His body half on hers, his leg thrown over her, his arm across her shoulders, his face close, when he wasn't popping up to check on the bear.

She had no doubt, from this position, that he planned on protecting her with his entire body if need be.

That did nothing for her hope of keeping him tucked away into the Just Friends zone. That, and the scratch of his whiskers against her cheek, his lips so close she could just . . . lean . . . in . . .

"Where is she?"

They'd been hiding/stuck/cuddling for nearly an hour, while Mama Bear and her cubs sat down for a tasty meal. It appeared that they just might be here for the rest of the winter. A breeze shook the trees, and a few bejeweled leaves scattered over their prone bodies. Pine needles scrubbed against her belly, old and prickly, and sap blackened her hands.

"Still about thirty feet away. The fact she hasn't seen us yet . . ." Pete shook his head and met her gaze with his, not a hint of fear in his beautiful eyes. He barely whispered, his voice just a breath in her ear. "We only have light for a couple more hours. We have to get out of here—if we don't, we'll have to hike down in the dark."

"And with the bear out there—"

"Exactly."

"What about a distraction? We could throw something, make a run for it?"

"Like we're action heroes? Where are my green arrows when I need them?"

"Funny. I'm trying here."

He gave her a slow smile, too much charm in his eyes. "I know. If anyone could be accused of manning up for the team, it's you."

She didn't know why his compliment—and she knew he meant it that way—gave her heart a little twist.

What was it about her that she could literally be in his arms for two hours and he still thought of her as one of the guys?

Okay, he might not be *quite* so cuddled up with one of the guys. With a flash, she got it. "Pete, are we still here because you're afraid I can't keep up with you if we run?"

He frowned at her. "No. We're here because running is a terrible idea."

"But if you were here with Gage . . ." She lifted her shoulder, a shrug that moved his arm.

Pete's smile dimmed, and he swallowed. "Right."

He went to shift away from her, and she hated herself for reminding him of their teammate status. But maybe it was for the best.

"I might have gotten a little overprotective."

"For a teammate, yeah," she said softly.

He looked at her then, no smile, his gaze solemn. Then he licked his lips and nodded. "I apologize."

Now that hadn't gone at all the way she wanted it to.

Or maybe it had. She shook her head, burying it into her arms.

"What?" he said.

"Nothing. We just need to get out of here."

"Okay, I do have an idea. We could keep moving away, then see if we could circle back to the trail. But we'd have to bushwhack down the mountain, along the ridge."

"Why didn't you say that before?"

"Because I thought she'd leave. And—"

"And it's risky."

"It sort of involves escaping through the trees to the ridgeline and, if necessary, going down the backside until we're out of range."

"Which you'd do with Gage or Ty or even Ben in a split second."

His mouth tightened.

"You're afraid I can't keep up."

"What if you get hurt?"

What if.

And that was Just. It.

"You know what, Pete? I'm tired of the what-ifs. Get up," she snapped. "I promise you, I can keep up."

"Jess."

She pushed him away and started to edge backward.

He got on all fours, his gaze on the bear. Then he turned and began to creep uphill, toward the ridge.

She crawled after him, staying low.

Pete glanced behind him, searching for the bear, then put his hand out to stop her.

She froze. Waited.

"She's sniffing the wind," he whispered.

She closed her eyes.

Finally, a tug on her jacket, and she followed Pete as he crawled under bushes and pine trees toward the top of the ridge.

Only when she reached it did she stand up, hiding behind a tall pine.

The bear had moved down the trail to nearly their previous position.

"Why didn't you tell me she was so close?"

Pete took her hand, glanced over the edge of the ridge. She held on to a branch, looked down.

The ridge fell away, not a sheer drop but still painfully steep, pine trees at forty-five-degree angles as they reached for the sun.

Pete looked over her shoulder. "She's going back to her cubs. I think we're okay, but let's walk along the ridge. Watch your footing." He still had ahold of her hand, a move that she doubted he'd make on Gage. But she tightened her grip in his.

He stepped along the edge, one eye on the bear, the other on his route.

"I suppose if you had your hang glider, we might just take a running jump."

He looked back at her, and she got a tight smile. "Next time."

Next time? "Really, that's a yes?"

"No. It's a . . . I don't think so. In my nicest of voices."

"Pete—"

"No."

"Seriously. You want me to be a teammate, but you don't treat me like one. Apparently, I'm the kind of teammate you have to protect, put your arm around, even hold hands with." She yanked her hand from his.

"Jess." He still kept his voice low, looked back. "Shh."

She narrowed her eyes but kept her voice down. "You can't have it both ways, Pete. Either I'm your teammate or I'm . . . whatever this is we're doing."

He stopped then, turned to face her. "Whatever this is?"

"This—you and me. This flirting thing we do—and don't tell me you don't feel it too."

"I feel it." He said it so quietly she nearly didn't hear him. "But it can't happen, Jess, because—"

"Because you're not the kind of guy who calls a girl the next day. And that makes it a little awkward when we work together."

He took a breath, his eyes so full of emotion it stole her breath. "Yes, okay. That's exactly it. I get people hurt."

"No, you don't—"

"Tallie. She's hurt."

"Tallie doesn't know you. She just likes you for—"

"For what, Jess?" He'd stopped whispering now, his voice tight.

Fine. "For exactly your reputation. For the fact that you are a good-time guy. But that's not you, Pete. You're the guy who shows up to paint a room or hangs out of a helicopter to scoop up a kid from a river or even sprints up a mountain to find his brother." Her voice pitched low. "You're the guy who would protect a girl with your own body in order to keep a bear from eating her."

He considered her a long moment. "Are you sure that's why I did that? Maybe I just like . . ."

Then his mouth twitched, and he looked away.

"What?"

"Holding you, okay? I just liked having you close to me!"

She froze. Really?

She heard herself, only an hour earlier. *"You'll forever live with the what-ifs. Wonder what you could have done differently."*

Suddenly, she wanted to do *this* differently. She found her voice, kept it soft. "I like having you, um, close to me too."

His eyes darkened then, and he swallowed. "Ah, Jess," he said softly, "don't say that to me. I've been trying to stay away from you all summer."

"I couldn't tell, what with you being at my house every day," she said just as softly, and took a step toward him.

Slowly, he smiled. Just a half-hitch, up one side, rueful. "Yeah, there's that."

"I didn't exactly slam the door in your face, did I?"

His smile faded. His gaze was on her face, roaming it, falling to her lips. "I don't want to hurt you." But he reached out, touched her face with his fingers, ever so lightly running them down her cheekbone.

Leaving a trail of tiny sparks.

She saw it in his eyes then, all the hunger, the longing not to be all-fun, all-the-time Pete but the guy who had asked her to help him with his résumé. The guy who stood in her living room and apologized. And the guy who, yes, would put his body between her and a grizzly.

That guy was the man who didn't want to hurt her, who now searched her eyes as if asking for something.

Yes. Oh *yes.*

She took a step closer, her heart thumping, and put her hands on his chest, that amazing, muscled chest, built from hours of labor at her house, in the gym, and even his extreme sports. Put her answer in her gaze, as her words had stopped working.

He slid his hand around her neck, his blue eyes holding hers. "Please don't let me hurt you," he whispered. Then he touched his mouth to hers.

She expected something molten; instead he simply brushed his lips on hers. A whisper, so achingly soft it caught her breath, stilled her heart. He tasted like Pete—a sort of sweetness over the hint of danger, the passion he reserved for BASE jumping or fighting fires, or even during a callout, simmering just under the surface.

She loved the tenderness but wanted a taste of that passion too. So she offered a little noise of desire, of approval.

As if surprised, Pete raised his head, met her eyes. "Oh, Jess."

If she didn't know better, she'd think she saw fear.

"What?"

"I just . . ." He shook his head, touched his forehead to hers. "If you only knew how much I thought of this."

She let a tiny smile nudge her mouth. And when he lifted his head, he matched it.

Then he kissed her again, and this time, he dove in. Really, *really* kissing her, so much of the Pete she knew and loved—oh, wait, maybe not *loved*—except in this moment, yeah. She was probably already desperately in love with Pete Brooks.

He kissed her like he meant it, as if he *had* been thinking about it for quite some time. He ran his hand along her jaw to angle her face to his, his lips nudging her mouth to surrender.

And she did. Stepping in closer, holding on to his jacket.

His whiskers brushed her face and he smelled of the woods, of adventure and fun and a thousand delicious hours of teasing her with his smile, his laughter.

Pete.

She could stay right here for the rest of her life, locked in his embrace.

He stilled in her arms. Broke their kiss.

She froze as he looked up over her shoulder.

"Oh no."

"What?"

He met her eyes. "Don't look back."

But she did look back.

She spotted the sow clearing the trees just as Pete took her hand and tugged her along the ridge.

And then she stopped thinking and ran.

10

SO MUCH FOR THEM GETTING HOME TODAY, before dark. Willow couldn't believe that her pitiful attempt at rescuing Sam ended up in her nearly drowning and Sam having to save *her*.

Not to mention the fact that she ended up in his arms.

Again.

Kissing him as if she would give him her heart, right there.

"It's okay. Willow. This time that was me kissing you."

Hardly.

She'd really made a mess of things now. Poor Sam—she'd seen the look on his face, the fear as she'd nearly gotten swept away in the whirlpool. When she'd dissolved into a hysterical puddle, the poor guy probably didn't know what else to do.

Well, she did.

No more risks with the kids. No more hiking out.

For the first time, she realized that they needed to send someone out alone.

Even if that meant Sam would leave her. Because he didn't belong to her anyway, and she had to get used to that.

Sam *would* leave her.

The sooner she stopped thinking about him, tasting his kiss, the sooner she'd stop feeling so undone.

"Here's what we're going to do," Sam said. He'd spent the past fifteen minutes sorting out their options with Josh and Willow.

They'd hiked back up the trail to the kids only to find them waiting by the river where they'd crossed, distraught, replaying the near tragedy.

Maggy rushed into Willow's arms, and even Zena looked worried. Dawson sat on a rock, holding his water bottle, looking dazed, and Riley had his arm around Vi.

Interesting.

Cold to the bone, her clothes soggy and frigid, Willow hunkered down, wanting to surrender to the exhaustion that had turned her brittle.

Josh came over, carrying an emergency blanket, but it did little good in her wet clothing.

Then he and Sam huddled up. She recognized a new confidence in Josh.

Well, he hadn't been the one swept downriver.

"We need to find a clearing, a good place to make camp, and then we hunker down for the night. Build a fire and find something to eat," Sam said. "Get these kids warm."

"And then what?" Josh said. "Stay out in the woods all night?"

Sam glanced at Willow. "Yeah. The road is still a mile or more away, and even if we get there, there's little chance someone will be on it this time of day. The park is nearly closed for the season."

"What about cell phone range?" Josh asked.

Sam looked around. "Anyone still got juice in their phone?"

Nothing.

"Exactly. Listen, we have matches, we'll get firewood, dry off. Willow—all of us—need to get warm, and soon. We'll be okay tonight. Tomorrow, we'll hike out."

No, tomorrow *Sam* would hike out.

Right out of her life.

"It's getting dangerous for us to travel together." She didn't have to mention the river, especially with it roaring behind them. "Maybe you should go by yourself, Sam. Or with a couple people."

"I'll go," Dawson said, raising his hand.

"Me too," Gus said.

But Sam was staring at her. "Let's find a place to camp," he said and then got up, leaving them behind.

Wasn't that what he wanted? To get home as fast as possible?

They walked in silence maybe two hundred yards until they came to a clearing—small but usable—and Sam declared it their campground for the night. "Find me some firewood," he said to the kids.

When Willow started to get up, he shook his head. "You stay there. You're shivering, and you need to get warm."

"I'll get warm by staying active."

He frowned, but she walked away.

She followed Maggy into the woods, surprised at the girl's sudden vigor as she picked up branches and broke them. "You okay, Maggy?"

"I can't believe I got through that river." She set a branch against a log and jumped on it, snapping it in half.

"Yeah, well, you probably can do a lot of things you didn't realize. You're stronger than you think."

Maggy glanced at her, a small smile on her face.

Willow gathered up birch bark off a downed tree and the inside of a rotted and dry log. Kindling.

By the time they returned, Sam had built a circle of river stone that outlined a hole he'd scraped into the ground, all the way to the mineral soil.

Gus and Quinn, too, had returned with their offering.

Dawson, however, hadn't moved, and sat away from the group. He looked exhausted.

"Is he okay?" Willow said to Zena, who arrived with a handful of berries.

"He's . . . fine. I guess." She showed the berries to Willow. "Are these edible?"

"Huckleberries," Willow said. "Where did you find them?"

"I'll show you." She gestured with her head, and Willow got up.

Sam glanced at her. "Don't go too far. Huckleberries mean bears. Keep an eye out."

She could have done with not hearing that. Just what they needed to add more excitement to the trip.

She caught up with Zena, her legs chafing in her wet clothes. The act of fetching firewood had helped, but she could curl up in front of a fire right now and sleep for a year.

Zena led her to a small clearing tangled with huckleberry bushes heavy with plump, purple berries. She took off her jacket, spread it on the ground, and began to fill it with the fruit.

"He's drunk." Zena said it so quietly Willow nearly didn't hear her.

"What?"

Zena glanced at her. The last twenty-four hours had stripped from Zena's face all the black eyeliner, the gray shadow, the darkened lips. She looked softer, more fragile. "I wouldn't say anything, but Dawson nearly fell going down the mountain yesterday and then today in the ravine. And he dropped Vi while crossing the river—I'm worried about him."

Zena dumped huckleberries into the jacket. Met Willow's gaze again, her eyes dark brown, piercing. "Dawson is drunk—or maybe high—but I'm guessing that water bottle he's toting around isn't just water."

Willow stilled. "Are you sure?"

"Yeah, I'm sure." She folded her arms over her chest. "I know you're probably thinking I gave it to him—"

"I'm not thinking anything, but . . . wow, Dawson?" Clean-cut twin brother of straight-A Vi?

"It's not easy being the stupid twin," Zena said. "He just wants to hide from the world a little like the rest of us."

That made sense. Because for all the pictures Zena took, Willow had never actually seen her in front of the camera.

And then there was Maggy, hiding her body under all the folds of sweatshirts and baggy pants.

Not to mention Riley and his computer games, and Gus and his football persona.

And Quinn. Willow didn't exactly know what Quinn was hiding, but Sam's cryptic words to her earlier niggled at her. *"Senator Starr isn't the kind of guy who would add a little physical incentive to get his way, is he?"*

"We need to get back."

Zena touched her arm. "Vi's watching him."

"Vi *knows*?" Of course she did.

"She's been helping him hide it for a while now. Does his homework, drives him around."

"I can't believe it."

"I'm not lying to you."

"Zena, I *believe* you. I'm just shocked. And not a little disappointed."

"Yeah, well, it's the ones you least expect, right? Rich, pretty Dawson is an alcoholic. While people like me get tried and convicted with a glance."

Where did that come from?

But, she got it. Because it just wasn't fair that people like Dawson, or really Sierra, had it so easy. And people like Zena and Willow spent life hoping and striving.

"I never thought you did drugs," Willow said quietly.

Zena looked away then, her mouth tight. "You'd be the first."

"Zena, my entire life people have been saying, Willow, daughter of that crazy hippie, grew up in a commune. Didn't even graduate from high school. She's a mess."

"I don't think you're a mess," Zena said.

Willow wanted to laugh at her sincerity, at the fact that probably she *was* a mess, especially right now. Instead, "And you're not either."

Zena looked up at her, and Willow had never seen so much emotion in her eyes, which were usually covered in layers of black, not to mention her natural hooded defenses. "I wish I could be like you," she said. "You're not afraid to be yourself. I just wish that . . ."

"That someone would care enough to want you around, even if you are a mess?" Willow slipped her arm over Zena's shoulders. "Yeah, well, guess what. We do. I do. You're creative and smart and beautiful and worthy of being loved, Zena. And not just by me, but by God, who sees you—the real you. You don't have to hide from him."

Zena wiped a hand under her eyes. "Listen, you can't tell Dawson I told you. He'd kill me. But that water bottle—you need to check it."

"How do you know this?"

"My big brother buys for him," she said. "I've seen him a few times outside church."

"Outside *church*?" She'd seen Zena's brother a few times, when he'd dropped Zena off for youth group, or even at the Gray Pony. Distinctive with his long dark hair and sleeve of tattoos, he worked at the Sweetwater Lumber Company and looked the spitting image of his father, or what Willow could remember of him before his arrest a few years ago for drug dealing.

Willow added more berries to the jacket, then knelt and folded it up. "He's drunk on a youth group trip. Beautiful."

"Who's drunk?"

She hadn't heard Sam come up.

His hair had dried, tousled, gold threads caught by the sun, and he wore a fatigue around his eyes she hadn't seen before. She could smell the forest, the campfire smoke on him, and was suddenly keenly aware of his strength, the memory of his arms around her, his kiss . . . *"We can't, Willow."*

And in that moment, she wanted to hate Sierra.

She stood up, glanced at Zena, who'd headed back to camp. Apparently not wanting to be a part of this conversation.

"According to Zena, Dawson is drunk."

Sam's mouth tightened a little around the edges. "Hmm."

"You're not surprised?"

"I'm a cop. Of course I'm not surprised. I'd be surprised if one of them weren't carrying a dime bag right now."

"Sam, these are Christian kids."

"These are *kids*. None of us are immune to the darkness, Willow. Except maybe you."

She opened her mouth, and he reached out for her jacket of berries.

But she didn't release them. "What do you mean?"

"I just think sometimes you're a little naïve to think these kids aren't up to their ears in trouble. That all they need is a little inspirational speech and they'll have their problems figured out."

She stared up at him. "Ouch. I didn't see that coming." She pushed past him, but he reached out for her.

"Willow—"

"Just let me pass, Sam."

He looked stricken as she strode by him.

He scrambled after her. "C'mon. I didn't mean to hurt you."

"No, it's true. You're completely right. I am naïve to believe I can help these kids. And you could probably add in reckless, idealistic, and if you want to take into account what happened at the river, impulsive and probably a bit of a boyfriend-stealer. Because I know you, Sam. You wouldn't kiss me unless it was an accident—"

"I kissed you on purpose, Willow!"

She stopped. Turned to look at him.

He stood, outlined by the falling sun, dark, solid, and not a little angry.

He stepped closer, his face now coming into view, his blue eyes stormy, his mouth set in a grim line. He lowered his voice. "I kissed you because I can't get you off my mind—and I haven't since you kissed me in the hospital."

He hadn't?

"And frankly, I want to kiss you again, right now. You are frustrating and beautiful and yes, everything Sierra isn't, and that's the problem. Sierra."

"I know," Willow said quietly. "I know you love her—"

"I don't love her!"

He drew in a quick, shaky breath, as if realizing the truth for himself for the first time.

The forest fell into silence around them, leaving behind only the thunder of her heartbeat.

His eyes were earnest in hers. "And I don't know that I ever will. Or could. Or even want to try anymore."

Oh. And that was her fault.

She looked up at him and hated the confusion on his face, the realization that she'd put it there with her inability to control her emotions or her actions.

"But you could, Sam. And you *should.* Sierra's the right one for you. She's smart and pretty and I'm nothing like her. I didn't even graduate from high school—"

"I know that. If you want, I'll help you get your GED. We'll study and . . ."

She stilled. And then she got it. Because, no, she wasn't Sierra, and he might be okay with that if he could rescue her, make her better. Fix her. Her jaw tightened, and he must have seen it.

"What?"

"Nothing. We have to get back." She turned away, but he grabbed her arm.

"Willow, what did I say?"

"Nothing." Fine. "Just listen. This is who I am. Willow. The barista, the waitress, the dog-sitter, and occasionally I get people lost in the park. I'm the girl who grew up in a commune. I'm not brilliant or organized, and yeah, I'm a dreamer, okay? I feed on hope, on inspirational views, I love cat videos and can't help but sing along to pop music. But that's okay, because I'm pretty sure that God loves me, even if I don't have a Bible degree. Even if I only serve French fries for the rest of my life."

He frowned at her.

She knew she wasn't making sense, so she simplified. "You don't have to rescue me. That's not your job. Let's just get these kids home, Sam. And then you'll come to your senses and realize that you don't really want me."

He stood there frowning as she turned, her heart breaking as she walked away.

———✦———

He didn't want her?

No amount of attempts to slow Willow down, make her stop, offer the slightest hint of clarity as to her cryptic words worked as Sam stumbled and tripped after Willow.

"Willow!"

"Leave me alone, Sam."

It couldn't get colder out here if they suddenly experienced an epic glacial event.

Whatever he'd said, he clearly couldn't fix it.

He could, however, do his job, starting with Dawson Moore, the little delinquent.

Sam had gotten a fire going—which was what he'd gone to tell Willow. Now the little company crouched around it, sitting on rocks. Josh was breaking up a couple soggy power bars he'd dug out of the emergency pack.

Riley sat next to Vi, his arm still around her—Sam could spot smitten from a mile away. And Gus and Maggy just might have the makings of another romance.

Quinn stood just outside the glow of the flames.

Willow set her jacket down next to the fire, and Zena came over, dropped a handful of berries into it.

Sam headed straight for Dawson.

He sat on the ground, his eyes closed, head back. As if he might be passed out.

"Sam?" Willow's voice, sharp, tight, bore an edge of warning.

"Stay out of this, Willow."

Dawson opened his eyes a second before Sam reached out, grabbed the water bottle from his hand.

"What the—"

Sam opened it, and the smell could knock him over, take him to his knees. "You've got to be kidding me!"

Dawson scrambled to his feet, and at closer look, his reddened eyes betrayed the fact that if he wasn't currently three sheets to the wind, he had been.

Probably sometime in the night. And since then nursed a comfortable buzz.

"Seriously? We nearly die and you're drunk?"

"That's not yours," Dawson said and took a swipe at the bottle. To which Sam stiff-armed him with a hand to his chest, pushed him back.

He poured the liquid on the ground, averted his nose to the odor. Dawson swore. "C'mon, man."

Sam pitched the entire bottle into the woods. "You c'mon. Have you lost your mind?"

Dawson's mouth closed, his jaw tight. He stumbled back to the rock.

"Oh no, you don't. You're sitting right here by this fire so I can keep an eye on you, make sure you're not going to pass out or die from alcohol poisoning." He put his hand on Dawson's arm.

Dawson came back swinging.

A scream—he didn't know from whom—and Sam stepped back. The kid just missed his jaw. The momentum turned Dawson around, and he landed with a thump on the earth.

Out of the corner of his eye, he spotted Gus and Quinn closing in.

Then he looked up, and as if drawn there, met Willow's gaze. Her mouth was tight, and her eyes glistened.

Yeah, well, she might think all these kids needed was a little inspiration, but he dealt in the real world. Where kids screwed up and got people killed. And it was his job to pick up the pieces.

Although, even now, he realized he'd poured too much of his cynicism into his comment. Why did he have to call her naïve?

Josh had come over, knelt next to Dawson, who pushed himself up from the ground and glared at Sam.

Sam shoved a water bottle into Josh's hands. "Make sure he has something to drink—all that booze is going to make him dehydrated."

He didn't want to remember how many times he'd had to nurse Pete back to sobriety. The memory stuck in his craw, tightened his jaw. Sam stood up, walked over to the fire, and stared into the flames, the residue of the argument simmering under his skin.

Maybe he should have left them behind, hiked out on his own. Except for Willow's voice in his head. *Don't leave me.*

He didn't want to.

What he wanted to do was take her in his arms, tell her that somehow over the last two days, she'd cut through all the darkness inside him and filled it with light.

Or at least tried to.

With the sun gone, shadow crept from the woods, the night air carrying a crispness to it that meant they'd have to huddle up together. He'd have to stay awake, keep the fire stoked.

Willow was dividing up the berries into even piles. Zena distributed them, and the kids ate them in strained silence.

A log fell, sparks escaped. Sam looked away, toward the milky darkness, the moon rising above the treetops. The parents were probably frantic by now, no idea where their children were or if they were safe.

He found himself staring again at Willow. At the way she had her arm around Maggy, the space blanket pulled around them for warmth.

The woman so desperately wanted to make an impact on these kids, on her world. What she didn't realize was how she'd made an impact on him. She lived with her heart dangerously on the outside of her body, but it was a pure heart.

"I'm not brilliant or organized, and yeah, I'm a dreamer, okay?"

Yes, actually, it *was* okay. Maybe he needed a dreamer, someone who helped him get a different perspective.

The right perspective.

He wasn't in love with Sierra.

But he could be falling for her sister.

Sam nearly got up, marched across the fire. Pulled her into his arms and told her that when they got home, they'd start over. This time without Sierra standing between them.

"You don't have to rescue me. That's not your job."

Maybe not, but maybe that's why God had put him here. For the first time, he could admit to being profoundly thankful that Sierra had goaded him into joining this ill-fated day trip with a bunch of delinquents.

At first light, he'd leave for help. Get them out of this mess, show the parents that Willow was the best thing that ever happened to this youth group.

Best thing that ever happened to him.

He didn't look at her when he got up. "All right. We're going to keep this fire lit all night. And then in the morning, you all are going to hunker down while I go get help."

They stared at him, digesting his words. But Quinn stepped

into the light and tossed another twig into the fire, the one he'd been peeling. "I'm going with you."

"Quinn—"

"I owe you, man."

Sam started to shake his head, but Quinn's dark expression stopped him, stared him down. "Please. For Bella."

What could Sam do when he recognized Quinn's expression as his own? A desperate desire to fix things, starting with perhaps Pete, and then Sierra, ending with Willow.

"Okay. We leave at first light."

———— + ————

Please don't let him kill them.

"Hurry, Pete!" Jess's voice slicked out behind him, tight and shrill, and he refused to glance up, his focus on tying the Prusik knot onto the rappel rope.

This had to work.

His brain had done the math the minute he saw the ledge jutting out from the ridgeline.

With the bear gaining ground, they couldn't outrun it. But maybe . . .

The ledge extended six feet across, and only adrenaline made him think they could jump down that fifteen feet without breaking an ankle.

Miraculously, that's exactly what they did, his hand in Jess's as he shouted "Jump!" and took them sailing over the edge.

They'd landed, hard, and for a second, he thought he might pitch right over the edge, his knees buckling, his body rolling.

He would be impaled on a pine spire, save for Jess's hand on his jacket, yanking him back.

Saving his life.

Then, while she'd scrambled for her bear spray, he whipped off his pack and grabbed out his rope.

"What are you doing?"

"We're going down the mountain," he'd said and she didn't argue. Just stood up and aimed the spray at the bear.

He caught a vision of her, just as he was setting the cam, her legs braced, her jaw tight, both hands on the spray, the wind blowing her blonde hair.

Planted between him and death.

The sense of it rattled him to his bones. *Please don't let her die on my watch.*

Now, fifteen feet above him, judging by the sound of the fury, the bear was beginning to recover from the bear spray. Jess had caught it in the snout and the eyes, and for a minute or three Pete had a chance to put two clear thoughts together.

Get down the mountainside.

And, he was such an idiot.

If he hadn't kissed Jess, he would have seen the sow alert to their presence, heard her charging up the ridge.

Instead, he'd been tangled inside his desires, losing himself in Jess's touch.

"Pete!" Her voice cut through his movements, and he tightened down the auto-block knot. Tested it.

His regrets could wait until after he got them over the edge and down the mountain.

"Get your harness on!" he yelled to her over his shoulder.

Overhead, the bear reached down and swiped at them. Any minute it would simply drop the fifteen feet onto the ledge and take them out.

Don't look.

He'd already anchored them into the rock, shoved the cam into a convenient horizontal crack, attached the rope to it, and hooked on the descender.

The pack contained only one webbed sling. He should have

checked before simply heading out and now cursed his reckless-ness again.

Like, say, kissing Jess when trying to outrun a bear.

Yeah, Pete, absolutely brilliant. He wouldn't hire him as incident commander either, with moves like that.

This next one just might get them killed.

Jess sat on the edge of the cliff, working on her harness. Below, the world dropped off at a brutal angle—not quite 90 degrees but close enough that the wrong step would send them careening down three hundred yards into trees and boulders.

Any other day, any other moment, the view would halt him, make him take a deep breath. The mountains around him jutted up bold, rugged, the sun glinting off high-altitude snow cover, turning it brilliant gold and orange in the afternoon light. Below them, that same light turned the valley into dusky dark greens, the pine forest lush and protective.

If they could get to it.

He was going to spider rappel and pray that Jess had the guts to hang on.

Above them, the bear made another swipe at them, saliva spray-ing from its teeth. And the rank feral odor—feces, blood, matted fur—could knock him right over.

Claws just barely missed Jess's shoulder, and Pete, hooked into the descender, sat down next to her. Pulled on his gloves.

"Listen very carefully," he said and kept his tone solid, without fear, his gaze holding hers.

She stared at him, panic around the edges of her beautiful eyes, but in the center, nothing but trust.

He hadn't expected that. *Okay.*

"This is how this is going to work." He shut out the roar of the bear above them, the sound of dirt and rock falling as the animal pawed the ground. "Get behind me, put your legs around my waist, and attach your harness to mine."

"What—wait. I thought we were rappelling—"

"We are. We're going face first." Her eyes widened then, and he nodded. "You can do this. Just hang on to me. I won't let you fall."

She inhaled fast, the resolve clicking in.

Especially when more rocks fell behind them.

She moved behind him, clipping into his harness.

"Put your arms around me and hang on. We'll go down together."

"I'm too heavy—"

"You're not, and this will work if you just trust me."

The grizzly gave a roar that found his bones and turned them brittle just as the ledge above gave way.

Jess clamped her arms and legs around him. "Let's go!"

The bear fell onto their ledge with a feral growl that cut through the canyon.

Pete didn't wait. With one hand on the Prusik knot to slow him down, he leaned up over the edge, Jess on his back, and started down the slope.

She held on, and for a second, with so much tension on his gloved hand, he thought they might just plunge forward, pitch down the incline.

Jess maybe had the same thought because she tried to put her feet down, tripped, nearly pushed him forward.

"Jess! Just hold on! I got this!"

He glanced over his shoulder. They were five feet down, and the bear gathered to take another swipe at them.

If the animal charged down the hill after them, it might fall on them and take them all to their deaths.

If ever Pete wanted to pray, to hearken back to the faith his father had tried to root in him, it was now. As if bidden, his father's words from the Bible stirred inside him. *Those who hope in the Lord will renew their strength.*

All right then, God. Get us out of this mess. And I'll stop making reckless choices.

Jess glued herself to him as he found his rhythm, nearly running downhill.

The rope whipped through his gloved hands, and as the roar above dimmed, Jess put her chin on his shoulder. "Wow."

"Right?" He loved rap jumping. He was breathing hard, but really, she weighed almost nothing, and the faster he went, the stronger he felt.

In fact, with a strange twist of his heart, he'd realized—he'd always wanted this. To bring Jess along on his adrenaline-laced adventures, to look over and see her grinning at him.

Even better, laughing.

"This is awesome! I mean, I know you're the one doing all the work, but—"

"It *is* awesome," he said, his chest about to explode with the freedom, the sense of triumph in the face of death. "The first time I did this, it was off a seven-story building in Seattle. Then I joined a rap-jumping group—now I go out whenever I can."

"You mean whenever you're not BASE jumping, or hang gliding, or skydiving."

She said it without judgment, however, as if she might want to tag along.

"Yeah. There's just something about facing death and winning, right?"

She gave a wry chuckle, sweet and low in his ears. "Sure, Pete."

The terrain began to level out, and he slowed. She put her feet down, began to walk in rhythm with him.

His impulsive promise to God not to make reckless choices came back to him.

Like kissing Jess.

Except, at this moment, it didn't feel so reckless.

Pete stopped them near a tall pine where he could brace himself, where she could unhook her harness.

Sixty yards above, the bear rooted around the ledge for a way back to the ridge, the call of her cubs turning her home.

Jess leaned against the tree, breathing hard, wearing a soft grin. "Pete Brooks, it can't be said that you don't show a girl a good time. Next time, however, let's try it without the bear."

He grinned, and wow, he wanted to kiss her again. But those kinds of impulses were exactly how people got hurt around him.

"Let's get going. We have to report in or they'll send a search team for *us*."

"Let them," she said. Oh boy. Because really, what was a guy to do with Jess looking at him like he might be a DC hero, her eyes full of spark and welcome?

He just had to taste that beautiful smile. So he kissed her, fast and short. Not pressing her up against the tree, not diving in, never to come up for air. And that had to count for something, right?

He dearly hoped that the Almighty took into account what it cost him to simply take her hand and run for the truck.

11

"WILLOW, ARE YOU AWAKE?"

Yes. No, or she had been, but as Willow stirred to the whispered voice, she realized she'd finally dropped off.

She'd watched Sam for what seemed like eternity across the flickering campfire.

He stared into the flames, occasionally looking over at her to meet her eyes with a piercing, bone-jarring gaze that could reach down to her soul and give it a shake.

"I kissed you on purpose, Willow!"

She didn't know if she believed him—she wanted to. But that couldn't possibly be right.

Not when he had Sierra waiting for him back home.

Maggy, Vi, and Zena all curled up together. Willow slept on one end, holding the blanket over them for warmth. She'd propped her head on a backpack and wore a lime-green bandanna Dawson had pulled out of his bag and offered her with a tight apology.

She had to give Sam credit. After his declaration that he planned on leaving—not abandoning—them in the woods, he galvanized the kids and built them a rudimentary windbreak, something to capture the heat from the fire. It was her idea to strip off the backpack straps and use them to secure a crossbar to a couple pine trees. Then, the kids gathered sticks and cut off lower pine branches to create a sort of wall against the wind.

Now, Dawson, Riley, and Josh slept under the protection of the windbreak. Gus sprawled out in the open, closer to the fire, on his back like a lumberjack. He emitted, now and again, a snore.

Quinn had sat up with Sam until he finally curled into a ball near the fire.

Somewhere in there, she'd fallen asleep, finally warm.

Willow stirred now at Sam's voice, found his breath on her skin, his mouth nearly to her ear. "Can I talk to you?" His hand touched her shoulder.

"Yeah," she whispered, her pulse awake now too.

She slipped out from under the warmth of the blanket and stood up. The fire still flickered, although with a dire cost to their firewood supply. The morning was still an hour away, the sky overhead a pewter gray, the stars fading.

Sam looked rough and tired, with tiny lines around his eyes, his jaw set tight as he reached out to take her hand and lead her away from camp.

She put her other hand on his to warm it up.

He pulled them out of earshot, into the fold of the woods. In the shadows like this, he appeared downright heroic, a champion about to say good-bye to his lady, although that was probably her imagination having its way this early in the morning.

In fact, she might still be asleep, evidenced by the way Sam wore so much tenderness in his gaze, the way he reached out, touched her face. His soft words. "I couldn't leave without telling you I'm sorry. I know I hurt you."

"Sam, you're not the one who needs to apologize. I shouldn't have gotten so angry at you. I am a little naïve. And yeah, maybe a little sensitive about not graduating from high school." She sighed. "It's just, sometimes I feel so . . . the fact is, I've tried to take my GED twice and failed. I'm just not smart—"

"And that's a lie. Just because you didn't pass a test doesn't mean you're not smart."

She looked away.

He put his hand on her face, guided her gaze back to his. "I only offered to help you with your GED because I thought it mattered to you. I was trying to tell you that when we get back, I want to figure this thing out."

She looked up at him. "What thing?"

He stared at her, his expression incredulous. "What thing? *This* thing—between us. This amazing, surprising, really scary thing that I should have figured out a long time ago—"

"Really scary?" she said, a small twist to her mouth. "Really?"

That stopped him, and he nodded. "Yeah, really scary. The truth is, ever since my dad died, I've had this . . . this anger inside me. I've spent the last twelve years trying to shake it free, and instead it's nearly consumed me. I thought it was about regret and blame, but it took getting lost with you—and I mean that in the best way—to figure it out."

He caressed her face, his thumb leaving little tingles on her skin. "But the strange thing is, the more that I'm with you, the more I feel free."

"Sam, you *can* be free. It's all about letting God in, with his grace to forgive, to heal. God's light can overtake the darkness."

He wove his fingers between hers, took her other hand and did the same. Met her eyes. "I want to believe that. And maybe I can start by letting *you* in. And that's the scary part."

Oh, Sam. She touched his face, seeing the man she'd kissed at the hospital, the one she'd fallen in love with.

His voice softened. "I don't know what it is about you, but you make me feel like the guy who I've tried so hard to be for the last decade. A guy who has half a chance of living again."

"Are you sure? I get it—we're out in the woods, and we nearly died a few times, and we're tired and maybe not thinking clearly."

His mouth tweaked up on one side, his gaze in hers. "I'm thinking clearly for the first time in years, Willow."

Oh, Sam.

"I meant it when I said I don't want Sierra—I want you."

He had so much honesty in his eyes, she couldn't escape it. "I want you too."

The smallest of delicious smiles crept up his face. "Good, because when we get back, I'm going to straighten everything out with Sierra, I promise."

Her eyes widened. "Oh, Sam—"

"Listen. I don't think Sierra is going to put up much of a fight for me."

"If she's smart she will."

"You're the smart one in the family," he said and moved his mouth to inches away from hers. "Smart and beautiful and kind and the one I should have been kissing from the first."

Then he did. Sweetly, his mouth soft on hers, an achingly tender caress. The warmth that had touched her at the fire curled right through her, seeped into her bones. He smelled of the campfire, the wild currents of the river, strength and determination and everything she'd discovered—and always known—about him.

Dependable, sacrificing, and heroic to the bone.

He lifted his head, met her eyes, a light in his expression she hadn't seen until now. "I'm coming back to you, I promise. So you promise me—don't go anywhere. Okay? Stay here."

She nodded, his words sliding through her, latching on. *"I'm coming back to you."*

He let her go, pushed away from the tree, took her hand, and led her back to camp.

Quinn stood by the fire, holding a water bottle. "Ready?"

"Let's go," Sam said, giving her a final look.

"I'm coming back to you."

Please.

———— + ————

Pete nursed his early morning coffee and stared at the search map on the wall. Darkness pressed against the windows, the dim light of the meeting room puddling on the floor.

They still needed a PLS—point last seen—to start their search.

The map was marked with the flyover areas and road markers Ty and Gage had stopped at yesterday. After finding nothing on Camas Road, they'd doubled back, hit McFarland Lodge for leads, then driven deeper into the park, stopping in at all the trailheads, searching for a clue. No one at any of the lodges or campsites had seen them.

Kacey and Ben had fruitlessly swept the areas along the Going-to-the-Sun Road in the chopper.

"Couldn't sleep either?"

Jess's voice was a sweet balm on his tired, raw places.

A dangerous balm. Because yesterday as they'd fled the bear, he remembered promising God not to make any more reckless mistakes.

She came into the room dressed in an oversized PEAK Rescue sweatshirt, a pair of yoga pants, and fuzzy wool socks. With her face scrubbed clean of makeup and her blonde hair down, she looked devastatingly innocent and sweet. But when she smiled at him, a hot blast of desire hit his heart, desire that had only grown since kissing her on a mountaintop.

Mistake, with a glaring neon capital M. Especially if he hoped to keep his head in this game and not blow his chance of being incident commander.

Although as she walked over to him, a sad smile tugging up her lips—those delicious, soft lips—he thought that maybe right now he didn't need his head in the game but rather Jess in his arms.

Oh boy.

"Trying to figure out where the park has cell service?" she asked.

He nodded and turned away fast because he didn't want her to know what was really roaming around in his brain at this hour.

This was why he probably shouldn't have kissed her. Sam's words from the Gray Pony jabbed at him. *"I swear, you're the most irresponsible person I've ever met."*

Oh, he didn't want to be.

"We know there's a cell signal at the Apgar Visitor's Center. And McDonald Lodge." He traced his finger along Lake McDonald. "It gets spotty from there along Going-to-the-Sun Road."

"I checked my phone. Sam called at 9:36, so that's about an hour and a half from when they left here. It takes about an hour to get to Huckleberry Mountain, so . . . Where could he go in thirty minutes that still had cell phone reception?"

"Maybe north." He traced the same distance on the inside North Fork Road, along the edge of the park. "Polebridge? That might be too far—"

"No. I'll bet Polebridge has a tower."

"You're right. They might lose signal between Huckleberry and Polebridge, but he could have reached the Polebridge signal by 9:36. But that seems so far. What's in Polebridge?"

"Willow's mom's commune is there." Jess pointed to a spot just southeast of Polebridge. "But that's the last place she'd take the kids."

"Why?"

"She doesn't like the commune. She felt trapped, and . . . it was a dark time for her."

Pete frowned, trying to fit that information into what he knew about Willow. Happy, life-is-fun Willow.

"No one is exactly what they seem, Pete," Jess said softly, as if reading his mind.

He glanced at her, nonplussed. Because he hadn't given any thought to what he might not see about Jess. She was so . . . easy to be with. No secrets, no agenda.

Except, they'd spent the entire summer talking about football, television shows, pizza toppings, their favorite Ben King songs and house repairs, in between training and hanging out at the Gray Pony and working together on callouts.

She never talked about her life before Mercy Falls. He couldn't pinpoint one conversation about her past.

"Jess, is there something you're not telling me?"

She swallowed, turned away. "Polebridge. Why would they go there?"

"Jess."

She headed to the kitchen area. "I need coffee."

He paused but couldn't seem to stop himself. "Okay, I get it. I know I haven't been the most . . . well, sensitive of guys. Or committed, maybe. But, Jess, you have to know that I . . ."

What? Loved her? He might not go that far—yet. But he *could* love her. Maybe. "I care." Yeah, that worked. "If you want to talk. About . . . anything."

She stood at the counter. Shook her head.

A rock sat on his heart. "Okay. But here's the thing. When we find Sam and the kids—and we will—I'm showing up on your doorstep. I'm calling you. I know I said I don't want more, but . . ."

He swallowed, found the words, refusing the nudge of warning inside. "With you, I do. I'm not just out for a good time, Jess. I want to know you and what matters to you—"

She frowned, and he held up his hand.

"I mean more than football and your house. Like, why you became an EMT, and where you're from, and I'll even meet your family if that's something you want."

She looked up at him, her eyes glistening, so much unshed emotion in them, it shook him.

"What is it, Jess? Please tell me."

The stairs creaked behind them, another teammate headed down from the upstairs sleeping quarters, and in that second, Jess moved away.

"Hey, guys," Ty said as he hit the landing. He'd showered, his dark hair still wet, his blue T-shirt clinging to his body. "Oh good, coffee."

Pete stood there, rattled. She was hiding something, a hurt that had flashed to the surface. Why hadn't he seen it earlier?

Because he *was* all about himself. Had he even once asked her about her past?

He wanted to order Ty from the room, or drag her away, get at the truth. For now, he met her eyes. *This isn't over, Jess.*

She looked away.

His heart heavy in his chest, he walked back to the map and stared at it, nearly unseeing.

"Working on your cell phone theory?" Ty said, coming to stand by him.

Pete had delivered the scenario to the team last night, when they returned to base frustrated, strung out, and not a little worried. Thankfully, the predicted storm hadn't rolled in, yet.

The fact that the temperatures held above freezing in the mid-forties last night, and Chet's reminder that Sam had taken emergency gear with him, were the only things that kept Pete from heading back out.

Besides, they'd find nothing in the dark.

Senator Starr had other ideas, but Sierra, who'd spent the evening with the congregation at the church, had calmed him down, kept them all abreast of the search.

The congregation was probably still holding their prayer vigil.

"We're thinking Polebridge," Pete said. "It seems to fit the window of the call." He turned to Ty. "Let's get the rest of the team in here. We have an hour before sunrise to figure this out."

His gaze landed on Jess, who was leaning against the table, but she looked away fast, set her coffee cup down, and headed upstairs to where Kacey Fairing slept in the women's bunk room.

"Gage is on his way down," Ty said. He had his cell phone out, probably to call Ben and Chet, who lived just down the road. "I think Miles is in Chet's office, on the sofa."

Pete headed to the office. Sure enough, Miles Dafoe lay on the sofa, his head at an awkward angle against the arm.

"I have an idea," Pete said into the darkness, and Miles opened one eye, as if he hadn't really been sleeping.

"Pour me coffee," Miles said as he sat up.

Twenty minutes later, with the night turning to grays, the moon low in the west, the team gathered around the map. To Pete's surprise, even Ian had shown up, unshaven, wearing a sweatshirt, cargo pants, and hiking boots, back in the SAR game.

Pete had already cleared his idea with Miles, who leaned against the table, on his second cup of java, watching.

"We have a very sketchy PLS, so we're going to have to get creative," Pete said. "Let's brainstorm probable scenarios. Given that they headed toward Polebridge, where did they go? The closest hikes are the Quartz Lake trail and the Hidden Meadow hike."

"How about the Logging Creek trail?" Gage said. "It's not as far north, but there's an unstaffed ranger station there—it could have cell service."

"We're assuming they stayed in the park," Ben said. He wore his baseball cap backward, his hands over his chest. "The Camas Road hooks up with the outside North Fork Road. They might have headed south, to the Big Creek Outdoor Education Center. There's also a ranger station there—with cell service."

"We'll call them, see if the kids were there," Pete said.

"It hit the news last night," Sierra said. She'd come over from the church. The stress of the last twenty-four hours and managing the terrified parents didn't show on her face. Although, admittedly,

226

Sierra never looked rattled. She carried Gopher, the cute golden retriever pup. He rested his snout on her shoulder, still sleepy. "Maybe someone will have seen them, will call in."

"What about . . . well, have we thought about the lookout tower?" Jess stepped up to the map, pointed at the Numa Ridge tower. "Willow—"

"Has a thing for lookout towers. You're right, Jess," Pete said and flashed her a smile.

His heart gave a little jump when she met his eyes, gave a quick grin in return.

So, maybe his words were sinking in. *I'm not just out for a good time, Jess.*

"What if they went up to the Numa hike and maybe got lost or hurt?" Sierra said.

"We did a flyby yesterday, but not nearly that far north," Kacey said. She wore her jumpsuit, had downloaded the weather reports for the day. Now she stepped up to the map, pointed to Bowman Lake and Numa Ridge. "We could start canvassing that area."

Pete shot a look at Miles, who leaned up from the table.

"All right," Miles said. "Gage, you and Ian take the medical van and head over to the Logging Creek trail and station. Ben and Kacey, establish an aerial search around the Numa Ridge Lookout hike, and include Bowman Lake. Pete, grab your truck and head up to Quartz Creek. Ty and Jess, take Ty's Silverado, go farther north, toward Polebridge. If you need to, head all the way to Bowman Lake. Call in everything you find—anything. We have about a six-hour window on this storm front. So, today, people, we bring these kids home."

The team began to disperse, including Jess, who headed out the door, her hair pulled back and cascading out of the opening in her baseball cap. She didn't even look Pete's direction as she followed Ty out the door.

Pete had the strangest urge to grab Ty. Tell him to keep her safe. And, right behind that, the irritating pinch of frustration.

"We'll find them," Chet said, coming over from his spot behind the team and clamping Pete on the shoulder. "You did a good job, there. Sam would be proud."

Pete managed a tight, grim smile and headed outside.

He caught Jess in the barn, checking her supply pack and getting water. Pete had passed Ty outside adding his gear to the truck; Gage was in the yard, checking supplies in the medical van.

Pete picked up a radio and a vest. Glanced at Jess.

Her mouth was a tight bud of concentration.

"Jess—"

"We'll talk when we get back."

"That's not what I was going to say."

She looked at him then, and he startled at the unfamiliar, skittish expression in her eyes.

He took a step toward her. Touched her cheek. "I was just going to say watch out for bears."

The wariness evaporated, leaving behind only her smile, and it reached in, chased away the chill, put him back together a little.

"You don't want me snuggling up with Ty?" she said, tease back in her beautiful eyes.

Pete cut his voice low. "I'd have to murder him, and figuring out where to hide the body might be a challenge with this crew."

He couldn't help it. Despite the yelling in his head, the fact he might be breaking promises to God, and all because she was still smiling up at him, he leaned down and kissed her. Sweetly, his fingers just barely touching her face.

She kissed him back, softness in her touch, as if, yes, everything would be fine.

He lifted his head, met her eyes. "Please be careful out there."

She nodded, and he watched her walk out to Ty.

"You're just out for yourself—always good-timin' Pete, right?"

228

Not anymore. And he planned on proving it.

"Okay, bro, I'm coming to find you."

———— ✦ ————

"Am I seeing things, or is there some hanky-panky going on with you and Pete?"

Ty sat in the truck, one arm propped over the steering wheel, wearing a wool cap, a blue PEAK fleece, a pair of cargo pants, and hiking boots—not at all his standard ranch wear. He hadn't shaved maybe for a few days, and his dark beard set off those piercing green eyes. Flash his cowboy smile, and he could reduce the average woman to a puddle. In fact, during their high school years when she'd spent spring break out west skiing with him and his family, he had that exact effect on Jess.

That was then. Now, she glanced at him, her entire body strung tight as she hung on to her seat belt. "No. Yes. I don't know. Maybe."

"Jess. Are you in trouble here?" His low baritone had a softness to it, that layer of understanding that he so loyally kept from everyone else.

She closed her eyes, then looked away to the forest, at the mist rising from the valleys, the low clouds that tufted the mountaintops. The sun had just begun to peek over the ridges, the sky a glorious striated gold and umber. She took another sip of her coffee, needing the bracing heat.

Especially after the way Pete had kissed her. Impossibly tender. Pete was all fun and passion, but the gentleness in him could undo her. And, the fact that he could turn her world silent with one look in his blue eyes scared her a little.

She just might be in over her head.

"I said something stupid," she said. "He mentioned something about Willow, and I responded with the fact that people keep secrets."

"What? Jess!"

"I *know*—I don't know what I was thinking. It just came out, and then he turned all curious on me and told me that he wanted to know me, about my life, and that after we found Sam, how he was planning to show up on my doorstep. That he wanted . . . more."

"*Pete* said that?"

"He even said that he wanted to meet my family."

Ty's eyebrows went up. "Oh. Bummer."

She pressed her hand to her forehead. "I should have seen this coming. I don't know how I got so stupid. I just thought—well, it's Pete. And he's not necessarily known for, I don't know, being a guy who wants a relationship."

"Right," Ty said. "But you're not one of Pete's normal girls, right? I mean, you're not just interested in—"

"No, of course not. I'm not that kind of girl. Really—"

Ty's hand on her arm stopped her. "Calm down, Jess. I know, okay?"

She took a breath, let the knot in her chest uncoil. "Okay."

"So, what are you going to do? Tell him about your dad, and New York, and the trial—"

"I don't know." She sighed. "I thought I left that behind two years ago. I mean, if you weren't here, no one would even know, right?"

"Not unless they went digging. No one would expect you to be hiding out in a small town in Montana."

"A few people—the right people—might."

He confirmed with his silence.

"If I haven't said so before, thank you. I'm not sure what I would have done had you not rescued me."

"I hardly rescued you, Jess. You would have been fine on your own. For the record, I'm glad you called. It's the least I could do. By the way, I *still* have your back. If Pete does you wrong, you let me know, okay?"

Sweet. But . . . "What if I do *him* wrong? I mean, I can't keep him in the dark forever, right? He could so easily look it up on the internet. Google me."

"Aside from the fact that Pete can barely use his cell phone, what's he going to do? He doesn't know your full name, and it's not like you have any connection to your life back in New York City. You're a different person now, Jess. Even I can see that."

Oh, she hoped so.

"But," he added, "if you want your life here to stay hidden and intact, you have to stay under the radar." He slowed as they passed the turnoff for Quartz Lake. "And that means the fewer people to keep your secret, the better. By the way, keep your eyes out for the van. Maybe it slid off the road."

She sighed, took another sip of coffee. "I can't lie to Pete. It's one thing to keep my past in the dark, it's another to invent something." Her gaze scanned the ditch, looking for skid marks. Here, forest edged the road, but as they ascended, it would drop away into valleys and harrowing cliffs.

She'd been up here once, with Willow, visiting her mother at her commune.

Ty had his eyes on the road. "So, what happens if you tell him?"

She stiffened. "I don't want him to see me like that—the woman who ratted out her father to save herself."

"Only you see it that way. Others see a woman who was trying to do the right thing." Ty slowed as he went around a curve, and shot her a look.

She didn't take her eyes off the shoulder. "It doesn't feel like the right thing. Not when I think of my father sitting in jail. And the fact I put him there."

"It's not that simple."

"It's *exactly* that simple, Ty. And, Pete's already been betrayed by his brother. Imagine how he would feel about me if he knew I betrayed my entire family."

Clearly she'd made her point because Ty grew silent beside her.

"The problem is, I never planned on telling anyone. I was perfectly happy just being one of the team, living my life, fixing my house. I didn't plan on—"

"Falling in love?"

They'd reached Polebridge, and now Ty paused at a stop sign.

"I'm not in love with Pete."

Ty gave her a look, then took a right, toward Bowman Lake.

"You've been in love with Pete Brooks since he walked into your life wearing a New York Giants T-shirt."

"That helped." She smiled at the sweet memory, the image of Pete, his blond hair tied back, his shoulders outlined in that royal blue shirt, wearing a pair of faded jeans and tossing a football to Ty.

Yeah, one look at those mesmerizing blue eyes and her heart had stopped cold.

It restarted with his delicious smile.

Oh. *No.* She couldn't be in love with Pete Brooks. He was supposed to be safe. A teammate. The exact wrong person for her to fall for.

"Like I said, you're in trouble, aren't you?"

She gave a sad nod.

"What's that?" She pointed to skid marks in the pavement, a churn of grass and brush along the side of the road.

Ty pulled into the ditch and had barely slowed before Jess hopped out.

She stood up and traced the path of debris left by a fast-moving vehicle as it careened off the highway and down the side of the mountain—bushes decimated, a tree splintered, another broken and bent over the path.

Ty came around, holding his pack and hers. She took it, clipped it on. "C'mon."

She picked her way down the slope, her heart lodged in her throat at the sight of scattered red taillight glass, the scrape of white paint across bark, and, just twenty feet from the edge of a cliff, a cell phone.

She picked it up, tried it. "No juice."

Ty stood at the edge of the cliff. "Oh no."

Jess had been in enough emergency situations with Ty for his tone of voice to turn her cold. She joined him. "Is that . . ."

"It looks like the church van."

Crushed, upside down, about sixty feet down. It looked like it had careened off the cliff, bounced off a ledge just below them, and slammed top down in the ravine below. Glass shattered out of the windows, but she didn't see any bodies.

"We gotta get down there," she said.

"I'll call it in," Ty said and moved away from the edge to get HQ on his radio.

She set up a rappel system to a nearby sturdy pine, climbed into her harness, and by the time Ty returned, had the descender attached.

She ignored the crazy urge to rap jump. She wasn't that brave, especially without Pete. She pulled on her gloves, put on her helmet. Looked up at Ty.

"Pete's on his way, and Miles is diverting the chopper this direction. Be careful. I'll be right behind you."

She nodded and stepped over the edge.

12

WITH THE SKY TURNING A DEEP PEWTER and the wind sharp as it snaked down his jacket, Sam could predict the forecast.

If he didn't find help today, tonight might be the last for his crew of survivors.

Maybe even himself. He glanced at Quinn just a few feet below as they climbed toward the road. They'd headed west, then north as the sun rose, and Sam had spotted the road, arching and curving above them, a ribbon cleft in the rock. They'd had to cross the river again to get to the road—this time finding a shallower passage—and he'd finally found a pass where the land arched up through pine and Fraser fir, where the cliff above was accessible through a tumble of boulder and ledge rock that had collapsed into a natural ladder.

With every step of the climb, Sam's breath burned in his lungs, the ache in his side burrowing deeper, turning to fire. Whatever he'd done in the accident, he'd only exacerbated the damage in his plummet down the river.

He could admit he might be getting dizzy, his body pushing itself past exhaustion.

Below him, on the rubble of rock, Quinn's foot slipped.

He caught himself before Sam could reach down.

"You okay, Quinn?"

He nodded. Quinn hadn't said much during their hike out and was back to his deeply brooding self as they'd trudged into the morning. Now, sweat dripped down his face, his dark hair plastered to his forehead, his breathing hard as he pulled himself from one handhold, one foothold to the next.

Maybe Sam wasn't as out of shape as he thought.

With the top of the cliff still forty yards or more above him, Sam turned around, sat on a perch, and pulled out a water bottle. He glanced at the darkening sky.

As Quinn sat down beside him, Sam handed him the bottle.

Quinn drank it, capped it. "You think we'll make it back before the storm hits?"

"I plan on it," Sam said.

Quinn handed him back the bottle.

"Thanks for tagging along."

"I couldn't stay there one more minute with Dawson Moore." Quinn shook his head. "It's a good thing you called him out, because I was about ready to shove him off a mountain."

"What are you talking about?"

Quinn's mouth tightened. "Dawson was at the pit party last weekend. He slipped Bella the weed. I didn't even know about it until we got to the party. I was going to give Bella this necklace, you know, sort of a homecoming gift. We'd been going out for four months. Then she started acting weird. But it wasn't until I kissed her that I figured it out. Then the bear came, and I lost the necklace . . ."

"And you got blamed."

Quinn raised a shoulder. "I can't figure it out. I land a varsity position on the team, get straight A's, and my dad still thinks I'm the guy who got his girlfriend high and tried to feel her up in the woods."

"He just wants the best for you, Quinn."

"No, he wants me to be like him. A Navy SEAL. A senator. A hero. But that's not me—"

"I disagree. You saved *my* life."

Quinn looked at him. Shrugged again.

"Just tell him that you don't want to go to the Naval Academy."

"I did. You walked in right about then—how do you think he took it?"

Sam had that feeling again, the one that gave his gut a twist. So, he had to ask. "Quinn, your dad isn't . . . he's not too tough on you, is he?"

It took a second, but Quinn shook his head. "No. Not like that."

Not like that?

"He's not. He's all bark, very little bite."

Sam stiffened. "Explain *very little* bite."

Quinn looked away, and Sam considered him a long moment, wishing he could rewind his conversation in the hospital a week ago, maybe take up for Quinn's side.

Quinn wasn't talking, so Sam got up, slid the bottle into his backpack, and began to climb. Quinn moved in behind him.

"He took me camping last summer. I should have known it wasn't a father-son bonding trip. He wanted me to see that I could survive on my own, so in the middle of the night, he just packed up and left me in the woods."

Sam was scrabbling over a sheer piece of ledge rock, leaning up for a handhold, his side pinching, so he couldn't react.

But he wanted to. Left him in the woods?

Except maybe his silence gave Quinn the space to keep talking.

"I was out there for two days. He expected me to hike out or something. I had no idea where I was, no food, hardly any water, and I nearly froze to death. I didn't know it, but Dad was out there, watching me, testing me. And I failed."

Sam reached the top of the ledge and stood on it, his hand gripped to a higher rock as Quinn followed him up.

Sure-footed, capable.

But certainly not able to handle himself alone in the woods. Yet.

Someday, however, yes. Sam could see Quinn as tall, broad-shouldered, and every inch a hero, given time.

"The fact you didn't know how to survive isn't a failure, Quinn. Sheesh, your dad was a SEAL. He trained for those things."

Quinn's mouth formed a tight bud of frustration. "I just want him to be proud of me."

Yep. It didn't matter how old Sam got, he still longed for his father to look down on him—even from heaven—with pride.

Maybe. Finally, he would. Because Willow's words this morning had loosened something in his chest.

"It's all about letting God in, with his grace to forgive, to heal. God's light can overtake the darkness."

Except, he didn't exactly know how to let God in.

Ten feet from the top. From there, the land sloped up at a brutal angle. At least Sam could see the road, maybe two hundred yards farther. Sam took another step—

His foot slipped.

Quinn caught it. "Right behind you, sir."

"Apparently," Sam said, giving him a half smile. He reset his foot and scrabbled to the top. With each breath, his chest turned to fire.

"You really don't look good," Quinn said as he landed next to him.

"I'm fine." Sam climbed to his feet. "But I'm not going to race you up the hill."

Quinn gave a low chuckle.

He began to hike up the slope, working his way through the pine trees, the boulders and ledge rock that scarred the land. "Why does your dad want you to go into the Navy?"

"Because my grandfather was in the Navy, and his father before that. It's what we Starr men do. Except me, of course."

"That's rough."

"Yeah, well, I used to want to be like him. When I was young, he was my hero. Then he became a senator and suddenly I couldn't do anything right. He kept pushing me, like I wasn't enough—or like he thought I'd mess up. It made me think, if he already thinks I'm a screw-up, why bother trying to impress him?"

"I don't know why I bother to try and impress you."

Pete's words at the Gray Pony slammed into Sam, along with the visual of his brother holding his bloody nose, his eyes filmed with hurt. Sam's chest tightened.

"He just sees me as irresponsible. A kid who gets his girlfriend high and lures her into the woods so she can be eaten by a bear. I wish I could prove to him that I'm not the guy he thinks I am."

Sam stopped, braced himself against a boulder, looked at Quinn.

"I'll always be a screw-up to you."

He gritted his jaw, pressed a hand to his chest, trying to catch his breath.

"Sam?"

Sam fell to his knees. Leaned over, his breaths coming hot, his chest tightening.

"Deputy Sam!"

He closed his eyes, leaned his forehead into the ground, sweat sliding down his back.

The sky opened up, began to weep. Icy rain slid into the trees, dripped down into his hair, his skin.

Quinn was beside him, his hand under his arm. "C'mon."

"I'm with you, kid," Sam said, fighting to get his feet under him.

He slipped. His chest slammed on the boulder beneath him. Pain spired through him, the world spinning, turning gray.

Black.

"Sam!"

Quinn's voice faded away into silence as Sam surrendered to the icy blades of the rain.

———— + ————

"I'm coming back to you, I promise."

Willow tried to cling to Sam's words as the youth huddled together at the edge of the forest, tucked under a massive white pine. The storm blew the flimsy shelter Sam had made right off its supports and into the fire, snuffing it out.

Of course.

Willow knew how to make a fire, but not in the driving rain.

Judging by the whitened faces of her kids, the way the air turned biting, the rain knifing through their layers, and the panic forming in crystalline puffs in the crisp air, they might all die of hypothermia before Sam returned.

If he returned.

No. She couldn't let herself think that.

Although, Dawson had mentioned it. "It's been six hours, maybe more. How long are we going to stay here and freeze to death?"

His question cut into all of them.

Especially Josh, who, despite his brave words last night, woke this morning moaning, his broken nose clearly as painful as it looked.

She shivered. "Sam will be back. He promised."

Josh got up and stormed away from the shelter of the trees.

"Everybody stay here," Willow said and glanced around at the kids. Maggy sat huddled under the fairly rainproof space blanket, along with Zena and Vi.

Riley hunkered next to the tree, his arms around his legs. Nearby, Gus crouched next to another tree. Dawson just stood at the edge of the forest, staring at the mountains, the forest, the rain dripping down the collar of his jacket.

"I mean it," she said to Dawson as she walked past him, a rare dark edge to her voice. "Josh!"

He didn't turn around but stalked toward the river, which was roaring as the rain whipped it to frenzy.

She found him standing at the river's edge, shivering. Admittedly, he looked like he'd been dropped off the edge of a cliff and landed on his face, then tossed about a river, tired, starving, and not a little shaken.

"Are you okay?"

"No." His voice emerged wrecked. "We're going to die out here. Even if Sam makes it out, how are they going to find us?" He turned to her, despair in his dark brown eyes. "And will we be alive when they do?"

"We're going to be fine."

"Willow, you are so—"

"What? Naïve?" The word came easily, raked up from her fight with Sam.

"Faithful," Josh said quietly. He glanced at her, a darkness on his face that rocked her back. "You just keep believing that God will save us."

"He will, Josh. I know it."

"How can you know that?"

"'Hear my cry, O God. Listen to my prayer.' Psalm 61. 'The Lord is near to all who call on him, to all who call on him in truth.' Psalm 145. 'Call on me in the day of trouble; I will deliver you.' Psalm 50."

"You just . . . you say it like you mean it." He shook his head. "I want to mean it, but—"

"Josh. It's right now that you have to dig down and ask yourself what you believe. Is God with us or isn't he? And yeah, maybe—I don't know, maybe we don't get rescued. But that doesn't mean that God has abandoned us."

She heard her own words, wanted to believe them too.

But her heart felt pretty numb these days. Tired of being battered and ignored. Tired of trying so hard to fit into a world that clearly didn't want her. Her father, her church.

Except for Sam. *"I want you."*

However, that left Sierra, where? Rejected by Ian. Rejected by Sam.

She couldn't lose Sierra. Her sister might be the only person who really *wouldn't* walk away from her.

Josh turned away from her, closed his eyes. "I can't do this."

His soft words brought Willow back to him. "What do you mean, can't do this?"

His expression was so wretched, it turned her cold. "I'm not cut out to be a youth pastor. I don't know what I was thinking." He sighed. "Dawson's got real problems—he's probably an alcoholic. And Zena, she's completely broken by her wretched family life. I have a horrible feeling she's been abused in some way."

"Her dad is in prison, and since then her mom goes through boyfriends like whiskey."

"And then there's Maggy, who tries to do everything right but feels like the world doesn't like her. She's pretty, but she hides behind all those layers. And Vi has the entire world on her shoulders trying to protect Dawson. Gus is a great kid, totally underappreciated, and it makes him feel like he's less. That's why he tries so hard to pull his weight—he just wants people to notice him. And then there's Riley, who wants to be the hero he plays in his video games. As for Quinn, he can't see beyond the label of failure his dad has put on him."

Willow just stared at him. In two days, he'd managed to do what it took her three years to do—get under the layers of each kid, understand them. In fact, it sort of felt like he knew them better than she did.

"I'm just not cut out to know how to help them. They're so different from the way I was raised." He stifled another shiver. "I came from a huge family—my dad was home every night, my mom kept the house running, my brothers and I courted our wives, my parents were a part of every decision. It was so easy for me to see that God loved me. And I thought . . . I don't know. I saw myself leading Bible studies, helping kids see that God loved them too, helping them make right choices. But they're already broken, and I don't know how to put them back together."

A log crashed into a boulder nearby and lodged there. Willow stared upriver at the froth and chaos. But farther downstream, the log made a tiny pool of calm, with the river rushing past it. Maybe that's all they were meant to do with these kids—give them a pocket of safety, feed them with truth while they could.

"I know you were supposed to have the job," Josh said quietly, cutting through her thoughts. "Pastor Hayes told me that you've been working with them for the last three years. I knew they were considering someone else, and it wasn't hard to do the math."

They'd been considering her? She'd hoped it, but after Carrie's words, the thought had died.

"I think they only gave it to me because of my Bible degree. Pastor Hayes seemed pretty impressed with that piece of paper. *I* was impressed with that piece of paper. But the truth is, a degree isn't as important as knowing the truth in your heart, right?"

She didn't know.

"And *you* know the truth. You believe it. You live it. You share it." Josh stared at her now, an earnestness in his eyes. "I don't know what to say to them. I don't know how to save them."

"We were crushed and overwhelmed beyond our ability to endure, and we thought we would never live through it," Willow said softly. "In fact, we expected to die. But as a result, we stopped relying on ourselves and learned to rely only on God, who raises the dead."

Josh just stared at her.

"It's from Second Corinthians, in a letter Paul wrote. He's telling the believers about being shipwrecked and how afraid he was."

Overhead, the sky hung low, dark. She was soaked through, her body a tight knot of ice. "I read the entire Bible through about four times in high school. I didn't go to high school, actually. I was homeschooled too—or sort of. I lived in a commune, not far from here, and my mother just let me pursue my own interests. I never actually finished any formal schooling. I was pretty lonely, so I spent a lot of time reading. You learn a lot when you just read through the Bible. Like the fact we're not supposed to save ourselves, but let God do the rescuing. It's a theme repeated over and over and over, from Abraham and Sarah to Joseph, to Moses, to David, and the nation of Israel, and finally through Jesus Christ. It's the entire point of the Bible, Josh. We're supposed to be over-whelmed. Because if we can save ourselves, we don't need God."

Josh frowned.

"If you think you're supposed to save these kids, you've missed the point. We can only point to the One who does the saving."

He swallowed. "From the ends of the earth I call to you, I call as my heart grows faint."

"Lead me to the rock that is higher than I."

A wry smile touched his lips.

She nodded, then startled as the log broke free, headed again downriver.

She watched it go.

Overhead, the sky was a bruised dark purple, with smoky gray thunderheads rolling in from the west. Snow glistened on the mountaintops of Rainbow Peak to the east.

And closer, to the southeast, the Cerulean Ridge.

"I know this view." She stared at the ridge, turned to get her bearings. "If we walk due west, stay south of this ridge, we'll hit Ainihkiwa."

She saw Josh considering her words and clarified. "We're about three miles from where I used to live. Where my mother *still* lives."

"Then let's go," Josh said. "What are we waiting for?"

She stilled. "Sam. He asked me to stay. And I promised him I would."

"I'm not staying here to freeze to death. We don't know where Sam is, or if he made it. C'mon, Willow. We *have* to go. These kids are our responsibility."

She stared at the churning river. "He said to stay, that he'd be back for us."

Josh's hand touched her arm. "Who knows but he needs *our* help? He wasn't in good shape when he left."

"Quinn will help him."

"If Sam goes down, what is Quinn going to do? No, Willow, Sam would want you to be safe. So if you know the way home, we need to go."

---- + ----

Jess had found the van.

Pete took just a moment to press the walkie to his forehead, brace himself for the rest of her report as he stalked back to his truck. He listened to the exchange between Miles and Jess.

"We're about six clicks up the highway to Bowman Lake. It looks like they may have taken a curve too quickly—they went right over the edge."

Pete got in his truck, held on to the steering wheel, closed his eyes.

"The van went down a hill, then over a cliff, landed wheels up."

Oh, please, God—

"But we're here, and there's no sign of any of them. No blood, no backpacks, just the debris from the fall. So either they got out before it went over, or somehow they all survived the fall and are hiking out."

Pete started up the truck, backed out.

"Ty and I are going to continue westward down the ravine. I don't think they would have walked east—too many natural bar-

244

riers, and my guess is that Sam would want to try and get back to the road."

"Roger that," Miles said.

Pete turned out onto the inside North Fork Road, put the gas to the floor.

Overhead, the sky had turned dark, and as he drove northward, the rain thickened, pelleted his windshield.

"Base to Brooks," Miles said, and Pete picked up.

"Brooks, Base. I'm on my way to Jess and Ty's location. Can you divert Kacey—"

"I'm sorry, but I'm bringing the chopper back to base—too much clutter with the weather rolling in. But Ian and Gage are headed your way," Miles said.

Pete signed off and kept his eyes on the road, trying to get into his brother's head.

How they'd walked away seemed impossible. Given the evidence, however, he had to assume they were all ambulatory, or at least most of them. Sam would want to find them a place to hunker down, stay safe. Then he'd want to get help, which meant he'd be hiking out to a place where he could get cell service. Except they'd been gone two days. It seemed unlikely anyone would have any juice left.

Pete passed the Polebridge ranger station and came to the turn to Bowman Lake.

He pulled over and reached for his terrain map. He traced his finger six miles up the road, found the nearly hairpin turn where they'd gone off.

Given the natural curve of the land, the rise in elevation to the east, yes, Sam would have walked the kids west until he hit Bowman Creek.

And then what? Cross the river at this time of year, after the ice storm? Better would be to walk along it, follow it to where it ran parallel to the highway. Although Sam might not know that from his position.

But Pete could start there, meet Jess and Ty by the river. He grabbed the radio. "Brooks to Watson. You there, Gage?"

"Watson here. We're just passing Hidden Meadow."

About ten miles behind him. "I'm going to park about four miles up road and start hiking in along the river. Call in when you reach my position."

He pulled back out onto the road. *Please, Sam, think like me. Be hiking along the river. Or better yet, hunkered down somewhere.* Although, knowing Sam, he'd have to have a couple broken legs to stay put.

"This search is not over."

Out of the past, Sam's words thundered into Pete's brain. That terrible moment when the searchers found him and Sam, frozen to the bone, strung out and horrified after six hours of searching the backwoods, and informed them that the blizzard had shut the search down.

With their dad still out there.

Sam had simply come apart. And most of the aftermath landed on Pete.

"I swear, you're the most irresponsible person I've ever met! You're just out for yourself."

Sam's words at the Gray Pony, but not the first time Pete had heard them.

"If Dad's dead, I'll never forgive you."

Pete's hands tightened on the steering wheel. Well, get in line, because he would never forgive himself, either.

He'd turned his wipers nearly on high now, along with the defrost, and slowed as the road turned slick. The wind buffeted the truck, and in the torrent, Pete nearly missed him.

A kid in a red jacket, running up the ditch behind the truck, waving his arms, yelling.

Not any kid, but Quinn Starr.

Pete pulled over and got out. The cold knifed down the neck of his jacket. He pulled up his hood as he ran. "Quinn!"

Grimy, sweaty, disheveled, and trembling, Quinn caught up to Pete. "He's—down—there." Quinn's breaths tumbled one over another. He bent over, clasped his hands to his knees.

"Who's down where?"

Quinn looked up. His dark hair was plastered to his head, and the rain ran in rivulets down his face. "Sam."

Sam.

"Where? Show me."

Quinn pointed behind him, and Pete dragged the kid back to his truck, turned it around, and drove back down the highway, pulling over onto a muddy lip of ditch. "Is he hurt?"

He tried not to react when Quinn nodded. "It's pretty bad."

Pete grabbed his walkie and his emergency pack. "Let's go."

Quinn was already out, slipping his way down the slope.

Pete started down after him, watching his footing as he worked his way down, squatting to brace himself on rocks, boulders, to catch a tree limb.

Quinn descended into the forest, Pete on his tail, and then— Sam.

He lay on a piece of ledge rock, pale, barely breathing by the looks of it. The rain pelted his face, and he didn't flinch, didn't move. He appeared battered, a bruise across his forehead, a cut on his cheek. He was probably hypothermic.

Pete had never seen his brother quite so taken apart.

Well, except for once.

"Sam." Pete knelt next to him, pulled off his emergency pack. He looked at Quinn. "What happened?"

"I don't know. He looked pretty bad this morning, but when we got to the ridge, he slipped and fell on the rock, and then he just sort of passed out."

Although not completely out of it, because Sam moaned as Pete took his pulse. He seemed to struggle to breathe, and Pete unzipped his jacket, pulled up his shirt.

A purple-black bruise covered his entire right side, starting at his chest, running under his arm, behind his back.

Pete put his hand on his sternum, watching Sam's chest move and how the bruised section stayed still, independent from the rhythm of the expiration.

"It looks like flail chest—ribs broken completely off the sternum. I've seen this a few times in motor accidents. It happens when you hit the steering wheel." He could only imagine the impact of going over the cliff. Even if Sam hadn't fractured his ribs completely, this second fall on the rocks could have finished the job. "We need to keep him from going into shock." He glanced at Quinn, nodded to his bag. "Get out the emergency blanket."

As Quinn rooted through the pack, Pete probed around the bruised area, searching for the edges of the flailed ribs. By the way Sam's chest moved, Pete guessed he had more than one fractured rib.

Quinn handed him the blanket, and he pulled it over Sam. "Now find me the gauze pads—all of them. And tape."

He pulled his walkie from the pouch. "Watson, where are you?"

"Just pulling onto the Bowman Lake Road."

"Look for my truck about two miles in. I'm about two hundred yards down. I found Sam—and he's pretty hurt. We'll need a stretcher, and you'll need to rope in. It's steep."

"On our way."

A moan, and Pete was just putting his radio away when he felt a hand grasp his wrist.

Sam's eyes opened, and for a second, he stared at Pete, unseeing, trying to get his bearings.

"Sam, just breathe. We've got you."

Then Sam's gaze focused, turned to Pete, startled.

When he began to sit up, Pete grabbed his shoulders. "Stop, bro—you're pretty hurt."

"Willow—she and the kids are out there—"

"I know. We'll find them." He eased Sam back down, took the pads from Quinn.

"The storm's only going to get worse. We have to go." But Sam's voice emerged on a hoarse whisper, as if dragged through the destroyed ribs of his chest. He winced, his breath catching.

Pete layered the gauze pads over the weakened ribs. Grabbed the tape. "Yeah, I don't think you're going anywhere, bro."

"Pete—"

"You have a pretty bad break here. Stop your yapping and let me get this secure."

Sam's jaw tightened, and he looked away, one eye closing in a wince as Pete secured the pads to his chest. He extended the long strips of tape across his chest and around his back.

"Quinn, get behind him. We need to elevate him, help him breathe."

Sam struggled to sit up, letting out a low groan between his teeth. Quinn sat behind him, his back to him as a prop.

"No, Quinn. Help me up. We need to get back to Willow."

Pete ignored him. "I need to check your blood pressure." He pulled out the wrist monitor and pushed up Sam's jacket.

Sam didn't fight him, but he said, "What we need to do is get going. I left Willow down by the river—which is probably uncrossable by now. We need to call Kacey, get the chopper in here—"

"Miles grounded them in this storm," Pete said, frowning at the numbers. "You're dangerously close to hypotension here, Sam. You're not going anywhere."

Gage's voice came through the radio. "Brooks, we're up top, coming down to you."

Pete picked up his radio. "Roger. Send a litter."

Sam grabbed Pete by the jacket, his grip surprisingly strong but not enough to menace. "I am not leaving."

Pete saw the look in Sam's eyes, and sure, Pete could wrestle him into the stretcher, get him up the hill, but he knew his brother.

He couldn't trust anyone else to find them.

Pete put his hand around Sam's wrist, cut his voice low. If he hoped to get Sam to listen to him, he couldn't do it at high decibels. He'd tried that, lived most of his life in the high decibels. But not Sam.

And maybe, being more like Sam, Pete might actually get through to him.

In fact, maybe he should have thought of that years ago.

"Bro. Listen to me. You're really hurt, going into shock, and frankly, you're not going to make it to Willow and the kids. I'm pretty sure you being dead is going to tick off a few people more than my not letting you tag along, starting with Sierra, right?"

Sam just stared at him, his eyes fierce, a muscle pulling in his jaw.

Pete glanced at Quinn sitting behind Sam. "You know where they are?"

Sam shook his head. "He's a kid—"

"I know where they are," Quinn said.

Sam glared at Pete. "You've got to be kidding me."

And that was just enough. "You've got to be kidding *me*! Do you seriously think I'm going to risk your life when I can find these kids without your help? I'm capable of finding them . . . and I'm not losing you, Sam. I know you hate me, but—" Pete bit back a word of frustration. "I don't hate *you*, okay?"

Sam blinked at him, clearly shaken.

Pete heard scrabbling above him and looked up, saw Gage descending, roped in, holding the litter. "Ian's up top with the winch. We'll get him up the slope."

Pete looked at Quinn. "Are you sure you're okay to go?"

Quinn nodded.

Sam blew out a breath, moaned, and looked away from them, so much emotion in his face Pete couldn't watch.

Gage landed next to Pete. "Let's get him packed up and tucked into the ambulance, and then you go. We've got this."

Pete eased Sam's grip from his jacket. "Stay alive, Sam, and I promise that I will find Willow and the kids and bring them home."

13

"JUST TRY TO RELAX, SAM. Pete *will* find them." Gage sat next to Sam in the Land Rover, which was outfitted to be a mountain ambulance, complete with cardiac monitor, oxygen supply, and drugs. "Let's go, Ian."

Sam could admit to some surprise seeing Ian Shaw meet him at the top of the cliff. Although the founder of PEAK Rescue, Ian rarely joined the team on callouts or even came over to HQ. Probably in fear of seeing Sierra and having his wounds raked open.

Although, given his most recent appearance at the Gray Pony, perhaps Ian had moved on.

That only made Sam want to wince.

He didn't relish the conversation with Sierra.

But, he'd meant it. He wanted Willow. Thinking of her, the fact that a fresh start waited after they got clear of this nightmare, might have been the only thing keeping him from howling as Gage and Pete carried the litter up the mountain slope. The rough terrain jostled him, and with every breath, pain knifed through him.

By the expression on Gage's face, he knew he was in bad shape. "We'd send in the chopper for you, but the ceiling is too low, even for Kacey."

Sam got it. A former Army rescue pilot, Kacey could probably fly their Bell 429 through the perfect storm, but with a brutal crash in PEAK's near history, Miles wasn't taking risks.

"I'm fine, Gage."

"No, actually, you're not. We'll need X-rays, and I'm no doctor, but you have striated bruises on your torso, and that, along with the dip in your chest as you breathe, tells me that you have at least three broken ribs, probably completely unattached breaks. Which means you might need surgery to pin these ribs and keep them from puncturing your lung." He slipped the oxygen mask over Sam's face. "For now, just breathe."

Sweet, fresh oxygen flowed into his mouth and his nose, and he closed his eyes.

"I'm going to roll you onto your side," Gage said and moved around beside him. "I know this will hurt, but lying on your injured side will actually help pin the bones in place, keep them moving with your chest." Gage put his hands behind him.

Sam let out a yell as Gage eased him up on his side.

He wanted to whimper. Instead, he wrapped his hand around the stretcher and held on.

"I'm driving as fast as I can in this weather," Ian said. "We'll get you to the hospital and pain meds as fast as we can."

Pain meds, actually, were only the third thing on his mind. Right behind the memory of Pete's words: *I know you hate me, but I don't hate you, okay?*

He didn't hate Pete.

He closed his eyes, the truth finding purchase. He loved his brother. Painfully, frustratingly. *That's why you're always so angry with him.*

He closed his eyes, and for some reason, memory stirred.

"Sam, come down the mountain with me! I'm going through the trees."

Pete, standing at the chairlift, glancing down at the deep powder and heavily treed off-road of the mountain. Pete's eyes shone, his smile wide.

Sam remembered looking over the edge, at all that dangerous, enticing white with its hidden disasters, and his stomach simply dropped.

In that second, Sam knew.

He was afraid. Maybe rightly so, but before he could lodge any sane rebuffs, there went his father, sidling up to Pete. Grinning at him, that same shine in his eyes. "Looks like fun!"

Wait . . .

"C'mon, Sam. Live a little!"

His father had pushed off, launching himself off the trail into the whitened back country.

Sam jerked, his eyes opening.

"Easy there, pal. Just breathe," Gage said.

"He went first," Sam said quietly. His breaths came quick, harsh. "He went first."

Gage had his fingers pressed to Sam's carotid artery. "I want you to slow your breathing down, Sam. In through your nose, out through your mouth. You've got a lethal heartbeat here."

All this time . . . Yes, it had been Pete's idea, but his father had launched off first.

Sam had, for the last decade, skimmed right past the most essential memory in favor of blaming his brother.

Because it was easier than forgiving him.

Forgiving himself.

And maybe that was the ultimate source of his darkness—his inability to forgive.

"It's all about letting God in, with his grace to forgive, to heal. God's light can overtake the darkness."

He didn't want to live in darkness anymore. Not when he had so much waiting for him in the light.

They turned onto the highway, and Sam closed his eyes and tried to relax his body.

He must have dozed off because when Ian turned again, he opened his eyes to discover they were exiting the park.

"That's affirmative, Sam. We found your campfire and the shelter blown down into it. But the camp is abandoned."

Sam wanted to throw the walkie across the room.

How could Willow have left?

He should have gone with Pete.

"He's hypotensive. Let's get him on an EKG."

"No! I have to go—" Sam dropped the walkie and reached for the IV neatly taped on his arm. Before Gage could stop him, he pulled it out.

Nurse Hudson shrieked, and the ER doc grabbed a gauze pad as blood spilled down his arm.

"Are you out of your mind?" Gage yelled as he pressed his hands to Sam's shoulders. "You're not going anywhere!"

"I promised Willow I'd come back for her!" He knew he sounded unraveled. "Willow is out there in the storm, and she needs . . ." *Me. She needs me.* "Help. I am not abandoning someone that I care about again."

He pushed himself up from the table.

"Sam—sit back down!"

The voice arrested him, and he looked around, found Sierra thundering into the room, her eyes dark. "Get back on that bed."

His bare feet landed on the floor even as he stiff-armed Gage. Swayed.

Gage caught his arm.

Ian supported the other side. "Sam! Get back in bed!"

"Listen, Pete's not going to give up," Gage said. "You're not the only one who can save these kids, Sam. You did your part. Let your team—your brother—do the rest. Trust us. Trust *Pete*."

Trust Pete.

Right.

At that moment, Sam's knees buckled. He landed on the floor.

Then, with a violent rush of heat and pain, he threw up.

Blood. It landed on the floor, gurgled out of him.

Sierra screamed, and it seemed everyone moved at once. E. Hudson shoved a pan under his chin, Ian and Gage dragged him up to the table.

"I think he's got broken ribs," Gage was saying as they pushed him back, pulled up an ultrasound machine. Gage picked up the walkie.

"I'm fine." But Sam coughed so hard blood pooled in his throat, choking him.

"Get that oxygen mask back on him!"

"You're not fine!" Sierra stood at the end of the bed, angry tears streaming down her face. "You've got to stop trying to save the world, Sam. Let someone help you!"

The ER doc put cold gel on his chest and ran a wand over him. "We have blood in the pleural cavity. He needs a chest tube right now. Tell surgery we're on our way."

Sam was shaking, his entire body turning cold. He grabbed the walkie from Gage. His voice had turned raspy, and he forced it through his closing lungs. "Pete!" An anvil sat on his chest. "Pete," he said again, his voice low, fading, "don't come home unless you find them."

Silence in the room, save for Pete's reply on the open line. "Affirmative," the voice said, dark and quick.

Gage regarded him with a sad look. "Nice, Sam."

Sierra shook her head, her face a mess of anger and fear. "One of these days you're going to figure out that you need to be rescued just as much as the next guy."

He looked away from her.

"Morphine, please," he said tightly.

"He didn't mean it, Pete."

Jess stood just outside the sodden campfire pit as Pete paced the clearing, searching for a clue, anything to tell him where Willow might have gone.

He knew Jess was trying to keep her voice soft, like he might be hurt and dangerous.

She might be right.

Don't come home. Simple words, with so many layers.

Don't come home, because you only hurt people. Don't come home, because you only cause trouble. Don't come home, because you don't belong here anymore.

"Pete—"

"He meant it, okay?" Pete rounded on her, his jaw tight. "I know my brother, and he definitely meant it. And I agree with him. I'm not coming home until I have Willow and the kids."

"Of course not. Everyone knows that."

"Yeah, well, I made a promise."

She had so much concern on her face that he added, "It's okay, Jess. He's like this when he's lost it. When he cares so much he simply unravels. It's not personal."

Except it had felt personal for too many years.

Maybe that was the problem. Pete had been too young back then to see otherwise.

Jess glanced at Ty, then back at Pete, and he didn't want to think about the fact that Ty and she had this sort of unspoken bond he couldn't get his brain around.

For a second, it jerked him out of the search and into his earlier conversation with Jess. What if *that* was the secret—that she and Ty had already dated? She *had* ruled Ty out awfully fast.

No. Pete couldn't care—not right now.

"I gotta think. Get me a map."

Quinn had sunk down onto a log, frustration in his demeanor as he curled his arms around himself, trying not to shiver.

They should have gotten here faster. But Pete hadn't wanted to take any chances at the river—not with Quinn. Or Jess, who had encountered impassable rapids when Bowman Creek bisected her path. She'd hiked downstream and met Pete, and he'd set up a belay system to get them across.

But they were soaked to the bone, shivering and possibly heading toward hypothermia, the way their breaths formed in the air.

"Where would they go?" Quinn said. "Sam told her to stay right here."

Pete got that part, loud and clear, given the commotion in the ER. Gage or someone had kept the walkie toggled, and he'd heard the main parts. Like "get back in bed" and "blood," and Sierra's voice—"You've got to stop trying to save the world, Sam. Let someone help you."

Clearly she didn't know his brother at all.

Ty brought over a topographical map divided into search grids, with known locations printed on it. He spread it out on the soggy ground. The rain had finally turned to a fine, merely bothersome drizzle, and moisture pooled on the washable surface. "All right, we're here, at the base of this ridge. She wouldn't have gone back over the river, not after what Quinn told me, and there's a kid who is hurt."

"Vi. She's got a broken leg," Quinn said, heading over to them.

"Okay, so following logic and natural barriers, Willow will probably keep heading west, under the cover of this ridge." Pete traced his finger along the markings. "The highway curls around here—she might even meet up with that."

"Wait," Jess said. "This is Bowman Campground, right?" She pointed to a designator on the map.

He had the strangest urge to reach out and take her hand. Just for a second pull her to himself, hold on. "Yeah."

"Then right here"—she put her thumb into the grid and measured it out, pointed to a valley in the map, not far from Polebridge—"is Ainihkiwa."

"What?" Ty said.

"Willow's mother's commune. It's just inside the park—officially billed as a travel hostel. Grandfathered inside the boundaries, southeast of the inner highway."

"That's about three miles from here," Pete said. "I suppose it's worth a shot."

"It absolutely is," Jess said. She looked at Quinn. "Although I'm worried about this one."

Quinn frowned at her. "I'm fine."

"Apparently. Outrun a bear, live through a van falling off a cliff, save Sam's life. Like father, like son, Quinn Starr." Jess winked at him.

Even Pete smiled at the way heat rose into the teen's face. "Okay, Captain America, let's get going."

Quinn led the way, Ty behind him. Pete fell back with Jess.

"I got the story from Quinn," Pete said to her. "They went over the edge, and believe it or not, a tree slowed them down, kept them from going over. The van apparently fell about fifteen feet to a little ledge, then the next day, they all managed to get out before it went over. Willow climbed down to get the ropes, and they belayed down."

"The van is completely flattened. No way they would have survived that fall if the tree hadn't stopped them," Jess said.

"Then apparently Willow and Sam got swept downstream. Then—get this. Dawson was drinking—"

"Dawson Moore? You're kidding me. His dad works in the ER over at Kalispell Regional Medical Center."

"I know."

"Wow." Jess had her hands in her pockets. She looked up at him then. "Hey, um, I wanted to tell you . . ."

He knew what was coming and wanted to make it easy for her, so he kept his tone light. "Listen, I think I figured it out. You and Ty dated, didn't you? That's what you didn't want to tell me."

Her mouth opened as if in surprise.

He gave her a grin. "I knew it. It was the way he looked at you." She frowned at him.

"Sort of possessive, maybe."

"Oh," she said.

The simmer inside ignited to a full, throat-scorching burn. "Wait, it's over, right? I mean, the other day when I said Ty had a crush on you, I meant—well, I never thought that you might—"

"He's my teammate," she said.

That shut him down, along with a sudden hollow desperateness that made him swallow. Worse, he couldn't stop himself from adding, pitifully, "Um, and . . . so am I?"

"Gotcha."

He looked back, and when she grinned at him, the rush of relief almost left him light-headed.

Then, invincible.

The lingering hold Sam's words had on him began to dissolve. Yes, he *would* find them. *Would* make it home.

Then he would show up on Jess's doorstep, start building a life . . . or at least a house with her.

"Hey! I found something!"

Pete looked up, spotted Quinn holding a lime-green bandanna. "It was here, tied to a tree."

"As if someone left it behind?" Pete ran up to him. Grabbed it.

"It's Willow's. I remember her wearing it," Quinn said.

"Another confirmed PLS," Pete said.

Jess took the bandanna out of Pete's hands. "Is this blood?"

Quinn nodded. "She hit her head on the windshield."

"How hard?"

"I don't know—hard enough. Sam washed it off—but there was glass in it, I think."

Jess looked at Pete. "Let's hurry."

———— + ————

Willow was calling herself a fool by the time they reached the back gardens of Ainihkiwa, with the tall cages that housed the now-harvested beds of pumpkin, corn, squash, tomatoes, cucumbers, cabbage, and row upon row of potato plants, the soil turned over and black, waiting for next year's eyes.

She should have recognized the area, realized how close they were. She blamed it on the stress of the accident and the residual adrenaline of being swept down river.

Not to mention ending up in Sam's arms.

"This is a commune?" Zena said. "It looks like a farm, with cabins."

"It is. Everyone lives in the rustic cabins—they used to be youth hostels back in the day. There are three small barns for goats, chickens, cows, and a few pigs. They grow their own food and in the winter mostly live in the main lodge."

She pointed to the log building, the one with the handmade rock chimney with smoke curling from it. "I'll bet my mother is inside, making soup."

Gus trudged up to her, carrying Vi. "I could eat some soup."

She directed them down the path, toward the lodge, standing for a second on the ridge, looking back. She'd left her bandanna tied to a tree just outside camp, hoping Sam would figure out where they'd gone.

She hated herself for not keeping her promise. Josh's words sat under her skin as they'd trudged through the woods. It could be that Sam needed *her* help.

As soon as they could get the Ainihkiwa truck, she'd drive to the ranger station, call in their location. No phones, no cell service at the commune.

"Willow? Is that you?"

The voice reached out through the drizzle, through the haze of the low-lying fog, and like a song fell upon her heart.

Her mother, her tawny brown hair tied up in an African-patterned duku and wearing an oversized knitted sweater and a pair of yoga pants, stood at the back door of the lodge.

Willow ran up and without a word fell into her arms.

"Oh my," her mother said, the warm smell of nutmeg and cinnamon in her skin flushing through Willow.

Despite their differences, Willow always relished the embrace of her mother.

"What's going on?" Her mother let her go and looked around at the crew. "You look like you've slept the night in the woods."

"We have," said Josh. He extended his hand. "Josh Blessing. I'm the youth pastor at Mercy Falls Community Church."

"Blossom Rose," her mother said. "Come inside, all of you."

Then it was over. Tangy pumpkin soup and hot cocoa. The fire blazing in the hearth. Fresh clothing and doctoring from her mother and a number of the other current residents, one who'd been a nurse somewhere. Willow inquired about the commune truck and discovered it was gone on errands, brother Arank at the wheel.

"He'll be sad he missed you," Blossom said as she sat down opposite Willow, setting a bowl of steamy orange soup in front of her. "He says you don't come back enough. I agree."

Willow was finally warm and dressed in a pair of her mother's yoga pants and an oversized sweatshirt, her head bandaged. They'd all availed themselves of the only shower, and now the crew congregated in the cozy lodge.

The former nurse had taken a look at Vi's ankle and confirmed her fear of a break. Now Vi sat with her leg propped up on the sofa by the fire, with ice in a towel wrapped around her ankle as she played a game of war with Riley. Her laughter trickled through the room. Funny, ever since Sam had confronted Dawson, Vi seemed less tightly coiled.

She wasn't the only one smiling. Maggy and Gus sat at the end of the table, eating soup—Willow didn't want to guess how many bowls Gus had consumed. Maggy was listening to him wax on about football and his hopes of playing for the University of Montana

Grizzlies, her eyes shiny with adoration. Judging by the expression on Gus's face, Willow thought the feeling might be mutual.

Maggy reached out and touched his arm.

Dawson sat in another chair by the fire, watching the flames, with Zena nearby, plucking on a guitar. Apparently, he knew a few chords and reached up and positioned her fingers. He hadn't asked who outed him, and Willow kept her secret.

Josh was in the kitchen, an ice pack on his face.

This was a healing place. Willow had forgotten that part.

She stirred the pumpkin seeds into her soup. The smell could reach in, make her whole, and when she tasted it, the butternut sweetness filled her hollow places.

Except . . .

She pushed it away.

"What's wrong?"

Willow pressed the heels of her hands into her eyes. "Oh Mom, I'm so worried about Sam. I should have never left our campground. He won't know where we are, and I promised I'd stay there—"

"Don't be silly, Willow. You were freezing to death, hurt and hungry. Sam will be grateful you got to safety."

"That's the point. He's going to come back, discover we're not there, and spend the next who knows how long searching for us. He's hurt, Mom."

Blossom's gaze went to Willow's forehead. She'd finally cleaned out the glass and grime as best she could. The wound still bled a little, since the cut was deep and in need of stitches. She'd have a scar that could tell tales.

"This is nothing. I'm fine. But I think Sam has a broken rib."

"Honey, is this Sam Brooks you're talking about? Your sister's boyfriend?"

There it was. The real reason Willow couldn't eat her soup or chase the chill from her bones.

Despite Sam's words about wanting to be with her, Willow had no illusions. Once he shook himself free of the bewitching hold the trauma had on him, he'd realize the mistake he'd made with Willow.

He'd forget Willow existed—or worse, live in a constant state of guilt and simply push her out of his life.

Which, frankly, might be for the best. Because her heart probably couldn't take being around Sam, seeing him hold Sierra's hand, turn his beautiful, devastating gaze on her. Knowing that Sierra was once again the focus of all his heroic attention.

She stared into her hot cocoa.

"Oh, Willow."

She looked up at her mother, her hazel-blue eyes so much like her own.

"You're in love with him."

Her mouth opened.

"Don't act surprised. It's not like your heart is difficult to read. You wear it on the outside of your body. I'd be surprised if you *weren't* a little in love with him after spending two days with him saving your life."

"It doesn't matter. He belongs to Sierra." But a knife went through her heart with her words.

"Really? Because last time I talked to Sierra, she spent the entire time telling me about Ian and his current search for his niece and how he'd shown up at the Gray Pony with some other girl, and . . . I think your sister is still terribly in love with her former boss. *Not* Sam Brooks."

Willow stared at her. "When did you turn into a romantic?"

"I've always been a romantic. I've just been a jaded romantic." Blossom gave her daughter a wry look. "Blame it on my parents and their brutal divorce. I saw what that did to my mother and decided never to be hurt that way. But, I hurt you anyway—you and Sierra."

Willow frowned. "You weren't married, Mom."

"But I should have been. My biggest regret is turning Jackson down when he asked. We had a nice family, and then I got scared and ran. I changed my name and threw myself into a new life, trying to reinvent myself. Again."

Indeed. Her mother had changed her name three times in her life from her original name—Charlene. Before Willow's birth, she'd been Meadow. Then she'd met Jackson, fallen in love, and changed her name to Lilly. She'd only become Blossom after the disastrous fallout of her breakup with Jackson.

"The truth is, I loved Jackson. I gave myself reasons why we shouldn't be married—but we all do that—we find excuses for people not to love us. Not to choose us because we're so afraid of being hurt. When, in fact, relationships mean *letting* yourself be loved, even if you don't think you deserve it."

Willow reached out, touched her mother's hand. "You deserve to be loved, Mom."

"I think I'm starting to believe that." She looked up, met Willow's eyes. "And you should too."

"Not at the cost of Sierra. She deserves to be happy, and Sam will make her happy."

"No. Sam makes *you* happy. Ian makes Sierra happy. Unfortunately."

"But she can't have Ian. Or won't."

"And it's a good thing too, because Ian has taken your sister for granted for years."

"Mom, she was his secretary."

Blossom gave her a withering look, and Willow conceded. "Okay, yes. She gave her heart to Ian. But that's why Sam is such a great catch for her. He appreciates how capable she is—"

"And how she doesn't need him?"

Well, yeah. "I'm just such a mess, Mom. I'm always doing stupid, reckless things. Sam is the sensible one."

"And that's why he's the right one—for *you*. Because love is about mutual dependence—I know that much. I didn't want to need Jackson. It scared me. So I ran from him. But it wasn't until I looked back, saw myself trying to raise two beautiful daughters alone, that I realized how much I needed him. His strength, his compassion. His loyalty. Jackson was my one true love."

Blossom was running her thumb up and down her coffee cup. Behind her, Zena had picked up a few chords, was strumming out a pattern.

Gus and Maggy entwined fingers.

Vi giggled as Riley declared war on her hand of cards.

"The problem is, you're fine with people needing you. That fills you right up. But needing them . . . you're too much like me. I'm sorry about that."

Willow looked up at her. "I need people."

"But you don't expect them to show up, to save you. To love you. That's probably my fault. You've been on your own since your daddy and I broke your heart. It only got worse when he joined the military full-time. You should know, he was hurting pretty badly, but for four years you didn't see him and I know you were devastated."

Willow blinked back a sudden, terrible heat in her eyes.

"And then, for a while, you let Sierra in to fill those hollow places. You needed her to take care of you, bring you to school. Until, of course, she left you too."

"She just moved to Mercy Falls—"

"She left you, Willow. Yes, she needed to build her own life, but again, you were abandoned by someone you needed."

"I had you, Mom."

Blossom gave her a tight smile. Shook her head. "Arank was more of a parent to you than I was. I know that. I came here to find myself, and I know I left you out of the equation. I am sorry for that."

Willow looked away, swiped her hand across her cheek.

"You learned that needing people only left you hurt and alone. Until this weekend, when Sam stepped into your life. He's strong and handsome and he's been rescuing you for two days." Blossom raised an eyebrow. "You were forced to need him. And it's scaring the wits out of you." She leaned forward. "Willow, be honest here. You know, deep in your heart, that Sierra and Sam aren't destined for each other. But it's an easy out. Much easier than giving him your heart, only to risk him abandoning it."

Willow looked away, her eyes burning.

She touched Willow's hand. "I love so many things about you, but the one thing I wish I had was your undaunted focus on loving others. It's not cluttered with agenda or envy or even resentment. Your love heals people. It makes them stronger, fills them with light. But you might consider letting down your guard and taking a risk on love yourself. Isn't that what you Christians call grace—letting God love you and letting that love change you?"

Willow offered a small grin. "Someday, Mom, you're going to figure out that Jesus loves you too."

"Well, it's enough that you do." She leaned back. "I'm guessing if Sierra knew how you felt about Sam—"

Footsteps thumped on the deck outside, and her mother scooted out her chair, rose just as the back door opened.

Just for a second, as Willow blinked against the light, she saw him standing in the frame, looking fierce and bold.

Sam.

He'd found her. Her heart gave a belligerent, traitorous leap.

Then he stepped into the room. Scanned it, and his gaze landed on Willow.

Pete. She stood up, her legs just a little weak, but she managed to head over to him.

"Willow." He pulled her into his arms, hard against his chest. "Sam is going to be so glad to see you."

She closed her eyes against his words, but they burrowed in and found her heart.

"Willow!"

She leaned away from him, and Jess rushed in. She pulled her friend into an embrace. "We were so worried." She leaned back. "Oh, your head."

"I'm fine."

"You will be," Jess said.

Around the room, the kids rose. Ty came in, shaking off the rain from his jacket, followed by Quinn.

He looked wrung out but wore a new confidence in his countenance.

"Let's get you warm," Blossom said to them.

Jess pulled out her walkie, walked away from them.

"Did you find Sam?" Willow asked, trying not to let too much panic in her voice.

Everything went quiet. She sensed the shift in the room, the way Pete's mouth tightened in a grim line.

"Yeah," he said quietly. Then, nothing.

"Pete—"

"He's in surgery, Willow. But I'm sure he's going to be fine."

Surgery. "What happened?"

"We got him to the hospital, but he freaked out when Pete couldn't find you," Ty said. "And injured himself."

Oh. She reached out for balance, her body turning liquid.

Then Gage's voice came over the line of Pete's walkie, breaking through the static, loud and clear. "Get back here, Pete, as soon as you can. Sam's out of surgery, but he's in critical condition."

Pete closed his eyes.

Willow echoed his low muttered words.

"Please, Sam, stay alive."

14

"So apparently, I didn't die." Sam's throat felt like a cement mixer had driven through it, gravelly and raw, and parked right in the middle of his chest.

Save for the cool, fresh oxygen, his entire body ached as if it had been kicked from a high cliff. His bones felt heavy in his skin. For the first time since rousing out of surgery, Sam got a good look at the person holding his hand.

Not Willow.

Sierra.

How long she'd been sitting at his bedside, he couldn't guess, but she too looked wrung out. Her head was tucked into her arms, her eyes closed.

She wasn't alone.

"No fault of your own," said Ian Shaw, who stood at the window wearing a wool cap, flannel shirt, cargo pants, and Scarpa hiking boots, looking like a billionaire who'd decided to go slumming in the back hills of Montana. He turned, offered a smile. He hadn't shaved either, and his eyes betrayed fatigue. "Good thing that Aaron Moore was the ER doc on shift last night. You flatlined on your way to surgery, twice."

"Scared us all to death," Sierra said now, lifting her head. She didn't smile. "I've never been so angry with someone in my entire life."

She glanced at Ian, her eyes narrowing as if she might be confirming her own words.

Ian raised an eyebrow. Shifted uncomfortably.

Then, "Nope. Never." Her expression softened. "But, good news. Pete found them."

For some reason, although Sam hadn't realized it, the knot that still held him together unraveled, and his entire body melted into the bed. "Please tell me they're okay."

Ian walked up to the bed, his gaze only stopping on the grasp Sierra had on Sam for a second. "They're all okay. Apparently Willow guided them all to her commune. Pete followed a hunch and found them a couple hours later. They should be here soon."

Sam closed his eyes, and Sierra's hand in his tightened.

He didn't move it, because, well, her grip kept him from doing something crazy like curling into a ball to weep.

Not that he didn't think Pete would find them, but . . .

"Don't come home unless you find them."

He wished he hadn't meant that, but . . . well, at least it was over.

"You'll love this part. The local press is in the ER, waiting for them to show up. Apparently, Tallie Kennedy has declared Pete a hero," Ian said. "She's got a cameraman and feed to the evening news, has already reported a preview segment. They want to talk to you, find out how it happened."

He'd been an idiot, that's how. Sam looked at Ian. "It was an accident. One second we were driving. *I* was driving. The next we just flew off the road." He cringed. "It was my fault."

"It was an accident, Sam," Sierra said. "Icy roads."

"No, I was at the wheel, and Willow started singing, and I took my eyes off the road for one lousy second." He couldn't tell them he'd actually been joining in. "They could have all died because of me."

"They didn't, because of you, Sam," Sierra said.

He looked away, his mouth tight. "The commune? Why did she take them there? I told her I'd come back. I promised her."

"Are you kidding me right now?" Sierra said.

"No." His voice emerged harsher than he meant. "That just wasn't . . . smart. She risked the lives of the kids. What if she hadn't found the commune—they'd be out there right now, the rain turning to ice and snow, and we would have no way to find them. It was just plain stupid."

It was then he heard the door click shut, the tiny rasp of metal into the latch, and he looked over.

Willow stared at him, her face stoic and pale. "I just got in. I wanted to see if you were . . . so, you're alive. Good."

Her glance went to Sierra's hand clasped into Sam's.

"Willow!" Sierra launched herself up from the bed, caught her sister in a full-on embrace. "I was so worried."

Willow surrendered to the force of her sister's relief.

Her beautiful, devastated gaze, however, stayed on Sam. Unshed emotion filled those hazel-blue eyes, and he heard his words like acid in his throat.

"It was just plain stupid."

"Willow . . ." he said, his voice broken.

She tore her gaze off him and onto her sister. "I'm fine, Sierra. Mom fed me her famous pumpkin soup and hot cocoa."

"Your head! That looks horrible!"

"I'm fine. I'm going down to the ER right now—Dr. Moore is still checking out the kids. I wanted to run up here and tell Sam . . . well anyway, we're home."

The smile she flashed him, hollow and distant, could bore a hole through him. "I see everything is back to normal here. I'm happy you got Sam back."

He closed his eyes. Trapped. Because yeah, he needed to talk to Sierra, but not here, not in front of Ian.

He owed Sierra that much.

"Me too," Sierra said, her voice a little odd. "But more, I'm glad you're back. You scared us."

"I think we've all pretty much figured out that me and a trip with the youth group into the mountains doesn't mix. I'm not going to stick around for strike three."

Her words made Sam look at her, but she didn't spare him a glance.

Still. "Willow, this wasn't your fault," he said.

She met his gaze then, a darkness in her eyes he hadn't seen before. Even after two days in the wilderness, after he'd nearly driven them over a cliff, after she'd been swept downriver, after discovering Dawson's drinking.

No, this darkness had to do with the fact that somehow he'd snuffed out the light she held on to so bravely. The light that told him she believed in him, in herself, in *them*.

That light that had pretty much kept him going until right now.

"Actually it is, and we both know it." She turned to Sierra. "I was trying to help these kids see that life wasn't as dark as they thought it was. That there was always a different perspective." She gave a harsh laugh. "I guess I did. I showed them that no matter how dark it is, it can always get worse."

Sam winced.

"I'll be downstairs, sis. I could probably use a ride home when you're ready to leave."

"Willow," Sierra said.

But she turned around, rushed from the room.

Sierra rounded on him.

"What?" he said.

"No, you tell me *what*?" Sierra snapped. "What happened out there that my sister looks like you took out her heart and stomped on it?"

He didn't know what to say. He glanced at Ian.

Not here. Not now.

"Nothing happened."

Silence, and Sierra looked at him as if she wanted to turn him to ash.

"Listen, okay, I might have . . ." *Fallen in love with your sister.*

The words moved inside him, took hold.

Oh. No.

Oh. *Yes.*

Because even as he looked at Sierra, searching for words, he longed to lift himself out of the bed and run—sprint—after Willow. To tell her—

What? Because he'd just called her stupid, practically to her face. How did he come back from that?

"Oh boy," Sierra said, shaking her head. "Something *did* happen, didn't it? And then you blew it. I can't believe I actually thought you would be good for her."

"What are you talking about?" Sam said quietly.

"I . . ." Sierra blew out a breath. "I set you up, okay? I wanted you to go hiking with Willow so that you could see how amazing and beautiful she is—and maybe I was a little bit of a coward. I didn't want to break your heart, Sam. So I thought if you fell in love with Willow, just a little, then maybe when I did cut you loose . . ."

Sam couldn't move. "You *wanted* me to fall for Willow?"

"You're so blind, Sam. Willow has loved you for I don't know how long. I didn't know it when we started dating, but the first time I let you kiss me, I knew the minute I told her that her heart was broken." She shook her head. "And I didn't know what to do about it. Until this weekend."

Really?

Willow loved him?

"And don't tell me that you didn't figure that out, Sam. You were out there with Willow for two days, and the girl doesn't exactly hide her feelings. Ever."

No. That she didn't. But wearing a crazy grin on his face probably wouldn't help. Especially since Sierra looked like she wanted to go for his throat.

Ian hadn't moved from his spot by the bed and now looked at Sierra, back at Sam. "Maybe I'll just, um . . . go."

"No, you stay right here, Ian Shaw, because this is for you too."

Ian glanced at Sam, something of panic in his eyes.

Sierra advanced on them. "You both drive me crazy, you know that? You're so consumed with blame and regret, it's practically choking both of you. Ian, you've got to face the truth that either way, Esme is gone. I'm sorry about that, but blaming yourself—or me—is not going to bring her back."

Ian stiffened.

"And Sam, you're completely missing the important part here. The kids are home safe. No one died—and that's a miracle. So you can either choose to see that and accept the amazing grace of God, or you can start pointing fingers and let all that darkness suffocate you."

He didn't want that, not anymore. He nearly spoke up, but Sierra cut him off, her gaze pinning him to the bed.

"You know why Willow is so amazing? It's because she's not afraid to let you see her heart and all the love inside it. And the amazing part is, that love isn't from her—it's from God. He's the source of the light that is in Willow."

"God's light can overtake the darkness."

Yes, that's *exactly* what had happened. Perhaps God had pushed him over a cliff to get his attention.

To part the darkness, draw him to the light.

Sierra's voice finally softened. "Sam. The only way you can escape the darkness is to stop looking at yourself and focus on someone greater. Someone who can *truly* set you free."

Sierra looked first at Sam, then Ian. Back to Sam. "But in order to be set free, you'd have to admit you can't fix it. That you are completely helpless. That you need rescuing. And you just can't do that, can you?"

Sam glanced at Ian, who was staring at his shoes.

In the hallway, he could hear the hum of voices, the rattle of a food cart.

"I'm going to find my sister and take her home. Tell her that she's the bravest person I've ever met." She looked at Sam then, ice in her eyes. "Frankly, Sam, you don't deserve her."

His throat thickened as she swept out of the room, the door closing with a soft click behind her.

He couldn't agree more.

———— ✦ ————

"The wound looks pretty clean."

Willow could barely hear the ER nurse over the echo of Sam's words in her brain.

"It was just plain stupid."

She knew it was his feelings of betrayal talking. She didn't blame him—she had broken her promise. Yes, she'd saved them, but what if she'd been wrong? What if the commune hadn't been where she thought?

By God's grace they weren't still wandering around in the woods, dangerously close to hypothermia.

"It's too late for stitches, and you'll have a scar, but otherwise, it's not infected." Nurse E. Hudson, by her badge, was in her mid-thirties, dressed in blue scrubs, wore her brown hair short, and didn't seem affected in the least by the press and chatter of the parents crowding into the ER.

Not that any of them had spoken to Willow.

She'd walked right past Pete, who was talking with Tallie and a number of other media, as well as Maggy and Gus. Inside the ER bay, she spied Vi with her father, who was taking a look at his daughter's splinted leg. Riley stood next to Vi, holding her hand.

Zena stood next to Dawson, who had planted himself at the foot of Vi's bed and barely looked up at Willow as she passed.

But it was long enough for his tight, grim look and a flash of fear to register.

She hadn't figured out what she was going to do yet. Carrie Hayes's words from last week speared through her. *"We trust you with our children."*

"I'm going to ask you to come back in a few days," Nurse Hudson said as she finished taping the bandage to Willow's head. "You're all set."

Willow slid off the table.

In another cubicle, she spotted Quinn, who sat with a blanket around his shoulders. She walked over. "You okay?"

He nodded but glanced down the end of the hallway, where his father stood with the media.

"You're a hero, Quinn," she said and squeezed his shoulder.

He offered a slim smile.

She, sadly, got it. Because despite their heroics, they'd returned, and their lives would reset. Which meant that, to the parents, she'd nearly gotten their kids killed.

Again.

"She risked the lives of the kids."

Sam was right. Absolutely, terribly right. No wonder he'd reached out for Sierra the minute he'd hit civilization.

She couldn't bear the memory of his hand clutched in Sierra's, their fingers entwined.

She was definitely some kind of stupid.

Josh sat on a table at the far end, right by the door, and a plastic surgeon was examining his nose. Gray-black bruises streaked across his face.

His cute wife, dressed in a pair of leggings and a pink shirt, stood at his bedside, holding his hand.

"Willow!" Josh said, but she kept her head down, not stopping as she strode out of the ER bay.

She knew what he was going to say. *Sorry, Willow, but we don't need you.*

That might be the kindest thing he could say.

She slipped out, hoping to sneak past the media still clustered inside the ER waiting room. She spotted Gus at the microphone, gesturing with his hands, telling a story.

At least someone had finally gotten the attention he deserved.

She'd nearly made it past the ER desk and was headed for the main doors of the lobby when she heard someone say, "Willow?"

She looked up, spotted Carrie and Pastor Hayes in the ER entryway. Bella walked with them, her arm in a bandage across her chest, looking frail and still recuperating from her ordeal.

Willow had a feeling they might all look like that for quite some time. "Hey, Bella."

Bella walked over, gave her an awkward hug. "I'm so glad you're safe."

"Quinn is in the ER bay," Willow said, and Bella caught her lip. Oh. Maybe she wasn't here to see him.

But Bella dashed a look toward the ER.

Even if she wanted to.

"Maggy is with Gus," Willow said a bit louder. Then she cut her voice low again. "And Quinn is fine."

Bella brightened and headed for the waiting room.

Carrie's eyes stayed on Willow, who took a breath.

"Willow," Carrie started.

She could save them all some time. "Listen, I know what you're going to say, and I agree. I shouldn't have anything to do with the youth group. I just get them into trouble with my harebrained ideas." She managed to swallow. "So I resign my position as youth leader. Not that you needed that—I'm a volunteer—but in case you were wondering, I know I'm done."

Pastor Hayes had the kindness to give her a sad, grim nod.

Carrie just cocked her head, lips tight, a slight knowing shake of her head.

Willow needed to leave before the heat in her eyes turned to full-on tears.

Oops, not fast enough. They filled and she turned, heading for the first door she could find.

The snack area. Perfect.

The room hummed with the sounds of the vending machines. Darkness pressed into the windows, and she touched her hand to the pane and closed her eyes. The day shook through her, right up to the moment when Gage's voice crackled through the radio.

"Sam's out of surgery, but he's in critical condition."

All she could think about—the *only* thing—was getting here as soon as she could. And praying, simply begging God to keep Sam alive.

Even if she couldn't have him. Even if he still belonged to Sierra.

Willow leaned her forehead against the cool window.

She should simply be grateful that God had answered her prayers.

She pressed her fingers to her lips, wishing she could wipe away the feel of Sam's arms around her, the way he made her feel brave and needed. And wanted.

She couldn't dislodge his words from her brain. *"You make me feel like the guy who has half a chance of living again."*

That should make her feel at least a little better. She'd done it—put Sierra and Sam back on the right path. Maybe Sam could eventually let go of his anger, let God into his life.

She curled her arms around her waist, willing herself to stop shaking.

"Willow?"

She hadn't heard her come in. Willow turned and saw Sierra

standing in the doorframe. "You okay? Pastor Hayes said you came in here."

Willow shook her head. "No. I'm—I'm so stupid, just like Sam said."

Sierra let the door close behind her. Stood there for a second, her expression turning fierce. "You are not stupid, Willow. You saved those kids."

"No, Sierra. Let's not fool ourselves and think that our getting out of the woods in one piece—mostly in one piece—wasn't God stepping in to deliver us, each step of the way." She whisked her tears from her cheeks. "I should have stayed and waited for Sam. I don't know why I left—"

"You left because you saw where you were, you weighed the options, and that was the right one." Sierra came into the room. "And yes, God saved you—but he used you and Sam and Josh to do it."

Willow wanted to believe her, but . . . "You should have seen Sam. He just didn't give up. He was so hurt and cold and he just—"

"Stop talking about Sam."

Willow recoiled. Oh. Right. Her breath caught. "Sorry." She sighed. "I know Sam probably told you that I . . ." She swallowed, turned back to stare out the window. "I kissed him. Right here, actually."

Sierra went quiet. Then, "No, he didn't."

Oh. Willow drew in a breath. Well.

Of course not. Because if he had, that would mean he *meant* his words about straightening things out with Sierra. About him wanting Willow.

She hadn't really believed Sam intended to break up with Sierra. He'd simply been caught up in the emotion of their survival, the momentum of the trauma, the need to cling to someone—anyone.

She'd been convenient, and painfully too easy. For Pete's sake, she'd practically given him her heart right here in this room.

Willow drew in a breath past the shattered pieces.

"Well," she said now, clearing her throat, "I did. And it was wrong. And I'm so sorry—"

Sierra was right there, arms around her waist, holding her close. "Willow. Shh. It's okay. I don't care."

She didn't care? Willow stiffened. "What are you talking about?"

"Oh, Willow, do you think I don't know you? Or how you feel about Sam?"

Sierra stepped back, gave her a sad smile. "I wanted you to go on that hiking trip with him. I knew that we weren't right for each other, and I admit I was selfish. I didn't want to break his heart. I was hoping he'd fall for you, and I'd be sort of off the hook." She took Willow's hands. "I just had no idea that he'd break *your* heart."

Willow just stared at her. "But he was holding your hand."

"No. I was holding *his* hand. Because I was worried about him. Nothing more."

Oh.

"I'm guessing, by the way he reacted in the ER, that my diabolical plot worked. I'd bet he does have feelings for you. He completely lost it when he discovered you weren't where he left you."

"And that's the point. I should have trusted him. Instead, I left."

"For the kids."

"Really? Because I've been going over and over it, and maybe I was just too afraid that he wouldn't keep his promise. That even though he said it, I'd be sitting there in the darkness. Alone."

Sierra tucked her hair behind her ear, sadness in her eyes. "You're not alone, Willow."

"Yes, I am. Because you left out the only important part. Whether you intended Sam to fall for me or not, he didn't tell you about us, did he?"

Sierra stared at her, the words finally landing. She shook her head.

Willow didn't think it could hurt any worse.

Until, Sierra added, "He told me that nothing happened."

Willow drew in a breath. "Yeah. Well, he's right. Nothing happened. Nothing that matters, anyway." She forced a smile, hated the way it quivered at the edges. One of these days she'd learn not to give away her heart quite so easily.

"Let's go home," she said. "Or whatever passes for home these days." She closed her eyes, shook her head. Gave a harsh laugh.

"C'mon, Eeyore. You need a bath—and I happen to know that Jess has working plumbing. I'll even spring for gelato." Sierra took Willow's hand. "By the way, I do know someone who has missed you desperately."

Willow looked at her, shook her head.

"Gopher."

Now that they'd gotten the crew home, Jess's lie sat under her skin like acid, sinking into her heart.

Yes, Pete, Ty and I dated. That was the big secret.

It could be just that easy.

Except, not even close.

She'd only made it worse by letting Pete believe it, if only for six hours. Because now, not only would she have to correct that assumption, but then she'd have to tell him why she'd let him believe it.

She pressed her hand to her gut just thinking about it.

"Hungry, Jess?"

Chet sat at the wheel of the pickup. He was driving her over to the hospital to check on Sam. And, of course, Pete would be there, having brought the kids in.

Later, Pete would want to drive her home, and this time when he walked her to her front door, she'd let him come in.

She wasn't so naïve not to admit she hoped he'd take her in his arms. Kiss her like he had on the mountain, or even with the sweetness of the kiss in the barn, the kind of kisses she hoped he reserved only for her.

Please, let her not be just one of the many.

"No, I'm fine," she told Chet and continued her hundred-yard stare out the window.

If she never told Pete the truth, she might as well be one of the many.

Because something real with Pete would mean letting him into her life. Really letting him in to see the mess, the debris, and the carcasses.

"I'm not just out for a good time, Jess. I want to know you, and what matters to you."

What mattered to her was him *not* knowing her.

No, she didn't just want all-fun, all-the-time, but Pete had suddenly gone from a safe guy, to a guy who threatened everything she'd built.

"You sure you want to go to the hospital? I could drop you off at home," Chet said. "You seem tired."

She'd had four hours of sleep in the last two days. Then there was the race against the grizzly that could still leave her weak if she let it.

Even more draining had been that moment when she discovered the van, despite the rush of relief when they'd finally located Willow and the kids.

So yeah, she might be a little wrung out.

And perhaps not thinking straight. "I think I have to tell Pete the truth," she said quietly.

Chet glanced at her.

"I know Ty told you everything when he called you."

"I had to know, Jess. I would have never given you a job if I didn't know the entire story or the fact that you have a medical degree. But I did understand why you didn't want to tell anyone else. It's not an easy thing you went through—testifying against your father, the scandal, your name in the papers. I know it took everything out of you to go through that."

"I can't be that naked again," she said softly. "I feel like I just got myself back."

She hadn't really admitted that to herself—how utterly bereft she'd felt when she moved to Montana, her Jeep and a couple suitcases to her name and her old pal Ty's number in her pocket.

Good thing Ty knew her before, way back to her carefree ski vacation days. Then later, when she was engaged to one of their best friends.

How far the rich and beautiful had fallen. But she wanted nothing to do with the Taggert name, had shortened it with the hopes that no one would ever associate her with Damien Taggert and the Great Embezzlement of the twenty-first century.

She should have learned from her notorious father that lies would only curl back and strangle her.

Chet, maybe, read her mind. "Why do you need to tell Pete?"

"Because, he and I . . ." What? Were in a relationship? She didn't exactly know what to call it. Maybe it was simply a mistake, and she was destroying her entire life because of an emotional friends-who-lost-their-minds moment.

"I'm not blind, Jess," Chet said. "I see the way Pete looks at you."

How did Pete look at her?

"For what it's worth, Pete might surprise you."

She glanced at Chet. "What if I tell him and—"

"And he sees you as the brave woman you are?"

Sweet Chet. She shook her head. "You and Ty, maybe. The rest of the world sees me as the daughter who testified against her father to save herself."

"You weren't to blame for your father's actions."

Oh, what he didn't know. And that was the problem, wasn't it? "I knew my father was embezzling all those people, Chet. I knew it years before the world found out."

There, she said it, and it was sort of a litmus test.

In his silence, he failed.

She reached up, wiped her cheek. Yep, she knew it.

"Jess," he said quietly. "I don't know what you're not telling me. But I do know this. Jesus is Lord. Full stop. That means he knows the past, the future, and the now. And he wants you to live in truth, trusting him to fix it. I know you feel naked. You came to Montana completely stripped of everything familiar. You've reinvented yourself on your terms. Maybe it's time to let Jesus reinvent you. Let him forgive you, give you a new name, heal you, and set you free."

He turned into the hospital parking lot, the light shining against his lined face and salt-and-pepper whiskers. "You aren't free when you're trapped inside guilt and lies."

He pulled up in a parking space and put a hand on her arm before she got out. "And I'll bet Pete understands that better than anyone."

She met his eyes in the glow of the dome light and saw compassion.

He gave her arm a squeeze.

He was probably—no, most assuredly right. If anyone understood being trapped by actions beyond your control, or even questionable choices, it would be Pete.

"I care. If you want to talk. About . . . anything."

Jess slid out and waited for Chet. They headed inside, and her gaze caught on the media vans parked near the entrance.

Oh no. It was déjà vu as she spotted Pete holding court in the middle of a media circus in the ER waiting room. At least three local news channels and Tallie stood closest to him, her arm touching the small of his muscled back as she leaned in to get his statement. Jess knew she was staring, rooted to the spot as Tallie smiled up at Pete, as he grinned down at her.

She recognized that grin, charming and sweet.

Admittedly, he looked every inch a hero, his long golden blond hair tied back, those baby blue eyes, the slightest hitch of a smile against his golden whiskers. He still wore his blue fleece jacket but now stood with his hands in the pockets, as if to say, *Aw, shucks, of course I saved those kids, ma'am. It's just what I do.*

Jess froze, not sure what to do, where to flee, because Chet was hobbling in behind her and she couldn't retreat.

Then Pete looked up past the cameras, past the mics and through the clutter of worried parents, and his gaze landed right on her.

Her world imploded.

"Jess—finally! Come here and tell everyone how you thought of the commune." Pete actually turned to Tallie. "She's the one who really saved them—she's the one who figured it out."

Every camera turned to Jess.

Oh.

Tallie slipped off the stool, headed her direction, and right behind her, Pete.

His eyes were shining as if he had just given her the best birthday present ever, maybe invited the Property Brothers over to remodel her home.

A camera was in her face, a microphone shoved into her airspace, and her feet were moving before she realized it.

"Jess!"

She pushed through the cameras, the reporters, parents, members of the youth group—even her own teammates. She spied Gage and Miles standing not far away, talking with Kacey.

"Jess." Pete had her by the arm now, and she turned, stared at him.

She couldn't breathe.

"What's the matter?"

"It's nothing." Oh no, please. Not right here.

Especially with Tallie advancing on them, still holding her mic. Seriously?

Jess yanked her arm away from Pete's grip. Shook her head. "I can't—I can't do this, Pete."

"What?"

"I'm not a hero! I don't want to be." She cut her voice low. "Trust me, you're hero enough for both of us."

He stared at her, his mouth closing, and for a second, hurt flashed across his face.

Oh. Everything inside her wanted to cry at his expression, because she hadn't meant it quite that way. But she couldn't tell him that it had nothing to do with him and everything to do with her and the fact that splashing her name across the news would destroy the fragile life she'd built in Mercy Falls.

She turned and practically fled down the hallway.

She crashed through to the lobby of the hospital, away from the ER, and simply stood there, breathing hard.

What had she just done? But she couldn't be in front of all those cameras. She didn't know how far the news might reach, but if it got picked up nationally . . .

Naked. Her life dismantled, again.

Footsteps behind her, and she whirled around, expecting Pete. Not Pete.

Ty came through the doors, his eyes darkened with concern. "Ty . . ."

"I saw what happened out there," he said quietly. "Are you okay?"

She wanted to say yes. That seeing everything she'd built here explode in her hands hadn't dismantled her. Hadn't threatened to send her to her knees.

But that's exactly what it did. She pressed her hands to her mouth, her eyes suddenly awash with heat and tears, her legs shaking. A terrible moan emerged from her mouth.

Ty caught her. Simply stepped up and put his arms around her. Strong, and capable, and no, they'd never been anything more

288

than friends, but he'd been her *only* friend for a while, and he knew what this meant.

What it all meant.

"Oh, Ty, what have I done?" She put her arms around him and held on, weeping. Sure, she could admit that it was probably fatigue as much as embarrassment, but for a second, she just didn't care.

She buried her face in his chest and let herself cry.

"Shh," Ty said, and she felt his lips on her head, a brotherly kiss. "I got you, honey. It's all going to be okay."

Probably not, but as long as she was lying, he could too.

———— + ————

"I'm sorry, but this interview is over." Pete glanced at Tallie, then back toward Jess's retreat and simply couldn't stand there one more minute.

"Trust me, you're hero enough for both of us."

Unfortunately, Jess hadn't chased her words with a smile or even given any hint that she didn't mean to reach in and rip out his heart. He even reached up and pressed his hand to his chest, as if she'd actually left a raw, empty hole there.

For the first time in his life, he'd been trying to pass along the kudos. To step out of the limelight, maybe not try so hard to be liked. At least not by people who didn't matter.

"Pete, we're not done," Tallie said, following him as he headed down the hall.

"I'll be right back," Pete said.

"I can't do this, Pete."

What couldn't Jess do?

Please let it not be *be with him.*

He strode past his team—Ben and Chet, Gage and Kacey all looking at him like they should be scrambling behind him.

So maybe he wore a little thunder on his face. He held up his hand. "I'm fine. Gage, go woo the press with your snowboarder charm. Tell them how you saved Sam's life."

Sam. He hadn't yet made it up to his brother's room.

Sam was out of surgery, and out of critical condition. So much that they moved him to a regular room.

Pete couldn't put a finger on why he hadn't made it up there yet.

Maybe it was easier to play the hero, like Jess said.

He shook the thought away as he reached the double doors that connected to the main lobby.

Stopped.

Because through the strip of glass, he could look right into the mostly empty space and see the truth.

Jess had run away from him right into the arms of her former boyfriend, Ty Remington. By the looks of things, whatever happened out in the field today had reignited old flames. Jess clung to Ty, her head nestled into his chest, and even from here Pete could see she was sobbing.

Pete put a hand on the door, the urge to push his way in and demand answers stirring to flame inside him.

Then he saw Ty lean down and kiss her. On the top of her head, but the gesture bespoke gentleness, compassion.

Love.

Pete hadn't seen that coming. Yes, Ty's gaze usually lingered on her longer than it might, say, Gage, but the softness in Ty's expression said much more.

Ty was still in love with her.

The way Jess clung to him, apparently she was too. Maybe hadn't been, but whatever had happened over the past ten hours . . .

"He's my teammate."

Her words, her laughing tone, burned inside him, an ember low in his gut.

Oh, he was an idiot.

Pete turned around and stalked back to the ER waiting room,

his brain churning with memories—Jess's smile when he showed up to fix her plumbing, the way she clung to him as they'd raced down the mountain, her laughter in his ears.

The way she'd pulled him into her vortex, making him believe that he could stop being all-fun, all-the-time Pete and instead be someone who actually hung around, showed up for the hard stuff, who could build a life with her.

Apparently, she'd finally figured out he wasn't that guy.

Except . . . And then he got it.

Tallie.

She stood waiting for him at the end of the hallway, her microphone put away. The cameramen were winding up cords, collecting their electronics. She smiled at Pete, so much welcome on her face.

It wasn't hard to rewind, to slow down and see Jess's expression as Tallie slipped her arm around him. His sins, returning to haunt him, and probably Jess could read the future.

All-fun, all-the-time Pete.

"Are you okay?" Tallie said now, her tone filled with real concern. She ran to keep up with him.

Admittedly, a dark, angry part inside him wanted to round on her. To tell her that, no, he wasn't okay. And maybe she could do something about that. Then the old Pete, the one from even a week ago, would have given her a charming, dangerous smile, something with spark and heat in it, and suggested that they get out of here and find someplace to, um, talk.

He considered it a long moment, in fact.

But it was too late. He'd already met Jess, already seen something beyond tonight, which was probably why a week ago he hadn't ended up making colossal mistakes with Tallie—a few yes, but nothing that required him to avoid the man in the mirror. Jess made him want to be that guy who stuck around. Fixed roofs and generally showed up the next day.

And the next.

"You're hero enough for both of us."

No, but maybe he would be someday.

Pete turned to Tallie, not sure what to say to her. She looked up at him with those amber eyes, her golden-brown hair down around her shoulders in tantalizing waves, a smile on her lips that hinted she'd like a go at trying to make him feel better.

And he knew, right then, it wouldn't. "I have to see my brother," he said, not trying to be rude. He chased his words with a smile.

"Oh. Okay. Well . . ." Her smile fell. "Give me a call, then."

He offered her a smile rather than lie to her.

Pete glanced at Gage, who was doing his part with the media stragglers, lifted his hand to Chet, and headed to the stairwell.

Pete stopped at the nurses' station on the third floor and checked in, and they gave him the go-ahead, despite the late hour.

Too late. Because as he eased the door open, he spotted Sam, the moonlight drifting over his sleeping, bruised, and broken form.

Pete sank down in a nearby chair and just took a good look at him.

Big brother Sam, his chest caved in, his head bandaged, an oxygen cannula affixed under his nose, an IV inserted into his arm, fluids dripping. In the wan light, Sam appeared frail and not at all the larger-than-life overbearing guardian that drove Pete to his last nerve.

In fact, Sam looked devastatingly human.

And Pete had nearly lost him.

In a rush, the day swept over him. No, the last week, starting with the grizzly, then their crazy fight, then finding Sam nearly dead—all the way to the moment when he thought he'd done it.

Saved them all.

He *had* wanted to be a hero. Wanted to save the day, wanted Jess and even Sam to see him as the guy who didn't cause trouble but *saved* people in trouble. The guy who said, "I'll bring them home," and meant it.

The guy who could redeem his sins.

Pete walked over to the window. He spotted Ty walking out of the hospital, Jess with him.

Ty had his hand on the small of her back. They disappeared into the darkness of the lot.

Nice. Perfect. Talk about colossal mistakes. He just hadn't seen that coming.

And Pete couldn't help it. Maybe it was the fatigue, maybe just the stress, but he cupped his hand over his eyes, fighting the burn in them.

Cosmically, he probably deserved it. Really, it wouldn't have taken him long to totally screw up anything good he had with Jess.

Still. He braced his hand on the window frame, nearly shaking. How he wanted to put his hand into something, *through* something.

Just somehow take the idiot inside who'd royally derailed his life, and slam him against the wall, knock some sense into him.

He turned around, slid down to the floor, his hands over his face. *I'm sorry, Dad. I'm so sorry. I just can't get it right.*

"Pete?"

He caught his breath. Across the room, Sam had opened his eyes, was now looking at him.

Pete scrubbed his hand down his face, thankful for the darkness that hid any remaining wetness there.

"Who are you apologizing to?"

Had he spoken aloud? Maybe. "No one." He found his voice, his feet. "I just came by to see—"

"Thank you, Pete."

He stilled, watching as his brother groped for a light above him. Sam caught the switch by his bedside, flicked it on.

In the puddle of light, Pete could see the last forty-eight hours on

293

Sam's face, his eyes, his body. He was unshaven, his eyes cracked, a bruise over his forehead—although yes, he had better color than he had by the side of the road.

The sight of him could send Pete back to his knees.

However, the devastation all broke away when Sam smiled at him.

Smiled.

Pete couldn't move, and his heart skidded to a full stop.

"You did it, Pete. You found them." Sam swallowed then, shook his head. "And I'm an idiot."

Huh? "Yeah, well, we all knew that."

"Right." Sam shook his head. "No, I mean I should have trusted you."

Pete's faux humor dropped away. "I . . ." Except, he had no words. He scraped a hand through his hair. "Yeah, well, when Willow wasn't where you said she'd be, I was pretty frustrated too. Although Gage tells me you tried to make a break for it."

"Not one of my best moments." Sam gave a shake of his head, looked away. "I've had a string of those lately. Starting with . . . the fight at the Pony." His gaze landed back on Pete. "I'm sorry about that too."

"Naw. I probably deserved that." No, he *knew* he'd deserved that.

"No, you didn't, Pete," Sam said. "Because it had nothing to do with Jess and your friendship—or whatever—with her."

"We're teammates, that's it," Pete said. But the words had teeth, bit in.

Sam frowned then. "Really? Because that's not what Sierra said. She seems to think you and Jess—"

"Nope," Pete said, looking away, and shoot, his eyes burned again. He should probably get out of here before he did something embarrassing. "Okay, well, I'm glad you're okay."

Two steps before the door—

"It wasn't your fault."

Sam's words stopped him. "What?"

"I know it wasn't your fault Dad fell, that we couldn't find him."

A beat. Pete frowned. "It was my idea to go off slope."

"Dad would have done it even without your suggestion. That's the thing. Dad was always the instigator. And you fell right in line."

Pete shook his head. "But you didn't go. You tried to stop us."

"I was afraid!" Sam drew in a tremulous breath. "I was afraid, okay? And I hated that my fear kept me from going with you. We should have stayed together. We *always* should have stayed together."

Pete had no words. He lifted a shoulder.

"I shouldn't have turned on you, Pete. Shouldn't have made you feel like you had to leave town."

Pete ran his fingers against his eyes, turned away. Walked to the window.

Silence.

"Pete?"

He held up a hand. "Just a sec, bro," he said, and hated the way his voice quavered. But he could hardly take a full breath.

"Maybe I have rubbed off on you, a little."

Huh? "How's that?"

"Sierra told me that I've let darkness consume me. And maybe she's right. I've spent the last twelve years angry and bitter. Unable to forgive anyone, including myself. But I don't want to be that man anymore. I won't." He took a long breath. "So, I'm sorry, Pete. And I can't make you forgive me, but it's important to me that you know I don't blame you anymore. I want to be in your corner, not fighting you . . ."

Sam swallowed, his expression stripped, as if he'd opened up his chest for Pete to take a good look.

Pete stared at him. Since Dad died, everything between them had been grief and fury and darkness.

Then, with a warmth Pete didn't know Sam possessed, he said, "You saved those kids, Pete. You're a good guy. Dad would be proud of you."

Pete emitted a sound, something harsh.

"What?" Sam said.

"Nothing. It's just . . ." He shook his head. "I highly doubt that Dad would like the things I've done."

He waited for Sam's agreement, the barrage of accusations, a litany of his sins and irresponsibility.

Nope. "Dad might not approve of all your choices, Pete, but he still would have been proud of who you are. The damage you've done in your relationships doesn't outweigh the person you are and what you do to save lives. That's who you are, Pete. A hero."

Oh.

Pete looked at his brother, then the floor. "So . . . We don't have to hug now, right?"

"Please, no."

Pete looked up. Sam was smiling.

Slowly, Pete matched his smile, his entire body filling with something he couldn't quite name.

Hope, maybe.

"So, about that incident commander job . . ." Pete said.

"We'll see."

"Hero. You said the word. I heard it. *Hero*. I'm sure that comes with a raise, an office, a new truck." Pete pulled up a chair, turned it around, straddled it.

Sam rolled his eyes. "Someday. Maybe you could start with remembering to pick up Mom from her appointments, okay?"

Pete made a face. "Sorry. I will."

"Good." Sam considered him, and a dark smile slid up his face. "So, 'just teammates,' huh?"

"What?"

"Really? That's all you got? *What?*"

Pete sighed. "Okay, fine. I blew it with Jess, but I'm not sure you and I are ready to give each other dating advice."

"If you want advice, you've come to the wrong brother." Sam's eyes turned shadowed. "I'm in big trouble."

"Really? Something happen in the woods?"

Sam looked away.

"Oh, dude. What, with Willow?"

"Nothing happened."

"Geez, at least I have the guts to admit it. Did you two hook up?"

"No, we didn't. Or, not like you mean—"

"I didn't mean . . . for Pete's sake, it's *Willow*. What happened?"

Sam shook his head. "Okay, yeah, we sort of . . . hooked up. In a non-Pete way."

"Hey—"

"But I said something stupid, and I hurt her, and now Sierra hates me too. I'm an idiot."

"And, we're back to that. Did you hear me say that I agree?"

Sam offered a smile. "Tell me about Jess."

Pete grinned back, the pinch in his chest suddenly not quite so blinding. "I messed up. Tallie's downstairs, and I think Jess might have seen me with her, maybe gotten the wrong idea. Anyway, she's back together with Ty. So." He lifted a shoulder.

Added a hollow smile.

Sam frowned. "I've known Ty his entire life—and Jess since she moved here. And I don't remember them dating. I mean, sure, Ty might be hoping, but—"

"No, they were definitely dating. She was all secretive about it, but I guessed it, and the way he had his hands on her . . ." Pete blew out a breath. "Yeah, well. I better not go there."

Sam was still frowning. "I don't know, Pete. Jess doesn't strike me as the girl who would run in Ty's circles. Playboy cowboy with his dad's jet and his fancy cars? His European ski vacations? Jess is normal and, I hate to say it, poor. You've seen her house."

Pete shook his head. "I can't put my finger on it, bro, but she doesn't seem destitute. I mean, she has a closet of Columbia weather gear, skis, and a pretty nice Mac computer, not to mention her Jeep."

Sam lifted his bed to a sitting position. Considered him. "And that's it? You're out? Handing Ty the game ball? Seems to me a guy who isn't afraid to throw himself off a mountain with nothing but a squirrel suit might consider putting up a fight for the girl he loves. Talk about the ultimate risk, right?"

Pete ran his hands along the back of the chair. "Love? Let's not go overboard here." Apparently, stupid things still came out of his mouth. Baby steps. But he had to say something to cover the sudden black hole in his chest before he broke out in unmanly tears. "I guess that means it's just you and me, batching it."

Silence, and he felt Sam's eyes on him. Then his brother smiled, slow and long. "Yep. So, how about you run out and smuggle us in a pizza? I'll see if I can catch a late-night hockey game."

He picked up the remote as Pete got up.

"Double sausage."

"I know. Sheesh," Pete said.

"And a pack of Mountain Dew."

On the way out, Pete ducked Tallie, who was still standing in the lobby.

But he stood in the wet parking lot, lifting his face to the rain, letting it wash over him, cleanse him.

Set him free.

15

NO MATTER HOW MUCH YELLOW PAINT THEY USED, everything seemed brutally gray.

"We need to get our hearts broken more often," Jess said, setting her roller into the antique yellow paint bin. "We'll have the house remodeled in record time."

"If I eat any more gelato, I'm going to roll down the stairs." Willow leaned on a paint-splattered stool, surveying the first truly finished bedroom. With the whitewashed antique fireplace, the window seat, and the pale yellow walls, it would be the perfect escape.

For any of them. Because Willow had noticed the distinct absence of one blond handyman around the house this week. Thankfully, Ty showed up once to help Jess put up Sheetrock in this very room, but for the most part, Jess had been upstairs, alone, the radio blaring, working out the kinks of her broken heart by spackling and sanding her walls, adding primer, and painting over the marks of her remodel.

She refused to talk about Pete or anything that might have happened to cause his sudden disappearance, and even Willow noticed her tight-lipped, dark moods when she returned from training at the ranch and probable run-ins with Pete.

Not that any of them had anything to say about their dismal love lives.

Jess mentioned seeing Ian at the hospital, and Willow could do the algebra. Ian plus Sam meant Sierra was probably swearing off men and dating for a while.

As for Willow, well, at least the dog still liked her.

From the doorway, where they'd affixed a baby gate, Gopher whined, pushing his snout into the holes.

"We'll be done in a minute, Goph," Willow said, standing up and grabbing a towel to wipe her hands. "I'll get you some food."

Which seemed to be the only thing she was good at—serving people their food. She'd picked up more hours at the Summit Café now that she didn't have youth group responsibilities to weigh her down.

Apparently, Pastor Hayes had taken her resignation to heart. She'd half hoped someone might call and beg her to return. She'd even kept her cell phone charged in the faint hope of a text.

Nope.

Clearly, everyone—from the parents, to the youth group, Josh, and even Sam—sighed in relief when she walked out of their lives.

Because no, Sam hadn't come back to her, despite his promise. Not that she expected him to.

Nothing happened, he'd told Sierra.

Except something *had* happened. At least for her.

She'd fallen in love with a man she couldn't have. Sure, she'd always had feelings for Sam, a high-level crush that she'd managed from afar.

Much different from getting up close and personal, inside Sam's way-too-intoxicating attention, discovering the man underneath the darkness, the one who wanted to start living again . . .

Who had, in her arms, seemed exactly the man she'd dreamed about. Honorable, brave, sacrificing. No, she might never be healed from the pain of loving Sam Brooks.

The fact was, maybe she didn't *want* to get over Sam. Didn't want to purge from her memory those pale blue eyes searching hers, the feel of his arms around her, his words still resounding in her head.

"You're smart and beautiful and kind and the one I should have been kissing from the first."

Which made her the most pitiful of all of the brokenhearted club.

She climbed over the gate, and Gopher started jumping up on her. She crouched down and petted the animal behind his ears. He leaned against her hand, and she laughed. "Oh, Gopher, you're so easy to love."

She got up and headed downstairs. Outside, a perfect blue sky pressed against the jagged, blackened Rocky Mountains.

A beautiful day for a walk in the park, one filled with sunshine, the last glimpse of fall, the smell of pine needles and the rich loam of autumn in the wind.

Willow choked back her own thought. With her luck, any step into the park would end up with a callout of the entire town in some sort of massive search for her.

She filled Gopher's water bowl, filled another with puppy food.

A knock sounded at the front door, and for a second her heart gave a traitorous leap.

Especially when she spied the hazy figure of a man through the glass.

She opened the door, probably too eagerly, and then fought to keep her smile when she spotted Quinn.

It faded at the look on his face. His jaw tight, his mouth in a grim line.

"Quinn, are you okay?"

He shook his head, frustration nearly radiating off him. In fact, if she didn't know better, she'd say she spotted tears in his eyes.

"Come in," she said.

He shoved his hands in his pockets, looked away. "I need your help."

She didn't know why his words rushed joy through her—invariably any help from her would only end up front page news. Still, "What's going on?"

"Bella's parents! They still won't let me talk to her. I show up every day on her doorstep, but they don't believe me."

Willow came out onto the porch. "Don't believe what?"

"That I wasn't trying to make out with Bella when I took her into the woods." He turned, walked out to the edge of the porch. "I love her. And I was going to give her a gift. A necklace. Then the bear showed up and I lost it and—" He closed his eyes, as if in pain. "And now everyone thinks I'm a jerk."

"Nobody thinks that."

"I need to find the necklace." He turned, his eyes in hers. "But my dad's taken the keys, and I need a ride up to the pit."

Oh.

"You're the only one who believes in me, Willow."

"That's not true, Quinn." Although, maybe . . .

"I just need to find the necklace, show them I'm not lying. Then maybe they'll let me apologize to her, tell her . . ." He looked like he might cry again, his mouth a bud of anger. "My dad is going to send me to a prep school out East to finish out my senior year, and I have to tell her that I'm not going to forget her."

His sweet gesture, the desperation in his voice . . . Oh, Willow was too much of a romantic.

"I'll need to get back in time for my shift at the Summit."

"I know exactly where I lost it," he said, his eyes brightening.

"Let me get changed. Come in and say hi to Gopher."

She heard the puppy barking as she changed into jeans, a sweatshirt, and hiking boots.

The sun turned her Jeep warm as they drove up to the pit.

"It's at the overlook—you know the one, right?"

"Mmmhmm."

They pulled into the pit, and she got out. The rain and snow from last weekend had stripped the remaining leaves from the oak and maple, leaving only the lush, rich pine. Still, the absence of leaves opened up the view of the mountain.

"It's even prettier in the fall, without the leaves," she said as she headed up the trail with Quinn. "I used to think the summer was the best time to hike the park, but fall gives you the best views when you're in the foothills." She shoved her hands into her pockets, the afternoon breeze filtering through her sweatshirt. "Sort of like getting a new perspective on your life."

"Oh, good, another inspirational talk," Quinn said. He looked over his shoulder, and she might have been offended, if not for his smile.

"Sorry."

"It's okay. You can't help it. And I might miss it a little when I move."

"Why is your dad sending you away?"

"He thinks I need to focus. I talked him into letting me stay through football season, but after that . . ." He shook his head. "He's not budging on the Naval Academy."

"Seems like a good place to hone those hero qualities," she said.

"I thought out of everyone, you'd be against it."

"Why?"

"Because . . . you always follow your heart. You don't live by the rules. You do what you want. Sheesh, you grew up in a commune. That's the coolest thing I've ever heard of."

Hardly. "You know what growing up in a commune is like? My mom renounced her parental role, and suddenly, I only had my own rules to follow."

"Awesome."

"Not really. Imagine you have no one to turn to for advice. No one who pays attention to what you're doing—or *not* doing. No one who shows up to make sure you're okay. Quinn—your dad is a United States senator, and yet he shows up in your life. He's been at the hospital, he led the parents in their vigil to find you, to pray, and frankly, the fact he cares enough about your future to hound you should tell you how much he loves you. It takes energy to show up—and yeah, maybe you don't like his influence, but he's not doing it to wreck your life. He's doing it because he cares."

Quinn said nothing.

"You have no idea what it feels like to know that there is no one who would go looking for you."

She made a face at her own words. She sounded a little too needy, too pitiful.

Too much heart pinned to the outside of her body.

"You have someone who would look for you, Willow," Quinn said.

She glanced at him, away from the breathtaking mountain views.

"When Sam was dying on the side of the mountain, he still begged Pete to let him go back to where you were waiting."

Um, where she *wasn't* waiting. "If he had, he would have died," she said quietly. "They wouldn't have gotten him out in time."

Now all the sunshine had gone out of her day.

Quinn stopped at the overlook and stood at the outcropping, staring up at the magnificent rise of Huckleberry Mountain.

"My dad talks to our football team every year, and he tells this story about his life in the SEALs during Operation Desert Storm. A buddy of his was wounded and they called for an extraction but were pinned down by the enemy and couldn't move. All he could do was wait for help. Said it was the longest six hours of his life as he waited for his fellow SEALs to get to them. But he talks about patience and trusting your team—he uses it as a metaphor for cooperation and teamwork." Quinn looked at her. "You're always helping everyone else. Maybe you should let someone else help you?"

She stared at him, her mother's words finding her, winding in from a week ago. *"Isn't that what you Christians call grace—letting God love you, and letting that love change you?"*

"When did you get so smart?" she said.

"Hey. I listen." Then he offered a crack of a smile. "Is this where we sing?"

She gave him a push. "Let's find that necklace for your one true love."

Funny, he didn't contradict her.

"We were sitting here," he said, moving over to a boulder, a natural seat in the overlook. "I had the necklace box in my hand, and that's when I spotted the bear. I don't remember much after that."

Willow had walked over to the boulder and began to search around it, then into the woods.

"You know, we all listen, Willow. Like Vi—she outed Dawson to their parents, and he's going into counseling, as well as getting a tutor. Zena applied to some photography school in Missoula. And Maggy and Gus are dating. Riley is organizing some kind of youth group event. I think even Josh listened to you. He told us in youth group meeting this week that we should remember that God kept us safe. And that if we think we can save ourselves, we're missing the point of the whole Bible, or something to that effect. It sounded like something you would say."

Quinn was on the other side of the trail, kicking through the weeds. The wind picked up, rushed through the woods, stirred up a scent.

Something feral.

She lifted her head.

"I found it!" Quinn said, bending to work from the wet soil the damp and mangled box.

"Quinn." She stepped toward him, searching for the source of the smell.

He stood, opened the box. "It's okay."

"Quinn." She put her hand on his shoulder, dug her fingers in. "It's still here."

"Uh, yeah, it is," she said quietly, her voice dropping to a guttural whisper.

Maybe it was the change in her tone, or perhaps her grip on his shoulder, maybe even the shift of wind carrying the rank scent, but Quinn slowly looked up.

Froze.

"You've got to be kidding me."

— + —

The ache in Sam's chest was only getting worse.

And it had nothing do with surgery, or the three broken ribs. Or the fact that his mother was determined to make him leave her condo about twenty-five pounds heavier than when he arrived a few days ago.

Sure, he could have gone home, but Pete seemed to think trading places with him—letting Mom fuss over him—might be exactly what Sam needed to get back on his feet.

The home-cooked chicken casseroles helped, but he needed a remedy for the bereft, hollow place inside. He didn't want to be a sap and label it as a broken heart, but with a bandage across his chest, with his ribs wired into place, the only explanation for the way the great cavity inside seemed to expand with each day was because he ached for the only remedy that would heal him.

Willow. Her smile, the way she could wheedle right through all his dark layers with her light, make him laugh, and cry, make him want to lose his mind with frustration and . . .

The idea of not having her in his life could drive him out of bed to pace the cold floor.

His mother found him this morning, staring vacantly out the back window at the mountains. She'd touched his back, taken the wooden spoon from his hand, and turned the heat off his overcooked eggs.

Sat him down in the chair to point out the obvious.

"You love this girl, don't you?"

Sadly, she thought she was talking about Sierra, and he couldn't take it. "No. I don't. But . . ."

It came out in a story that took three cups of coffee and his mother making him a fresh omelet, bacon, and three pancakes.

"So, you *are* in love, just with the *other* sister," she said, handing him syrup.

Love? "If love means feeling as if I'm drowning or can't take a full breath or even as if there's something alive and burning in my chest—I don't know if I want it."

His mother slid her hand over his. "It's just because you're afraid, Sam. You're terrified of giving away your heart. But if you give it to the right person—Willow—she'll keep it safe."

"She doesn't want to see me."

"You'll never find out if you don't get out of that recliner and go after her. C'mon, it's time for you to live a little."

He retired to his recliner, her words cooking inside him.

Until a knock at the front door, sometime after he'd woken up from a nap.

His mom came down the stairs. *Please let it not be Chet.* The man had been awkwardly here for the past three evenings, watching television, eating his mother's dinners, and generally making Sam want to run from the room.

Since when did his mother have male friends? Especially a widower? He didn't buy the "we're just friends" line from Chet. Not at all. Chet might be nearing his sixties, but he was still a man.

"Sam, you have guests," his mother said, and Sam pushed pause on the remote, stilling the current *Arrow* episode. His brother had him hooked on all things comic book.

Reliving the years they'd missed together, apparently.

"Hey, Deputy Sam." Gus's voice led his way up the stairs. He wore a Mercy Falls Mavericks sweatshirt and had his hat on backward, his blond curly hair spilling out the sides and back. He flashed his signature good-ole-boy grin. "We came to pry you out of your chair."

We?

Maggy appeared right behind him, looking cute in a pink T-shirt and a fresh haircut, a soft curly bob that took about ten pounds off her face. And makeup. Huh.

"Josh and Riley are putting together a pizza thing. We're on strict orders to drag you down to the Summit."

The Summit. Where Willow worked. Sam kept his voice easy. "Really? Now?"

Gus grabbed the remote off the edge of the chair. "I hate to drag you away from Oliver Queen, but your fans are calling."

His fans?

Maggy set his cowboy boots next to the chair, held his leather jacket. "We never got to thank you for saving us out there. It's a fan party."

His mother stood by the door, wearing a strange smile.

"I wasn't the only one who saved you. We all worked together—the team, and Josh, and, of course, Willow." In fact, he'd been sitting here for five days rolling Sierra's words through his thick skull. *"One of these days you're going to figure out that you need to be rescued just as much as the next guy."*

Maybe more than the next guy. "And God."

"Yeah, yeah, we know. Put your boots on."

He pulled on his boots, grabbed his jacket, and refused to ask if Willow would be joining them.

But as they drove into town, him sitting on Gus's bench seat, Maggy behind them, he couldn't help but notice that the simmer in his chest only stirred to life.

If she was there, he'd . . . what? Apologize, yes. And then . . .

He wanted to tell her that she was beautiful and smart and brave and that he'd been a coward—a problem he didn't realize he'd had in spades until last weekend.

He'd meant what he said to Pete. He wasn't going to live in darkness anymore. *So, God, if you're listening, please. Rescue me. Please help me put this thing between Willow and me back together.*

They pulled up to the Summit and Sam got out, took a breath of crisp late-afternoon Saturday air. Maybe Willow would be inside and be willing to forgive him.

It couldn't be that easy, of course, because when he walked in, Willow wasn't at the long soda bar, wasn't waiting tables.

Instead, Zena stood near the door to the party room. She waved at him, and he headed to the back, followed by Maggy and Gus.

Inside, three pizzas sat on elevated serving platters, pitchers of Coke all around. Josh and Ava sat at the head of the table, Josh looking better than he had last time Sam saw him, his nose bandaged.

"Surprise!" said Vi, who was sitting in a chair with her leg in a cast.

"He knew about it, Vi," Gus said, letting go of Maggy's hand. "We told him."

"It was supposed to be a—oh, forget it. Where's Willow?" Vi asked.

"She's not at home." This from Dawson, who came in with Riley, right behind Gus. "Jess said she left a couple hours ago with someone—she didn't see who. A guy, she thought."

Sam tried not to let Riley's words find footing.

"I can't get ahold of Quinn." Bella came into the room, holding her cell phone. "It keeps ringing like it's on but then goes to voice mail." She slid onto a chair, bit her lip. "He was so mad after he left my parents' house. I'm afraid he's going to do something stupid. Like run away."

That caught Sam's attention. "What do you mean, so mad?"

"They still won't let us talk to each other. Quinn stood outside on the stoop for a half hour trying to reason with my dad. He finally left. Now I can't get ahold of him, and I'm worried. He wouldn't do something stupid, would he?"

For a woman he loved? It seemed that a man couldn't love a woman *without* doing something spectacularly stupid.

"Where could he have gone? My dad accused him of terrible things. Said Quinn had taken me up to the overlook to . . ." She made a face. "Quinn was so mad."

"I just wish I could prove to him that I'm not the guy he thinks I am."

"I know where he is," Sam said before he could stop himself. Bella looked at him, surprise on her face.

"He was going to give you a necklace that night—but it got lost. I'll bet he's up at the overlook searching for it."

As he watched, Bella's expression turned white, her hand moving almost instinctively toward her bandaged arm.

Sam glanced at Gus, who nodded.

"Can I grab some pizza on my way out?" Gus reached for a napkin.

Sam was reaching for his phone when it came alive in his hand. He read the number.

And then he didn't know what to think. "Willow?"

He could barely hear her; her voice cut into a whisper. "Sam?"

"Yeah, I'm here." He closed his eyes.

Just hearing Willow's voice allowed him to take a full, fresh breath. To calm the swirl inside. He turned away from the kids, toward the door. "I need to talk to you—"

"Sam—"

"I know I hurt you—"

"Sam—"

"—and I'm so sorry, I'll never—"

"Sam!"

"—do it again, if you'll just let me—*what*?"

He stopped talking when she took a deep, ragged breath.

"I'm with Quinn. We're up at the pit—and we're in trouble."

That's when he heard it—the guttural, feral growl reverberating through the phone.

He froze as he imagined Willow putting her hand over her mouth, maybe trying not to scream.

He was trying not to scream.

"Willow, stay where you are. Don't move. I'm coming to you."

Then he hung up, looked at Gus, and started moving toward the door. Pressed speed dial as he hit the street.

Pete picked up on the second ring. "'Sup?"

Sam held out his hand for Gus's keys. Good boy, he handed them over.

Sam only took a quick breath, skipping right over the past, into the present. No, the future, to the truth. "Pete, get the tranq gun and meet me at the pit. I need you, bro."

"We should run."

Quinn spoke quietly in Willow's ear, his voice so muffled she almost didn't hear it.

Or maybe she'd simply thought it. Because as the sun began to set, she did the math. Once the sun went completely to bed, darkness would descend.

They'd have no idea where the bear would be. Make that bears, plural, because right behind Mama Grizzly, with the silver mane and the gray-black jowls, lingered two cubs about six months old.

Not a small grizzly, either. Maybe four hundred pounds, the size of a buffalo. Her powerful limbs had ripped apart a downed tree, and she was rooting through the log for insects.

The cubs dove in, ate their fill, then lay in the middle of the path, out for a lazy sunning.

Quinn hunkered down next to Willow, who was hidden in the

brush and looking for a nearby tree to climb. He'd dropped his phone on the path, and every time it vibrated, a thread of terror tightened around Willow.

So far, the animal hadn't come over to investigate, but as it moved toward them up the trail, she prayed the battery would die.

The cell phone ringing did press into her brain one thought.

Sam.

Nothing else but that emerged, and even as she pulled out her phone and dialed his number, she had to roll her eyes at the sheer absurdity of calling Sam to her aid, again.

Certainly she was the last person he'd want to hear from.

Except, he was a rescuer—and even if he didn't love her, he'd show up.

"I know I hurt you, and I'm so sorry, I'll never do it again . . ."

She barely registered his words until *after* she'd hung up the phone, after he'd said the most important part.

"Don't move. I'm coming to you."

How she wanted to believe that it wasn't just his heroism that ignited those words.

But she'd gladly take just heroism at the moment.

She watched through the foliage as the bear wandered past them, stopped for a moment at the overlook, then moved up the trail. Mud matted its fur, and she could smell the rank odor of feces and rot and not a little blood. It wore a jagged scar on its shoulder, which was infected and seeping.

Willow covered her nose to keep herself from gagging.

"It's moving up the trail. If we don't go now, we'll be stuck here all night." Quinn started to move, but she grabbed his shirt.

He looked back at her, his eyes wide, probably from fear but also the adrenaline pulsing in his veins. She felt it too, the bolt impulse.

Especially since the animal and the cubs had moved past them, maybe kept going.

Except: *"Don't move."*

She couldn't get Sam's words, his soft, solid voice, out of her head.

No, not Sam. Because the words went deeper, into her bones, resounding through her.

Be still.

Yes, there it was again, finding her heart, her soul.

That was her problem, wasn't it? She just couldn't . . . wait. Couldn't curb her fear that no one would *want* to rescue her. So she jumped out ahead, on her own. Saving herself.

Quinn edged forward, his breath shallow.

Be still.

She put her hand on Quinn's back. "Shh."

Quinn hunkered down next to her, his voice low. "We need to go now, before we lose the light. With the bear and her cubs behind us, we can outrun—"

"No."

"Willow."

"We're staying." She pitched her voice as low as she could make it. "First, now we're upwind, so if we go out there, we're going to smell like a piece of pizza that's been sitting under the warmers. Second, bears can run something like forty miles an hour. I'm not sure about you, but I can't top a seven-minute mile."

The old saying about not being able to outrun a bear as long as you could outrun the person behind you flickered through her mind.

Yeah, well, she'd be bear bait.

"Run if you want, but I'm not leaving. As your former youth leader, I don't want to see you become a tasty snack. Stay here. Sam is on his way."

"That was fifteen minutes ago."

"He'll be here."

She pressed her head into the forest floor.

Be still.

She counted her heartbeat, forcing herself not to panic, even when she heard the rooting of the bear, a low growl, way too close.

Quinn hadn't moved, but he'd begun to tremble.

"Quinn," she whispered. "We're going to live through this. You're going to give Bella the necklace and tell her that you love her. Then you'll find your dad and thank him for offering you a decent education."

Quinn looked at her, his golden brown eyes shining in the fading light. "And you're going to tell Deputy Sam that you love him."

She froze, and the slightest smile tweaked up Quinn's face.

"I don't—"

"Oh yes, you do. It doesn't take a genius to figure that out."

Okay, yes. But, "He doesn't want me. If he did, he would be—"

"On his way to save you?"

"That's his job."

"He could have sent Pete. Or Gage. Or Ty." He lifted a shoulder. "But it was *his* panicked voice that said"—and Quinn affected Sam's low baritone—"I'm coming for you."

Huh. "You heard that?"

"Hard not to—he was practically shouting."

Branches snapped not far from them. The darkness had fallen to almost lethal shadows, and she strained to look out onto the path.

Then, a feral roar lifted into the night, the kind that could strip the bones from her skin and leave her crumpled.

It happened so fast, Willow struggled to sort it out.

Branches breaking, something barreling through the forest. Something—no, *someone*—landed on her and covered her entire body with his warm, solid protection. He put his arms around her head. "Don't move."

On the trail, feet thundered and shouts rang out.

Another roar shredded the twilight; the grizzly exploded down the trail toward them.

Then, the voice beside her. "Now, Pete!"

The thump of a tranquilizer gun—one dart, two, another.

And all that time, Sam hunched over her, his elbows bracketing her shoulders, his head down beside hers, his long legs tucked around her.

Shielding her body with his.

"She's down!" Pete said. Two more shots. "Cubs are hit."

Only then did Willow realize that she was shaking.

"Shh," Sam said softly, his voice in her ear, steady, tender. "It's over."

Next to her, Quinn got up, launched himself out through the forest, to the trail.

Sam, however, simply held her, his hands on her arms, his forehead against her neck. He seemed to be trembling. "It's okay," he said, his voice roughened. "You're okay."

He took a breath and sat back.

She rolled over, sat up.

He was sitting on the forest floor, breathing hard, looking a little stripped. He wore a flannel shirt, his jeans, his hair rucked up as sweat trickled down his face. Such a handsome face, even in the purples of twilight. The bruises from last week had healed, just the slightest gray over his eye, and the cut on his cheek was now a thin line. The barest layer of whiskers darkened his jaw, and his eyes were so devastatingly blue and filled with something she couldn't quite place.

Or maybe . . . love? Shining out from a heart that he wore right there, on the outside of his body. "Willow, you really scared me."

She couldn't speak. Couldn't move. Then, in a whisper, "You came for me."

"I told you I would." The warmth in his eyes elicited a shiver, right down her spine, and he reached out, cupping her face with his hand. "I'm so sorry it took me so long."

"You got here just in time—"

"No, Willow. I'm sorry it took me so long to stop being a fool. To come to you and tell you that I love you." He said it without pause, no fear, and even chased it with a smile. "I love you so much that I can't breathe if you're not around me. If you don't say you love me back, I might just—"

"I love you, Sam. I have for a while now. You make me feel smart and beautiful and—"

"It's because you *are* smart and beautiful. And brave. And—"

She kissed him. Curled her hand in his shirt and pulled him to herself, just in case he thought he could escape.

Which, apparently, he had no intention of doing because he put his arms around her and dove in. The kind of kiss that told her that, while she'd started it, he'd take it from here. That she didn't have to worry about who wanted whom, or if he'd show up.

He poured everything he had into his touch, all his heart, no fear, no darkness. Pure light.

All Sam.

He finally gave a soft, sweet groan of desire and broke away, just as she decided that she could stay forever tucked into the piney forest of the Rocky Mountains with Sam in her arms.

"We'd better get going before Pete decides you need rescuing," Sam said, winking.

"Or you."

"Oh," he said, helping her up, catching her in his arms, his eyes sparking with mischief, with life, "I've already been rescued."

Epilogue

"ARE YOU SURE ABOUT THIS? Because we don't have to—"

"Willow. Take a breath. Yes, I'm sure." Sam put his truck into park, then turned to her.

The sun hung low, gilding the parking lot of the Gray Pony a rich amber and streaking the horizon with tones of magenta and lavender. With the twilight sparkling in Willow's hazel-blue eyes, Sam knew Sierra was right.

He didn't deserve Willow. Not the way she reached out and loved him, so much abandon in her smile, her laughter, her heart right there for him to hold. She'd taken all the darkness in his life, turned it inside out, and left only light.

And so much life he could hardly take a full breath, even still, with the enormity of loving her.

She gave him a shy grin, and he cupped his hand on her cheek, ran his thumb down her impossibly soft skin. "I am crazy about you," he said, the words dropping from him easily.

"Just remember, I kissed you first," she said.

He took her hand, pressed it to his mouth. "Maybe we can keep that to ourselves."

Then he got out, went around, and opened her door. She tucked her hand into the pocket of his arm and headed inside.

The music—Ben's hot new single, only three weeks old—spilled out through the doors. Sam spotted Ben King and his daughter, Audrey, at the mic, playing dueling guitars. Then Ben stepped back to the mic.

> *Girl, I see you across the dance floor*
> *And when you smile, I can't take it no more*
> *The music is low, the beat has a name*
> *It's singing our song, no more waiting game . . .*

Glancing to the front, Sam met Ben's gaze. The singer nodded a greeting mid-chorus. Sam spotted Kacey seated at the front on her regular stool, sipping a signature root beer.

Sam headed for the table in back, near the dart board, where Gage was trying to teach Sierra how to throw, and was standing behind her, lifting her arm.

Ian leaned against the wall, not far away, his arms folded across his chest, mouth tight, watching. He glanced at Sam.

Sam interlaced his fingers through Willow's, pulling her along. It was about time they made their debut.

Jess sat in the booth, laughing, and it only took a second to see why—Gopher the puppy squirmed on her lap, fighting for a slurp on her chin. Jackson, Terri, and the kids had extended their vacation yet another week more.

Ty sat beside her, his arm up over the top of the booth. Not exactly with his arm around her, but . . . Sam now understood why Pete stood away from them, at the bar, near Ian. Close enough to be a part of the group but far away enough to be able to make a quick escape.

Sam wasn't going to let him get too far.

Ben's song ended to the applause of the crowd, and he announced a break.

Sierra tossed the dart, and it landed in the outer circle. She high-fived Gage, then turned and spotted Sam and Willow.

Grinned, not a hint of malice.

Beside him, Sam could feel Willow relax. Sam pulled her in, his lips to her ear. "Told ya," he said, then kissed her cheek.

She offered a smile, but when her gaze flickered past him into the crowd, it faded.

He turned, spotted Josh and Ava, who were lifting their hands in a wave.

Not far away, Senator Starr sat with Carrie and Pastor Hayes.

Which meant, hopefully, Quinn and Bella hadn't had to pull a Romeo and Juliet to get back together.

However, Sam said to Willow, "I'll be right back," and let go of her hand. He weaved through the crowd.

Sam had overheard Quinn those few precious seconds when he'd waited for Pete to get into position.

"He could have sent Pete. Or Gage. Or Ty . . . But it was his panicked voice that said, I'm coming for you."

Right then, Sam had wanted to pick up Quinn and give him a swat on the back—okay, maybe even a man hug. Because his words clicked into place for Sam too.

He *had* been panicked. Nothing was going to stop him from finding and rescuing Willow. Not just because she needed him, but because he loved her.

Suddenly, everything that Chet and Sierra and even his mother had been trying to say to him clicked into place.

He *did* need rescuing—not because he made stupid mistakes, although yeah, that was a given. And not because he was reckless or took chances, but because if he didn't occasionally fall, then he'd never be saved.

And if he was never rescued, then he would never know how much God loved him. He'd never experience grace.

Maybe Quinn needed a little grace on his side too.

"Hey, Senator Starr," Sam said, holding out his hand. The senator got up, met his grip.

"I wanted to thank you for saving Quinn, again," the senator said.

"No, actually, I should thank you. See, when I was hiking out after the van crash, Quinn saved my life. He kept me alive and got help. Apparently, he learned those survival skills from you."

Starr looked at him, without aplomb. "He saved you?"

"Absolutely. He's got a good head on his shoulders." He clamped the senator on the shoulder. "He's exactly the hero you hoped he would be."

Then he turned to Carrie, his smile fading.

"Before you start, Deputy," she said, "you should know that Josh told us how Willow and you saved them—"

He did?

"And we're going to ask Willow to come back and volunteer—"

"And I think she should politely decline."

Shock flickered in Carrie's eyes.

"Willow deserves a *job*—as another youth leader. These kids need more than Josh. They need someone who knows how to inspire. Who lives with light pouring out of her, even in the darkness. Someone who won't give up trying to figure out how to help them triumph. And I'm not just talking in the woods, but in their life, in their faith."

"I can't—"

"Oh, I think you can, Carrie. I'm a long-time member and I see the budget reports. The right people just need to recommend it to the board." He looked at the senator. "Right?"

Starr gave him a slow smile. "Ever thought of running for sheriff?"

"I have a job," Sam said. "And still have some official business, so if you'll excuse me."

"What was that all about?" Willow asked when he returned. She was leaning over the booth, Gopher jumping up to love her.

"Hey, Gopher, wait your turn," Sam said, pressing a kiss to the side of her neck. Willow laughed, and the sound was like music.

He walked over to Pete, who was now picking at a basket of curly fries. "So," Sam said, cutting his voice low enough for the chatter of the crowd to cover it, "what are you going to do about Jess?"

Pete glanced over his shoulder at Ty, then back to Sam. A slow smile worked over his face. "Get her back, of course. I've got a strategy. Just sit back and watch the master, bro."

"How about if I watch the incident commander?"

Pete's smile slacked into a look of disbelief. "Really?"

"I already talked to Chet, and he agrees we need someone to fill in if Miles isn't available. I've already filed the paperwork." He held out his hand, and Pete took it.

"No new truck, though. And forget the big raise. I'll let you make an extra ham sandwich on your shift."

Pete was just nodding, and for a second looked away. Sam was probably mistaken, but he thought he saw his brother's eyes glisten.

Next to Pete, Ian glanced over to his cell phone buzzing on the counter. He grabbed it, stared at the number with a frown.

He set it down, clearly letting it go to voice mail. When it vibrated again, he put the phone to his ear, listening, pressing a hand to his other ear. Sam guessed that Ian probably vetted all his calls.

It was the expression on his face, the sudden slack of his jaw, the way he looked up and met Sam's eyes, that made Sam still.

Ian motioned him over.

"What?"

Ian's hand trembled as he handed the phone to Sam. "Listen."

Sam put the phone to his ear. The voice that came over the line, recorded just moments ago, turned his entire body cold.

Then, of course, hot, as he realized who was speaking.

Please, Uncle Ian, you have to stop looking for me. I'm fine, I promise. But I won't be if you keep trying to find me. So for my sake, please— don't. I love you.

Ian had stepped away from him with the palms of his hands pressed to his temple, as if trying to keep his head from exploding.

Well, Sam too.

Alive. Finally, proof, because even Sam could recognize her voice. Soft, with the slightest Texas accent. *Esme Shaw.*

Sierra came over to Ian, clearly still tuned to his station. "What is it?"

Ian drew in a breath, shook his head.

So Sam spoke for him. "Esme just left a message." He could hardly believe his own words. "She's alive."

Sierra blinked at him, then turned her gaze back to Ian.

She wore so much compassion in her eyes that Sam knew.

Of course Sierra could never have loved Sam. Not when she so clearly loved Ian.

Ian glanced down at Sierra, then at Sam.

Offered a sad, bewildered smile.

Sierra put her arms around Ian in a rare but appropriate moment of comfort between them, probably a long time coming.

Willow came up to Sam, put her arms around his waist. "You okay?"

He closed her in an embrace. Slowly nodded.

Very okay.

On the stage, Ben stepped up again to the mic. "We need all the couples on the floor—this one's for you."

Willow smiled up at him. "Is that us?"

Oh baby. Sam leaned down then and kissed her, just a soft,

sweet kiss, a hint of everything he felt, all the light stored inside him.

Ben started into the song.

"I love you, Sam Brooks," Willow said.

And Sam realized he wasn't just living a little but enough to declare himself whole.

Acknowledgments

DECEMBER 1, 2105. A year after giving me the idea for the Montana Rescue series around the Thanksgiving table, my sweet mother lost her battle with leukemia and advanced to heaven. To say that time was a challenge is an understatement. I took the month off, grieving with our family as we prepared for Christmas without my mother, then pulled myself up to the keyboard, ready to start writing.

And had nothing. Maybe it was the grief, or perhaps the stress of wanting to follow up *Wild Montana Skies* with a story worthy of my readers. But as I stared at the screen, I had nothing.

Normally, when I write a story, I have the entire story mapped out ahead of time. I know what I want to write, can already see the scenes before I sit down to write. I even "tell myself the story" in a long summary ahead of time to make sure it works.

In short, I like to be in control. But suddenly my planning wasn't working; the story was locked in my brain, refusing to emerge. And I started to panic.

And then I realized that I was living Sam's fear—my carefully scripted life had spiraled out of control and I had nothing to hold on to. Nothing to pin my creativity on. I couldn't rescue myself.

I love the scene when Sierra tells Sam that he needs to admit he can't rescue himself. That he, too, needs help, because frankly, that was my epiphany. Here I was, writing a story about a man who refuses to realize he needs rescuing . . .

Aha. After a few days of wildly grasping for a muse that didn't want to show up, I realized what I needed was to fall on my knees and ask for the only thing that could save me. Divine anointing and story from the Lord.

The scenes and ideas began to flow, and within three weeks, I'd fleshed out the shell of the story. Six weeks later, I turned it in.

And I learned something. That Jesus has what we need—whether it is story, or direction, or even just hope to carry us when we've fallen and can't get up. He is enough.

I guess that's what Paul meant when he said, "But he said to me, 'My grace is sufficient for you, for my power is made perfect in weakness.' Therefore I will boast all the more gladly about my weaknesses, so that Christ's power may rest on me."

If we never ask for help, we never get to see God show up to save us.

God showed up to save me not only in providing words on the page but also with people to help me develop this story. My deepest gratitude goes to:

MaryAnn Lund, my beloved mother, who showed me the meaning of *rescue* by adopting me and loving me her whole life. I miss you.

Curt Lund, for your continued ideas, guidance, and support in helping me research the PEAK team. I'm so grateful for your creativity and wisdom!

David Warren, who knows how to manage the erratic emotions of his crazy author mother with fantastic ideas, brilliant storycrafting, and wonderful encouragement. Thank you for seeing my vision and helping me flesh out characters and scenes. I know I've said this before, but really, you're brilliant.

Rachel Hauck, my writing partner. What would I do without you? Thank you for walking this journey with me. I am so blessed to be your bestie!

Andrew Warren, who is kind enough to feed me when I forget to eat, lost in a story, and wise enough to know when to pull me away because my brain is about to explode. You rescue me every day, and I am crazy about you.

Noah Warren, Peter Warren, Sarah and Neil Erredge, for being my people. I know I can always count on you, and that is a rare and beautiful thing. I love you.

Steve Laube, for always being in my corner. I'm blessed to have you on my team!

Andrea Doering, for seeing my vision and for your gentle prodding to "make it a little shorter." Because of your wisdom, I write better books. I am so grateful for you!

The *amazing* Revell team, who believe in this series and put their best into making it come to life—from editing to cover design to marketing. I'm so delighted to partner with you!

To my Lord Jesus Christ, who shows up to protect, provide, and lead me home. You are my rescuer.

Susan May Warren is the ECPA and CBA bestselling author of over fifty novels with more than one million books sold. Winner of a RITA Award and multiple Christy and Carol Awards, as well as the HOLT and numerous Readers' Choice Awards, Susan has written contemporary and historical romances, romantic suspense, thrillers, romantic comedy, and novellas. She can be found online at www.susanmaywarren.com, on Facebook at SusanMayWarrenFiction, and on Twitter @susanmaywarren.

Don't miss the next
MONTANA RESCUE
COMING SUMMER 2017

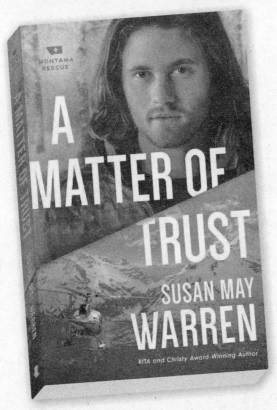

When a US Senator's brother goes missing, Gage Watson is tasked to save him. He only has one problem: the bossy and beautiful young senator wants to come with him.

Connect with
Susan May Warren

Visit her website and sign up for her newsletter to get a free novella, hot news, contests, sales, and sneak peeks!

ISBN: 978-1-57972-990-5
Printed in the United States of America